D0443651

LEGAL
FICTIONS

LEGAL FICTIONS

SHORT STORIES ABOUT

Lawyers and the Law

EDITED BY
JAY WISHINGRAD

THE OVERLOOK PRESS
WOODSTOCK • NEW YORK

First published in 1992 by
The Overlook Press
Lewis Hollow Road
Woodstock, New York 12498

Library of Congress Cataloging-in-Publication Data

Legal fictions: short stories about lawyers and the law / edited, with an
   introduction by Jay Wishingrad.

    p.   cm.

   1. Law—Fiction. 2. Lawyers—Fiction. 3. Short Stories
   I. Wishingrad, Jay.

PN6120.95.L33L4   1992
808.83'9355—dc20

              91-46664
              CIP

ISBN #0-87951-455-8

Set in Palatino by AeroType, Inc.

Contents

III. Lawyers & the Law: 1850–1900

IV. Lawyers & the Law: Humor

V. Lawyers & The Law: Other Voices, Other Countries

ACKNOWLEDGMENTS

Even an editor has an editor. Mine was Tracy Carns, the Editorial Director at Overlook, who had the idea for an anthology of stories about lawyers and the law. Tracy was educated as a lawyer. But that did not get in her way in helping me shape and balance this literary collection.

Words fail to express my debt for the incalculable contributions of my wife, Susan Leshe Wishingrad, to the publication of *Legal Fictions*.

For my wife, Susan

and

my daughter, Mara

Introduction

This is the first anthology of short stories solely about lawyers and the law. It is for the general reader — a category that presumably includes lawyers.

The collection includes stories about young lawyers, junior partners, senior partners, and name partners. There are stories about lawyers, law firms, and the law from the mid-nineteenth century to the 1990s, here and around the world. Some of the stories are about successful lawyers; others are about lawyers struggling through professional or personal crises. And in some stories there are lawyers without much talk of law and in some there is law without lawyers.

Yet all the stories have at least two things in common: They are all about law or lawyers or both, and, equally important, they all illuminate more than just lawyers and the law. Taken together, these fictions are compelling documentary evidence — as lawyers are wont to say — of the interrelations of lawyers, the law and literature.

The natural affinities between law and literature have long been evident. Since ancient times legal themes have permeated myth and literature. The story of Orestes is a classic example of the clash of law and morality. In the *Oresteia* Athena ends a blood-feud by establishing a "jury" of citizens (perhaps the first) to "judge" Orestes, who was "charged" by the Furies for killing his mother Clytemnestra, who, in turn, had killed Agamemnon, her husband and Orestes's father. Centuries later in Rome, Cicero, a lawyer and an orator, made eloquent, literary arguments for Justice on behalf of capital defendants.

The law and literature connection has intrigued many writers including Chaucer, Shakespeare, Dostoyevsky, Dickens, and, of course, Kafka. A few legal advocates, such as Daniel Webster and Clarence Darrow, and jurists, such as United States Supreme Court Justices Oliver Wendell Holmes and Benjamin N. Cardozo, have also made distinctly literary contributions to the law.

More than thirty years ago, civil liberties lawyer Ephraim London edited a two-volume anthology titled *The World of Law,* now out of print. Volume I was "The Law in Literature" and Volume II was "The Law as Literature." *The World of Law* included many extracts from longer works, such as plays, novels, or judicial opinions. It also included short stories. None of the short stories from *The World of Law* are repeated here. What is more, *Legal Fictions* purposely extends the very loose and ever expanding boundaries of the field of law and literature to encompass many stories where there may be little or no law, but a lawyer is a protagonist.

I read many of these stories long before collecting them for this anthology. Not surprisingly, I found some of them still scattered about the shelves of my library.

The rest of the stories I searched out and, on occasion, was referred to by literary friends and my editor. One story, "Congress in Crisis: The Proximity Bill," was suggested by Garrison Keillor as a substitute for an equally humorous Keillor fiction which I was considering. Another story, "Still Life," by my friend Marian Thurm, was personally delivered to me.

For me, no collection of stories about lawyers and the law would be complete without a piece by Kafka. For others, what is required is a story by the prolific writer, and Wall Street lawyer, Louis Auchincloss. Ironically, these two writers, and their fictions, could not be more dissimilar. Kafka's "Before the Law" is frightening. But no one can even begin to fathom our labyrinthine and bureaucratic legal system without reading his parable. As for Auchincloss, no one else gives the non-lawyer the substance and feel of the mega-firms that handle the legal affairs of the *Fortune* 500 corporations and *Forbes'* 400 richest individuals and families.

The stories range from one and one-half pages for Kafka's "Before the Law" to more than thirty pages for Melville's "Bartelby, The Scrivener." For this collection of short stories I decided that nothing would be too short — whether a short short, a comic sketch, or even a parable. At the long end of the spectrum, however, some arbitrary page limit was necessary. This excluded Herman Melville's "Billy Budd, Sailor" which has become a talismanic law and literature text.

Each of these stories stands ably on its own. By bringing them together I hope that each will be enriched by its proximity to the others. In addition, lawyers and law firms — albeit fictive ones — of different eras can be compared and contrasted. Styles of practice and the profound impact of money on lawyers' ethics and their loyalty (to clients and even to their own law partners) can also be viewed across time.

How different is the gentlemanly nineteenth-century Wall Street lawyer's office where, in Melville's "Bartelby, The Scrivener," the unfailingly polite Bartelby ("I would prefer not to") toiled as a copyist, from the 1940s Wall Street law firm of Forbes, Hathaway, Bryan & Devore, depicted by James Reid Parker in "The Most Outrageous Consequences"? And how, in turn, does the 1950s Wall Street law firm of Tower, Tilney & Webb, described in Auchincloss's "The Colonel's Foundation," differ from both? For one thing, in the legal world of 1950s junior partner Rutherford Tower, who rode most comfortably into the partnership on the coattails of his famous uncle, the Tower of Tower, Tilney & Webb, must now struggle to make his "social-register practice" pay off.

How do these seemingly genteel and gentile Wall Street firms differ from the archetypal Park Avenue (i.e., Jewish) mergers and acquisitions and litigation firms that mushroomed in the 1960s, 1970s and 1980s? Initially, the tickets to a Park Avenue law partnership were academic merit or business generation, rather than social status, the "old boy" network or family connections. Eventually the differences between "white shoe" Wall Street and Park Avenue law firms began to blur. And by the 1980s greenbacks, not bluebloods, reigned at most large corporate law firms.

In "The Tender Offer," for example, Auchincloss chronicles a senior partner's personal, professional and ethical crisis at the 1980s mid-town Manhattan corporate law firm of Treanor, Saunders, Arkdale, Rosen & Shaw. Auchincloss shows how law firm economics and increased competition for clients have dramatically altered the legal landscape: knowledge of the law becomes secondary to billings, new business generation, and bottom-line profits-per-partner.

What happens to the brilliant, hard-working senior associate who, after seven years or so of toil, is highly praised but not offered a partnership? "About Boston," by Ward Just, is also about a lawyer passed over for partnership by a prestigious law firm and how he then goes about building his own firm and a successful divorce and trusts and estates practice. What is more, that lawyer's solitary bachelor lifestyle is called into question when an old girlfriend asks him to represent him in a divorce action. While on the subject of bachelor lawyers, one might compare the lawyerly fellowship Melville uncovered in nineteenth-century London, and which he tells us about in "The Paradise of Bachelors," with that of the 1980s legal protagonist in "About Boston."

Let us not forget the bright young associate, fresh out of a prestigious law school, where he or she was an editor on the Law Review. That young associate typically spends days, nights, and most weekends researching precedents to support the unconscionable legal position staked out by a senior partner for a corporate client. Marian Thurm's "Still Life" describes such a young associate who billed an incredible number of hours at a major New York law firm for "the most unworthy cases." "Still Life" also exposes the professional and personal consequences of that bright young associate's decision to get off the fast-track and give up the big firm's big bucks for an idyllic small-town practice and lifestyle.

Irwin Shaw used "Justice" rather than "Law" in his title. This raises the question of the difference between "Justice" and "Law." A client seeking Justice is well advised of the difference by Mr. Page of Paget & Page, in Thomas Wolfe's "Justice Is Blind." Mr. Page repeatedly tells his client, who is seeking Justice, that Law, not Justice, is the standard by which his case will be decided. To make his point indelible, Mr. Page tells his client: "You are laboring under a grave misapprehension if you think you have to do something to be sued about.... *Anybody* — can sue — *anybody* — about *anything!*"

Is there any humor in the law or lawyers? I think so. And I think the reader will agree and relish the humorous pokes that Garrison Keillor takes at lawmakers, who are mostly lawyers, and that William Gaddis, in "Szyrk v. Village of Tatamount et al.," and Ian Frazier, in "Coyote v. Acme," take at the law and the legal system.

Several of the stories were written by practicing lawyers. Others are by writers who, for better or for worse, had some legal training or education. Louis Auchincloss, as many readers know, was a practicing lawyer at an old-line Wall Street firm. James Reid Parker was, and Lowell B. Komie is, a practicing lawyer. The nitty gritty level of the legal practice described in their stories makes that legal background apparent.

Where do women lawyers fit in? A somewhat surrealistic answer is revealed by Cynthia Ozick in "Puttermesser: Her Work History, Her Ancestry, Her Afterlife." In the 1970s feminist Puttermesser, the only woman but not the only Jewish associate, put in her billable hours "and three years of meticulous anonymous research [and] deep deep nights going after precedents" for the blueblood Wall Street firm of Midland, Reid & Cocklebury. However, as a woman and a Jew, Puttermesser knew that a partnership would not be in the cards. But Puttermesser finds little solace thereafter as an Assistant Corporation Counsel for the City of New York, while she wanders about her cavernous Bronx apartment "in the world without a past."

For Alice Adams in "After You've Gone" and Margaret Atwood in "Weight," the law can be for some women an insidious passion. To these writers law can be a way of thinking and talking that is alien to society's norms or expectations. Thus Adams's woman lawyer, whose two-year live-in relationship with a poet has ended, tries "with [her] orderly lawyer's mind [to put] events — or 'matters,' as [lawyers] say — in order." But her too "fair-minded" lawyerly way of thinking masks her true emotional loss. One of Atwood's woman lawyers, on the other hand, has simply left the legal profession for business. The other is literally destroyed by her husband — a lawyer — as she pursued her idealistic law school values: "Knocking herself out, and for peanuts. The kind of woman she represented never had money."

Continuing efforts are being made in the 1990s to increase the number of minority lawyers in general and minority law partners in particular. So Charles W. Chesnutt was truly a remarkable person — a successful black lawyer and celebrated writer who practiced law and published critically acclaimed stories and novels toward the end of the nineteenth, and early in the twentieth, century. His "The Web of Circumstance" is a terrific and appalling exposition of "southern justice."

Tales of lawyers and the law are not limited to writers steeped in the litigious American culture. Lawyers and legal themes abound in stories of writers from around the world.

Thus in "Heart of a Judge," by F. Sarif Easmon of Sierra Leone, there is a phantasmagorical and comical "courtroom" confrontation between colonial British Justice and West African superstition. The 1991 winner of the Nobel prize in literature, Nadine Gordimer of South Africa, in contrast, uses the realistic setting of a political trial to tell a contemporary tale of deceit and deception in "Crimes of Conscience," "The Judge's Wife," by Isabel Allende who was born in Chile but who now lives in Venezuela, is a gripping tale of "frontier justice." Karel Čapek's "The Clairvoyant" juxtaposes a wonderfully pompous district attorney with a clairvoyant; and Benjamin Peret's "The Condemned Man's Last Night" takes us on a short walk to the guillotine.

Does the short story bear any similarities to any of the myriad legal documents that lawyers produce? Surprisingly the answer is yes.

"Above all," writes V.S. Pritchett, a modern British master of the short story, "more than the novelist who is sustained by his discursive manner, the writer of short stories has to catch our attention at once not only by the novelty of his people and scene but by the distinctiveness of his voice, and to hold us by the ingenuity of his design." So too must the effective advocate. For this and other reasons, a short story is in many ways akin to the so-called "fact statement" in a legal brief — a lawyer's written argument to the court on a client's behalf.

Both the short story writer and the lawyer must succinctly give the reader — whether at home or in a judge's chamber — a concrete sense of time and place. The short story writer must then swiftly paint a vivid word picture of the fictive protagonists; the lawyer, too, must, in the opening pages of the fact statement in the brief, explain the context out of which the lawsuit arose and identify the parties to the lawsuit so that they stand out sharply against the abstract landscape of the legal arguments that follow. Finally, the short story writer and the lawyer must, through the characters' or parties' words and actions, as juxtaposed against the circumstances they are mired in, delineate character traits and motivations.

The lawyer gets the "facts," or, better yet, the "story" (or often several versions of the story) from the client. In the case of a corporate client, of course, there will always be several stories — many, if not most, of which will differ markedly from the others. But the lawyer must nevertheless write a harmonious and internally consistent tale — rather a fact statement. To do so, the lawyer, like the short story writer, calls on personal and professional experiences, also real and imagined.

In both the short story and the fact statement of the legal brief, the writer/lawyer shapes, arranges and supplements the basic facts or story. Each does so with logic, illogic where necessary and, most important, imagination. (Yes, lawyers do use their imagination).

A goal of many short story writers is to create a basis for the reader to "judge" the protagonist's actions. Similarly, a lawyer strives, and sometimes strains, to create a believable, probable, or at least possible story to convince one special reader — the judge — of the truthfulness of the client's story and thus the client's entitlement to a favorable legal ruling.

For the lawyer, and the court, a critical issue is often the client's motive or intent in taking, or refraining from taking, certain actions. The protagonist's motives are equally important to the writer and the short story reader. And this state of mind is typically inferred — by the judge or the short story reader — from the narrative of the actions and the protagonist's or parties' words.

The short story is, of course, fundamentally a work of fiction. But the respective fact statements in the legal briefs of the opposing parties to a lawsuit are, in a sense, competing fictions. A judge deciding the case stamps one version as representing the "true facts." That version belongs to the winner of the lawsuit. By implication, the version of the facts, or story, set out in the other brief is found to be less credible or less believable. That is to say, the fact statement or "story" of the losing party is, in effect, treated as a work of "legal fiction."

The field of law and literature is now the subject of several law reviews and journals as well as The Law and Humanities Institute, founded in 1979 by Professor Richard Weisberg of Yeshiva University's Benjamin N. Cardozo School of Law. The field is also being tilled by leading literary critics such as Professor Stanley E. Fish, Chairman of the Department of English and a member of the law faculty at Duke University, along with a growing number of law professors and practicing lawyers. Even judges, including Circuit Judge Richard A. Posner of the United States Court of Appeals for the Seventh Circuit, and the author of *Law and Literature: A Misunderstood Relationship* (Harvard, 1988), have acknowledged the benefits to law and to literature from this mutual exploration. These interdisciplinary scholars have harvested a provocative crop of imaginative readings and theories about reading, law, and literature.

The stories in this collection deal with themes of guilt and innocence, right and wrong, morality and legality, and they naturally bring up questions that are central to "deconstruction." This controversial critical literary theory asserts, among other things, that all the world is a text and that historical "truth" is impossible to arrive at and therefore irrelevant. Yale University Comparative Literature English Professor Paul de Man was considered deconstruction's foremost guru in the United States. But his reputation went — and remains — on trial when his pro-Nazi and anti-semitic war-time writings came to light in 1987 nearly four years after his death. Professor de Man wrote the following about the indeterminancy of all texts:

> It is always possible to face up to any experience (to excuse any guilt), because the experience always exists simultaneously as fictional discourse and as empirical event and it is never possible to decide which one of the two possibilities is the right one. The indecision makes it possible to excuse the bleakest of crimes because, as fiction, it escapes from the constraints of guilt and innocence. [*Allegories of Reading* at 293, Yale University Press, 1979]

Says Gordon S. Wood, Professor at Brown University:

> The blurring of fact and fiction is part of the intellectual climate of our postmodern time — dominated as it is by winds of epistemological skepticism and Nietzchean denials of the possibility of objectivity that are sweeping through every humanistic discipline, sometimes with cyclonic ferocity. Historians are usually the last to know about current fashions, but so powerful have the postmodern, decon-

structive theories become that even historians can no longer remain ignorant of them."[1]

Law and lawyers too, though slow to change, have been buffeted by these deconstructive winds. The Critical Legal Studies movement (CLS) is, in part, legal deconstruction. So it has at its center the same conundrum, namely the indeterminacy and the ambiguity of the statutes and precedents that make up the texts of the law. Thus, according to CLS theory — and the "legal realists" of the 1920s and 1930s — a judge must choose either of two conflicting interpretations in every case that comes before the court; the judge is allowed to choose which one to accept — there are no standards on which the judge must base the decision and therefore no criteria for determining the correctness of that decision.

A problem with CLS theory is that since it ends up deconstructing the law itself, there is no longer a rational framework or any objective standards to work within. For CLS, the law appears, or becomes, rather, a means to maintain the rights and privileges of the dominant societal groups, arbitrarily and capriciously. Of course the truth about the legal system lies somewhere between the extremes of blind, impartial Justice and instrument of the privileged class.

But neither literary nor legal theory is the concern here. This collection is for reading. However, if the stories stimulate readers to consider the interrelations of law and literature, or the myriad roles of lawyers and the law in literature and in our public and private cultures, so much the better.

Jay Wishingrad
New York City
October, 1991

---

[1] G. Wood, reviewing *Dead Certainties (Unwarranted Speculations)* (Knopf, 1991), by Simon Schama, Mellon Professor of Social Sciences at Harvard University, 38 *New York Review of Books* at 12 (June 22, 1991).

HERE AND NOW

The Tender Offer

LOUIS AUCHINCLOSS

V alerian Shaw, a member of the flourishing midtown Manhattan corporate law firm of Treanor, Saunders, Arkdale, Rosen & Shaw, had long assumed that, by the time he should have reached the age of sixty-four, he would have achieved a modicum of emotional and financial security. Although, like most of his heavily taxed generation, he had scanty savings, he had figured that his ultimate pension should be adequate to keep him comfortably as a widower in his small apartment on Riverside Drive where, surrounded by his books and collection of New York iconography, he would be able peaceably to pursue to the grave his hobby of metropolitan history.

But in his sixty-fourth year, with only three to go before his mandatory retirement, a strange thing happened. He began to lose his professional nerve. Valerian found himself now uncomfortably conscious of a widening discrepancy between the pace of his working efforts and that of his partners and associates. The image that seemed to stick in his mind was of them all engaged in a forced march across the slushy bog of the endless legal technicalities of the seventies, a quagmire of statutes and regulations and judicial opinions, and of himself sticking in the slime, falling behind the resolutely progressing backs of the others. He began at last to be afraid that he would not be able to pull his weight in the firm until the retirement age.

And then, as if to justify this gloomy foreboding, the basket in which for thirty years he had toted most of his legal eggs burst its bottom and dropped its cargo on the street. Standard Bank

& Trust Company, the small but reliable depository of the for-
tunes of some of New York's oldest families for which he had
so long labored, first as an associate and then as a partner, on
whose board of directors he had conscientiously served, and all
of whose principal officers he had come to regard as his particular
friends, was merged, taken over, consumed, raped, by First National Merchants' Loan. The new amalgamate ("Thank you very
much, old Val!") would be quite adequately represented in the
future by Lockridge, Kelly, First National's old-time, hard-nosed
legal experts, who had designed the plan that had resulted in
Standard's sudden siege and quick, fluttering surrender.

Valerian at first tried desperately to persuade himself that the
blow was not a fatal one to his position in the firm. Might another
bank not seek a general retainer? Might his friends at Standard not
yet gain control of the amalgamate? And surely he had other clients.
Was the vault not full of wills? The partners were very kind. But
it was a matter not of months but of weeks, and very few of them,
before the computer began remorselessly to show the steady increase of unbilled time and the widening discrepancy between
the overhead of Valerian's little department and the revenues that
in engendered. He could not fool himself that he would long
escape that "soul-searching" interview with the senior partner.

Cecil Treanor and Valerian had been classmates at Andover,
Yale and Harvard Law, but Cecil was not a man to be too much
counted on, even by so old an acquaintance. He had a convenient way of packing noble ends with rather less noble means in
the same box without any seeming awareness of the least impro-
priety or even inconsistency. At Yale, for example, he had written
a series of controversial columns for the *News* attacking the powerful senior societies, only to end by accepting the bid of Skull and
Bones. At law school he had composed a brilliant note for the
Review on legal restraints to anti-Semitism, and had then joined
a club in Boston that excluded Jews. Years later, as president of
the New York State Bar Association, he had thunderously preach-
ed the gospel of *pro bono publico* while keeping his own clerks
so busy they hadn't a minute left for the needy. And always these
compromises, if such they were, seemed to be effected without
any interrupting cough in that emphatic tone, without the inter-
position of a single cloud over that beaming countenance.
Sometimes of late Valerian had begun to feel that that beam was
more like a hard electric light.

That Cecil should come to Valerian's office for the soul-searching talk was in itself indicative of its importance, but his tone was milder than Valerian had expected.

"We've never been just a 'money firm,' and we're never, at least while I'm around, going to be one. We measure a partner's contribution by many factors other than the fees he brings in. In your case, Val, there are qualities of experience and wisdom and compassion and integrity—yes, sir, good old-fashioned integrity— that are indispensable to a firm like ours. Some of our younger partners don't know the value of those things, but they'll learn."

"It's good of you to say that, Cecil."

"Nonsense! You and I go back together to the flood. One doesn't forget that. But, as Hamlet said to Horatio, 'something too much of this.' What I came in to suggest, now that you have a little more time on your hands, is that maybe you could help me out a bit."

"In what?" Val was instantly alert.

"Well, how about giving me a hand on a new piece of business?" Cecil paused here to assume a graver look. "My client Zolex is casting a hungry eye in the direction of Pilgrim Publishers."

"Pilgrim! But that's one of the finest houses in the book business! What does Zolex know about literature?"

"Oh, Zolex knows a bit about everything. Don't forget they acquired the Heller chain last year. Department stores sell books, don't they?"

"I suppose they do." Val saw the sudden gleam in his partner's eye and knew that he must be careful. "Simeon Andrews in Pilgrim is an old friend of mine."

"I'm aware of that." Cecil was watching him carefully now. "I thought that might come in handy. You've always taken an interest in publishing, have you not?"

"Oh, nothing special." Val began to feel very nervous. "Not enough to be any real help to you. Frankly, Cecil, I don't see myself working on a corporate takeover. Even the vocabulary gets me down. Terms like 'bear hug' and 'blitzkrieg' and 'shark repellent'!"

But there was no answering smile from Cecil. "I use those terms, Val. They are merely technical. Are you suggesting there is anything illegal about the acquisition by Zolex of a controlling share of Pilgrim's common stock?"

"Oh, no, of course not."

"Are you suggesting, then, that I am violating any of the canons of ethics by advising Zolex how most expeditiously to acquire that stock within the law?"

"No, no, you're perfectly ethical. I guess it's the huggermugger of the whole thing that sticks in my craw. The way we go about it. First checking the files to see if we have ever had any legal connection with the target company. And then the stealthy lining up of stockholders and the secret approaches. And finally— *bang*—the unleashing of the tender offer, like a Pearl Harbor attack!"

"Of course, if it's all so distasteful to you, you needn't have anything to do with it. I can see I'm wasting your time."

"No, please, Cecil, of course I'll do it! I'm just shooting my big mouth off. You know how I am."

Cecil nodded briskly to accept his partner's collapse. It had been wholly anticipated. He then proceeded to a more delicate matter: a proposed fifty percent reduction in Valerian's share of the firm's profits. This was accompanied by what was known jocularly among the partners as the "old fart" formula: "We old farts have to keep moving over to make room for the younger men!"

But Val knew perfectly well that only one old fart would be taking the cut.

* * *

Nothing had added more to Valerian's malaise in the firm than Cecil's development of a large department, highly trained and specialized, to be dedicated to the art of corporate acquisitions. When the practice of company raiding on a large scale had begun, Cecil had denounced it as dirty business, and had loftily told his partners at a firm lunch that they should act only as defenders in such cases. The "snide art," he stoutly maintained, of preparing and launching a surprise attack against some unsuspecting company, whose officers, about to be stripped of their livelihood, might like as not be numbered among one's closest friends, ill fitted gentlemen supposedly devoted to the pursuit of justice and the reverence of law. But when Cecil's own corporate clients had begun to look to other firms for just this service, he had performed more than a volte-face. He had made his firm the first in the field! Like Philippe-Égalité in the French Revolution, he wore the lilies of France on his liberty cap with perfect aplomb. History to Cecil, Valerian sometimes mused, must have seemed like a fancy-dress ball. Was there any reason that Justice Holmes and Al Capone should not have had a friendly drink together?

Valerian was somewhat relieved to discover that his role in the preparation of Zolex's project was confined to a study of all the material on Pilgrim Publishers that the firm had been able, with the necessary discretion, to lay its hands on. He did not quite see what value this would have in a proxy fight, but Cecil assured him that he needed someone at hand with the overall picture in mind. He suspected that the senior partner might be making up work for him, but even if this were so, why should he complain? He only hoped that he would not have to be present at any meeting, once the matter became public, with his old friend Simeon Andrews.

Ordinarily he lunched with the editor of Pilgrim every couple of weeks, but now he discontinued the practice, and at his club in the Pan Am Building he frequented the buffet, knowing that his friend was apt to lunch in the main dining room. But one day at noon, crossing the lobby, he felt a firm pull on his sleeve and turned to confront the countenance that he had been avoiding.

"Where have you been hiding, Val?" Simeon demanded. "I've been looking out for you all week."

"I've been having a sandwich sent in to my office. I'm keeping pretty busy these days, Sim."

"Too busy for a little business talk? Too busy for a proposition I want to put to you? How about the regular dining room? I hate just to eat and run."

Valerian submissively followed his friend to the latter's regularly reserved table in a corner of the green-walled room hung with Audubon prints. Simeon's table was directly under a print that depicted two red-tailed hawks fighting in the air over a bleeding rabbit clutched by one. Valerian, unpleasantly reminded of the impending fate of Pilgrim, shuddered. Was it possible that Simeon had got wind of the raid?

But Simeon seemed wholly absorbed in gravely applying a piece of lemon peel to the rim of his pre-iced martini glass. Bald, wide-eyed, he was as still, except for his moving fingers, as some great bird of prey on a bare limb. Valerian had always associated this stillness with his friend's reputation for being able to pick the best as well as the most popular books without even reading them. His secret, Simeon used to boast, was that if his eyes were sometimes closed, his mind was always open. Nothing was too refined, too esoteric, too vulgar, or too pornographic for his consideration.

"Do you remember, Val, that you once mentioned to me that it would be a great idea if some house were to publish the unexpurgated diaries of Philip Hone and George Templeton Strong in a joint edition?"

"Why, yes," Valerian replied, astonished at his friend's memory. "Allan Nevins published only half of each of them. And Strong really begins where Hone leaves off. Put together, they'd make a week-by-week, almost a day-by-day account of life in New York from eighteen twenty-five to eighteen seventy-five."

"Precisely. Well, that idea of yours stuck in my mind. That's how a good publisher operates. Those fifty years represent the transition of New York from a minor seaport to a great metropolis. By eighteen seventy-six the job was pretty well done. Fifth Avenue boasted as many châteaux as the Loire Valley, and all the great cultural institutions had been founded or at least planned."

"And do you know something else, Sim? I've read the manuscripts of those diaries in the New-York Historical Society. The unpublished parts are just as good as the published. Nevins simply had to cut because his editors wouldn't give him the space he needed. But imagine, if he'd had an editor with your vision!"

Simeon sipped his drink complacently. "Well, I've been looking into it. It seems to me perfectly feasible. I don't say it would be a great money-maker, but any publishing house that's worth its salt should be willing to stick its neck out from time to time. We owe it to the public. We owe it to history!"

"Oh, Sim, that's wonderful!"

"*If* we decide to go ahead with it, would you consider serving on some kind of advisory board? On questions of how much explanatory text we need and how many footnotes? We wouldn't be able to pay you much, but then, it shouldn't take too much of your time."

"Pay me! I'd pay *you* for the privilege! My God, man, this project has been my dream of dreams!"

Simeon smiled, pleased at such a display of enthusiasm, although probably considering it a bit on the naive side. But Valerian didn't care. He ordered a second martini, although he knew it would make him tiddly in the middle of the day. He began to calculate how many volumes would be needed—not too many, not more than ten. His mind was already a gallery of possible illustrations. His second cocktail came, and he swallowed it in a couple of minutes. He started to run off to his friend the names of possible editors...

And then, when Simeon had suddenly sprung up from the table to buttonhole a former mayor whose memoirs he had his eye on, a terrible thought came to Valerian. The radiant dome of his new fantasy was shattered.

Zolex!

Was it conceivable that a massive corporate conglomerate, controlled by men concerned with profit alone, would countenance such a project? Of course not! The mere suggestion might cost its proponent his job.

Valerian deliberately reached over now to pick up Simeon's half-finished cocktail, and finished it for him. His heart was beating rapidly, and the big crowded room blurred before his eyes. Through his mind throbbed the slow, marching melody of the old hymn: "Once to-o ev-er-y man a-a-and na-a-tion, comes the-e-e mo-o-ment to-o decide." Simeon came back to the table.

"Sorry, old boy, but I had to have a word with Tom. He's given me an option on his autobio. Of course, he can't write a word of English. Seen any good ghosts lately?"

"Simeon!" Valerian exclaimed sharply and then abruptly paused. His friend eyed him curiously.

"What is it, Val?"

Valerian seemed to be looking at the editor from the other side of a deep crevice. Could he jump it? Would he stumble? He lowered his eyes to the tablecloth as with an audible gasp he took the mental leap. But he fell! He fell and fell!

"Val, are you feeling all right?"

Valerian looked up, dazed, from the bottom of his pit. "I'm all right, Sim," he said in a flat voice. "I want to tell you something about a client of ours."

Simeon's big watery eyes stared as he listened to Valerian's tale in absolute silence. But when the latter had finished, and the editor responded, his tone was curiously emotionless. He shook his head.

"Well, I'll be damned. It seems we live in a new age of piracy. Thanks for the tip, old boy."

"Of course, you realize I've put my professional life in your hands."

Simeon gave him a shrewd look. "Of course, I do," he said softly. "But never fear. I shall be discreet. And now, I think, everything points to a very good lunch."

Valerian reflected that it was indicative of the strength of the man that he could even think of lunch at such a moment! He tried to quell the rising surge of panic in his stomach by telling himself that he had only done his duty as a friend. And as a citizen. And as a student of New York history.

* * *

Valerian soon heard at the office that somebody besides Zolex scouts was picking up Pilgrim stock, but this was not an unusual development. No matter how secret a raider's precautions, there were always nostrils keen enough to pick up the scent of impending war. What disturbed him was that the lawyers working on the matter did not seem more disturbed. The general expectation that Pilgrim would go down with only a few bubbles continued unabated.

On the Sunday afternoon before the filing of the tender offer Valerian took a long walk with his frayed and shaggy poodle in Central Park. As he circled the reservoir and let his eyes rest on the southern skyline, his mood was one of static resignation. It seemed to him now that his little gesture was merely symbolic of his own uselessness and futility in the modern world. There was no law but that of the market, no right but that of the strong. The irresistible and unresisted materialism of the day was a flooding river that had penetrated every fissure and cranny of his world, inundating poor and rich, unions and management, the most popular entertainment and the greatest art. He visualized, tossing on its raging surface, the torn pages of the diaries of Philip Hone and George Templeton Strong.

On Monday he did not go to the office until the afternoon. He had no function in the filing of the tender offer or in the subsequent call on the target. Was it his imagination that the receptionist's greeting was saucy?

"Mr. Treanor wants to see you immediately, Mr. Shaw. He said for you to go right in the moment you arrived."

Valerian, his overcoat on his arm, his heart pounding, entered the office of the senior partner. Cecil jumped up at once, without greeting him, and strode to the window where he stood with his back to his visitor.

"How did things go at Pilgrim, Cecil?"

"Very well, no thanks to you," the bitter voice came back to Valerian. "In fact, I've never seen a smoother takeover. They capitulated at once. It was positively friendly! Your friend, Simeon Andrews, played his cards with the greatest astuteness. He sold his own stock for ten million plus an agreement that he would be chairman of the board of Zolex-Pilgrim for three years! It seems to be a question of who took over whom!"

Valerian felt his panic ebb away as he stood silently contemplating the wide, tweeded back of his former friend and about-to-be former partner. He took in the surprising fact that he was not surprised. There was something almost comforting in the flatness, the totality of his desolation.

"Andrews had another condition," the voice continued. "If we are to continue as counsel to Zolex-Pilgrim, the price will be your resignation from this firm. He informed me all about your indiscretion. He had already flared the Zolex project, so you told him nothing he didn't know, but he says he cannot afford to be represented by a firm with such a leak. Of course, I had to agree with him. I told him that you would cease to be a member of the firm as of today. I assured him that, if you refused to resign, we would dissolve the firm and re-form without you."

"That won't be necessary, Cecil. I resign. As of this moment."

Cecil whirled around. "How could you do it, Val?" There was actually some feeling in his voice now. "How could you do it to me? After all I've done for you? Looking after you and inventing things for you to do? And saving your stupid neck from our ravenous younger partners?"

"There's no point talking about it."

"Of course, I'll have to tell the firm about it. I'm afraid there can be no idea now of a regular pension. But if you will let me negotiate the matter for you, I'll see that you get something. We don't want you to starve, after all. I'll put it to the partners as a kind of aberration on your part. Perhaps even that you've had a small stroke."

"Any way you want it, Cecil. I leave that entirely to you."

"But, Val, how *could* you?" Cecil's voice now rose to a wail.

"How could you betray a client? How could you violate the most sacred of the canons of ethics? What are the younger men to think of us? When I tell them at firm meetings what the ideals of Treanor, Saunders mean to me, to clients, to the bar, to the public? Won't they simply laugh at me?"

"I guess they may, Cecil," Valerian replied wearily as he turned now to the door. "I guess they really may. Why don't you just tell them you've gotten rid of a rotten egg?"

About Boston

WARD JUST

BETH WAS TALKING and I was listening. She said, "This was years ago. I was having a little tryst. On a Thursday, in New York, in the afternoon. He telephoned: 'Is it this Thursday or next?' I told him it was never, if he couldn't remember the *week*. Well." She laughed. "It makes your point about letters. Never would've happened if we'd written letters, because you write something and you remember it. Don't you?"

"Usually," I said.

"There isn't a record of anything anymore, it's just telephone calls and bad memory."

"I've got a filing cabinet full of letters," I said, "and most of them are from ten years ago and more. People wrote a lot in the sixties, maybe they wanted a record of what they thought. There was a lot to think about, and it seemed a natural thing to do, write a letter to a friend, what with everything that was going on."

"I wonder if they're afraid," she said.

"No written record? No," I said. "They don't have the time. They won't make the time and there aren't so many surprises now, thanks to the sixties. We're surprised-out. They don't write and they don't read either."

"That one read," she said, referring to the man in the tryst. "He read all the time — history, biography. Sports books, linebackers' memoirs, the strategy of the full-court press." She lowered her voice. "And politics."

"Well," I said. I knew who it was now.

"But he didn't know the week." She lit a cigarette, staring at

13

the match a moment before depositing it, just so, in the ashtray. "You always wrote letters."

I smiled. "A few close friends."

She smiled back. "Where do you think we should begin?"

"Not at the beginning."

"No, you know that as well as I do."

I said, "Probably better."

"Not better," she said.

"I don't know if I'm the man —"

"No," she said firmly. She stared at me across the room, then turned to look out the window. It was dusk, and the dying sun caught the middle windows of the Hancock tower, turning them a brilliant, wavy orange. In profile, with her sharp features and her short black hair, she looked like a schoolgirl. She said, "You're the man, all right. I want you to do it. I'd feel a lot more comfortable, we've known each other so long. Even now, after all this time, we don't have to finish sentences. It'd be hard for me, talking about it to a stranger."

"Sometimes that's easiest," I said.

"Not for me it isn't."

"All right," I said at last. "But if at any time it gets awkward for you —" I was half hoping she'd reconsider. But she waved her hand in a gesture of dismissal, subject closed. She was sitting on the couch in the corner of my office, and now she rose to stand at the window and watch the last of the sun reflected on the windows of the Hancock. A Mondrian among Turners, she called it, its blue mirrors a new physics in the Back Bay. And who cared if in the beginning its windows popped out like so many ill-fitting contact lenses. The Hancock governed everything around it, Boston's past reflected in Boston's future. And it was miraculous that in the cascade of falling glass the casualties were so few.

I watched her: at that angle and in the last of the light her features softened and she was no longer a schoolgirl. I checked my watch, then rang my assistant and said she could lock up; we were through for the day. I fetched a yellow legal pad and a pen and sat in the leather chair, facing Beth. She was at the window, fussing with the cord of the venetian blind. She turned suddenly, with a movement so abrupt that I dropped my pad; the blind dropped with a crash. There had always been something violent and unpredictable in her behavior. But now she only smiled winningly, nodded at the sideboard, and asked for a drink before we got down to business.

I have practiced law in the Back Bay for almost twenty-five years. After Yale I came to Boston with the naïve idea of entering politics. The city had a rowdy quality I liked; it reminded me of Chicago, a city of neighborhoods, which wasn't ready for reform. But since I am a lapsed Catholic, neither Irish nor Italian, neither Yankee nor Democrat nor rich, I quickly understood that for me there were no politics in Boston. Chicago is astronomically remote from New England, and it was of no interest to anyone that I had been around politicians most of my life and knew the code. My grandfather had been, briefly, a congressman from the suburbs of Cook County, and I knew how to pull strings. But in Boston my antecedents precluded everything but good-government committees and the United Way.

Beth and I were engaged then, and Boston seemed less daunting than New York, perhaps because she knew it so intimately; it was her town as Chicago was mine. I rented an apartment in the North End and for the first few months we were happy enough, I with my new job and she with her volunteer work at the Mass. General. We broke off the engagement after six months — the usual reasons — and I looked up to find myself behind the lines in enemy territory. I had misjudged Boston's formality and its network of tribal loyalties and had joined Hamlin and White, one of the old State Street firms. I assumed that H,W — as it had been known for a hundred years — was politically connected. An easy error to make, for the firm was counsel to Boston's largest bank and handled the wills and trusts of a number of prominent Brahmin Republicans, and old Hamlin had once been lieutenant governor of Massachusetts. In Chicago that would have spelled political, but in Boston it only spelled probate. There were thirty men in the firm, large for Boston in those days. The six senior men were Hamlin and Hamlin Junior and White III, and Chelm, Warner, and Diuguid. Among the associates were three or four recognizable Mayflower names. The six senior men were all physically large, well over six feet tall and in conspicuous good health, by which I mean ruddy complexions and a propensity to roughhouse. They all had full heads of hair, even old Hamlin, who was then eighty. Their talk was full of the jargon of sailing and golf, and in their company I felt the worst sort of provincial rube.

Of course I was an experiment — a balding, unathletic Yale man from Chicago, of middling height, of no particular provenance, and book-smart. I was no one's cousin and no one's ex-roommate. But I was engaged to a Boston girl and I had been first in my class at Yale and the interview with Hamlin Junior had gone well. All of them in the firm spoke in that hard, open-mouthed bray peculiar to Massachusetts males of the upper classes. The exception was Hamlin Junior, who mumbled. When it was clear, after two years, that their experiment had failed — or had not, at any event, succeeded brilliantly — it was Hamlin Junior who informed me. He called me into his dark brown office late one afternoon, poured me a sherry, and rambled for half an hour before he got to the point, which was that I was an excellent lawyer mumble mumble damn able litigator mumble mumble but the firm has its own personality, New England salt sort of thing ha-ha mumble sometimes strange to an outsider but it's the way we've always done things mumble question of style and suitability, sometimes tedious but can't be helped wish you the best you're a damn able trial man, and of course you've a place here so long's you want though in fairness I wanted mumble make it known that you wouldn't be in the first foursome as it were mumble mumble. Just one question, I've always wondered: 'S really true that you wanted to go into politics here?

It was my first professional failure, and in my anger and frustration I put it down to simple snobbery. I did not fit into their clubs, and I hated the North Shore and was not adept at games. I was never seen "around" during the winter or on the Cape or the Islands or in Maine in the summer. I spent my vacations in Europe, and most weekends I went to New York, exactly as I did when I was at law school in New Haven. New York remains the center of my social life. Also, I was a bachelor. Since the breakup of my engagement, I had become an aggressive bachelor. Beth was bitter and I suspected her of spreading unflattering stories. Of course this was not true, but in my humiliation I believed that it was and that as a consequence the six senior men had me down as homosexual. In addition, I was a hard drinker in a firm of hard drinkers, though unlike them I never had whiskey on my breath in the morning and I never called in sick with Monday grippe. I could never join in the hilarious retelling of locker room misadventures. They drank and joked. I drank and didn't joke.

When I left H,W, I opened an office with another disgruntled provincial — he was from Buffalo, even farther down the scale of things than Chicago — half expecting to fail but determined not to and wondering what on earth I would do and where I would go, now that I'd been drummed out of my chosen city: blackballed. Young litigators are not as a rule peripatetic: you begin in a certain city and remain there; you are a member of the bar, you know the system, you build friendships and clientele and a reputation. Looking back on it, Deshais and I took a terrible risk. But we worked hard and prospered, and now there are twenty lawyers in our firm, which we have perversely designed to resemble a squad of infantry in a World War II propaganda movie: Irish, Italians, Jews, three blacks in the past ten years, one Brahmin, Deshais, and me. Of course we are always quarreling; ours is not a friendly, clubby firm. In 1974, we bought a private house, a handsome brownstone, in the Back Bay, only two blocks from my apartment on Commonwealth Avenue. This is so convenient, such an agreeable way to live — it is my standard explanation to my New York friends who ask why I remain here — that we decided not to expand the firm because it would require a larger building, and all of us love the brownstone, even the younger associates who must commute from Wayland or Milton. Sometimes I think it is the brownstone and the brownstone alone that holds the firm together.

I suppose it is obvious that I have no affection for this spoiled city and its noisy inhabitants. It is an indolent city. It is racist to the bone and in obvious political decline and like any declining city is by turns peevish and arrogant. It is a city without civility or civic spirit, or Jews. The Jews, with their prodigious energies, have tucked themselves away in Brookline, as the old aristocrats, with their memories and trust funds, are on the lam on the North Shore. Remaining are the resentful Irish and the furious blacks. Meanwhile, the tenured theory class issues its pronouncements from the safety of Cambridge, confident that no authority will take serious notice. So the city of Boston closes in on itself, conceited, petulant, idle, and broke.

I observe this from a particular vantage point. To my surprise, I have become a divorce lawyer. The first cases I tried after joining forces with Deshais were complicated divorce actions. They were women referred to me by Hamlin Junior, cases considered — I think he used the word "fraught"— too mumble "fraught" for H,W. In Chicago we used the word "messy," though all this was a long time ago; now they are tidy and without fault. However, then as now there was pulling and hauling over the money. Hamlin Junior admired my trial work and believed me discreet and respectable enough to represent in the first instance his cousin and in the second a dear friend of his wife's. He said that he hoped the matter of the cousin would be handled quietly, meaning without a lengthy trial and without publicity, but that if the case went to trial he wanted her represented by a lawyer ahem who was long off the tee. You know what it is you must do? he asked. I nodded. At that time divorces were purchased; you bought a judge for the afternoon. Happily, the cousin was disposed of in conference, quietly and very expensively for her husband. The success of that case caused Hamlin Junior to send me the second woman, whose disposition was not quite so quiet. Fraught it certainly was, and even more expensive.

I was suddenly inside the bedroom, hearing stories the obverse of those I had heard after hours at H,W. The view from the bedroom was different from the view from the locker room. It was as if a light bulb joke had been turned around and told from the point of view of the bulb. Hundred-watt Mazda shocks WASP couple! I discovered that I had a way with women in trouble. That is precisely because I do not pretend to understand them, as a number of my colleagues insist that they "understand women." But I do listen. I listen very carefully, and then I ask questions and listen again. Then they ask me questions and I am still listening hard, and when I offer my answers they are brief and as precise as I can make them. And I never, never over-promise. No woman has ever rebuked me with "But you *said*, and now you've broken your word."

The cousin and the wife's friend were satisfied and told Hamlin Junior, who said nothing to his colleagues. He seemed to regard me as the new chic restaurant in town, undiscovered and therefore underpriced; it would become popular soon enough, but meanwhile the food would continue excellent and the service attentive and the bill modest. For years he referred clients and friends to me, and I always accepted them even when they were routine cases and I had to trim my fees. And when Hamlin Junior died, I went to his funeral, and was not at all startled to see so many familiar female faces crowding the pews.

My divorce business was the beginning, and there was a collateral benefit — no, bonanza. I learned how money flows in Boston, and where; which were the rivers and which were the tributaries and which were the underground streams. Over the years, I have examined hundreds of trusts and discovered a multiformity of hidden assets, liquid and solid, floating and stationary, lettered and numbered, above ground and below. The trusts are of breathtaking ingenuity, the product of the flintiest minds in Massachusetts, and of course facilitated over the years by a willing legislature. And what has fascinated me from the beginning is this: the trust that was originally devised to avoid taxes or to punish a recalcitrant child or to siphon income or to "protect" an unworldly widow or to reach beyond the grave to control the direction of a business or a fortune or a marriage can fall apart when faced with the circumstances of the present, an aggrieved client, and a determined attorney.

This is not the sort of legal practice I planned, but it is what I have. Much of what I have discovered in divorce proceedings I have replicated in my trust work, adding a twist here and there to avoid unraveling by someone like me, sometime in the future. Wills and trusts are now a substantial part of my business, since I have access to the flintiest minds in Massachusetts. Turn, and turn about. However, it is a risible anomaly of the upper classes of Boston that the estates have grown smaller and the trusts absurdly complex — Alcatraz to hold juvenile delinquents.

So one way and another I am in the business of guaranteeing the future. A trust, like a marriage, is a way of getting a purchase on the future. That is what I tell my clients, especially the women; women have a faith in the future that men, as a rule, do not. I am careful to tell my clients that although that is the objective, it almost never works; or it does not work in the way they intend it to work. It is all too difficult, reading the past, without trying to read the future as well. It is my view that men, at least, understand this, having, as a rule, a sense of irony and proportion. At any event, this is my seat at the Boston opera. It is lucrative and fascinating work. There was no compelling reason, therefore, not to listen to the complaint of Beth Earle Doran Greer, my former fiancée.

She said quietly, "It's finished."

I said nothing.

She described their last year together, the two vacations and the month at Edgartown, happy for the most part. They had one child, a boy, now at boarding school. It had been a durable marriage, fifteen years; the first one had lasted less than a year, and she had assumed that, despite various troubles, this one would endure. Then last Wednesday he said he was leaving her and his lawyer would be in touch.

"Has he?"

"No," she said.

"Who is he?"

She named a State Street lawyer whom I knew by reputation. He was an excellent lawyer. I was silent again, waiting for her to continue.

"Frank didn't say anything more than that."

"Do you know where he is?"

"I think he's at the farm." I waited again, letting the expression on my face do the work. There were two questions. Is he alone? Do you want him back? She said again, "It's finished." Then, the answer to the other question: "There is no one else." I looked at her, my face in neutral. She said, "Hard as that may be to understand."

Not believe, *understand;* a pointed distinction. I nodded, taking her at her word. It was hard, her husband was a great bon vivant.

"That's what he says, and I believe him. His sister called me to say that there isn't anybody else, but I didn't need her to tell me. Believe me, I know the signs. There isn't a sign I don't know and can't see a mile away, and he doesn't show any of them. Five years ago — that was something else. But she's married and not around anymore, and that's over and done with. And besides, if there was someone else he'd tell me. It'd be like him."

I nodded again and made a show of writing on my pad.

"And there isn't anyone else with me either."

"Well," I said, and smiled.

"Is it a first?"

I laughed quietly. "Not a first," I said. "Maybe a second."

She laughed, and lit a cigarette. "You were afraid it would be another cliché, she would be twenty and just out of Radcliffe. Meanwhile, I would've taken up with the garage mechanic or the gamekeeper. Or Frank's best friend; they tell me that's chic now." She looked at me sideways and clucked. "You know me better than that. Clichés aren't my style."

I said, "I never knew you at all."

"Yes, you did," she said quickly. I said nothing. "You always listened; in those days you were a very good listener. And you're a good listener now."

"The secret of my success," I said. But I knew my smile was getting thinner.

"The mouthpiece who listens," she said. "That's what Nora told me when she was singing your praises. Really, she did go on. Do they fall in love with you, like you're supposed to do with a psychiatrist?"

Nora was a client I'd represented in an action several years before, a referral from Hamlin Junior. She was a great friend of Beth's but a difficult woman and an impossible client. I said, "No."

"It was a pretty good marriage," she said after a moment's pause. "You'd think, fifteen years..." I leaned forward, listening. Presently, in order to focus the conversation, I would ask the first important question: What is it that you want me to do now? For the moment, though, I wanted to hear more. I have never regarded myself as a marriage counselor, but it is always wise to know the emotional state of your client. So far, Beth seemed admirably rational and composed, almost cold-blooded. I wondered if she had ever consulted a psychiatrist, then decided she probably hadn't. There was something impersonal about her locution "like you're supposed to." She said abruptly, "How did you get into this work? It's so unlike you. Remember the stories you told me about your grandfather and his friend? The relationship they had, and how that was the kind of lawyer you wanted to be?"

I remembered all right, but I was surprised that she did. My grandfather and I were very close, and when I was a youngster we lunched together every Saturday. My father drove me to the old man's office, in an unincorporated area of Cook County, near Blue Island. I'd take the elevator to the fourth floor, the building dark and silent on Saturday morning. My grandfather was always courteous and formal, treating me as he would treat an important adult. On Saturday mornings my grandfather met with Tom. Tom was his lawyer. I was too young to know exactly what they were talking about, though as I look back on it, their conversation was in a private language. There was a "matter" that needed "handling," or "a man" — perhaps "sound," perhaps "a screwball" — who had to be "turned." Often there was a sum of money involved — three, four, fi' thousand dollars. These questions would be discussed sparely, long pauses between sentences. Then, as a signal that the conversation was near its end, my grandfather would say, "Now this is what I want to do," and his voice would fall. Tom would lean close to the old man, listening hard; I never saw him make a note. Then: "Now you figure out how I can do it." And Tom would nod, thinking, his face disappearing into the collar of his enormous camel-hair coat. He never removed the coat, and he sat with his gray fedora in both hands, between his knees, turning it like the steering wheel of a car. When he finished thinking, he would rise and approach me and gravely shake hands. Then he would offer me a piece of licorice from the strand he kept in his coat, the candy furry with camel hair. He pressed it on me until I accepted. I can remember him saying good-bye to my grandfather and, halting at the door, smiling slightly and winking. Tom would exit whistling, and more often than not my grandfather would make a telephone call, perhaps two, speaking inaudibly into the receiver. Finally, rumbling in his basso profundo, he would make the ritual call to the Chicago Athletic Club to reserve his usual table for two, "myself and my young associate."

In those days children were not allowed in the men's bar, so we ate in the main dining room, a huge chamber with high ceilings and a spectacular view of the lakefront. We sat at a table by the window, and on a clear day we could see Gary and Michigan City to the southeast. Long-hulled ore boats were smudges on the horizon. Once, during the war, we saw a pocket aircraft carrier, a training vessel for navy pilots stationed at Great Lakes. The old man would wave his hand in the direction of the lake and speak of the Midwest as an ancient must have spoken of the Fertile Crescent: the center of the world, a homogeneous, God-fearing, hardworking *region*, its interior position protecting it from its numerous enemies. With a sweep of his hand he signified the noble lake and the curtain of smoke that hung over Gary's furnaces, thundering even on Saturdays. Industry, he'd say, *heavy* industry working at one hundred percent of capacity. Chicagoland, foundry to the world. His business was politics, he said; and his politics was business. "We can't let them take it away from us, all this..."

When the old man died, Tom was his principal pallbearer. It was a large funeral; the governor was present with his suite, along with a score or more of lesser politicians. Tom was dry-eyed, but

I knew he was grieving. At the end of it he came over to me and shook my hand, solemnly as always, and said, "Your grandfather was one of the finest men who ever lived, a great friend, a great Republican, a great American, and a great client." I thought that an extraordinary inventory and was about to say so when he gripped my arm and exclaimed, "You ever need help of any kind, you come to me. That man and I..." He pointed at my grandfather's casket, still aboveground under its green canopy, then tucked his chin into the camel hair. "We've been through the mill, fought every day of our lives. I don't know what will happen without him." He waved dispiritedly at the gravestones around us, stones as far as the eye could see, and lowered his voice so that I had to bend close to hear. "The world won't be the same without him," Tom said. "The Midwest's going to hell."

Tom died a few years later, without my having had a chance to take him up on his offer. But from my earliest days in that fourth-floor office I knew I would be a lawyer. I wanted to be Tom to someone great, and prevent the world from going to hell. Tom was a man who listened carefully to a complex problem, sifting and weighing possibilities. Then, settled and secure in his own mind, he figured a way to get from here to there. It was only an idiosyncrasy of our legal system that the route was never a straight line.

"I mean," she said brightly, leaning forward on the couch, "listening to a bunch of hysterical women with their busted marriages, that wasn't what I expected at all."

"They are not always hysterical," I said, "and some of them are men."

"And you never married," she said.

That was not true, but I let it pass.

"No," she said, rapping her knuckles on the coffee table. "You *were* married. I heard that a long time ago. I heard that you were married, a whirlwind romance in Europe, but then it broke up right away."

"That's right," I said.

"She was French."

"English," I said.

"And there were no children."

"No," I said. We were silent while I walked to the sideboard, made a drink for myself, and refilled hers.

"Do you remember how we used to talk, that place on Hanover

Street we used to go to, all that pasta and grappa? I practiced my Italian on them. Always the last ones out the door, running down Hanover Street to that awful place you had on — where was it?"

"North Street," I said.

"North Street. We'd get to dinner and then we'd go to your place and you'd take me back to Newton in your red Chevrolet. Three, four o'clock in the morning. I don't know how you got any work done, the hours we kept."

I nodded, remembering.

"And of course, when I heard you'd been sacked at H,W, I didn't know what to think, except that it was for the best." She paused. "Which I could've told you if you'd asked." I handed her the highball and sat down, resuming my lawyerly posture, legs crossed, the pad in my lap. "Do you ever think about your grandfather? Or what would've happened if you'd gone back to Chicago instead of following me here? Whether you'd've gone into politics, like him?"

"I didn't follow you," I said. "We came together. It was where we intended to live, together."

"Whatever." She took a long swallow of her drink. "Chicago's such a different place from Boston, all that prairie. Boston's close and settled and old, so charming." I listened, tapping the pencil on my legal pad. It was dark now. At night the city seemed less close and settled. The cars in the street outside were bumper to bumper, honking. There was a snarl at the intersection, one car double-parked and another stalled. A car door slammed and there were angry shouts. She looked at me, smiling. "I don't want anything particular from him."

I made a note on my pad.

"I have plenty of money; so does he. Isn't that the modern way? No punitive damages?" She hesitated. "So there won't be any great opportunity to delve into the assets. And Frank's trust. Or mine."

I ignored that. "Of course there's little Frank."

She looked at me with the hint of a malicious grin. "How did you know his name?"

"Because I follow your every movement," I said, with as much sarcasm as I could muster. "For Christ's sake, Beth. I don't know how I know his name. People like Frank Greer always name their children after themselves."

"Don't get belligerent," she said. "A more devoted father —" she began and then broke off.

"Yes," I said.

"— he's devoted to little Frank." She hesitated, staring out the window for a long moment. She was holding her glass with both hands, in her lap. She said, "What was the name of that man, your grandfather's lawyer?"

"Tom," I said.

"God, yes," she said laughing lightly. "Tom, one of those sturdy Midwestern names."

"I think," I said evenly, "I think Tom is a fairly common name. I think it is common even in Boston."

She laughed again, hugely amused. "God, yes, it's common."

I glared at her, not at all surprised that she remembered which buttons worked and which didn't. Beth had an elephant's memory for any man's soft spots. Why Tom was one of mine was not easily explained; Beth would have one explanation, I another. But of course she remembered. My background was always a source of tension between us, no doubt because my own attitude was ambiguous. She found my grandfather and Tom...quaint. They were colorful provincials, far from her Boston milieu, and she condescended to them exactly as certain English condescend to Australians.

"It's a riot," she said.

"So," I said quietly, glancing at my watch. "What is it that you want me to do now?"

"A quick, clean divorce," she said. "Joint custody for little Frank, though it's understood he lives with me. Nothing changes hands, we leave with what we brought, status quo ante. I take my pictures, he takes his shotguns. Except, naturally, the house in Beverly. It's mine anyway, though for convenience it's in both our names. He understands that."

"What about the farm?"

"We split that, fifty-fifty."

"Uh-huh," I said.

"Is it always this easy?"

"We don't know how easy it'll be," I said carefully. "Until I talk to his lawyer. Maybe it won't be easy at all. It depends on what he thinks his grievances are."

"He hasn't got any."

"Well," I said.

"So it'll be easy," she said, beginning to cry.

We had agreed to go to dinner after meeting in my office. I proposed the Ritz; she countered with a French restaurant I had never heard of. She insisted, Boylston Street nouvelle cuisine, and I acceded, not without complaint. I told her about a client, a newspaperman who came to me every six years for his divorce. The newspaperman said that the nouvelle cuisine reminded him of the nouveau journalisme — a colorful plate, agreeably subtle, wonderfully presented with inspired combinations, and underdone. The portions were small, every dish had a separate sauce, and you were hungry when you finished. A triumph of style over substance.

She listened patiently, distracted.

I was trying to make her laugh. "But I can get a New York strip here, which they'll call an entrecôte, and there isn't a lot you can do to ruin a steak. Though they will try."

"You haven't changed," she said bleakly.

"Yes, I have," I said. "In the old days I would've been as excited about this place as you are. I'd know the names of the specialties of the house and of the chef. In the old days I was as al dente as the veggies. But not anymore." I glanced sourly around the room. The colors were pastel, various tints of yellow, even to a limp jonquil in the center of each table, all of it illuminated by candles thin as pencils and a dozen wee chandeliers overhead. It was very feminine and not crowded; expensive restaurants rarely were in Boston now; the money was running out.

"I'm sorry about the tears," she said.

I said, "Don't be."

"I knew I was going to bawl when I made that remark about Tom and you reacted."

"Yes," I said. I'd known it too.

"It made me sad. It reminded me of when we were breaking up and all the arguments we had."

I smiled gamely. "I was al dente then, and I broke easily." I knew what she was leading up to, and I didn't want it. When the waiter arrived I ordered whiskey for us both, waiting for the little superior sneer and feeling vaguely disappointed when he smiled pleasantly and flounced off. I started to tell her a story but she cut me off, as I knew she would.

"It reminded me of that ghastly dinner and how awful everything was afterward."

I muttered something noncommittal, but the expression on her face told me she wanted more, so I said it was over and forgotten, part of the buried past, et cetera. Like hell. We had argued about the restaurant that night, as we had tonight, except I won and we went to the Union Oyster House. My parents were in town, my father ostensibly on business; in fact they were in Boston to meet Beth. The dinner did not go well from the beginning; the restaurant was crowded and the service indifferent. My parents didn't seem to care, but Beth was irritated — "The Union Oyster Tourist Trap" — and that in turn put me on edge, or perhaps it was the other way around. Halfway through dinner, I suspect in an effort to salvage things, my father shyly handed Beth a wrapped package. It was a bracelet he had selected himself; even my mother didn't know about it. It was so unlike him, and such a sweet gesture, tears jumped to my eyes. Even before she opened it, I knew it would not be right. Beth had a particular taste in jewelry and as a consequence rarely wore any. I hoped she could disguise her feelings, but as it happened she giggled. And did not put the bracelet on, but hurried it into her purse after leaning over the table and kissing my father. He did not fail to notice the bracelet rushed out of sight. Probably he didn't miss the giggle, either. In the manner of families, after a suitable silent interval my father and I commenced to quarrel. On the surface it was a quarrel about businessmen and professional men, but actually it had to do with the merits of the East and the merits of the Midwest and my father's knowledge that I had rejected the values of his region. The Midwest asserted its claims early, and if you had a restless nature you left. It forced you to leave; there were no halfway measures in the heartland, at that time a province as surely as Franche-Comté or Castile, an interior region pressed by the culture of the coasts, defensive, suspicious, and claustrophobic. When I left I tried to explain to him that a New Yorker's restlessness or ambition could take him to Washington as a Bostonian's could take him to New York, the one city representing power and the other money. No Midwesterner, making the momentous decision to leave home, would go from Chicago to Cleveland or from Minneapolis to Kansas City. These places are around the corner from one another. The Midwest is the same wherever you go, the towns larger or smaller but the culture identical. Leaving the Midwest, one perforce rejects the Midwest and its values; its sense of inferiority — so I felt then — prevented any return. In some way it had failed. What sound reason could there be for leaving God's country, the very soul of the nation, to live and work on the cluttered margins? It had failed you and you had failed it, whoring after glitter. My father's chivalry did not allow him to blame "that girl" publicly, but I knew that privately he did. Too much — too much Boston, too much money, too determined, too self-possessed. He hated to think that his son — flesh of my flesh, blood of my blood! — could be led out of Chicagoland by a woman. The image I imagine it brought to his mind was of an ox dumbly plodding down a road, supervised by a young woman lightly flicking its withers with a stick. That ghastly dinner!

"The thing is." She smiled wanly, back in the present now, that is, her own life, and what she had made of it. "It's so — *tiresome.* I know the marriage is over, it's probably been finished for years. But starting over again. I don't want to start over again. I haven't the energy." She sighed. "He's said for years that he's got to find himself. He's forty-eight years old and he's lost and now he wants to be found. And I'm sure he will be."

"Usually it's the other way around," I said. "These days, it's the women who want to find themselves. Or get lost, one or the other."

"Frank has a feminine side." I nodded, thinking of Frank Greer as a pastel. Frank in lime green and white, cool and pretty as a gin and tonic. "But the point isn't Frank," Beth said. "It's me. I don't want to start over again. I started over again once and that didn't work and then I started over again and it was fun for a while and then it was a routine, like everything else. I like the routine. And I was younger then."

I did not quite follow that, so I said, "I know."

"Liar," she said. "How could you? You've never been married."

"Beth," I said.

She looked at me irritably. "That doesn't count. You've got to be married for at least five years before it's a marriage. And there have to be children, or at least a child. Otherwise it's just shacking up and you can get out of it as easily and painlessly as you got into it, which from the sound of yours was pretty easy and painless."

I looked away while the waiter set down our drinks and, with a flourish, the menus.

"How long ago was it?"

"Almost twenty years ago," I said.

"Where is she now?"

I shrugged. I had no idea. When she left me she went back to London. I heard she had a job there; then, a few years ago, I heard she was living in France, married, with children. Then I heard she was no longer in France but somewhere else on the Continent, unmarried now.

"That's what I mean," she said. "You don't even know where she *is*."

"Well," I said. "She knows where I am."

"What was her name?"

"Rachel," I said.

Beth thought a moment. "Was she Jewish?"

"Yes," I said.

Beth made a little sound, but did not comment. The amused look on her face said that my father must have found Rachel even more unsuitable than Beth. As it happened, she was right, but it had nothing to do with Rachel's Jewishness. She was a foreigner with pronounced political opinions. "And you like living alone," Beth said.

"At first I hated it," I said. "But I like it now and I can't imagine living any other way. It's what I do, live alone. You get married, I don't. Everyone I know gets married and almost everyone I know gets divorced."

"Well, you see it from the outside."

"It's close enough," I said.

"Yes, but it's not *real*." She glanced left into Boylston Street. It was snowing, and only a few pedestrians were about, bending into the wind. She shivered when she looked at the stiff-legged pedestrians, their movements so spiritless and numb against the concrete of the sidewalk, the sight bleaker still by contrast with the pale monochrome and the fragrance of the restaurant. Outside was a dark, malicious, European winter, Prague perhaps, or Moscow. "We might've made it," she said tentatively, still looking out the window.

I said nothing. She was dead wrong about that.

She sat with her chin in her hand, staring into the blowing snow. "But we were so different, and you were so bad."

The waiter was hovering and I turned to ask him the specialties of the day. They were a tiny bird en croûte, a fish soufflé, and a vegetable ensemble. Beth was silent, inspecting the menu; she had slipped on a pair of half-glasses for this chore. I ordered a dozen oysters and an entrecôte, medium well. I knew that if I ordered it medium well I had a fair chance of getting it medium rare. Then I ordered a baked potato and a Caesar salad and another drink. The waiter caught something in my tone and courteously suggested that medium well was excessive. I said all right, if he would promise a true medium rare. Beth ordered a fish I never heard of and called for the wine list. The waiter seemed much happier dealing with Beth than with me. They conferred over the wine list for a few moments, and then he left.

She said, "You're always so defensive."

"I don't like these places, I told you that." I heard the Boston whine in my voice and retreated a step. "The waiter's OK."

"You never did like them," she said. "But at least *before*..." She shook her head, exasperated.

"Before, what?" I asked.

"At least you were a provincial, there was an excuse."

I pulled at my drink, irritated. But when I saw her smiling slyly I had to laugh. Nothing had changed, though we had not seen each other in fifteen years and had not spoken in twenty. The occasion fifteen years ago was a wedding reception. I saw her standing in a corner talking to Frank Greer. She was recently divorced from Doran. I was about to approach to say hello; then I saw the expression on her face and withdrew. She and Greer were in another world, oblivious of the uproar around them, and I recognized the expression: it was the one I thought was reserved for me. Now, looking at her across the restaurant table, it was as if we had never been apart, as if our attitudes were frozen in aspic. We were still like a divided legislature, forever arguing over the economy, social policy, the defense budget, and the cuisine in the Senate dining room. The same arguments, conducted in the same terms; the same old struggle for control of our future. Her prejudice, my pride.

"You have to tell me one thing." She turned to inspect the bottle the waiter presented, raising her head so she could see through the half-glasses. She touched the label of the wine with her fingernails and said yes, it was fine, excellent really, and then, turning, her head still raised, she assured me that I would find it drinkable, since it came from a splendid little château vineyard near the Wisconsin Dells. The waiter looked at her dubiously and asked whether he should open it now and put it on ice, and she said yes, of course, she wanted it so cold she'd need her mittens to pour it. I was laughing and thinking how attractive she was, a woman whose humor improved with age, if she would just let up a little on the other. Also, I was waiting for the "one thing" I would have to tell her.

I said, "You're a damn funny woman."

"I have good material," she said.

"Not always," I replied.

"The one thing," she said, "that I can't figure out. Never could figure out. Why did you stay here? This isn't your kind of town at all, never was. It's so circumspect, and sure of itself. I'm surprised you didn't go back to Chicago after you were canned by H,W."

"I like collapsing civilizations," I said. "I'm a connoisseur of collapse and systems breakdown and bankruptcy — moral, ethical, and financial. So Boston is perfect." I thought of the town where I grew up, so secure and prosperous then, so down-at-heel now, the foundry old, exhausted, incidental, and off the subject. We lived in Chicago's muscular shadow and were thankful for it, before the world went to hell. "And I wasn't about to be run out of town by people like that," I added truculently.

"So it was spite," she said.

"Not spite," I said equably. "Inertia."

"And you're still spending weekends in New York?"

I nodded. Not as often now as in the past, though.

"Weird life you lead," she said.

I said, "What's so weird about it?"

"Weekdays here, weekends in New York. And you still have your flat near the brownstone, the same one?"

I looked at her with feigned surprise. "How did you know about my flat?"

"For God's sake," she said. "Nora's a friend of mine."

It was never easy to score a point on Beth Earle. I said, "I've had it for almost twenty years. And I'll have it for twenty more. It's my Panama Canal. I bought it, I paid for it, it's mine, and I intend to keep it."

She shook her head, smiling ruefully. She said that she had lived in half a dozen houses over the years and remembered each one down to the smallest detail: the color of the tile in the bathroom and the shape of the clothes closet in the bedroom.

She and Doran had lived in Provincetown for a year, and then
had moved to Gloucester. That was when Doran was trying to
paint. Then, after Doran, she lived alone in Marblehead. When
she was married to Frank Greer they went to New York, then
returned to Boston; he owned an apartment on Beacon Hill. They
lived alone there for two years, and then moved to Beverly —
her idea; she was tired of the city. She counted these places on
her fingers. "Six," she said. "And all this time, you've been in
the same place in the Back Bay." She was leaning across the table,
and now she looked up. The waiter placed a small salad in front
of her and the oysters in front of me. The oysters were Cotuits.
She signaled for the wine and said that "Monsieur" would taste.
She told the waiter I was a distinguished gourmet, much sought
after as a taster, and that my wine cellar in Michigan City was
the envy of the region. She gave the impression that the restaurant
was lucky to have me as a patron. The waiter shot me a sharp
look and poured the wine into my glass. I pronounced it fine.
Actually, I said it was "swell," and then, gargling heartily, "dandy."
I gave Beth one of the oysters and insisted that she eat it the way
it was meant to be eaten, naked out of the shell, without catsup
or horseradish. She sucked it up, and leaned across the table once
again. "Don't you miss them, the arguments? The struggle, always
rubbing off someone else? The fights, the friction —?"

I laughed loudly. "Miss them to death," I said.

* * *

We finished the bottle of white and ordered a bottle of red; she
said she preferred red with fish. I suspected that that was a
concession to my entrecôte, which at any event was rare and
bloody. She continued to press, gently at first, then with
vehemence. She was trying to work out her life and thought that
somehow I was a clue to it. At last she demanded that I describe
my days in Boston. She wanted to know how I live, the details,
"the quotidian." I was reluctant to do this, having lived privately
for so many years. Also, there was very little to describe. I had
fallen into the bachelor habit of total predictability. Except to travel
to the airport and the courts, I seldom left the Back Bay. My
terrain was bordered by the Public Garden and the Ritz, Storrow
Drive, Newbury Street, the brownstone where I worked, and
Commonwealth Avenue where I lived. I walked to work, lunched

at the Ritz, took a stroll in the Garden, returned to the brownstone, and at seven or so went home. People I knew tended to
live in the Back Bay or on the Hill, so if I went out in the evening
I walked. Each year it became easier not to leave the apartment;
I needed an exceptional reason to do so. I liked my work and
worked hard at it.

She listened avidly, but did not comment. The waiter came to
clear the table and offer dessert. We declined, ordering coffee
and cognac.

"What kind of car do you have?" she asked suddenly.

I said I didn't own one.

"What kind of car does she own?"

I looked at her: Who?

"Your secretary," she said. "I hear you have a relationship with
your secretary."

"She's been my assistant for a very long time," I said.

"Her car," Beth said.

I said, "A Mercedes."

"Well," she said.

"Well, what?"

"Well, nothing," she said. "Except so do I."

"Two cheers for the Krauts," I said.

"Is she a nice woman?"

I laughed. "Yes," I said. "Very. And very able."

"She approves of the arrangement."

"Beth," I said.

Beth said, "I wonder what she gets out of it."

"She won't ever have to get divorced," I said. "That's one thing
she gets out of it."

"Was she the woman in the outer office?"

"Probably," I said.

Beth was silent a moment, toying with her coffee cup. There
was only one other couple left in the restaurant, and they were
preparing to leave. "You were always secretive," she said.

"You were not exactly an open book."

She ignored that. "It's not an attractive trait, being secretive.
It leaves you wide open."

For what? I wondered. I looked at her closely, uncertain whether
it was she talking or the wine. We were both tight, but her voice
had an edge that had not been there before. I poured more coffee,
wondering whether I should ask the question that had been in my

mind for the past hour. I knew I would not like the answer, whatever it was, but I was curious. Being with her again, I began to remember things I had not thought of in years; it was as if the two decades were no greater distance than the width of the table, and I had only to lean across the space and take her hand to be twenty-five again. The evening had already been very unsettling and strange; no reason, I thought, not to make it stranger still.

I said quietly, "How was I so bad?"

"You never let go," she said. "You just hung on for dear life."

"Right," I said. I had no idea what she was talking about.

"Our plans," she began.

"Depended on me letting go?"

She shrugged. "You tried to fit in and you never did."

"In Boston," I said.

She moved her head, yes and no; apparently the point was a subtle one. "I didn't want to come back here and you insisted. I was depending on you to take me away, or at least make an independent life. You never understood that I had always been on the outs with my family."

I stifled an urge to object. I had never wanted to come to Boston. It was where she lived. It was her town, not mine. Glorious Boston, cradle of the Revolution. I had no intrinsic interest in Boston; I only wanted to leave the Midwest. Boston was as good a city as any, and she lived there —

"You were such a damn good *listener.*" She bit the word off, as if it were an obscenity. "Better than you are now, and you're pretty good now. Not so good at talking, though. You listened so well a woman forgot that you never talked yourself, never let on what it was *that was on your mind.* Not one of your strong points, talking."

"Beth," I said evenly. She waited, but I said nothing more; there was nothing more to say anyhow, and I knew the silence would irritate her.

"And it was obvious it would never work; we never got grounded here. And it was obvious you never would, you could never let go of your damn prairie *complexe d'infériorité.* And as a result you were" — she sought the correct word — "*'louche.'*"

"I am not André Malraux," I said. "What the hell does that mean?"

"It means secretive," she said. "And something more. Furtive."

"Thanks," I said.

"It's a mystery to me why I'm still here. Not so great a mystery as you, but mystery enough. You had to lead the way, though, and you didn't. And I knew H,W was a mistake."

"It was your uncle who suggested it," I said.

"After you asked him," she said.

"At your urging," I said.

"When it looked like you wouldn't land anything and I was tired of the griping."

"You were the one who was nervous," I said.

"I didn't care where we lived," she said. "That was the point you never got." Her voice rose, and I saw the waiter turn and say something to the maître d'. The other couple had left and we were alone in the restaurant. Outside, a police car sped by, its lights blazing, but without sirens. The officer in the passenger seat was white-haired and fat, and he was smoking a cigar. It had stopped snowing but the wind was fierce, blowing debris and rattling windows. The police car had disappeared. I motioned to the waiter for the check. But Beth was far from finished.

"So I married Doran."

"And I didn't marry anybody."

"You married Rachel."

"According to you, Rachel doesn't count."

"Neither did Doran."

The waiter brought the check and I automatically reached for my wallet. She said loudly, "No," and I looked at her, momentarily confused. I had forgotten it was her treat. I had become so absorbed in the past; always when we had been together, I had paid, and it seemed cheap of me to let her pay now. But that was what she wanted and I had agreed to it. She had the check in her hand and was inspecting it for errors. Then, satisfied, she pushed it aside along with a credit card. She exhaled softly and turned to look out the window.

She said quietly, talking to the window, "Do you think it will be easy?"

"I don't know," I said.

"Please," she said. She said it hesitantly, as if the word were unfamiliar. "Just tell me what you think. I won't hold you to it if you're wrong."

"His lawyer," I began.

"Please," she said again, more forcefully.

"You're asking me for assurances that I can't give. I don't know."

"Just a guess," she said. "In your line of work you must make guesses all the time. Make one now, between us. Between friends."

"Well, then," I said. "No."

"The first one was easy."

"Maybe this will be too," I said.

"But you don't think so."

"No," I said. I knew Frank Greer.

She said, "You're a peach." She put on her glasses.

I did not reply to that.

"I mean it," she said.

Apparently she did, for she looked at me and smiled warmly. "I have disrupted your life."

I shook my head no.

"Yes, I have. That's what I do sometimes, disrupt the lives of men."

There was so much to say to that, and so little to be gained. I lit a cigarette, listening.

With a quick movement she pushed the half-glasses over her forehead and into her hair, all business. "Get in touch with him tomorrow. Can you do that?"

"Sure," I said.

"And let me know what he says, right away."

"Yes," I said.

"I don't think it's going to be so tough."

"I hope you're right," I said.

"But I've always been an optimist where men are concerned."

I smiled and touched her hand. I looked at her closely, remembering her as a young woman; I knew her now and I knew her then, but there was nothing in between. That was undiscovered territory. I saw the difficulties ahead. They were big as mountains, Annapurna-size difficulties, a long slog at high altitudes, defending Beth. I took my hand away and said, "You can bail out any time you want if this gets difficult or awkward. I know it isn't easy. I can put you in touch with any one of a dozen —" She stared at me for a long moment. In the candlelight her face seemed to flush. Suddenly I knew she was murderously angry.

"I think you're right," she said.

"Look," I began.

"Reluctant lawyers are worse than useless." She took off her glasses and put them in her purse. When she snapped the purse shut it sounded like a pistol shot.

"I'll call you tomorrow," I said. I knew that I had handled it badly, but there was no retreat now.

She stood up and the waiter swung into position, helping her with her chair and bowing prettily from the waist.

Outside on Boylston Street the wind was still blowing, and the street was empty except for two cabs at the curb. We stood a moment on the sidewalk, not speaking. She stood with her head turned away, and I thought for a moment she was crying. But when she turned her head I saw the set of her jaw. She was too angry to cry. She began to walk up the street, and I followed. The wind off the Atlantic was vicious. I thought of it as originating in Scotland or Scandinavia, but of course that was wrong. Didn't the wind blow from west to east? This one probably originated in the upper Midwest or Canada. It had a prairie feel to it. We both walked unsteadily with our heads tucked into our coat collars. I thought of Tom and his camel-hair coat. At Arlington Street she stopped and fumbled for her keys, and then resumed the march. A beggar was at our heels, asking for money. I turned, apprehensive, but he was a sweet-faced drunk. I gave him a dollar and he ambled off. Her car was parked across the street from the Ritz, a green Mercedes convertible with her initials in gold on the door. The car gleamed in the harsh white light of the streetlamps. She stooped to unlock the door, and when she opened it the smell of leather, warm and inviting, spilled into the frigid street. I held the door for her, but she did not get in. She stood looking at me, her face expressionless. She started to say something, but changed her mind. She threw her purse into the back seat and the next thing I knew I was reeling backward, then slipping on an icy patch and falling. Her fist had come out of nowhere and caught me under the right eye. Sprawled on the sidewalk, speechless, I watched her get into the car and drive away. The smell of leather remained in my vicinity.

The doorman at the Ritz had seen all of it, and now he hurried across Arlington Street. He helped me up, muttering and fussing, but despite his best intentions he could not help smiling. He kept his face half turned away so I would not see. Of course he knew me; I was a regular in the bar and the café.

Damn woman, I said. She could go ten with Marvin Hagler.

He thought it all right then to laugh.

Not like the old days, I said.

Packed quite a punch, did she, sir? Ha-ha.

I leaned against the iron fence and collected my wits.

Anything broken? he asked.

I didn't think so. I moved my legs and arms, touched my eye. It was tender but there was no blood. I knew I would have a shiner and wondered how I would explain that at the office.

Let's get you into the bar, he said. A brandy —

No. I shook my head painfully and reached for my wallet. The doorman waited, his face slightly averted as before. I found a five, then thought better of it and gave him a twenty. He didn't have to be told that twenty dollars bought silence. He tucked the money away in his vest and tipped his hat, frowning solicitously.

You wait here one minute, he said. I'll fetch a cab.

No need, I replied. Prefer to walk. I live nearby.

I know, he said, looking at me doubtfully. Then, noticing he had customers under the hotel canopy, he hurried back across the street. I watched him go, assuring the people with a casual wave of his hand that the disturbance was a private matter, minor and entirely under control.

I moved away too, conscious of being watched and realizing that I was very tight. I was breathing hard and could smell my cognac breath. I felt my eye beginning to puff and I knew that I would have bruises on my backside. I decided to take a long way home and walked through the iron gate into the Garden. There was no one about, but the place was filthy, papers blowing everywhere and ashcans stuffed to overflowing. The flurries had left a residue of gray snow. I passed a potato-faced George Washington on horseback on my way along the path to the statue facing Marlborough Street. This was my favorite. Atop the column a physician cradled an unconscious patient, "to commemorate the discovery that the inhaling of ether causes insensibility to pain. First proved to the world at the Mass. General Hospital." It was a pretty little Victorian sculpture. On the plinth someone had scrawled UP THE I.R.A. in red paint.

I exited at the Beacon Street side. A cab paused, but I waved him on. I labored painfully down Beacon to Clarendon and over to Commonwealth, my shoes scuffing little shards of blue glass, hard and bright as diamonds; this was window glass from the automobiles vandalized nightly. While I waited at the light a large

American sedan pulled up next to me, its fender grazing my leg, two men and a woman staring menacingly out the side windows. I took a step backward, and the sedan sped through the red light, trailing rock music and laughter. Tires squealed as the car accelerated, wheeling right on Newbury.

My flat was only a few blocks away. I walked down the deserted mall, my eyes up and watchful. Leafless trees leaned over the walkway, their twisted branches grotesque against the night sky. I walked carefully, for there was ice and dog shit everywhere. The old-fashioned streetlights, truly handsome in daytime, were useless now. It was all so familiar; I had walked down this mall every day for twenty years. Twenty years ago, when there was no danger after dark, Rachel and I took long strolls on summer evenings trying to reach an understanding, and failing. I remembered her musical voice and her accent; when she was distressed she spoke rapidly, but always with perfect diction. I looked up, searching for my living room window. I was light-headed now and stumbling, but I knew I was close. The Hancock was to my left, as big as a mountain and as sheer, looming like some futuristic religious icon over the low, crabbed sprawl of the Back Bay. I leaned against a tree, out of breath. There was only a little way now; I could see the light in the window. My right eye was almost closed, and my vision blurred. The wind bit into my face, sending huge tears running down my cheeks. I hunched my shoulders against the wind and struggled on, through the empty streets of the city I hated so.

The Balloon of William Fuerst

LOWELL B. KOMIE

ILLIAM FUERST WAS VERY TIRED. He'd been a lawyer for twenty years and he was very tired. He'd been dragging himself to the office. He could barely make his morning court call. The telephone had become his enemy. The minute he walked into the office the receptionist would hit him with a sheaf of calls. Little urgent notes on red and white message paper. Monday mornings were the worst. All the crazies were waiting for him. The lonely widows: "Oh, Mr. Fuerst, I hope I'm not disturbing you. I had the most awful experience with one of the delivery boys from the drugstore. I gave him a fifteen-cent tip for bringing me a package" — probably a bottle of bourbon— "and he called me a bitch. Now isn't that insolence? Don't you think so? You do think I'm right in reporting him, don't you?"

As soon as he'd hang up and reach for his cup of coffee, the receptionist would hit him again. She knew just when he was at his early morning ebb and she'd let all the crazies come pouring through the switchboard. Finally he'd open his office door and scream at her, "No more calls! Not one, goddamit!"

Then there was the matter of the time book. His was a little black book that he filled with squiggles—time records of his phone calls. After he shut off the calls at the board he'd have to reconstruct time for the time book. It was like taking the calls all over again. "Mrs. Hardiman, .25—call." Fuerst had invented the office decimal system. He remembered when he'd called the special meeting of his partners. He was convinced that a phone call couldn't take less than fifteen minutes. We should keep track

40

of the phone calls at a decimal value of .25. One had to consider the interruption in flow of the lawyer's work, the break in rhythm of the lawyer's concentration. He still remembered his little speech. The way he gracefully used his hands at the conference table, gesturing, holding the red pencil like a conductor's baton. Every call should be treated uniformly as .25. One of the three partners wasn't even recording phone calls. He pointed the red pencil at the offender. He tapped the red pencil impatiently and stared. He was only forty then, still bright-eyed, interested in efficiency. Adamant. At $60 an hour, each call was worth $15. Ten accurately recorded calls a day were worth $150. He smiled at his three partners. That would pay the receptionist's salary for a week. The partners agreed to the Fuerst decimal system. For five years he'd been proud of it. He'd put it across with the red pencil baton like a conductor leading a reluctant quartet, positively, deftly, with graceful gestures. The Fuerst decimal system had worked. Now he was forty-five and very tired. He just didn't give a damn. In fact, his head was leaking time and he was glad about it. He didn't tell any of his partners about the time leak. He always now had the feeling that there was a slight hissing of air from his ears. No one else could hear it, though. A hiss of all the useless acts he performed every day. His vitality, his intelligence, his youth, all being drained away from this secret rent in his head. He knew there was a tiny leak in his head and he'd have to repair it. How to fix it though he didn't know. He'd think about it.

He tried to reconstruct the calls for his time book this morning before he left for the morning court call. There was the woman and the delivery boy. Oh yes, then the man who bought a lemon. The engine was falling out. Some lawyer out in the suburbs had referred him. The man had no money, so Fuerst told him to call Legal Aid or Consumer Fraud. The man called back three more times for advice. He couldn't mark those calls down. Why had he taken them? Why couldn't the receptionist have screened them out?

Then there was the glazier he'd represented in a divorce. Now the glazier was remarried to a younger woman and his first wife was suing for back support. The first wife had taken a lover, though, and they were living in the glazier's house with the glazier's eight-year-old boy. The glazier wanted Fuerst to take the child and the house away. He listened to his client screaming that his ex-wife was a whore. Fuerst hummed to himself and, as the man screamed, doodled patterns—whirlpools of the client's frenzy, circles, triangles, and hexagons. Fuerst could hear a buzz saw in the background cutting glass. Finally the man hung up. When the phone clicked off, Fuerst immediately sensed the hissing sound of air escaping from his ears. He wondered if anyone else heard it. He looked around the office. The stenographers were busy typing. The receptionist was staring at her switchboard.

Fuerst sat down and stared out the window at the lake. The phone rang again. An officer from his bank. Maybe he should put two Band-Aids over his ears to stop the hissing. He took the call from the banker. Fuerst was ten days overdue on his term loan. In twenty years as a lawyer, he'd managed to accumulate a bank debt of $15,000. When he thought about it, he began to sweat. The perspiration was barely perceptible but it was like a fine mist across his forehead. The young man from the bank had been polite: "Perhaps, Mr. Fuerst, there's been a mistake? We haven't received your payment. There was $2,000 due on principal and $950 on interest ten days ago." Fuerst lied to the young banker and told him the check was in the mail. Now the only problem was where to get $3,000? Maybe he'd go to another bank and borrow it. But then he'd have to lie about the $15,000 owed to the first bank because no bank in Chicago would give him another three when he was still out with fifteen. He could just imagine the conversation. Another young loan officer, another pinstriped suit, silk tie, shoes gleaming. "And what did you say you did with the $15,000, sir?"

"Taxes, it mostly went for taxes. And then some remodeling on the house. I don't know. It just grew. But I can handle it." (It was none of this kid's business whether he could handle it.)

Fuerst put his hat on the back of his head and his raincoat over his shoulder and took one more call. He was ready to leave for court. The call was from a man who wanted new instructions in his will.

"I want to be cremated," he said plaintively to Fuerst without saying hello. "And I want it in the will. No urn, Fuerst, do you understand? No *urn*. I want my ashes taken up in a plane and scattered over Lake Michigan. Scattered to the winds. I want my eyes given to Northwestern. I want my heart and my liver given to the University of Chicago."

"I don't know if we can do all that," Fuerst said quietly.

"Why not?"

Fuerst could hear the familiar whine toward frenzy in the client's voice.

"Why not?" the man shouted. "Don't tell me that can't be done. My friends are doing it."

"Giving parts of their bodies away?"

"Everything, hearts, lungs, eyes. What's the big deal?"

"Nothing. I'll take care of it for you." Fuerst hung up. He had a vision of a pilot in an old biplane, struggling with the box containing the client's ashes. The pilot has a white silk scarf streaming around his throat, and, when he tosses the ashes into the slipstream, they blow back into his face and smudge his immaculate white scarf. Fuerst smiled.

At the courthouse, William Fuerst kept his eye on his hat and coat. They don't teach a course about that in law school. Hat and Coat Watching 103. In the divorce courts in particular it's always important to keep one's hat and coat in full view. Hung out of sight in a back room . . . the lawyer returns from losing a motion at the bench . . . whisk . . . he's also lost his hat and coat. A double loss. So Fuerst sat at the divorce motion call carefully watching the slim tapered obelisk where he'd hung his raincoat and his hat. The clothes post reminded him of the obelisk in the Place de la Concorde and the lawyers scurrying around the courtroom reminded him of automobiles in Paris. No, that was not really true. They reminded him of fish he'd seen in a lagoon in the Florida Keys—barracudas, sharks, stingrays, lethal fish that will prey on you and rip your throat open. They don't teach divorce law either in the law schools, like how to drop $1,000 to a judge's campaign fund. (Drop a dime and make out like a bandit on motions for fees and child support.) Fuerst can remember his constitutional law professor in the wrinkled suit with the glasses on his nose droning on and on for a semester about *Marbury v. Madison*. Nothing about how to schmeer in the divorce courts. Fuerst would drop a dime, too, if he had any money to schmeer. The banks have all his money on overdue notes. Anyway, he was specializing now in keeping his eye on his hat and coat on the obelisk. He couldn't think clearly about bribery. Also there was the matter of the slow leak in his head.

After the divorce courtroom he walked slowly over to Probate where the judges were more honest but still it was necessary to protect your hat and coat from the lawyers. He hung his raincoat and hat on a Probate Obelisk. Here you only schmeered the clerks at Christmas with bottles of Scotch and maybe a box of cigars. There were a few well-dressed women lawyers seated in the courtroom. Fuerst could tell by the exchange of glances between a young woman and an older man that there was a special relationship between them. They were too animated. Her cheeks were flushed. She touched the top of his fingers and swept her hair back over her shoulders and laughed. There was byplay.

Fuerst watched them and then he remembered a young woman at law school. She'd sat next to him in the first semester of contracts and there'd been byplay between them. At least Fuerst had thought so. He remembered her long eyelashes, her reticence, the very pale face and silken auburn hair. Occasionally they'd speak between classes, in the basement with paper cups of coffee. She was having a hard time. She was reluctant to talk about it. She just didn't understand some of the courses. He tried to get her to join a study group, but she never came around. In the second semester she disappeared, and they found her one afternoon in her room hanging from the noose she'd made of her bathrobe cord. She'd stepped off her wastebasket and choked herself to death because she couldn't handle law school.

In those days there was no student health service with therapists. Fuerst had thought that all women law students eventually hung themselves or else became librarians. Then suddenly they reappeared as confident young women with silk bows on their blouses and gold rims around the soles of their shoes. Eyes flashing, some of the young ones had even whipped him badly in argument in the Federal Court. So now, in the Probate Court, he would only nod to the women and sit at one side far away from them, remembering the lovely young girl with auburn hair who stepped off her wastebasket. His eyes were on the coatrack, his hands just playing with the hair at his ears, feeling for the movement of escaping air. His face showed no sign. He had a smile, a confident smile.

After court, he took the elevator down and walked out on the Civic Center Plaza. The sun was beginning to break through the morning fog, and, as he crossed the plaza, he removed his hat. There was a man in front of the Picasso statue selling helium-filled balloons. Fuerst bought one and a spray can of helium for his youngest child. As he walked back to his office, on impulse he filled the balloon and then, just at the entrance of his building, he let the balloon drift away. No one paid attention to him. He watched the balloon surge up past the girders of a high-rise under construction.

When he returned to his office, the receptionist handed him another sheaf of messages. He carefully hung his hat and coat and went back to his office and closed the door. He tried to see his balloon out the window rising above the Chicago skyline. He couldn't find it. Then it occurred to him that he could patch the leak in his head with the same can of helium he'd used to inflate the balloon. At least he could replace the lost air. He didn't realize that helium would change the timbre of his voice. He gave himself a trial squirt. When the receptionist hit him with the first call back to the new sheaf of crazies, he answered with a high, tiny voice that sounded just like Mickey Mouse.

"Hello," William Fuerst squeaked in the Mickey Mouse voice.

It was the same man who called previously about his ashes. "Is that you, Fuerst?"

"It's me," the Mickey Mouse voice said.

"It don't sound like you."

William Fuerst opened his mouth wide and gave himself another squirt of helium. He could feel a slow cessation of the hissing in his head, as if the rent were sealing.

"Fuerst. Do you understand? No urn. My ashes. No urn. Do you understand? Get a plane. A pilot."

"I understand," William Fuerst squeaked.

The hissing sound had stopped, though. He held the phone away and felt for movement of air at his ears. There was nothing. He put the client on hold. He knew that if he was silent for a while, the timbre of his voice would return to normal. He dropped the can of helium into his pocket and wondered what would happen if he lit a cigarette. He wanted a cigarette badly but he didn't want to end his career by immolating himself. He couldn't remember whether it was the *Hindenburg* or the *Graf* or was it the *Graf Spee*? Was it helium or hydrogen? He couldn't remember. The phone buzzed again. He gave himself another squirt. "Hello," he answered in the tiny squeaking voice.

"Is that you, Fuerst?"

He put a cigarette in his mouth and struck a match. He held the match in his fingers for a moment and stared at the sudden brightness of the flame and then touched it to the cigarette. Nothing happened. "Okay," he said into the phone, "you have my attention."

The Contract

HARVEY JACOBS

MARTIN HARLEN, A YOUNG MAN who believed in responsibility, took on the job of going through his aunt's papers and possessions a few weeks after she died. Annie Harlen Fine had lived for eighty-five years, sixty of them in the same Brooklyn flat. The family had tried to pry her loose from the "old neighborhood," which was turning into a slum, but the old lady would not budge.

Everyone assumed her decision to remain was sentimental. She had come to the little court off Flatbush Avenue as a bride, lived there through her marriage and raised two children in those rooms. The slow inventory of Aunt Annie's accumulations now made Martin Harlen think it was not so much sentimentality as gravity.

As he sorted through ancient documents, saved advertisements for products long since gone from the market, as he moved past heavy upholstered furniture, as he explored closets filled with dresses, coats, shoes, bags, as he brewed coffee in a kitchen loaded with pots, pans, dishes, cups, plates, utensils, an incredible collection of drinking glasses decorated with pictures of Shirley Temple, Snow White and the Seven Dwarfs, glasses that once held cottage cheese, memorial candles, Lord knows what, as he sorted mustard jars, horseradish bottles, tubby ketchup bottles, slender wine bottles, aristocratic seltzer bottles that perched like birds on high shelves, as he fumbled through drawers holding receipts, rubber bands, balls of foil, single stockings, hairpins, curlers, paper clips, clothespins, bottle caps, souvenir spoons from the 1939 World's Fair...the combined weight of Annie Fine's personal property added to enormous tonnage.

How could she move? It would have taken a caravan. Where could she move? To Radio City Music Hall? He had already filled ten cartons from the A&P with his aunt's leftovers and marked them for the Salvation Army. And there was hardly a dent in the mysterious glut.

When Martin Harlen volunteered to dismantle his aunt's apartment (Annie's son lived in Phoenix, her daughter in Santa Barbara, and neither could spare the time nor cared for the fate of the objects that remained after rings, watches, bonds, and the will had been removed from the safety deposit), he never expected such trouble. Still, someone had to do it. The apartment had to be vacated by the end of the month.

The work was slow and tedious. It was the fault of the *things* themselves. It was somehow necessary to stop and muse over the tiniest objects. Martin Harlen decided that possessions are transformed at the moment of their owner's death. Bits of ghost enter unlikely containers like empty jewelry boxes covered in plush, compacts, lamps, ashtrays, even rusty Flit guns and cans that held mothballs. *Why did she keep it?*

Martin Harlen loved his aunt. She was a tough lady, like a military jeep rolling from place to place on thick tires. She was the only one in the family who would tell him about the past. She admitted that her father went senile. She called her brother, Sol, a miser. She was glad when her children married and moved out of town. So if Aunt Annie's ghost had fractured and fragmented into a pile of junk, her nephew was determined to give the pile its due. He saw that as the fair price for the stories, the holiday meals, the brutal advice about the "world," the tours through albums of brown photographs.

When the bell rang, Martin Harlen thought it was another furniture dealer. He had suffered through three so far. They came in shabby clothes to look like poor men, they sniffed around the bed, the dresser, the end tables, the sofa, isolated mounds of towels and linen, scatter rugs, they browsed the kitchen, they sighed, wheezed, moaned, suffered, then quoted a ridiculous price for "the whole shebang." They told Martin Harlen *he* should pay *them* for the carting. Their names and offers were jotted down on a pad. Part of the responsibility was to get the best price he could for his aunt's heritage. That was not just because a dollar is a dollar. Annie Harlen Fine was a hard bargainer. Since it was to be that her *things* would go to strangers, dispersed to flea markets and second-hand shops, then price had to do with pride. She deserved a good deal.

What the Salvation Army didn't get would be converted to cash and the cash would be used carefully for necessities and pleasures. The guilty son and daughter said the whole ball of wax should go to some charity. Martin Harlen argued for keeping a share. Aunt Annie was a practical woman. Some to charity, then, and some to divvy up. It had to do with Annie's fresh ghost and what would bring peace.

The intercom to the downstairs door was broken. Martin Harlen could hear only a crackled voice in response to his yells. But he buzzed the visitor. It could be a furniture dealer or a thug with a hammer or a dragon. Life in the city demands chances. Besides, the greatest favor would be an arsonist in a mask. No such luck.

A knock, a tap, a clearing of the throat, was heard at the apartment door. A small, rotund, puffing man wearing a heavy overcoat and a Russian hat of Persian lamb (Aunt Annie had a stole like that) stood in the doorway holding a wooden box with a black handle.

"They said snow," he said. "It is cold. I should wear a scarf and gloves but I lose them. Like umbrellas."

"This is the Fine apartment," Martin said.

"I know. I read the obituary. I'm sorry. My condolences. Can I come inside?"

"Come in."

"I can't believe she passed. That was some lady. How are you related?"

"My aunt. Actually, my great-aunt."

"I met her children years ago. They didn't look like you. Maybe around the eyes. My name is Jack Pinsky. Pleased to make your acquaintance. Better on a happier occasion."

Martin Harlen introduced himself and shook a thin hand. Jack Pinsky slowly took off his coat and hat and laid them over a chair. He carried his wooden box with him to the sofa and placed it between his feet.

"I'm sitting without an invitation. You wouldn't believe it, but I am a seventy-seven-year-old man."

Jack Pinsky looked a hundred. His face was a pale triangle

blotched in red and blue from the weather. His lips were lavender, like Aunt Annie's drapes.

"So you knew my aunt?"

"Knew her? From a girl. At least, a very young woman. Beautiful woman. I once offered her plenty just to take off her clothes and let me gaze. She wouldn't do it."

"Excuse me, but are you talking about Mrs. Fine?"

"Fine is right. Delicious. What a face. What a body. So what are you doing here? Are you the executor of her estate?"

"Is that any of your concern, Mr. Pinsky?"

"I asked in a nice way. It is my business. My name don't ring any bells?"

"I'm afraid not."

"Then you didn't find the contract yet? It wasn't in her vault? I would think she'd keep it in the vault."

"I'm not aware of any contract. Look, I don't know what you're after, but..."

"But? But it is your responsibility to find the contract. That upon the death of the principal the contract should be returned to Jack Pinsky. It's in the contract. I need something hot to drink. You got coffee?"

"I'll make some instant. Mr. Pinsky, you're going to have to explain yourself. And I'm telling you, I am aware of scavengers who follow the death notices and show up with false claims, if you know what I'm getting at."

"Scavengers? Soap in your mouth. I can't believe she didn't mention the contract. Did she die sudden? Unexpected?"

"She died suddenly, yes."

"Ah. Ah. That explains that. You mind if I go in the bedroom?"

"Yes, I mind."

"Hey, I have been in there plenty of times. I'll prove it. There is a bed with posts. There is a window with a curtain of hand-embroidered angels holding harps. There is wallpaper with a scene from France of sheep with a lady and plenty flowers. Next to the bed, two tables with curvy legs. And across from the bed is a fantastic painting in a gold frame of a sunset over the Brooklyn Bridge. And in the lower righthand corner of that painting is the signature in gray of one Jack Pinsky. No saucer. No spoon. No napkin. Just in a cup is sufficient. Did I convince you?"

"I'll make the coffee."

While Jack Pinsky sipped hot coffee, Martin Harlen verified the signature.

"So?"

"You're that Jack Pinsky?"

"You want credentials? What do you want? Diners Club? Social Security? Medicare? What? Jack Pinsky in the lower righthand corner near the organ grinder with the ape written like it was in cement on the sidewalk. Right or wrong?"

"I saw it."

"You know when I painted that picture for Annie? Guess. The month she moved in here. I was still a kid in high school. Her friend, Hannah, knew my mother, may she rest in peace. Annie Fine needed a picture, so they sent me over with a picture and she bought it. My first sale. Three dollars. 'Sunset on the Brooklyn Bridge.' Painted from life. I don't begrudge Mrs. Fine the three dollars. Not the lousy price. The contract."

"What contract?"

"She made me sign a piece of paper. What did I know? I was a kid. I would have signed anyhow for that girl. She was very gorgeous."

"You told me."

"Terms and conditions. What did I know about terms and conditions? I signed. You're interested in the terms and conditions? The terms and conditions were that whenever your aunt changed her drapes or bedspread or the walls she could call Jack Pinsky to run over and fix the painting to match her new colors. And for nothing. No pay except the cost of the oil paint. Can you imagine? You know how many times that woman called me? In 1930 she got pink crazy. All pink in there. In 1939 she bought all new. God knows where she got the money. In the middle of World War Two she changed again. Beige. I hated it. During Truman, yellow. Eisenhower, she went green. During Nixon, blue with purple. Six times she called me. Change. Fix. The sun. The sky. The water. The bridge. The ape's jacket. She yelled at me. She cursed me. I came. And between you and me, I gave up art during Franklin D. Roosevelt's second term. But I came. I fixed. I honored the contract, which was probably illegal, since I was eighteen when I signed it. But I am an honorable man, maybe the last. Jack Pinsky signs his name, he means it. He changes. He fixes."

"I almost sold that painting to a dealer this afternoon."

"For how much?"

"It's hard to say. It was part of a parcel that included lamps, a gown, ornaments."

"You didn't sell. Something in you, a little voice, said don't sell."

"Exactly right."

"You got an eye. Like your aunt. Congratulations."

In the bedroom, Jack Pinsky ran fingers over the surface of "Sunset on the Brooklyn Bridge."

"It seems to have held up well, considering," said Martin Harlen.

"Considering the abuse. See here? In the original the bridge was more black. The sky was before a storm. Now it looks like a gypsy birthday cake. The damn wallpaper with the French sheep. Fix, change. But I did it. I am a successful man. Textiles. Flocking. I could buy and sell the whole Fine Family ten times. But I came. I remember when her husband died. Her children moved. I got the whole story. She stood over my shoulder telling me colors. Please, get me my box."

Martin Harlen brought in the box from the living room and watched Jack Pinsky open it to remove a smock and a small palette.

"What are you doing, Mr. Pinsky?"

"Terms and conditions. Upon the death of Mrs. Fine the artist shall have the right to fix back his painting titled 'Sunset on the Brooklyn Bridge' to its first combination of colors. Furthermore, the artist should get back the contract to rip up once and for all. I made her put that in the document, because while I was a kid I was smart. A term and condition was she could sell the painting with me to fix it. I knew she would never sell. I let her have that if when she died I would get back my rights. She died. Who can believe it? Rest in peace for a thousand years. But I'm not taking chances. I don't want any claims on me or my painting. I don't want any calls. That contract must be found and destroyed by me personally, and I will not leave until I have it in my hand."

"Be realistic, Mr. Pinsky. Look around you. I'm sure your contract is somewhere in those mounds, but how long will it take to find? If I find it."

"The stipulation is clear. In the event..."

"Calm yourself. I'll go through everything. I'm not promising to spend my life here, but if I find the contract, I personally will send it to you or burn it or whatever you want."

"Not enough. I'm getting back what I gave away and I am entitled."

"I agree to allow you to fix the painting."

"Restore. Not fix."

"In fact, Mr. Pinsky, I insist that you take the painting as a gift."

"Are you crazy? That painting is worth plenty today. I'm not interested in robbing the dead. Now, let me go to work. I would appreciate more coffee, not so dark. But let me work."

Martin Harlen put more water in his aunt's kettle and set it to boil. He went to the living room, where he had stacked a random ton of papers gathered from around the apartment. At the top of the pile was a *Daily News* with a headline about Eleanor Roosevelt feeding hot dogs to the King and Queen of England. Under the paper was a letter, under the letter an ad for Fairy soap, under that a lease, under the lease a song sheet, under that a recipe for honeyed sweet potatoes.

He heard Jack Pinsky humming from the bedroom. An old sunset would throw shadows on a still-young bridge. Under the recipe was some fabric, maybe cut from the bottom of somebody's pants. Under the fabric, a chart of stars, under the chart a map of New Jersey.

"Are you looking? Is there coffee?" said Jack Pinsky. "You think there was something between me and Annie? Your uncle was no Cary Grant. You want to ask me questions?"

Under the map of New Jersey was a collection of coupons and under the coupons a *Reader's Digest* contest letter with gold seals, more letters and a photograph of Annie Harlen Fine eating a jelly apple on a boardwalk. Martin Harlen sat on the floor near the papers. He examined a toaster lying there, a big Emerson radio, some books and a white plaster head of Mozart.

"When I rang downstairs you shouldn't have let me in without knowing who was coming up. That's the most dangerous thing," said Jack Pinsky. "You know, I'm surprised she didn't keep the contract in her vault. She must have had a vault."

"She trusted people," said Martin Harlen.

"A big mistake," said Jack Pinsky.

Still Life

Marian Thurm

A T HIS EX-IN-LAWS' THIRTY-FIFTH wedding anniversary party, Brad is the only guest to arrive in faded corduroy pants and a sweater that has seen better days. All the men are in ties and jackets, and most of the women are wearing dresses and lots of jewelry. But in a crowd of fifty people, it is doubtful whether anyone will notice him, and, anyway, he's not planning to stay long. He's only here because Nina followed up a written invitation with a phone call begging him to come. Nina, his ex-wife, has a new husband and a new baby and is the happiest person she knows. When she told all this to Brad over the phone last week, he immediately fell silent, though he knew that she was waiting for him to congratulate her on having achieved with someone else what had been only a painful subject for discussion when she was married to him. Listening to her go on about her happiness had exasperated him, and he cut the conversation short, perhaps was even the slightest bit rude, telling her the toaster oven had just popped open with his dinner and that he couldn't talk anymore. To make up for his rudeness he bought her parents a pair of carved wooden candlesticks that cost him more than he'd intended to spend. And for the baby he settled on a bear dressed in a blue hooded coat, red rubber boots, and a broad-brimmed yellow felt hat. The bear came in three sizes; he quickly decided on the largest, wondering later just whom he'd been trying to impress.

When he was first married to Nina, Brad had done very well at the large corporate law firm he worked for. But working for what seemed to be a thousand hours a week on what he was sure were the most unworthy cases in the world made him miserable. Understanding this, Nina encouraged him to quit. Given a choice between misery and happiness, it would be crazy to make the wrong decision, she said.

They left the city and moved up the Hudson to a tiny rented house in Garrison so Brad could be a country lawyer with Nina working as his secretary in an office they shared at the front of the house, just off the kitchen. At lunchtime, they went into the living room and ate their sandwiches on a black vinyl couch while they laughed at ancient reruns of "I Love Lucy." The couch had been borrowed from Nina's parents, and it was the one where she and Brad made love every Saturday night before their wedding. Brad found himself remembering their whispered conversations and the time Nina had said she loved him, her voice so soft he hadn't caught the words. "You what?" he'd asked her more than once (probably sounding a little cranky), but Nina was too embarrassed to repeat it. Later, whenever one of them mentioned love, the other always answered, "You what?"

They'd been in Garrison almost a year when the transmission in their Toyota went, and their stereo system and TV set needed major repairs, all in the same month.

"I just can't live like this anymore," Nina said one afternoon in the office, laying her head down on the typewriter so that her mahogany-colored hair streamed over the edge of the desk dramatically. "It kills me to admit it, but I was brought up to want things." Her voice was apologetic, even embarrassed. None of the things she named seemed unreasonable: a house with rooms larger than closets; vacation trips to interesting places; and, most important, children.

When he came around to her and caught her hair in his hands, Brad could see that she was crying. "Our marriage," she said, lifting her face to look at him. "I can't imagine letting it go."

That night, in bed, they talked about Nina's wanting to have a child, both of them trying hard to see how a baby might fit comfortably into their life together, but they came to the same conclusion: there wasn't any way they could manage it in the near future.

"It's only a matter of being patient," he soothed her, "of waiting for things to fall into place." For Brad, what mattered most was that he loved his work, that he was actually providing a useful service to a handful of ordinary, honorable people.

The following year, which turned out to be the last year of their marriage, Nina had an accidental pregnancy which ended in early miscarriage. She insisted on showing Brad exactly what they had lost. Looking at a book of magnified photographs of an eight-week-old fetus with pudgy hands and fingers and an indistinct face, Brad felt nothing but confusion—the photographs were like a display of abstract paintings. He wasn't as patient with Nina as he ought to have been, he realized. He was disappointed in her for having all but given up on their small-town, small-time life (her words), for having convinced herself that neither of them was adventurous enough or romantic enough to live from hand to mouth with any degree of grace or pleasure.

He waited for her to leave him, and when she did he could make no sense of her explanation. She just didn't want to be married, she said, to a man who showed so few signs of ever being happy. Refusing to meet his eyes, she said, "I fantasize about some kind of happiness for you, but I can't figure out where it's going to come from."

"You're talking about yourself," Brad told her, staring at the little opal ring she twirled around her finger. "You're the one to whom everything looks imperfect, impossible."

Now, nearly two years later, as he eases his way through Nina's parents' crowded living room and discovers Nina waving to him from a high-backed satin chair that looks like a throne, he has to smile. But his smile is vague, as if he were approaching someone he knew only slightly and couldn't remember from where.

"Didn't I get you that sweater for Christmas about a hundred years ago?" she asks him, but pleasantly.

He bends to kiss her, and as he does, the baby against her shoulder grabs a fistful of his hair and pulls so hard tears spring to Brad's eyes. Holding his breath, he unfolds the baby's tiny damp hand saying, "Is this what they call love at first sight?"

"Don't feel special," Nina says, laughing. "She does that to just about everyone."

The baby, a little bald girl in a knitted white dress and white tights, looks at Brad with wide-open eyes and then yawns.

"It *is* kind of a boring party," Nina says. "Lots of fourth cousins I've probably seen twice in my life. I'm sorry Ken's not here. I think you guys might have been able to strike up a conversation or two." The baby hiccups. "Well, maybe not," Nina says. "Maybe it's just as well."

"He's at the hospital?"

"His beeper went off the minute we got here, and that was that."

"It must be hard, never knowing when your plans are going to be disrupted."

"Not so hard. You make the best of it, that's all."

"Unbelievable," Brad says. "Is that your new philosophy of life I'm hearing?"

"Baby doll," a voice says. "Brad!" He turns to see Nina's grandmother smiling in his direction. Approaching him, Evelyn puts a hand over each of his ears and kisses him on the forehead. "You know, I'm very disappointed in you," she says. "Come over here so I can talk to you." Leading him into a spare bedroom full of coats, she closes the door behind them and leans against a plastic-mesh playpen.

"I should have called you," Brad says. "I'm sorry I dropped out of sight like that."

"You know, when Nina told me she was going to marry this other young man, I just felt sick," says Evelyn. "It makes you sick to your stomach to hear a story like that. 'What's so terrible about Brad,' I asked her, 'that you couldn't make an effort to keep your marriage in one piece?'"

Nina's grandmother is five feet tall, but broad and fleshy. She is wearing black leather Space shoes, the only shoes that fit her at all, and a fancy silk dress with swirls of magenta and gray. "How do you like these new cataract glasses they've got me wearing?" she asks Brad. "They keep slipping down on my nose and all day long I'm annoyed with them."

"I didn't even know you'd had the surgery. Nina and I haven't really been in touch." He hangs his head, feeling bad that he's neglected her. When he was married to Nina, her grandmother used to send him a soft, battered-looking ten-dollar bill on his birthday, slipped between a large index card folded in half. Front and back, the index card said "With 'love'"—no signature. He and Nina had never figured out what the quotation marks meant, though near the end of their marriage, Nina admitted she'd always assumed her grandmother was mocking him, letting him know that in her eyes he would forever be an in-law, never the real thing. Brad, who was touched by her gifts (which he could never bring himself to spend), considered that ridiculous. There were four bills in all, one for each year of their marriage. He kept them in a coffee mug on the top of his dresser, along with some loose buttons, a set of tarnished cuff links, and a torch-shaped National Junior Honor Society pin that he'd given Nina as a joke when they'd got engaged.

"At the end of my life, I'm seeing things differently," Evelyn tells him. "I look through these dumb glasses and everything is bright and glittery, like diamonds." She says this with a mixture of amazement and disgust, shaking her head slowly. Now her voice has softened to a whisper. "Do you want me to tell you about Nina's new husband? I see things there that keep me up at night, if you understand what I'm saying."

Sitting at the edge of a bed piled with coats, Brad trails his hand through someone's mink. "She claims to be very happy," he says.

"For some people, women especially, the loneliness is too much. They'll do anything to avoid it," says Evelyn. She looks up at Brad, her eyes exaggerated and blurred behind the lenses of her glasses. "And you?"

"I work very hard," he says quickly, feeling defensive. "And after work, I'm usually in the basement, puttering around, refinishing furniture—that kind of thing." He stands up, sticks his hands in front of her face, lets her see that his fingers are stained a reddish brown.

Evelyn takes a step back from him. "So you're down in the basement all night. So that's what you've been up to."

"There's more," he says, but won't elaborate. There are friends he occasionally drinks with, women he occasionally sleeps with; there's no point in telling her any of this. Still, he hates it that his life sounds so stark, so needy. "I'm getting by," he says. "Sometimes it seems almost enough."

"This new husband," says Evelyn, "is a toothpick of a man. All sharp bones and about ten feet tall. Do you want to see a picture of him?"

"Are you kidding?" Brad says. "Not even a snapshot."

"He doesn't talk to her nicely. Even before they were married, he was speaking to her the wrong way, as if she were a salesgirl in some store wasting his time, showing him all the wrong things."

"Listen to me," Brad says. "You can't contradict someone when they say they're happy. It just can't be done."

"You stubborn mule," Evelyn says sadly. "I could just kill you. I could put my hands around your throat and..."

* * *

At Nina's suggestion, she and Brad are going to take the baby for a walk around the block in her carriage. Outside in front of the house, one of Nina's cousins is washing his new car, a Datsun 280ZX with a red leather interior. The cousin, who is called Bobby, is dressed in a zippered jump suit, despite the cold. Underneath a mimosa tree across from the Datsun is a portable tape deck playing David Bowie songs.

"Perfect day for a car wash," Bobby says, pointing to the cloudless sky with a dripping sponge.

"I just love your jump suit," Nina says. She winks at Brad. "Ideal for any occasion, no matter how formal."

"Did you get the invitation to my wedding?" Bobby asks.

"We're looking forward to it."

"Well, tear it up," says Bobby. "The wedding's off."

"That's a shame. I don't know what else to say."

"Yeah, well, to thine own self be true and all that jazz," Bobby says. "From now on, it's just me and my Z."

"Beautiful car," Brad says.

"You bet." Spinning around and facing the hood, Bobby opens his arms wide, as if in an embrace.

Brad and Nina walk slowly along a sharply curving street past houses set close together on frozen, gray-brown lawns. "Cousin Bobby's clearly a man who knows his own heart," Brad says after a while.

"Pathetic," Nina hisses. She stops the carriage and leans in to look at the baby, who's already asleep. An angora hat with two small, peaked mouse ears covers the baby's head. "Am I prejudiced, or would anyone in the world agree this is one spectacular three-month-old?"

"Oh, I'm sure," says Brad.

"Of what?"

"Wait," he says. "Watch out," and he lifts the carriage over a large patch of swollen concrete, then sets it down gently.

"You're so funny," Nina says. "What a father you'd make."

He assumes she is being ironic, and feels insulted. "You're always doubting me, hinting that I'm incompetent. Even now, when you have no stake at all in anything I do."

"Sweetie pie," Nina says, and grabs his arm urgently. "That was a compliment back there. I was very moved, thinking what a devoted father you'd be. And actually, I've missed you," she says, leaning her head against his coat sleeve. "Though I guess not our life together."

"In another setting I'd be very desirable, is that what you're telling me?"

"I don't know what I'm telling you."

Rushing toward them from the other side of the street, a gray-haired man in a long tweed coat yells, "Do I see a baby?" He takes a large, awkward step over the curb and looks into the carriage.

"So what do you think, Dr. Glassman?" Nina explains to Brad that Dr. Glassman was her childhood dentist. "One year I had seventeen cavities and spent a whole summer in his office, clenching my fists and staring at the plaid curtains he had up over the window," she says.

"That's not seventeen teeth we're talking about, just seventeen surfaces," Dr. Glassman says. "Now tell me about your wonderful baby. Am I looking at a boy or a girl?"

"Her name is Amanda," Nina says, and pauses. "This is Seymour."

Dr. Glassman shakes Brad's hand. "I congratulate you on your lovely little family, Seymour. And my professional advice is that you enjoy to the fullest these years as a young family. It all passes like a dream; in the blink of an eye it's gone."

Brad nods. He feels Nina's hand slipping into his own. He is light-headed, thinking of his secret life as a husband and father. Soon his child will be grown and he and Nina will be middle-aged, comforting each other in the silence of their empty house.

"Seymour," Nina is saying.

"I'm right here."

"Don't you think we ought to be heading home?"

"Home?"

"Let me just suggest that you wipe the baby's gums with a wet washcloth at least once a day," Dr. Glassman says. "Even at this age." With his back turned to them, he raises a hand high over his head and waves good-bye.

"I'm feeling very lonely all of a sudden," Brad says, and sighs, watching Dr. Glassman disappear into a white Cadillac parked not too far up the street.

"What's the matter?"

"It's the empty-nest syndrome, striking a little early."

"You must think I'm a Looney Tune," Nina mumbles, "trying to pass you off as my husband."

"Don't you know you're talking to a man who drove ninety miles to a party he'd been dreading all week?" And then he is imagining, with astonishing ease, the two of them as lovers, their affair stretching effortlessly over a lifetime, accommodating her marriage, his marriage, children, grandchildren—every obstacle thrown (or carefully placed) in their path. As he envisions it, they won't ever be free to marry each other; really a very romantic notion, he thinks—just what is needed to keep things passionate. Not that he would want to be married to Nina again; he wouldn't dream of altering his life to suit her expectations. But at this moment, looking at her small, round winter-pale face, her eyes large and grave as a child's, he sees that what he has missed most these past two years is the thrill of desire. It seems incredible now that he's managed so long without it, indifferent to nearly everything except his work: women, friendship, the food he prepares for himself, the music he listens to as he falls asleep at night.

"Ninety miles," he says, and puts a hand over hers on the velvety roof of the carriage. He rubs his palm back and forth across her knuckles, no farther. Toward the end of his trip today, crossing the Throgs Neck Bridge, he'd been in such a panic that he missed the outstretched hand of the toll collector entirely, his quarters and dimes falling to the ground and rolling in all directions over concrete. The toll collector, a black woman about his age, looked on with amusement as he jumped from the car and on his knees gathered the coins together breathlessly, as if his life depended upon it. "You one desperate son of a bitch," the woman said, taking the money from him with both hands. Her hair was in dozens of little braids, decorated with beads and leather and thin gold coins. She shook her head at him, and the braids made a tinkling sound, like wind chimes. It was only later, when he arrived at the house and got out of the car, that he noticed his knuckles were bleeding slightly, the skin scraped in layers so delicate they were almost imperceptible.

Drinking champagne punch from clear plastic cups, Brad and Nina sit close to each other on a couch in her parents' den, their knees touching. On the other side of the room people are crowded around an aluminum folding table filled with platters of food. The room is uncomfortably warm. Too many people, too many chairs wherever you walk, too many hanging plants blocking your view out the jalousie windows.

A little girl, about four or so, wearing a long flowered skirt and white patent-leather clogs, is crouched on the step that leads into the den. She stares at Nina. "Where's your baby?" she says. She puts a cocktail frankfurter into her mouth and chews on it a long time. "My mother told me I could play with her."

"The baby's asleep in a bassinet in one of the bedrooms," Nina says. "And you know, the last time I saw you, Janey, you were a baby yourself."

"You have milk in your bosoms?" the little girl says.

Nina and Brad think this is very funny (they look at each other and smile), but Gloria, Janey's mother, who comes along at just the right moment, does not; she yanks her up from the step and says, "Watch your mouth, Lady Jane." Then she taps Brad on the knee, saying, "Terrific to see you."

"If you have any influence at all with your brother," Brad says, "maybe you could get me a whirlwind tour of the neighborhood in his new car."

"Oh, sure." Gloria rolls her eyes. "You came to just the right person."

"What happened to his girlfriend?" says Nina. "Or can't you tell us?"

"She traded him in for a better model, so to speak." Gloria looks startled, as if she can't believe what she's just heard. "Can I talk to you for a minute?" she asks Nina. She pulls at Nina's hand. "It's absolutely imperative."

As Nina rises from the couch and turns so that she is facing him, Brad sees what it is that has unnerved Gloria: two wet stains are spreading across the front of Nina's shiny, off-white blouse. She is leaking milk, he realizes, and then, unexpectedly, he is overwhelmed by a longing to shelter her, to shield her from the husband who speaks to her in a voice that has nothing to do with love.

"I have an announcement to make," Nina's grandmother hollers from the middle of the dining room. "The bride and groom will now cut the cake. I'd like everyone at the table right now. And that includes all those men who locked themselves away to watch football on TV."

Nina has disappeared. From all directions people begin moving toward the dining room table, which has been cleared of everything except a white sheet cake decorated with pink roses set in green-gray leaves, and stacks of dessert plates and silverware. Brad finds himself almost directly behind Nina's mother and father, to whom he hasn't said a word all afternoon. The candles are lit and blown out, then Nina's father is asked to make a speech. What does he have to say after thirty-five years of marriage, Nina's grandmother wants to know.

"Ah, well," Leon says, and clears his throat theatrically. "Life has its little disappointments." A few people, mostly men, laugh uneasily. Then there is silence. "A joke," Leon says, raising both arms in the air. "A *joke!*"

"You'll hear from me later, you stinker," Nina's mother says, but of course she is teasing him, her voice light and friendly as she guides cake into his open mouth with an ornate silver fork.

Leon has just spotted Brad and is motioning to him to come closer to the table. "Hey, buddy," he says. "Are you friend or foe?"

"Happy anniversary," Brad says. Nina's father seems slightly drunk. His smile is goofy, his face flushed and shiny. Brad doesn't like the feel of Leon's hand clamped on his wrist.

"Happy anniversary," says Leon. "And many more."

Nina's mother passes a plate of cake to Brad. "I'm going to cry," she whispers, tipping her head so that it's nearly resting on Brad's shoulder. "If anyone wants to know where I am, just tell them I'll be hiding in the bathroom for the remainder of the party."

Leon sighs as he lets go of Brad's arm. "Can I ask you a personal question? Yes? Did I invite you to this party? And if so, why?"

"It was Nina."

"Nina," Leon says, snapping his fingers in front of his face. "Who else." He blinks at Brad. "She's not a happy person, buddy. I don't know how she got that way, and I don't know what to do about it. I spend a lot of time thinking about it, though." His eyes are closed now. "Do you think I'm wasting my time?" When he doesn't get a response, Leon says, "At least there's a baby this time. That's something, I suppose."

Brad says, "I don't think you want to talk to me now. I think what you want to do is slice up the cake and pass it around to your guests, don't you?"

"The thing is," Leon says, "I don't think of it as a waste. There's no such thing as wasting your time when it comes to your children." Accepting the wedge-shaped knife Brad offers him, Leon runs his finger over the serrated edge. "When she was a little girl," he says, "Nina always had to have a rose."

Brad reaches for the knife and skims it along one side of the cake, collecting a row of perfect pink roses. Slowly, with a second knife, he transfers them to a plate that Leon holds solemnly in his hands.

Walking along the narrow hallway that leads to the bedrooms, his fingers curved around the thin china, Brad can feel his hands shaking slightly. Amazed, he stares at his strange coppery fingers, stained, he realizes now, the color of Nina's hair. He presses the rim of the plate into his middle, hugs it delicately, his elbows stiff at his sides.

He finds Nina in her parents' room, nursing Amanda in a blond bentwood rocker. Late-afternoon sunlight falls in narrow bands across Nina's thighs. The baby is asleep; Nina raises a finger to her lips in warning to Brad. She smiles at him, at the roses, but says nothing. The smile has not left her face as Brad settles on the floor with his back against the edge of the rocker. In his mind, they are a still life: a mother nursing her child in a sunlit room, while at her feet a man waits patiently, motionless, with a plate of bright roses.

After You've Gone

ALICE ADAMS

T HE TRUTH IS, for a while I managed very well indeed. I coped with the house and its curious breakages, and with the bad nights of remembering you only at your best, and the good days suddenly jolted by your ghost. I dealt with the defection of certain old friends, and the crowding-around of a few would-be new best friends. I did very well with all that, in the three months since your departure for Oregon, very well indeed until I began to get these letters from your new person (I reject "lover" as too explicit, and, knowing you, I am not at all sure that "friend" would be applicable). Anyway, Sally Ann.

(You do remember encouraging me to write to you, as somewhat precipatately you announced your departure—as though extending me a kindness? It will make you feel better, you just managed not to say. In any case, with my orderly lawyer's mind, I am putting events—or "matters," as we say—in order.)

The house. I know that it was and is not yours, despite that reckless moment at the Trident (too many margaritas, too palely glimmering a view of our city, San Francisco) when I offered to put it in both our names, as joint tenants, which I literally saw us as, even though it was I who made payments. However, your two-year occupancy and your incredibly skillful house-husbanding made it seem quite truly yours. (Is this question metaphysical, rather than legal? If the poet-husband of a house is not in fact a husband, whose is the house?) But what I am getting at is this. How could you have arranged for everything to break the week you left? Even the Cuisinart; no one else even heard of a broken Cuisinart, ever. And the vacuum. And the electric blanket. The dishwasher and the Disposal. Not to mention my Datsun. "Old wiring, these older flats," the repair person diagnosed my household problems, adding, "But you've got a beautiful place here," and he gestured across the park—green, pyramidal Alta Plaza, where even now I can see you running, running, in your eccentric non-regular-runner outfit: yellow shorts, and that parrot-green sweatshirt from God knows where, both a little tight.

My Datsun turned out simply to need a tune-up, and since you don't drive I can hardly blame that on you. Still, the synchronism, everything going at once, was hard not to consider.

Friends. Large parties, but not small dinners, my post-you invitations ran. Or very small dinners—most welcome, from single women friends or gay men; unwelcome from wives-away husbands, or even from probably perfectly nice single men. I am just not quite up to all that yet.

People whom I had suspected of inviting us because of your poet fame predictably dropped off.

Nights. In my dreams of course you still are here, or you are leaving and I know that you are, and there is nothing to do to stop you (you already told me, so sadly, about Sally Ann, and the houseboat in Portland). Recently I have remembered that after my father died I had similar dreams; in those dreams he was dying, I knew, yet I could not keep him alive. But those father dreams have a guilty sound, I think, and I truly see no cause for guilt on my part toward you. I truly loved you, in my way, and I did what I could (I thought) to keep us happy, and I never, never thought we would last very long. Isn't two years a record of sorts for you, for maybe any non-marrying poet? Sometimes I thought it was simply San Francisco that held you here, your City Lights–Tosca circuit, where you sought out ghosts of Beats. Well, in my dreams you are out there still, or else you are here with me in our (my) bed, and we awaken slowly, sleepily to love.

Once, a month or so ago, I thought I saw you sitting far back in a courtroom; I saw those damn black Irish curls and slanted eyes, your big nose and arrogant chin, with that cleft. A bad shock, that; for days I wondered if it actually could have been you, your notion of a joke, or some sort of test.

In all fairness, though—and since I mention it I would like to ask you something. Just why did my efforts at justice, even at seeing your side of arguments, so enrage you? I can hear you shouting: "Why do you have to be so goddam *fair*, what *is* this justice of yours?"

But as I began to say, in all fairness I have to concede that I miss your cooking. On the nights that you cooked, that is. I really liked your tripe soup and your special fettuccine with all those wild mushrooms. And the Sunday scrambled eggs that we never got to till early afternoon.

And you are a marvel at fixing things, even if they have a tendency not to stay fixed.

And, most importantly, a first-rate poet; Yale and now the Guggenheim people seem to think so, and surely as you hope the MacArthur group will come around. Having read so little poetry other than yours, I am probably no judge; however, as I repeatedly told you, to me it was magic, pure word-alchemy.

I do miss it all, the house-fixing and cooking, the love and poetry. But I did very well without it all. Until recently.

The letters. The first note, on that awful forget-me-not paper, in that small, tight, rounded hand, was a prim little apology: she felt badly about taking you away from me (a phrase from some junior high school, surely) but she also felt sure that I would "understand," since I am such a fair-minded person (I saw right off that you had described my habits of thought in some detail). I would see that she, a relatively innocent person, would have found your handsomeness-brilliance-sexiness quite irresistible (at that point I wondered if you could have written the letter yourself, which still seems a possibility). She added that naturally by now I would have found a replacement for you, the natural thing for a woman like me, in a city like San Francisco. That last implication, as to the loose life-styles both of myself and of San Francisco, would seem to excuse the two of you fleeing to the innocence of Portland, Oregon.

A couple of false assumptions lay therein, however. Actually, in point of fact, I personally might do better, man-wise, in Portland than down here. The men I most frequently meet are young lawyers, hard-core yuppies, a group I find quite intolerable, totally unacceptable, along with the interchangeable young brokers—real-estate dealers and just plain dealers. Well, no wonder that I too took up with a poet, an out-of-shape man with no CDs or portfolio but a trunk full of wonderful books. (I miss your books, having got through barely half of them. And did you really have to take the *Moby-Dick* that I was in the middle of? Well, no matter; I went out to the Green Apple and stocked up, a huge carton of books, the day you left.)

In any case, I felt that she, your young person, your Sally Ann, from too much evidence had arrived at false conclusions. In some ways we are more alike, she and I, than she sees. I too was a setup, a perfect patsy for your charm, your "difference."

But why should she have been told so much about me at all? Surely you must have a few other topics; reading poems aloud as you used to do with me would have done her more good, or at least less harm, I believe. But as I pondered this question, I also remembered several of our own conversations, yours and mine, having to do with former lovers. It was talk that I quite deliberately cut short, for two clear reasons: one, I felt an odd embarrassment at my relative lack of what used to be called experience; and, two, I did not want to hear about yours. You did keep on trying, though; there was one particular woman in New York, a successful young editor (though on a rather junky magazine, as I remember), a woman you wanted me to hear all about, but I would not. "She has nothing to do with us," I told you (remember?). It now seems unfortunate that your new young woman, your Sally Ann, did not say the same about me.

Next came a letter which contained a seemingly innocent question: should Sally Ann go to law school, what did I think? On the surface this was a simple request for semi-expert advice; as she went on and on about it, though, and on and on, I saw that she was really asking me how she could turn herself into me, which struck me as both sad and somewhat deranged. Assuming that you have an ideal woman on whom Sally Ann could model herself, I am hardly that woman. You don't even much like "lady lawyers," as in some of your worst moments you used to phrase it.

Not having answered the first note at all (impossible; what could I have said?), I responded to this one, because it seemed required, with a typed postcard of fairly trite advice: the hard work involved, the overcrowding of the field, the plethora of even token women.

And now she had taken to writing me almost every day; I mean it, at least every other day. Does she have no other friends? No relatives, even, or old school ties? If she does, in her present state of disturbance they have faded from her mind (poor, poor Sally Ann, all alone with you, in Portland, on a Willamette River houseboat), and only I remain, a purely accidental, non-presence in her life.

The rains have begun in Portland, and she understands that they will continue throughout the winter. She does not really like living on a houseboat, she finds it frightening; the boat rocks, and you have told her that all boats rock, there is nothing to be done. (You must be not exactly in top form either. I never heard you admit to an inability to remedy anything—even my Datsun; you said you could fix it and you did, temporarily.)

You have found some old friends over at Reed College, she tells me; you hang out a lot over there, and you tell her that she would be very much happier with a job. Very likely she would, but you have taken her to an extremely high unemployment area.

She doesn't understand your poetry at all, and doesn't know what to say when you read it to her. Well, this is certainly a problem that I too could have had, except that I dealt with it head-on, as it were, simply and clearly saying that I didn't understand poetry, that I had not read much or ever studied it. But that to me your poems sounded marvelous—which they did; I really miss the sound of them, your words.

You talk about me more and more.

You are at home less and less. And now Sally Ann confesses to me that she used to be a waitress at the Tosca; on some of the nights when I was at home, here in San Francisco (actually I used to be grateful for a little time to catch up on work), when I assumed you were just hanging out in North Beach, you were actually courting Sally Ann, so to speak. Well, at this point I find this new information quite painless to absorb; it simply makes me miss you even less. But Sally Ann wonders if I think you could possibly be seeing someone else now? She says that you've mentioned a French professor at Reed, a most talented woman, you've said. Do I think—?

Well, I most certainly do think; you seem to prefer women with very respectable professions, poor Sally Ann representing the single rule-proving exception, I suppose. Some sort of lapse in calculation on your part—or quite likely Sally Ann had more to do with me than with herself, if you see what I mean, and I think you will. In any case, a fatal error all around.

Because it is clear to me that in an emotional sense you are battering this young woman. She is being abused by you. I could prove it to a jury. And, unlike me, she is quite without defenses.

You must simply knock it off. For one thing, it's beneath you, as you surely in your better, saner, kinder moments must clearly see (you're not all bad; even in my own worst moments I recall much good, much kindness, even). Why don't you just give her a ticket to somewhere, along with some gentle, ego-preserving words (heaven knows you're at your best with words), and let her go? Then you can move in your Reed College French professor and live happily there on your houseboat—almost forever, at least until the Portland rains let up and you feel like moving on.

As for myself, it seems only fair to tell you that I have indeed found a new friend—or, rather, an old friend has reappeared in my life in another role. (*Fair.* As I write this, I wonder if in some way, maybe, you were right all along to object to my notion of fairness? There was always a slightly hostile getting-even element in my justice? Well, I will at least admit that possibility.) In any case, I am taking off on a small trip to Jackson, Wyoming, day after tomorrow, with my old-new friend. About whom I can only at this moment say so far so good, in fact very good indeed— although I have to admit that I am still a little wary, after you. However, at least for me he is a more known quality than you were (we were undergraduates together, in those distant romantic Berkeley days), and I very much doubt that you'll be getting any letter of complaint regarding me. He already knows what he's getting, so to speak.

And so, please wish me well, as I do you (I'll keep my fingers crossed for the MacArthur thing).

And, I repeat, let Sally Ann go. All three of us, you, me, and Sally Ann, will be much better off—you without her, and she without you. And me without the crazy burden of these letters, which, if I were *really* fair, I would send on to you.

Weight

MARGARET ATWOOD

I AM GAINING WEIGHT. I'm not getting bigger, only heavier. This doesn't show up on the scales: technically I'm the same. My clothes still fit, so it isn't size, what they tell you about fat taking up more space than muscle. The heaviness I feel is in the energy I burn up getting myself around: along the sidewalk, up the stairs, through the day. It's the pressure on my feet. It's a density of the cells, as if I've been drinking heavy metals. Nothing you can measure, although there are the usual nubbins of flesh that must be firmed, roped in, worked off. *Worked.* It's all getting to be too much work.

Some days, I think, I'm not going to make it. I will have a hot flash, a car crash. I will have a heart attack. I will jump out the window.

This is what I am thinking as I look at the man. He's a rich man, that goes without saying: if he weren't rich, neither of us would be here. He has excess money, and I'm trying to get some of it out of him. Not for myself; I'm doing nicely, thank you. For what we used to call charity and now call good causes. To be precise, a shelter for battered women. Molly's Place, it's called. It's named after a lawyer who was murdered by her husband, with a claw hammer. He was the kind of man who was good with tools. He had a workbench in the cellar. The lathe, the vise, the buzz saw, the works.

I wonder if this other man, sitting so cautiously across the tablecloth from me, has a workbench in the cellar too. He doesn't have the hands for it. No calluses or little nicks. I don't tell him about the claw hammer, or about the arms and legs hidden here and there about the province, in culverts, in wooded glades, like Easter eggs or the clues in some grotesque treasure hunt. I know how easily frightened such men can be by such possibilities. Real blood, the kind that cries out to you from the ground.

We've been through the ordering, which involved the rueful production of the reading glasses, by both of us, for the scanning of the ornate menu. We have at least one thing in common: our eyes are going. Now I smile at him and twiddle the stem of my wineglass, and lie judiciously. This isn't even my thing, I tell him. I got sucked into it because I have a hard time saying no. I'm doing it for a friend. This is true enough: Molly was a friend.

He smiles and relaxes. *Good,* he's thinking. I am not one of those earnest women, the kind who lecture and scold and open their own car doors. He's right, it's not my style. But he could have figured that out from my shoes: women like that do not wear shoes like this. I am not, in a word, *strident,* and his instinct in asking me to lunch has been justified.

This man has a name, of course. His name is Charles. He's already said: *Call me Charles.* Who knows what further delights await me? *Chuck* may lie ahead, or *Charlie. Charlie is my darling. Chuck, you big hunk.* I think I'll stick with Charles.

The appetizers arrive, leek soup for him, a salad for me, endive with apples and walnuts, veiled with a light dressing, as the menu puts it. *Veiled.* So much for brides. The waiter is another out-of-work actor, but his grace and charm are lost on Charles, who does not reply when ordered to enjoy his meal.

"Cheers," says Charles, lifting his glass. He's already said this once, when the wine appeared. Heavy going. What are the odds I can get through this lunch without any mention of the bottom line?

Charles is about to tell a joke. The symptoms are all there: the slight reddening, the twitch of the jaw muscle, the crinkling around the eyes.

"What's brown and white and looks good on a lawyer?"

I've heard it. "I'll bite. What?"

"A pit bull."

"Oh, that's terrible. Oh, you are awful."

Charles allows his mouth a small semicircular smile. Then apologetically: "I didn't mean woman lawyers, of course."

"I don't practice anymore. I'm in business, remember?"
But maybe he meant Molly.

Would Molly have found this joke funny? Probably. Certainly at
first. When we were in law school, working our little butts off
because we knew we had to be twice as good as the men to end
up with less than the same, we used to go out for coffee breaks
and kill ourselves laughing, making up silly meanings for the
things we got called by the guys. Or women in general got called:
but we knew they meant us.

"*Strident.* A brand of medicated toothpick used in treatment
of gum disease."

"OK! *Shrill.* As in the Greater Shrill. A sharp-beaked shorebird
native to the coasts of . . . "

"California? Yes. *Hysteria?*"

"A sickly scented flowering vine that climbs all over Southern
mansions. *Pushy?*"

"*Pushy.* That's a hard one. Rude word pertaining to female
anatomy, uttered by drunk while making a pass?"

"Too obvious. How about a large soft velvet cushion . . . "

"Pink or mauve . . . "

"Used for reclining on the floor while . . . "

"While watching afternoon soaps," I finished, not satisfied.
There should be something better for *pushy.*

Molly was pushy. Or you could call it determined. She had
to be, she was so short. She was like a scrappy little urchin, big
eyes, bangs over the forehead, tough little chin she'd stick out
when she got mad. She was not from a good home. She'd made
it on brains. Neither was I, so did I, but it affected us differently.
I for instance was tidy and had a dirt phobia. Molly had a cat
named Catty, a stray of course. They lived in cheerful squalor.
Or not squalor: disorder. I couldn't have stood it myself, but I
like it in her. She made the messes I wouldn't allow myself to
make. Chaos by proxy.

Molly and I had big ideas, then. We were going to change
things. We were going to break the code, circumvent the old boys'
network, show that women could do it, whatever it might be.
We were going to take on the system, get better divorce settle-
ments, root for equal pay. We wanted justice and fair play. We
thought that was what the law was for.

We were brave, but we had it backwards. We didn't know you had to begin with the judges.

But Molly didn't hate men. With men, Molly was a toad-kisser. She thought any toad could be turned into a prince if he was only kissed enough, by her. I was different. I knew a toad was a toad and would remain so. The thing was to find the most congenial among the toads and learn to appreciate their finer points. You had to develop an eye for warts.

I called this compromise. Molly called it cynicism.

Across the table, Charles is having another glass of wine. I think he's deciding that I am a good sport. So necessary in a woman with whom you're considering having an illicit affair; because that's what this lunch is really about. It's a mutual interview, for positions vacant. I could have made my charity pleas in Charles's office, and been turned down shortly and sweetly. We could have kept it formal.

Charles is good-looking, in the way such men are, though if you saw him on a street corner, lacking a shave and with his hand out, you might no think so. Such men always seem the same age. They were longing to be this age when they were twenty-five, and so they imitated it; and after they pass this age they will try to imitate it again. The weightiness of authority is what they want, and enough youth left to enjoy it. It's the age called *prime*, like beef. They all have that beefy thing about them. A meaty firmness. They all play something: they begin with squash, progress through tennis, end with golf. It keeps them trim. Two hundred pounds of hot steak. I should know.

All of it swathed in expensive dark blue suiting, with a thin stripe. A conservative tie down the front, maroon with a little design. This one has horses.

"Are you fond of horses, Charles?"

"What?"

"Your tie."

"Oh. No. Not particularly. Gift from my wife."

I'm putting off any renewed mention of Molly's Place until dessert—never make the heavy pitch till then, says business etiquette, let the guy suck up a little protein first—though if my guess is right and Charles too is concerned for his weight, we'll both skip dessert and settle for double espresso. Meanwhile I listen to Charles as I dole out the leading questions. The ground rules are being quietly set forth: two mentions of the wife already, one of the son at college, one of the teenage daughter. Stable family, is the message. It goes with the horse tie.

It's the wife who interests me most, of course. If men like Charles did not have wives they would have to invent them. So useful for fending off the other women when they get too close. If I were a man that's what I'd do: invent a wife, put one together from bits and pieces—a ring from a pawnshop, a photo or two snuck out of someone else's album, a three-minute sentimental drone about the kids. You could fake phone calls to yourself. You could send postcards to yourself, from Bermuda, or better, Tortuga. But men like Charles are not thorough in their deceptions. Their killer instincts are directed elsewhere. They get snarled up in their own lies or give themselves away by shifty eye movements. At heart they are too sincere.

I on the other hand have a devious mind and little sense of guilt. My guilt is about other things.

I already suspect what this wife will look like: overtanned, overexercised, with alert, leathery eyes and too many tendons in her neck. I see these wives, packs of them, or pairs or teams, loping around in their tennis whites, over at the Club. Smug, but jumpy. They know this is a polygamous country in all but name. I make them nervous.

But they should be grateful to me for helping them out. Who else has the time and expertise to smooth the egos of men like Charles, listen to their jokes, lie to them about their sexual prowess? The tending of such men is a fading art, like scrimshaw or the making of woolen-rose mantelpiece decorations. The wives are too busy for it, and the younger women don't know how. I know how. I learned in the old school, which was not the same as the one that gave out the ties.

Sometimes, when I have amassed yet another ugly wristwatch or brooch (they never give rings; if I want one of those I buy it myself), when I've been left stranded on a weekend in favor of the kids and the Georgian Bay cottage, I think about what I could tell and I feel powerful. I think about dropping an acerbic, vengeful little note through the mailbox of the wife in question, citing moles strategically placed, nicknames, the perverse habits of the family dog. Proofs of knowledge.

But then I would lose power. Knowledge is power only as long as you keep your mouth shut.

Here's one for you, Molly: *menopause.* A pause while you reconsider men.

At long last here come the entrées, with a flashing of teeth and a winsome glance from the waiter. Veal scaloppine for Charles, who has not evidently seen those sordid pictures of calves being bleached in the dark, seafood en brochette for me. I think: now he'll say *Cheers* again, and then he'll make some comment about seafood being good for the sex drive. He's had enough wine for that by now. After that he'll ask me why I'm not married.

"Cheers," says Charles. "Any oysters in there?"

"No," I say. "Not a one."

"Too bad. Good for what ails you."

Speak for yourself, I think. He gives a meditative chew or two. "How is it that you never got married—an attractive woman like you?"

I shrug my shoulder pads. What should I tell him? The dead fiancé story, lifted from the great-aunt of a friend? No. Too World War I. Should I say, "I was too choosy?" That might scare him: if I'm hard to please, how will he manage to please me?

I don't really know why. Maybe I was waiting for the big romance. Maybe I wanted True Love, with the armpits airbrushed out and no bitter aftertaste. Maybe I wanted to keep my options open. In those days I felt that anything could happen.

"I was married once," I say, sadly, regretfully. I hope to convey that I did the right thing but it didn't work out. Some jerk let me down in a way too horrible to go into. Charles is free to think he could have done better.

There's something final about saying you were married once. It's like saying you were dead once. It shuts them up.

It's funny to think that Molly was the one who got married. You'd think it would have been me. I was the one who wanted two children, the two-car garage, the antique dining table with the rose bowl in the center. Well, at least I've got the table. Other women's husbands sit at it and I feed them omelets, while they surreptitiously consult their watches. But if they even hint at divorcing the wife I have them out the door so fast they can't even remember where they left their boxer shorts. I've never wanted to make the commitment. Or I've never wanted to take the risk. It amounts to the same thing.

There was a time when my married friends envied me my singleness, or said they did. I was having fun, ran the line, and they were not. Recently though, they're revising this view. They tell me I ought to travel, since I have the freedom for it. They give me travel brochures with palm trees on them. What they have in mind is a sunshine cruise, a shipboard romance, an adventure. I can think of nothing worse: stuck on an overheated boat with a lot of wrinkly women, all bent on adventure too. So I stuff the brochures in behind the toaster oven—so convenient for solo dinners—where one of these days they will no doubt burst into flame.

I get enough adventure right around here. It's wearing me out.

Twenty years ago I was just out of law school. In another twenty I'll be retired and it will be the twenty-first century, for whoever's counting. Once a month I wake in the night, slippery with terror. I'm afraid, not because there's someone in the room, in the dark, in the bed, but because there isn't. I'm afraid of the emptiness, which lies beside me like a corpse.

I think: what will become of me? I will be alone. Who will visit me in the old-age home? I think of the next man as an aging horse must think of a jump. Will I lose my nerve? Can I still pull it off? Should I get married? Do I have the choice?

In the daytime I am fine. I lead a rich full life. There is of course my career. I shine away at it like an antique brass. I add onto it like a stamp collection. It props me up: a career like an under-wired brassiere. Some days I hate it.

"Dessert?" says Charles.

"Will you?"

Charles pats his midriff. "Trying to cut down," he says.

"Let's just have a double espresso," I say. I make it sound like a delicious conspiracy.

Double espresso. A diabolical torture devised by the Spanish Inquisition, involving a sack of tacks, a silver bootjack, and two three-hundred-pound priests.

Molly. I let you down. I burnt out early. I couldn't take the pressure. I wanted security. Maybe I decided that the fastest way to improve the lot of women was to improve my own.

* * *

Molly kept on. She lost that baby-fat roundness, she developed a raw edge to her voice and took to chain-smoking. Her hair got dull and her skin looked abraded and she paid no attention. She began to lecture me about my lack of seriousness, and also about my wardrobe, for which I overspent in her opinion. She began to use words like *patriarchy*. I began to find her strident.

"Molly," I said. "Why don't you give it up? You're slamming your head against a brick wall." I felt like a traitor saying it. But I'd have felt like a traitor if I hadn't said it, because Molly was knocking herself out, and for peanuts. The kind of women she represented never had any money.

"We're making progress," she'd say. Her face was getting that ropy look, like a missionary's. "We're accomplishing something."

"Who is this *we?*" I'd say. "I don't see a lot of people helping you out."

"Oh, they do," she said vaguely. "Some of them do. They do what they can, in their own way. It's sort of like the widow's mite, you know?"

"What widow?" I said. I knew, but I was exasperated. She was trying to make me feel guilty. "Quit trying for sainthood, Molly. Enough is enough."

That was before she married Curtis.

"Now," says Charles. "Cards on the table, eh?"

"Right," I say. "Well, I've explained the basic position to you already. In your office."

"Yes," he says. "As I told you, the company has already allocated its charitable donations budget for this year."

"But you could make an exception," I say. "You could draw down on next year's budget."

"We could, if—well, the bottom line is that we like to think we're getting something back for what we put in. Nothing blatant, just what you might call good associations. With hearts and kidneys, for instance, there's no problem at all."

"What's wrong with these battered women?"

"Well, there would be our company logo, and then right beside it these battered women. The public might get the wrong idea."

"You mean they might think the company was doing the battering itself?"

"In a word, yes," says Charles.

It's like any negotiation. Always agree, then come at them from a different angle. "You have a point," I say.

Battered women. I see it in lights, like a roadside fast-food joint. *Get some fresh*. Sort of like onion rings and deep-fried chicken. A terrible pun. Would Molly have laughed? Yes. No. Yes.

Battered. Covered in slime, then dipped into hell. Not so inappropriate, after all.

Molly was thirty when she married Curtis. He wasn't the first man she'd lived with. I've often wondered why she did it. Why him? Possibly she just got tired.

Still, it was a strange choice. He was so dependent. He could hardly let her out of his sight. Was that the appeal? Probably not. Molly was a fixer. She thought she could fix things that were broken. Sometimes she could. Though Curtis was too broken even for her. He was so broken he thought the normal state of the world was broken. Maybe that's why he tried to break Molly: to make her normal. When he couldn't do it one way he did it another.

He was plausible enough at first. He was a lawyer, he had the proper suits. I could say I knew right away that he wasn't totally glued together but it wouldn't be true. I didn't know. I didn't like him very much, but I didn't know.

For a while after the wedding I didn't see that much of Molly. She was always busy doing something or other with Curtis, and then there were the children. A boy and a girl, just what I'd always expected, for myself. Sometimes it seemed Molly was leading the life I might have led it if hadn't been for caution and a certain fastidiousness. When it comes to the crunch I have a dislike for other people's bathtub rings. That's the virtue of married men: someone else does the maintenance.

"Is everything all right?" asks the waiter, for the fourth time. Charles doesn't answer. Perhaps he doesn't hear. He's the sort of man for whom waiters are a kind of warm-blooded tea trolley.

"Wonderful," I say.

"Why don't these battered women just get a good lawyer?" says

Charles. He's genuinely baffled. No use telling him they can't afford it. For him that's not a concept.

"Charles," I say. "Some of these guys *are* good lawyers."

"Nobody I know," says Charles.

"You'd be surprised," I say. "Of course, we take personal donations too."

"What?" says Charles, who has not followed me.

"Not just corporate ones. Bill Henry over at ConFrax gave two thousand dollars." Bill Henry had to. I know all about his useful right buttock birthmark, the one shaped like a rabbit. I know his snore pattern.

"Ah," says Charles, caught unawares. But he will not be hooked without a struggle. "You know I like to put my money where it's doing some real good. These women, you get them out, but I've been told they just go right back and get battered again."

I've heard it before. They're addicted. They can't get enough of having their eyes punched in. "Give it to the Heart Foundation," I say, "and those ungrateful triple bypasses will just croak anyway, sooner or later. It's like they're asking for it."

"Touché," says Charles, Oh good. He knows some French. Not a complete oaf, unlike some. "How about I take you out for dinner on, say—" he consults his little book, the one they all carry around in the breast pocket— "Wednesday? Then you can convince me."

"Charles," I say, "that's not fair. I would adore to have dinner with you, but not as the price of your donation. Give first, and then we can have dinner with a clear conscience."

Charles likes the idea of a clear conscience. He grins and reaches for his checkbook. He is not going to look cheaper than Bill Henry. Not at this stage of the game.

Molly came to see me at my office. She didn't phone first. It was right after I'd left my high-class flunky company position and set up on my own. I had my own flunkies now, and I was wrestling with the coffee problem. If you're a woman, women don't like bringing you coffee. Neither do men.

"Molly, what's wrong?" I said. "Do you want coffee?"

"I'm so wired already I couldn't stand it," she said. She looked it. There were half circles under her eyes the size of lemon wedges.

"It's Curtis," she said. "Could I sleep over at your place tonight? If I have to?"

"What's he done?" I said.

"Nothing," she said. "Not yet. It isn't what he's done, it's how he is. He's heading straight for the edge."

"In what way?"

"A while ago he started saying I was having affairs at work. He thought I was having an affair with Maurice, across the hall."

"Maurice!" I said. We'd both gone to law school with Maurice. "But Maurice is gay!"

"We aren't talking rational here. Then he started saying I was going to leave him."

"And were you?"

"I wasn't. But now, I don't know. Now I think I am. He's driving me to it."

"He's paranoid," I said.

"*Paranoid*," said Molly. "A wide-angle camera for taking snapshots of maniacs." She put her head down on her arms and laughed and laughed.

"Come over tonight," I said. "Don't even think about it. Just do it."

"I don't want to rush it," said Molly. "Maybe things will work out. Maybe I can talk him into getting some help. He's been under a lot of strain. I have to think about the kids. He's a good father."

Victim, they said in the papers. Molly was no victim. She wasn't helpless, she wasn't hopeless. She was full of hope. It was hope that killed her.

I called her the next evening. I thought she would've come over, but she hadn't. She hadn't phoned either.

Curtis answered. He said Molly had gone on a trip.

I asked him when she'd be back. He said he had no idea. Then he started to cry. "She's left me," he said.

Good for her, I thought. She's done it after all.

It was a week later that the arms and legs started turning up.

He killed her in her sleep, I'll give him that much credit. She never knew. Or so he said, after he got around to remembering. He claimed amnesia, at first.

Dismemberment. The act of conscious forgetting.

I try not to think of Molly like that. I try to remember her whole.

Charles is walking me to the door, past white tablecloth after white tablecloth, each one held in place by at least four pinstripe elbows. It's like the *Titanic* just before the iceberg: power and influence disporting themselves, not a care in the world. What do they know about the serfs down in Steerage. Piss all and pass the port.

I smile to the right, I smile to the left. There are some familiar faces here, some familiar birthmarks. Charles takes my elbow, in a proprietary though discreet way. A light touch, a heavy hand.

I no longer think that anything can happen. I no longer want to think that way. *Happen* is what you wait for, not what you do; and *anything* is a large category. I am unlikely to get murdered by this man, for instance; I am unlikely to get married to him either. Right now I don't even know whether I'll go so far as dinner on Wednesday. It occurs to me that I don't really have to, not if I don't want to. Some options at least remain open. Just thinking about it makes my feet hurt less.

Today is Friday. Tomorrow morning I'll go power-walking in the cemetery, for the inner and outer thighs. It's one of the few places you can do it in this city without getting run over. It isn't the cemetery Molly's buried in, whatever of her they could put together. But that doesn't matter. I'll pick out a tombstone where I can do my leg stretches, and I'll pretend it's hers.

Molly, I'll say. We don't see eye to eye on some things and you wouldn't approve of my methods, but I do what I can. The bottom line is that cash is cash, and it puts food on the table.

Bottom line, she will answer. What you hit when you get as far down as you're going. After that you stay there. Or else you go up.

I will bend, I will touch the ground, or as close to it as I can get without rupture. I will lay a wreath of invisible money on her grave.

Puttermesser:
Her Work History,
Her Ancestry,
Her Afterlife

CYNTHIA OZICK

P UTTERMESSER WAS THIRTY-FOUR, a lawyer. She was also something of a feminist, not crazy, but she resented having "Miss" put in front of her name; she thought it pointedly discriminatory, she wanted to be a lawyer among lawyers. Though she was no virgin she lived alone, but idiosyncratically—in the Bronx, on the Grand Concourse, among other people's decaying old parents. Her own had moved to Miami Beach; in furry slippers left over from high school she roamed the same endlessly mazy apartment she had grown up in, her aging piano sheets still on top of the upright with the teacher's X marks on them showing up to where she should practice. Puttermesser always pushed a little ahead of the actual assignment; in school, too. Her teachers told her mother she was "highly motivated," "achievement oriented." Also she had "scholastic drive." Her mother wrote all these things down in a notebook, kept it always, and took it with her to Florida in case she should die there. Puttermesser had a younger sister who was also highly motivated, but she had married an Indian, a Parsee chemist, and gone to live in Calcutta. Already the sister had four children and seven saris of various fabrics.

Puttermesser went on studying. In law school they called her a grind, a competitive-compulsive, an egomaniac out for aggrandizement. But ego was no part of it; she was looking to solve something, she did not know what. At the back of the linen closet she found a stack of her father's old shirt cardboards (her mother was provident, stingy: in kitchen drawers Puttermesser still discovered folded squares of used ancient waxed paper, million-creased into whiteness, cheese-smelling, nesting small unidentifiable wormlets); so behind the riser pipe in the bathroom Puttermesser kept weeks' worth of Sunday *Times* crossword puzzles stapled to these laundry boards and worked on them indiscriminately. She played chess against herself, and was always victor over the color she had decided to identify with. She organized tort cases on index cards. It was not that she intended to remember everything: situations—it was her tendency to call intellectual problems "situations"—slipped into her mind like butter into a bottle.

A letter came from her mother in Florida:

Dear Ruth,

I know you won't believe this but I swear it's true the other day Daddy was walking on the Avenue and who should he run into but Mrs. Zaretsky, the thin one from Burnside not the stout one from Davidson, you remember her Joel? Well he's divorced now no children thank God so he's free as a bird as they say his ex the poor thing couldn't conceive. *He* had tests he's O.K. He's only an accountant not good enough for you because God knows I never forget the day you made Law Review but you should come down just to see what a tender type he grew up into. Every tragedy has its good side Mrs. Zaretsky says he comes down now practically whenever she calls him long distance. Daddy said to Mrs. Zaretsky well, an accountant, you didn't overeducate your son anyhow, with daughters it's different. But don't take this to heart honey Daddy is as proud as I am of your achievements. Why don't you write we didn't hear from you too long busy is busy but parents are parents.

Puttermesser had a Jewish face and a modicum of American distrust of it. She resembled no poster she had ever seen: with a Negroid passion she hated the Breck shampoo girl, so blond and bland and pale-mouthed; she boycotted Breck because of the golden-haired posters, all crudely idealized, an American wet dream, in the subway. Puttermesser's hair came in bouncing scallops—layered waves from scalp to tip, like imbricated roofing tile. It was nearly black and had a way of sometimes sticking straight out. Her nose had thick, well-haired, uneven nostrils, the right one noticeably wider than the other. Her eyes were small, the lashes short, invisible. She had the median Mongol lid—one of those Jewish faces with a vaguely Oriental cast. With all this, it was a fact she was not bad-looking. She had a good skin with, so far, few lines or pits or signs of looseness-to-come. Her jaw was pleasing—a baby jowl appeared only when she put her head deep in a book.

In bed she studied Hebrew grammar. The permutations of the triple-lettered root elated her. How was it possible that a whole language, hence a whole literature, a civilization even, should rest on the pure presence of three letters of the alphabet? The Hebrew verb, a stunning mechanism: three letters, whichever fated three, could command all possibility simply by a change in their pronunciation, or the addition of a wing-letter fore and aft. Every conceivable utterance blossomed from this trinity. It seemed to her not so much a language for expression as a code for the world's design, indissoluble, predetermined, translucent. The idea of the grammar of Hebrew turned Puttermesser's brain into a palace, a sort of Vatican; inside its corridors she walked from one resplendent triptych to another.

She wrote her mother a letter refusing to come to Florida to look over the divorced accountant's tenderness. She explained her life again; she explained it by indirection. She wrote:

I have a cynical apperception of power, due no doubt to my current job. You probably haven't heard of the Office for Visas and Registration, OVIR for short. It's located on Ogaryova Street, in Moscow, U.S.S.R. I could enumerate for you a few of the innumerable bureaucratic atrocities of OVIR, not that anyone knows them all. But I could give you a list of the names of all those criminals, down to the women clerks, Yefimova, Korolova, Akulova, Arkhipova, Izrailova, all of them on Kolpachni Street in an office headed by Zolotukhin, the assistant to Colonel Smyrnov, who's under Ovchinikov, who is second in command to General Viryein, only Viryein

and Ovchinikov aren't on Kolpachni Street, they're the ones
in the head office—the M.V.D., Internal Affairs Ministry—
on Ogaryova Street. Some day all the Soviet Jews will come
out of the spider's clutches of these people and be free. Please
explain to Daddy that this is one of the highest priorities of
my life at this time in my personal history. Do you really think
a Joel Zaretsky can share such a vision?

Immediately after law school, Puttermesser entered the firm of
Midland, Reid & Cockleberry. It was a blueblood Wall Street firm,
and Puttermesser, hired for her brains and ingratiating (read:
immigrant-like) industry, was put into a back office to hunt up
all-fours cases for the men up front. Though a Jew and a woman,
she felt little discrimination: the back office was chiefly the
repository of unmitigated drudgery and therefore of usable youth.
Often enough it kept its lights burning till three in the morning.
It was right that the Top Rung of law school should earn you the
Bottom of the Ladder in the actual world of all fours. The wonderful thing was the fact of the Ladder itself. And though she was
the only woman, Puttermesser was not the only Jew. Three Jews
a year joined the back precincts of Midland, Reid (four the year
Puttermesser came, which meant they thought "woman" more
than "Jew" at the sight of her). Three Jews a year left—not the
same three. Lunchtime was difficult. Most of the young men went
to one or two athletic clubs nearby to "work out"; Puttermesser
ate from a paper bag at her desk, along with the other Jews, and
this was strange: the young male Jews appeared to be as committed to the squash courts as the others. Alas, the athletic clubs
would not have them, and this too was preternatural—the young
Jews were indistinguishable from the others. They bought the
same suits from the same tailors, wore precisely the same shirts
and shoes, were careful to avoid tie clips and to be barbered a
good deal shorter than the wild men of the streets, though a bit
longer than the prigs in the banks.

Puttermesser remembered what Anatole France said of Dreyfus:
that he was the same type as the officers who condemned him.
"In their shoes he would have condemned himself."

Only their accents fell short of being identical: the "a" a shade
too far into the nose, the "i" with its telltale elongation, had long
ago spread from Brooklyn to Great Neck, from Puttermesser's
Bronx to Scarsdale. These two influential vowels had the uncanny

faculty of disqualifying them for promotion. The squash players, meanwhile, moved out of the back offices into the front offices. One or two of them were groomed—curried, fed sugar, led out by the muzzle—for partnership: were called out to lunch with thin and easeful clients, spent an afternoon in the dining room of one of the big sleek banks, and, in short, developed the creamy cheeks and bland habits of the always-comfortable.

The Jews, by contrast, grew more anxious, hissed together meanly among the urinals (Puttermesser, in the ladies' room next door, could hear malcontent rumblings in the connecting plumbing), became perfectionist and uncasual, quibbled bitterly, with stabbing forefingers, over principles, and all in all began to look and act less like superannuated college athletes and more like Jews. Then they left. They left of their own choice; no one shut them out.

Puttermesser left too, weary of so much chivalry—the partners in particular were excessively gracious to her, and treated her like a fellow-aristocrat. Puttermesser supposed this was because *she* did not say "a" in her nose or elongate her "i," and above all she did not dentalize her "t," "d," or "l," keeping them all back against the upper palate. Long ago her speech had been "standardized" by the drilling of fanatical teachers, elocutionary missionaries hired out of the Midwest by Puttermesser's prize high school, until almost all the regionalism was drained out; except for the pace of her syllables, which had a New York deliberateness, Puttermesser could have come from anywhere. She was every bit as American as her grandfather in his captain's hat. From Castle Garden to blue New England mists, her father's father, hat-and-neckwear peddler to Yankees! In Puttermesser's veins Providence, Rhode Island, beat richly. It seemed to her the partners felt this.

Then she remembered that Dreyfus spoke perfect French, and was the perfect Frenchman.

For farewell she was taken out to a public restaurant—the clubs the partners belonged to (they explained) did not allow women—and apologized to.

"We're sorry to lose you," one said, and the other said, "No one for you in this outfit for under the canvas, hah?"

"The canvas?" Puttermesser said.

"Wedding canopy," said the partner, with a wink. "Or do they make them out of sheepskin—I forget."

"An interesting custom. I hear you people break the dishes at a wedding too," said the second partner.

An anthropological meal. They explored the rites of her tribe. She had not known she was strange to them. Their beautiful manners were the cautiousness you adopt when you visit the interior: Dr. Livingstone, I presume? They shook hands and wished her luck, and at that moment, so close to their faces with those moist smile ruts flowing from the sides of their wafer-like noses punctured by narrow, even nostrils, Puttermesser was astonished into noticing how strange *they* were—so many luncheon Martinis inside their bellies, and such beautiful manners even while drunk, and, important though they were, insignificant though she was, the fine ceremonial fact of their having brought her to this carpeted place. Their eyes were blue. Their necks were clean. How closely they were shaven!—like men who grew no hair at all. Yet hairs curled inside their ears. They let her take away all her memo pads with her name printed on them. She was impressed by their courtesy, their benevolence, through which they always got their way. She had given them three years of meticulous anonymous research, deep deep nights going after precedents, dates, lost issues, faded faint politics; for their sakes she had yielded up those howling morning headaches and half a dioptre's worth of sight in both eyes. Brilliant students make good aides. They were pleased though not regretful. She was replaceable: a clever black had been hired only that morning. The palace they led her to at the end of it all was theirs by divine right: in which they believed, on which they acted. They were benevolent because benevolence was theirs to dispense.

She went to work for the Department of Receipts and Disbursements. Her title was Assistant Corporation Counsel—it had no meaning, it was part of the subspeech on which bureaucracy relies. Of the many who held this title most were Italians and Jews, and again Puttermesser was the only woman. In this great City office there were no ceremonies and no manners: gross shouts, ignorant clerks, slovenliness, litter on the floors, grit stuck all over antiquated books. The ladies' room reeked: the women urinated standing up, and hot urine splashed on the toilet seats and onto the muddy tiles.

The successive heads of this department were called Commissioners. They were all political appointees—scavengers after spoils. Puttermesser herself was not quite a civil servant and not quite *not* a civil servant—one of those amphibious creatures hanging between base contempt and bare decency; but she soon felt the ignominy of belonging to that mean swarm of City employees rooted bleakly in cells inside the honeycomb of the Municipal Building. It was a monstrous place, gray everywhere, abundantly tunnelled, with multitudes of corridors and stairs and shafts, a kind of swollen doom through which the bickering of small-voiced officials whinnied. At the same time there were always curious farm sounds—in the summer the steady cricket of the air-conditioning, in the winter the gnash and croak of old radiators. Nevertheless the windows were broad and high and stupendously filled with light; they looked out on the whole lower island of Manhattan, revealed *as* an island, down to the Battery, all crusted over with the dried lava of shape and shape: rectangle over square, and square over spire. At noon the dark gongs of St. Andrew's boomed their wild and stately strokes.

To Puttermesser all this meant she had come down in the world. Here she was not even a curiosity. No one noticed a Jew. Unlike the partners at Midland, Reid, the Commissioners did not travel out among their subjects and were rarely seen. Instead they were like shut-up kings in a tower, and suffered from rumors.

But Puttermesser discovered that in City life all rumors are true. Putative turncoats are genuine turncoats. All whispered knifings have happened: officials reputed to be about to topple, topple. So far Puttermesser had lasted through two elections, seeing the powerful become powerless and the formerly powerless inflate themselves overnight, like gigantic winds, to suck out the victory of the short run. When one Administration was razed, for the moment custom seemed levelled with it, everything that smelled of "before," of "the old way"—but only at first. The early fits of innovation subsided, and gradually the old way of doing things crept back, covering everything over, like grass, as if the building and its workers were together some inexorable vegetable organism with its own laws of subsistence. The civil servants were grass. Nothing destroyed them, they were stronger than the pavement, they were stronger than time. The Administration might turn on its hinge, throwing out one lot of patronage eaters and gathering in the new lot: the work went on. They might put in fresh carpeting in the new Deputy's

office, or a private toilet in the new Commissioner's, and change
the clerks' light bulbs to a lower wattage, and design an extra-
vagant new colophon for a useless old document—they might
do anything they liked: the work went on as before. The organism
breathed, it comprehended itself.

So there was nothing for the Commissioner to do, and he knew
it, and the organism knew it. For a very great salary the Commissioner shut his door and cleaned his nails behind it with one
of the shining tools of a fancy Swiss knife, and had a secretary
who was rude to everyone, and made dozens of telephone calls
every day.

The current one was a rich and foolish playboy who had given
the Mayor money for his campaign. All the high officials of every
department were either men who had given the Mayor money
or else courtiers who had humiliated themselves for him in the
political clubhouse—mainly by flattering the clubhouse boss, who
before any election was already a secret mayor and dictated the
patronage lists. But the current Commissioner owed nothing to
the boss because he had given the Mayor money and was the
Mayor's own appointee; and anyhow he would have little to do
with the boss because he had little to do with any Italian. The
boss was a gentlemanly Neapolitan named Fiore, the chairman
of the board of a bank; but still, he was only an Italian, and the
Commissioner cared chiefly for blue-eyed bankers. He used his
telephone to make luncheon appointments with them, and
sometimes tennis. He himself was a blue-eyed Guggenheim, a
German Jew, but not one of the grand philanthropic Guggenheims. The name was a cunning coincidence (cut down from
Guggenheimer), and he was rich enough to be taken for one
of the real Guggenheims, who thought him an upstart and
disowned him. Grandeur demands discreetness; he was so
discreetly disowned that no one knew it, not even the Rockefeller
he had met at Choate.

This Commissioner was a handsome, timid man, still young,
and good at boating; on weekends he wore sneakers and
cultivated the friendship of the dynasties—Sulzbergers and War-
burgs, who let him eat with them but warned their daughters
against him. He had dropped out of two colleges and finally
graduated from the third by getting a term-paper factory to
plagiarize his reports. He was harmless and simple-minded, still
devoted to his brainy late father, and frightened to death of news

conferences. He understood nothing: art appreciation had been his best subject (he was attracted to Renaissance nudes), economics his worst. If someone asked, "How much does the City invest every day?" or "Is there any Constitutional bar against revenue from commuters?" or "What is your opinion about taxing exempt properties?" his pulse would catch in his throat, making his nose run, and he had to say he was pressed for time and would let them have the answers from his Deputy in charge of the Treasury. Sometimes he would even call on Puttermesser for an answer.

Now if this were an optimistic portrait, exactly here is where Puttermesser's emotional life would begin to grind itself into evidence. Her biography would proceed romantically, the rich young Commissioner of the Department of Receipts and Disbursements would fall in love with her. She would convert him to intelligence and to the cause of Soviet Jewry. He would abandon boating and the pursuit of bluebloods. Puttermesser would end her work history abruptly and move on to a bower in a fine suburb.

This is not to be. Puttermesser will always be an employee in the Municipal Building. She will always behold Brooklyn Bridge through its windows; also sunsets of high glory, bringing her religious pangs. She will not marry. Perhaps she will undertake a long-term affair with Vogel, the Deputy in charge of the Treasury; perhaps not.

The difficulty with Puttermesser is that she is loyal to certain environments.

Puttermesser, while working in the Municipal Building, had a luxuriant dream, a dream of *gan eydn*—a term and notion handed on from her great-uncle Zindel, a former shammes in a shul that had been torn down. In this reconstituted Garden of Eden, which is to say in the World to Come, Puttermesser, who was not afflicted with quotidian uncertainty in the Present World, had even more certainty of her aims. With her weakness for fudge (others of her age, class, and character had advanced to Martinis, at least to ginger ale; Puttermesser still drank ice cream with cola, despised mints as too tingly, eschewed salty liver canapés, hunted down chocolate babies, Kraft caramels, Mary Janes, Milky Ways, peanut brittle, and immediately afterward furiously brushed her teeth, scrubbing off guilt)—with all this nasty self-indulgence, she was nevertheless very thin and unironic. Or: to postulate an afterlife was her single irony—a game in the head not unlike a melting fudge cube held against the upper palate.

There, at any rate, Puttermesser would sit, in Eden, under a middle-sized tree, in the solid blaze of an infinite heart-of-summer July, green, green, green everywhere, green above and green below, herself gleaming and made glorious by sweat, every itch annihilated, fecundity dismissed. And there Puttermesser would, as she imagined it, *take in*. Ready to her left hand, the box of fudge (rather like the fudge sold to the lower school by the eighth-grade cooking class in P.S. 74, The Bronx, circa 1942); ready to her right hand, a borrowed steeple of library books: for into Eden the Crotona Park Branch has ascended intact, sans librarians and fines, but with its delectable terrestrial binding-glue fragrances unevaporated.

Here Puttermesser sits. Day after celestial day, perfection of desire upon perfection of contemplation, into the exaltations of an uninterrupted forever, she eats fudge in human shape (once known—no use covering this up—as nigger babies), or fudge in square shapes (and in Eden there is no tooth decay); and she reads. Puttermesser reads and reads. Her eyes in Paradise are unfatigued. And if she still does not know what it is she wants to solve, she has only to read on. The Crotona Park Branch is as paradisal here as it was on earth. She reads anthropology, zoology, physical chemistry, philosophy (in the green air of heaven Kant and Nietzsche together fall into crystal splinters). The New Books section is peerless: she will learn about the linkages of genes, about quarks, about primate sign language, theories of the origins of the races, religions of ancient civilizations, what Stonehenge meant. Puttermesser will read Non-Fiction into eternity; and there is still time for Fiction! Eden is equipped above all with timelessness, so Puttermesser will read at last all of Balzac, all of Dickens, all of Turgenev and Dostoevski (her mortal self has already read all of Tolstoy and George Eliot); at last Puttermesser will read *Kristin Lavransdatter* and the stupendous trilogy of Dmitri Merezhkovski, she will read *The Magic Mountain* and the whole "Faerie Queene" and every line of *The Ring and the Book*, she will read a biography of Beatrix Potter and one of Walter Scott in many entrancing volumes and one of Lytton Strachey, at last, at last! In Eden insatiable Puttermesser will be nourished, if not glutted. She will study Roman law, the more arcane varieties of higher mathematics, the nuclear composition of the stars, what happened to the Monophysites, Chinese history, Russian, and Icelandic.

But meanwhile, still alive, not yet translated upward, her days given over to the shadow reign of a playboy Commissioner, Puttermesser was learning only Hebrew.

Twice a week, at night (it seemed), she went to Uncle Zindel for a lesson. Where the bus ran through peeling neighborhoods the trolley tracks sometimes shone up through a broken smother of asphalt, like weeds wanting renewal. From childhood Puttermesser remembered how trolley days were better days: in summer the cars banged along, self-contained little carnivals, with open wire-mesh sides sucking in hot winds, the passengers serenely jogging on the seats. Not so this bus, closed like a capsule against the slum.

The old man, Zindel the Stingy, hung on to life among the cooking smells of Spanish-speaking blacks. Puttermesser walked up three flights of steps and leaned against the crooked door, waiting for the former shammes with his little sack. Each evening Zindel brought up a single egg from the Cuban grocery. He boiled it while Puttermesser sat with her primer.

"You should go downtown," the shammes said, "where they got regular language factories. Berlitz. N.Y.U. They even got an *ulpan*, like in Israel."

"You're good enough," Puttermesser said. "You know everything they know."

"And something more also. Why you don't live downtown, on the East Side, fancy?"

"The rent is too much, I inherited your stinginess."

"And such a name. A nice young fellow meets such a name, he laughs. You should change it to something different, lovely, nice. Shapiro, Levine. Cohen, Goldweiss, Blumenthal. I don't say make it *different*, who needs Adams, who needs McKee, I say make it a name not a joke. Your father gave you a bad present with it. For a young girl, Butterknife!"

"I'll change it to Margarine-messer."

"Never mind the ha-ha. *My* father, what was your great-great-grandfather, didn't allow a knife to the table Friday night. When it came to *kiddush*—knifes off! All knifes! On Sabbath an instrument, a blade? On Sabbath a weapon? A point? An edge? What makes bleeding among mankind? What makes war? Knifes! No knifes! Off! A clean table! And something else you'll notice. By us we got only *messer*, you follow? By them they got sword, they got lance, they got halberd. Go to the dictionary, I went once. So help me, what don't one of them knights carry? Look up in the book, you'll see halberd, you'll see cutlass, pike, rapier, foil, ten dozen more. By us a pike is a fish. Not to mention what nowadays they got—bayonet stuck on the gun, who knows what else the poor soldier got to carry in the pocket. Maybe a dagger same as a pirate. But by us—what we got? A *messer! Puttermesser*, you slice off a piece butter, you cut to live, not to kill. A name of honor, you follow? Still, for a young girl—"

"Uncle Zindel, I'm past thirty."

Uncle Zindel blinked lids like insect's wings, translucent. He saw her voyaging, voyaging. The wings of his eyes shadowed the Galilee. They moved over the Tomb of the Patriarchs. A tear for the tears of Mother Rachel rode on his nose. "Your mother knows you're going? Alone on an airplane, such a young girl? You wrote her?"

"I wrote her, Uncle Zindel. I'm not flying."

"By sea is also danger. What Mama figures, in Miami who is there? The dead and dying. In Israel you'll meet someone. You'll marry, you'll settle there. What's the difference, these days, modern times, quick travel—"

Uncle Zindel's egg was ready, hard-boiled. The shammes tapped it and the shell came off raggedly. Puttermesser consulted the alphabet: *aleph, beys, gimel*; she was not going to Israel, she had business in the Municipal Building. Uncle Zindel, chewing, began finally to teach: "First see how a *gimel* and which way a *zayen*. Twins, but one kicks a leg left, one right. You got to practice the difference. If legs don't work, think pregnant bellies. Mrs. *Zayen* pregnant in one direction, Mrs. *Gimel* in the other. Together they give birth to *gez*, which means what you cut off. A night for knifes! Listen, going home from here you should be extra careful tonight. Martinez, the upstairs not the next door, her daughter they mugged and they took."

The shammes chewed, and under his jaws Puttermesser's head bent, practicing the bellies of the holy letters.

Stop. Stop, stop! Puttermesser's biographer, stop! Disengage, please. Though it is true that biographies are invented, not recorded, here you invent too much. A symbol is allowed, but not

a whole scene: do not accommodate too obsequiously to Puttermesser's romance. Having not much imagination, she is literal
with what she has. Uncle Zindel lies under the earth of Staten
Island. Puttermesser has never had a conversation with him; he
died four years before her birth. He is all legend: Zindel the
Stingy, who even in *gan eydn* rather than eat will store apples
until they rot. Zindel the Unripe. Why must Puttermesser fall
into so poignant a fever over the cracked phrases of a shammes
of a torn-down shul?

(The shul was not torn down, neither was it abandoned. It
disintegrated. Crumb by crumb it vanished. Stones took some
of the windows. There were no pews, only wooden folding chairs.
Little by little these turned into sticks. The prayer books began
to flake: the bindings flaked, the glue came unstuck in small
brown flakes, the leaves grew brittle and flaked into confetti. The
congregation too began to flake off—the women first, wife after
wife after wife, each one a pearl and a consolation, until there
they stand, the widowers, frail, gazing, palsy-struck. Alone and
in terror. Golden Agers, Senior Citizens! And finally they too flake
away, the shammes among them. The shul becomes a wisp, a
straw, a feather, a hair.)

But Puttermesser must claim an ancestor. She demands
connection—surely a Jew must own a past. Poor Puttermesser
has found herself in the world without a past. Her mother was
born into the din of Madison Street and was taken up to the
hullabaloo of Harlem at an early age. Her father is nearly a Yankee:
his father gave up peddling to captain a dry-goods store in Providence, Rhode Island. In summer he sold captain's hats, and wore
one in all his photographs. Of the world that was, there is only
this single grain of memory: that once an old man, Puttermesser's
mother's uncle, kept his pants up with a rope belt, was called
Zindel, lived without a wife, ate frugally, knew the holy letters,
died with thorny English a wilderness between his gums. To him
Puttermesser clings. America is a blank, and Uncle Zindel is all
her ancestry. Unironic, unimaginative, her plain but stringent
mind strains beyond the parents—what did they have? Only day-
by-day in their lives, coffee in the morning, washing underwear,
occasionally a trip to the beach. Blank. What did they know?
Everything from the movies; something—scraps— from the
newspaper. Blank.

Behind the parents, beyond and before them, things teem. In

old photographs of the Jewish East Side, Puttermesser sees the teeming. She sees a long coat. She sees a woman pressing onions from a pushcart. She sees a tiny child with a finger in its mouth who will become a judge.

Past the judge, beyond and behind him, something more is teeming. But this Puttermesser cannot see. The towns, the little towns. Zindel born into a flat-roofed house a modest distance from a stream.

What can Puttermesser do? She began life as a child of an anti-Semite. Her father would not eat kosher meat—it was, he said, too tough. He had no superstitions. He wore the mother down, she went to the regular meat market at last.

The scene with Uncle Zindel did not occur. How Puttermesser loved the voice of Zindel in the scene that did not occur!

(He is under the ground. The cemetery is a teeming city of toy skyscrapers shouldering each other. Born into a wooden house, Zindel now has a flat stone roof. Who buried him? Strangers from the *landsmanshaft* society. Who said a word for him? No one. Who remembers him now?)

Puttermesser does not remember Uncle Zindel; Puttermesser's mother does not remember him. A name in the dead grandmother's mouth. Her parents have no ancestry. Therefore Puttermesser rejoices in the cadences of Uncle Zindel's voice above the Cuban grocery. Uncle Zindel, when alive, distrusted the building of Tel Aviv because he was practical, Messiah was not imminent. But now, in the scene that did not occur, how naturally he supposes Puttermesser will journey to a sliver of earth in the Middle East, surrounded by knives, missiles, bazookas!

The scene with Uncle Zindel did not occur. It could not occur because, though Puttermesser dares to posit her ancestry, we may not. Puttermesser is not to be examined as an artifact but as an essence. Who made her? No one cares. Puttermesser is henceforth to be presented as given. Put her back into Receipts and Disbursements, among office Jews and patronage collectors. While winter dusk blackens the Brooklyn Bridge, let us hear her opinion about the taxation of exempt properties. The bridge is not the harp Hart Crane said it was in his poem. Its staves are prison bars. The women clerks, Yefimova, Korolova, Akulova, Arkhipova, Izrailova, are on Kolpachni Street, but the vainglorious General Viryein is not. He is on Ogaryova Street. Joel Zaretsky's ex-wife is barren.

The Commissioner puts on his tennis sneakers. He telephones. Mr. Fiore, the courtly secret mayor behind the Mayor, also telephones. Hey! Puttermesser's biographer! What will you do with her now?

Centaurs

J.S. MARCUS

T HE SMARTEST MAN in our law-school class told me he
wanted to be an actor. He is short and awkward, and he
has a comical problem with his "R"s. Once, he grabbed
my hand and said, "Sheila, I made a terrible mistake leaving the
stage." I like the idea of private failure. There must be chief executive officers who harbor secret dreams of teaching high-school
English.

Inertia seems to be getting me through law school. I don't move
much. I wait for a professor to intimidate me into the suject at
hand: arson, divorce, whatever. I am particularly fascinated with
the predicament of battered husbands. Not fascinated enough
to do anything about it, but I don't mind reading the cases. My
tax professor told me that I am not so different from my classmates. I suppose he meant the remark to be comforting.

If some man—say, X—runs a mink farm, and another, Y, is ex-
ploding dynamite next door, Y does not have to pay X in the event
the mink eat their kittens from the shock of the explosion. It's
the law.

I have a private life but not a personal one. Mostly, I smoke
Dunhill cigarettes, put unwhipped cream on things, and reread
early Evelyn Waugh novels. In private, I'm English.

A man from Yale who wants to go into entertainment law offered to buy me dinner. We chatted about the various apartments
he'd had in New York, his stint in television, his Midwestern roots.
When we got back to his apartment and undressed, he said, "Do
it to me, sweetie." Now when we see each other, which is about

twelve times a day, he acts as if we were once partners in some sort of class project.

If a railroad employee, X, thinks he is tripping over a bundle of newspapers, but is in fact tripping over a can of dynamite, and the explosion causes Y to drop a valuable family heirloom, could Y sue the railroad company for the cost of her grandmother's Hummel figurine? I don't know, because I wasn't paying attention that day.

At a mandatory law-school party, a lady law professor from another university asked me to show her which were the law students and which were the dates. She just assumed I wasn't a date. After most of the guests had left, she broached the subject of alternative families. She said that lesbian motherhood was fascinating but doomed as an institution. I told her that I liked her Laura Ashley dress.

I have one friend. He's a homosexual and also likes Evelyn Waugh. Sometimes he even does imitations of the characters. He calls most people philistines, and often walks into Evidence and says, "I got positively no sleep last night." I usually believe him.

At a mandatory tea at the Dean's house, I met the Dean's wife. She's an illustrator of children's books and a gourmet cook. After a few preliminary remarks, she asked if I wanted her receipe for *crème brûlée*. I suppose she thought I was different from the other law students.

The editor of the law review lives across the street. She used to be a nun, but now she wears hiking boots and smokes mentholated cigarettes. After she left the convent, and before she entered law school, she worked at the men's cologne counter of a large department store. Sometimes she has dinner parties and drinks a lot of Scotch. I guess another "terrible beauty is born." But how and when? Did she just wake up one morning and head for the nearest men's cologne counter? Perhaps it happened gradually (she's about forty-five)—a rosary in one hand, a Budweiser in the other; half saint, half goat.

People in law school, like people in general, try to be pleasant, and like people in general they often fail. Law students, I have noticed, tend to eat three-quarters of a sandwich and then wrap the remainder in foil, right there out in the open. One law student who is handicapped asks people to buy him hot chocolate around lunchtime; his wheelchair can't get near the vending machines. The other law students, busy wrapping, usually don't hear him.

My Jurisprudence professor decided to hold class in his apartment so it could turn into a party. He had a copy of *Soviet Life* in the bathroom and talked about how much money he'd be making if he weren't a law professor. He lives with one of his former students. She's a judge and wears the same clothes as he does: boots, blue-jeans, blazers. They are both, as fate would have it, from the same Chicago suburb. She came up to me with a plate full of cucumbers and smiled. I wanted to tell her that while insanity may be a defense for homicide, it is not a defense for a plate full of cucumbers; she always has a ravaged, insane look on her face.

As a child, I wanted to be an actress. More recently I've toyed with the idea of becoming a chief executive officer.

Each year, we eagerly await the Malpractice party and the White-Collar Crime party. The Malpractice party comes in October and is made up of law students and medical students. The White-Collar Crime party comes in February and is made up of law students and business students. One wonders: Left to their own devices, do the medical students and business students meet on their own? Is there such an animal as the Hospital Administrators' party?

Soon we will be reading about a woman who signed up for thirty thousand dollars' worth of dance lessons. I'm not sure if she was hit by a car on the way to her first lesson and wanted all her money back, or if she never learned to dance and blew up the studio with dynamite. Perhaps she was black, or a man, or handicapped, and they gave her inferior lessons. I just don't know.

In law school, you can feel boredom go from the benign to the malignant. You can see people run around with a quarter of a tuna-salad sandwich in their briefcase and argue about mink farms. You can, with a little patience and finesse, get yourself invited to a party where the food and liquor are free.

Law students, unlike other students, tend to have umbrellas. I feel even more English when it rains, and often say things like "Excuse me, I have to go to the loo."

Some of the more interesting stereotyped characteristics of law students: unshaven, impotent, dirty, overweight, devout, narrow-minded, humorless. Or if they're women: frigid, tall, overweight, giddy. If you've ever seen a law-school catalogue, you know there are very few pictures.

I could be wrong, of course. Perhaps the man from Yale said, "Do it to me, Mama," not "sweetie." This would make more sense, since I am taller than he is. But if I had to go through it all over again and he did say "sweetie," I would tell him never under any circumstances to use both an imperative and a diminutive in the same sentence—especially in bed.

The other day, I was on my way to class when the man from Yale came out of nowhere and said to me, "Where are you galloping off to?"

At law-school parties, men and women talk to each other as if there were no difference between men and women. The law students and the dates act as if there were no difference between the law students and the dates. Of course, the dates don't understand all this talk about law, unless they happened to be judges. Sometimes the women talk about feminism, and sometimes the men talk about sports. But we eventually leave those topics to the extremists and drift off onto the less sacred subjects. I have never heard Evelyn Waugh's name brought up at a law-school party—not even at the ex-nun's house. My homosexual friend has better things to do, and I usually don't open my mouth, even though I am a baseball fan.

Transformations, sublimations, things becoming other things. Yesterday, I had a Reuben potato—certainly the centaur of modern delicatessen food. Prodding the melted cheese for some trace of Russian dressing, I tried to recall if any of the law-school parties so far had been catered. I am becoming a lawyer.

Discipline

LARRY BROWN

P| LEASE TELL THE court again, Mr. Lawrence.

We were tortured in pairs, singly, that is individually, but only on Saturdays, or in groups of not more than four.

Let me see if I have this straight. Now, you said you were only tortured on Saturdays, is that right?

No. You misunderstood me. What I said was that we were only tortured individually on Saturdays.

And why do you suppose that was?

I have no idea.

[*Turns, facing the room, head shaking in mock wonderment, small malicious smile of feigned chagrin or imagined bond of friendship obvious*] You have no idea. I see. Well then, let me ask you something else. [*Referring to notes*] You said that on the evening of March twelfth, yourself and a man named Varrick? I believe? were taken from your quarters and allowed intercourse, blindfolded, with two obese women?

Well, that's partly correct....

And where do you suppose—no wait. *Who* do you suppose these two women were?

I told you we were blindfolded.

Ah, yes.

And we weren't al*lowed*. We were forced. That's all in my deposition. I don't see any need to—

Just answer yes or no, please. How well did you know this Mr. Varrick? Was he a close friend?

Well. [*Perhaps hedging here?*] No. I wouldn't say he was a close friend, no. I mean we ate lunch together a few times. We read a few of each other's stories.

And you took a few showers together, too, didn't you? Yes. Did you at any time of your last period of incarceration engage in a sexual act with Mr. Varrick?

I did not.

You're under oath here, sir. Need I remind you?

Never.

Did you ever catch Mr. Varrick watching you in the shower? While you were there together? Naked?

I never noticed.

Never noticed. I'm constantly amazed at how much you didn't notice over a period of—what was it? Five?

Four. Four years.

Four years, five years, whatever. All right. Now back to Mr. Varrick. How long did you know him?

Let's see. Let me think. I think it was...four, no, three years. Yes, three years [*Nodding vigorously, hands clasped in lap*]

I think we've already established your capacity for not noticing things, but during the time you knew Mr. Varrick, did you ever happen to notice what his first name was?

I believe it was Howard.

You *believe* it was Howard.

Yes.

Under the contention of cruel and unusual punishment, the defense would like for us to believe that this alleged torture actually took place without due cause. Without being deserved, in other words. All right, Mr. Lawrence. Doyle Huey, isn't it? [*Titters from crowd; judge's gavel rapped lightly, perfunctorily*] You have already stated, under oath, that you and Mr. Varrick had sex with these two unidentified women. I would like for you to explain to the jury and to this court exactly how you knew this act was being consummated while you were blindfolded and, apparently, engaged simultaneously in the same alleged action.

What do you mean? I don't know what you mean.

Forgive me. Let me make it simple enough for you to understand it. I mean, how did you know Mr. Varrick made love to this woman while you were blindfolded? I believe in your deposition you also stated that you were equipped with earplugs? And nose plugs? Is that correct?

That's correct. We...we had to breathe through our mouths. So there was no kissing. Involuntary sex, well, for involuntary sex that's required. It was just one of the rules.

And you always followed the rules.

Always tried to, yes. I mean, we were at the mercy of these people. Every time we tried to—

Let's not go off on that particular tangent again, please. Please. Just. Answer the question. How do you know Mr. Varrick had sex with this woman?

Well. I could just tell.

You could just tell. That's interesting. A prisoner for four years doesn't know why he was individually tortured only on Saturdays, doesn't know a close friend was a homosexual—

That hasn't been proved.

—isn't sure what the friend's first name was; in short, doesn't notice a whole lot about what is going on immediately around him for four years. Not very good recommendations for a writer, are they? Right?

[*Silence*]

I said, Isn't that RIGHT!

Yes. Yes. That's right.

Yet you knew without the shadow of a doubt what was going on in a cot twenty feet away, *clear across the room*, while you were blindfolded and literally deprived of any other sensory perception. Is that what you're saying?

Yes.

You're a liar. Aren't you?

No.

You *are* a liar. You've been a liar all your life, haven't you?

No.

Isn't it true that you were classified as a pathological liar by the United States Navy as early as 1966? Didn't you lie about your age to get into the Writers' Institute? Didn't you lie about the mileage on a 1963 Chevrolet Impala that you traded in Shreveport, Louisiana, for a Dodge Dart?

I...I don't—

Remember? Let me refresh your memory. Didn't you also take a Delco twelve-volt battery in good condition from that same Impala and replace it with a battery that actually had two dead cells, that you had been using with a trolling motor for three years?

Yes. [*With head hung*]

All *right*. Now we're getting somewhere [*Speaking to jury*] Look at him, ladies and gentlemen! How'd you like to curl up on Christmas Eve with a good novel by him? [*Taking twenty seconds to stroll back to desk, pour glass of water, sip, reflect, study notes carefully, walk back to front*] Mr. Lawrence. Let's go back to the day you and Mr. Varrick were taken from your quarters. Why don't you just tell us about it?

Which part? You mean when we went over there? I mean, which part do you want to know about?

Why were you and Mr. Varrick selected for this alleged 'involuntary sex'? Was it because of something you had done?

I'm not sure. They never told us.

Was anybody else ever forced to perform involuntary sex with obese women? Did they just pick people out at random? Did they walk down the line and say, "Well, let's get him today"?

I don't know. We were kept isolated.

How did you and Mr. Varrick manage to read each other's stories and eat lunch a few times if you were isolated? How did you and Mr. Varrick manage to take showers together?

We had visitation. Everybody did.

Well, which was it?

Which was what?

Was it isolation or was it visitation? Why do you keep changing your story?

I'm not changing my story! I'm trying to tell the truth!

I don't think you are. I think you're lying. I think you've been lying since the first day of this hearing. You'd do anything to get paroled. Wouldn't you?

No.

Yes, you would. You'd perjure yourself to save your own neck, wouldn't you?

I'm telling you the truth!

I don't think so.

You weren't there! You didn't have to live through it! You don't know what they made us do! [*Rising from chair halfway, hands gripping armrests*]

Control yourself, Mr. Lawrence. Just tell us. Go on.

[*Easing back. A little flustered, confused. Slight licking of lips*] Well. I guess it was about—four o'clock in the afternoon. I was working on some revisions in my study. I remember it was almost time for beer call and I was trying to get through my revisions.

What kind of revisions are we discussing here?

Several different kinds. Some poetry. And I think, ah. Some short stories. Yes. I believe that's what it was. Well anyway. It was fifteen till four or something, and I was trying to hurry up and get through so I could turn in my revisions. We had so many each week we had to turn in for grading. But they turned on the siren ten minutes early. So, I just scooped everything up, boxed it up, then locked my study and went out to the yard.

Was Mr. Varrick in the yard when you got there?

Yes, he was.

Did you know the reason Mr. Varrick was in the camp?

Yes. [*Uneasy look. Shifting around in chair. Unable to find a comfortable position*] I did.

Would you like to tell us why Mr. Varrick was in the camp?

[*Extremely uneasy. Rubbing palms together, averting his face, appearing to be searching for something at his feet*] Well. It was common knowledge, I suppose. He was in for plagiarism. Like seventy-five percent of the other inmates.

Was this a first offense for Mr. Varrick?

I'm...I'm not sure. [*Obviously lying*]

Right. Not sure. Can't remember. Didn't notice. Isn't it true that Mr. Varrick had in fact had his probation revoked for plagiarism?

Well...yes. But it wasn't the same author.

Oh? Your memory seems to be improving. I don't suppose you'd remember who he plagiarized the first time, would you?

I believe it was Flannery O'Connor. I think it was a line out of "A Good Man Is Hard to Find."

A line? Is that right? One line?

I believe so. Yes. I'm sure that's what it was.

[*Shaking his head. Wry humor touched with pity*] Mr. Lawrence. Didn't Mr. Varrick actually copy, verbatim, every single word from the time the grandmother's family went into The Tower, until they had the wreck? And turn it into *Playboy* as his own?

[*Shaken badly now*] I don't know. I—didn't know it was that bad.

Bad? You don't think it's bad to steal from a dead woman? Pilfer words from a sick, dying writer, who barely had the strength to work three hours a day? Who had more guts and talent in one little finger than you and your buddy Varrick have in your whole bodies?

I didn't mean that! I meant I didn't know he stole that much!

Stole! That's the right word. Robbed. [*With vigor*] Extorted. That's a better word. But even that. Even *that* wasn't as bad as what he did later. Was it? It wasn't as bad as what got him thrown in hacks' prison for five years, was it?

No. [*Almost whispering*] It wasn't.

Well. You're telling it. Your memory's coming back now, isn't it? Why don't you just tell us what he did do? After he was already on probation for the same crime?

I told you. It was plagiarism. Why do I have to say all this? You know it already. You know what he did!

Didn't it ever strike you that Mr. Varrick might have been just a little bit stupid?

Well. I suppose so.

You suppose so? Is that all you can say? You suppose so?

All right. It was stupid.

Who did he plagiarize the next time, Mr. Lawrence? The five-year sentence. And please don't tell me what you believe.

[*Grim, fatalistic conviction of lethargic hopelessness*] It was Cormac McCarthy.

Well, well. Now we're getting somewhere again. Now we're talking about *living* writers. Now we're getting up to a new level of theft. We're getting up into grant country now. Now we're talking about the American Academy of Arts and Letters. The big time.

Yes. [*Whispered*]

You're telling it so good I think I'll just let you go on. Why don't you just tell us what Mr. Varrick did to Mr. McCarthy?

[*Studying fingernails*] He stole different passages from three of his novels.

And?

And submitted—

Wait, wait. First—

First he put them into his own novel.

It was actually a novella, wasn't it?

I don't know. I never read it.

You never read it because it was never published. It was never published because it was submitted to the same house that originally published those same three novels. Ladies and gentlemen, the act of a stupid man. He stole ten thousand words, whole, uncut scenes, dialogue, ripped them up a little, tore them up some, and mixed them with ten thousand of his own miserable words and called it his own. Didn't he?

Yes. Yes, he did.

And he got caught.

Yes.

Just like you got caught.

Yes.

In a blatant, vicious act of plagiarism. Literary theft. And it got him five years.

Yes.

Did Mr. Varrick ever confide in you? Did he ever tell you any of his secrets?

Secrets? [*Shrugs shoulders, still studying nails*] We talked. Some.

Did he ever say to you that he thought his sentence was unfair?

[*Looking up*] Yes. He did.

What exactly did he say?

He said...he said he thought it was too long. And he said he thought the regimen was too strict. He said he thought we should have more beer and more recreational reading. More contemporary reading.

Like what?

Oh, you know. More new stuff. He thought we should have been allowed to read what was on the best-seller lists.

In short, he didn't want to have to read the classics, correct? He just wanted to skip Melville and Twain and Tolstoy, didn't he?

Essentially, yes. That's correct.

He thought they were a bunch of old geezers, didn't he?

Well. Not in so many words. I guess you could put it like that.

Didn't he actually say that once, though? Didn't he once, in the presence of two other prisoners, call Sophocles 'a dried-up old fart'?

I...

You don't remember.

No.

Your memory just comes and goes, doesn't it? Well, why don't you just see if you can remember what happened on the afternoon you met Mr. Varrick in the yard, before you were taken in for involuntary sex? I'm, sure everybody would just love to hear that.

It may take a while.

I've got all day.

[*Deep breath, gathering will*] Well. Like I said, we thought it was beer call. I mean, it was almost four o'clock. We just thought they were a little early.

Were they ever early for a beer call?

Not usually, no.

Up until that time, had you ever seen an early beer call?

No.

Wasn't everything timed to a very strict schedule, right up to the minute?

Yes. Well anyway. I saw How—Mr. Varrick, standing in line on the yellow footprints, and I went over to him. We talked for a minute. He'd been writing some poetry—

Whose? Raymond Carver's?

and he said he thought something funny was going on. He said they'd been heavy on his grading. He said all his papers were coming back with red marks on them, and they'd caught him with three comma splices in one week. And he'd lost his thesaurus. He was worried.

Under oath, Mr. Lawrence. Did he mention anything to you at that time about involuntary sex?

He said...he said he thought we were in for it. Those were his words.

He didn't specifically mention involuntary sex?

No. Not in so many words. I just told you what he said.

But you knew. You knew what was coming.

We didn't know for sure. They hadn't told us anything.

You knew it wasn't beer call yet. Didn't you?

Well, everybody else was beginning to line up. They all had their papers. We hadn't been given any reason to suspect. We...we thought they'd let us slide. At least, I did.

And why was that? Had they ever let anybody slide before?

[Ghastly smile, horrific remembrance, flood of emotions rapidly flickering across face] No. They never had.

Then why did you think this time would be any different? Why did you think they weren't going to take you out and torture you? Were you friendly with any of the guards?

No. Certainly not. They were all former editors. That was one of the requirements.

I'm well aware of the requirements. This court is not questioning the integrity of the guards.

It should! If you call yourselves lawmakers! This hearing is a farce! Howard Varrick was a humorist! If he'd been published he'd have been one of the greatest writers of this century! He was on his way! He was making some real progress until he was tortured! I read his drafts! I laughed!

[General confusion, buzzing from peanut gallery, rapping of gavel, uneasy order quickly restored. Small gaping faces at door swiftly pushed outside] Thank you. [Turning, pausing, acknowledging appreciation to judge] If we can proceed....Tell us about that afternoon. Tell us what happened after you and Mr. Varrick discussed your problems.

We had to turn our papers in. That came first. Dr. Evans was the personal guard and senior editor.

Did Dr. Evans review your revisions in the exercise yard?

Yes. He did. But that was common practice. We had to get the initial okay from him before we could go to beer call.

And how long did that usually take?

[*Ruminating, chin in hand*] Not long, usually. He'd just give it a quick glance. He wouldn't read all the way through.

How long would you say? Ten minutes? Five?

Probably about five. Maybe a little less.

And how many words of copy are we talking about here?

Well. It varied.

How much?

It depended. On what we were revising.

How many words would you say, on the day in question?

Between us?

Yes, Between you.

Oh. Probably. About six thousand. Somewhere around that.

He was a fast reader, wasn't he?

Fairly quick, I suppose. I'm sure he'd had a lot of practice.

But you didn't go to beer call that day. Did you?

No. We didn't.

What did it, Mr. Lawrence?

I don't understand.

Whose work was it that caused Dr. Evans to cancel your beer break and send you in for involuntary sex instead?

[*Mad panic now, sudden, furious, eyes searching the court, hands gripping chair arms wildly*] What?

I said whose work was it?

I don't have to answer that question!

Answer it.

No.

Answer it!

Damn you! Damn you and your court. I'm not saying anything else. I want to see my lawyer.

Well, there he is. Sitting right there at that table.

[*Unable to decide. Fear. Horror. Mouth chewing knuckle*] I...

Answer the question. Wasn't it in fact *your* work that got Mr. Varrick sent in for involuntary sex along with you? Hadn't he been cribbing your notes? Didn't you drag him down with you? Weren't you still secretly copying Faulkner, at *night*, under the covers, with a flashlight?

Eee....yes! Damn you! Yes!

Weren't you laboring along, in the 'great southern gothic tradition,' using heavy frightening imagery?

Yes! [*Beaten. Whipped. Chastised. Chastened. Cowed. Diminished. Uncertain. Afraid. Tentative. Sick*]

Ignoring punctuation, running whole pages of narrative together, incorporating colons, semicolons, hyphens, making your characters talk like Beeder Mackey on LSD?

[*Softly*] Yes.

All right. What happened after Dr. Evans finished reading your...*work*?

[*Trying to regain composure*] He became irrational.

Irrational? Was it irrational for him to show displeasure over unacceptable work?

No.

Was it irrational for him to have little patience with two longtime inmates who refused to be rehabilitated? Repeaters?

No.

Then why did you say he became irrational?

He... [*shifting in chair, crossing legs, uncrossing legs*] he started taking the paper clips off the papers. He was shouting.

What was he shouting?

Obscenities.

Were these obscenities pertaining to the work at hand?

Yes.

Did he tell you he was about to take you in for involuntary sex?

No. He didn't. He just told us to wait, that we weren't going to beer call with the rest.

What happened then?

Well. We waited. We waited in the yard.

Did everybody else take a beer break?

Yes. They did. We could hear them. They sounded like they were having a good time.

Really whooping it up, eh?

Yes.

And that really bothered you. Didn't it?

Yes. It did.

You thought you weren't being treated fairly, didn't you? You thought even a convicted copycat should have rights, didn't you?

Yes. I do. I mean I did.

When did you first realize that you were about to be taken in for involuntary sex?

When they brought the blindfolds out.

Were the earplugs and the nose plugs applied at this time, also?

Yes. They were. [*Eyes downcast*] We knew, then.

Were you afraid?

I... [*Ashamed*] I was very afraid. I'd never had to do anything like that before in my life.

But you'd been given plenty of warning.

Yes.

You'd been told to pick up the level of your writing. Both of you.

Yes.

Were you blindfolded before you were taken inside?

No, they—made us look at them first. For several minutes.

And then.

[*A whisper*] Then they blindfolded us. [*Whole court straining forward to catch words, reporters scribbling furiously*] I tried to hold Howard's hand but I couldn't find it. I told him...I told him to be brave. He was crying. I was, too. We were both...at the lowest point of our lives. They'd reduced us to animals.

What happened then?

[*Eyes closed. Huge gulp*] Someone touched me. She said—she said she was a member of a book club. And a poetry society. She put her arms around me. They were big arms. Huge.

Were you scared?

I was terrified.

Can you describe it?

Describe *what*? Do you want to hear about the *act*? Oh, you filthy animal. You dirty, dirty man. You want to hear about it? I'll tell you about it. I'll tell you all what you want to hear. If it'll keep one person from going through what I went through. She was fat, okay? She was big, and fat, and heavy, and she sweated, all right? [*Rising from chair, face heated, turning red, carotid artery protuberant, teeth gritted*] She couldn't have sat down in two chairs, okay? She didn't have any teeth. She was covered with tattoos and she was hairy, and she had bad breath. Now. You want to hear some more?

Bailiff?

No! She got on top of me! They'd told her I was famous! She was mashing me! I was trying to get out from under her but she was too big! It was horrible, do you hear me? Horrible! I can't forget about it! I wake up in the middle of the night screaming from it, screaming from it, screaming huh huh huh...[*Complete breakdown, hands over face, gradual grading off to racking sobs loud in hushed awe of courtroom*]

All right, Mr. Lawrence. [*Going back to table for manuscript pages, waving them in the air*] The state has one more piece of evidence to present in this parole hearing. [*Approaching witness stand, thrusting papers rudely forward*] Read this. Out loud.

[*Looking up, face still contorted, eyes wet, nose snuffling*] What?

[*Shaking pages belligerently*] You wrote it. I should think you'd be proud to get a chance to read it in public. I want this court to hear the real reason your parole should be denied. Go on, read it.

[*Taking papers slowly, recognizing them*] Oh. God, no. [*Head shaking, papers trembling slightly in fingers*] You can't mean...I don't want to read this. Please. It isn't fair to make me read this. If you have one shred of decency...

Read it.

This...this is just a rough draft.

I thought you'd revised it, Mr. Lawrence.

I was drunk when I wrote this.

Wasn't beer call yet, Mr. Lawrence. Remember? Read it.

You. You got this out of my files somehow. This was locked up in my study. [*Looking up, amazed*] You won't stop, will you? It's never going to end, is it? You want to keep me in there forever, don't you? You don't really believe in rehabilitation. It's just a way to keep us out of print. [*Soft, unbelievable horror. Pause. Bitter resignation. Determination*] All right, I'll read it. I'll read every damn word of it. It may be the only time I'll get to [*Bracing himself, adjusting tie, one hand on knee, beginning...*] And it was with a timorous expression of the wide upturned Afro-American nostrils that, arched and slightly hissing, Otis McQuay paused and turned toward his eating, sitting, brother, the twin, the Aquarius, the one with whom he had shared the dark bloody nacreous unlighted cavern of his mother's womb, and sniffed, hesitantly, not blatantly or in open astonishment or anything so challenging as that, at the malodorous gases drifitng cloudlike and thick as turtle soup down the rough unplanned splintered wobbly table to where he sat eating his butter beans and cornbread, his stance like that of a bluetick on a mess of birds. For it was not in his nature to be challenging. Then he heard it, the slight thin whistle like steam escaping, and his eyes shifted quickly in their sockets, huge and white and rolling. Trapped, with him now, his own supper but half eaten, frozen in that indecision or flight or willingness to endure, to stand, the muscles of his legs coiled tight as screen-door springs, his hands on either side of his plate like dead or wounded or dying blackbirds, while all around him the fumes grew stronger and more malodorous, more pungent. The air grew rank, grew right funky. There came a long ragged sound like paper tearing and it was chopped off short, immeasurably loud in the close silence. Then like two toots on a bugle came the next two toots: toot, toot. But it was not the brass mouth of a trumpet, not an instrument of music that played that sorry scale. It was something deeper, more sinister—

I think that will do.

a sound born not of clean air and lungs but a fecund, a ripe smell, like burning shoes...

Your Honor, I think we've proved our point.... Bailiff, would you show this man to his seat?

...like dead rattlesnakes, like soured slops, like contaminated sheepdip—

Could we get the bailiffs to perform their duties, please?

[*Bailiffs surging forward, babble of voices rising from courtroom, judge rapping gavel*]

Like moldy mattress stuffings! Like bad cheese!

Your Honor! Could we have order restored! Please!

[*Judge rapping gavel louder, bailiffs grappling with defendant on witness stand, now wild-eyed, smiling! Defiant! Eyes ablaze!*] Like putrid prairie dog meat! Wait! There's more! Do you hear me! Just listen!

Witness

MADISON SMARTT BELL

T HE DAY HE HEARD that Paxton Morgan was released, Wilson had been planning to revise a will. It was a slack period for him and he didn't expect to be in court until late in the following week, but he'd come in early just the same. The door to his inner office was open on the lateral hallway, and he could hear the whisk of a letter opener as Mrs. Veech, behind the front desk, sliced into the morning mail. Mostly bills or offers of subscriptions, he'd glanced through it quickly on his way in.

There was a jingle as the front door opened and Wilson raised his head to listen, but it was a man he didn't want to see, and Mrs. Veech denied his presence. A grumble, sound of pacing, scrape of a match and a faint distant odor of tobacco. Mrs. Veech coughed. The voice grudgingly inquired if the smoke bothered her. Mrs. Veech said nothing but coughed again, more signifi cantly. Her allergy to cigarettes was highly selective—Wilson, for instance, smoked himself. When the front door released a jangle of departure, he picked up his pencil and went back to the will. Mrs. Veech, he could hear, was dealing with the remains of the mail.

"Mr. Wilson, did you know they were letting Pax Morgan go?"

He heard her voice without immediately understanding it, registering only the anxiously rising note at the end. The task in his hand was complicated, though almost entirely frivolous: the testament of a woman some forty years old who would prob ably live at least forty more, revising her bequests more or less semiannually. Still, it was an amusement she could afford if it pleased her, harmless enough, and he had use for the fee.

He drafted another line or two on the long yellow pad and broke the point of his pencil. Then the sense of Mrs. Veech's question reached him and he stood up, taking a cigarette from his shirt pocket as he stepped into the hall. Mrs. Veech sat bolt upright in her desk chair, clamping some sort of form in both her hands. Wilson took it from her and walked to the front window, setting the unlit cigarette in the corner of his mouth as he moved. It was a slick gray photocopy of a release form from Central State, with the name of Paxton Morgan typed along with other information and the illegibly scrawled signature of some doctor or official in the lower right-hand corner. He noted that the box for the date was not filled in.

"They might have already turned him out," Mrs. Veech said.

"Or they might just still be thinking about it." Wilson turned to face her. Round, plain and comfortable, she was a clean fifteen years older than he and normally unfazeable, though now she seemed perceptibly disturbed.

"I wonder who sent us this," he said.

"There wasn't any cover letter." Mrs. Veech frowned.

Wilson stepped across and picked up the slit envelope from the stack of circulars on the desk and paced back to the window, turning it over in his hands. It was letterhead stationery from the hospital, with his own address unremarkably typed and a postmark from two days before. Absently he folded it in three and peered out the window, around the hanging vines of the plants Mrs. Veech had insisted on stringing up there. The office was on the ground floor at the corner of the square, and sighting through the letter *O* of his own reversed name on the glass, Wilson could see a couple of cars and one mud-splattered pickup truck revolving lazily around the concrete Confederate soldier on his high pedestal at the center. Opposite, the usual complement of idlers lounged around the courthouse steps. The office had a southern exposure, and he could feel a slight sunny warmth on the side of his face through the pane.

"Well, damn their eyes," he said, and then, as he noticed Mrs. Veech again, "Excuse me."

Back in his inner office, Wilson lit the cigarette and set it in an ashtray to burn itself out, then began dialing the phone with the butt end of his pencil. In some fifteen minutes he had variously heard that Pax Morgan had already been released, was not going to be released at all, or had never been admitted. He hadn't expected to discover who had sent the anonymous notification, and so was not surprised when he didn't. Although he did learn that a Dr. Meagrum was supposed to be presiding over the case, he could not get through to him. He left a message asking that his call be returned. The central spring of his revolving chair squealed slightly as he leaned back, away from the phone. On the rear wall of the room, behind the triangle of clients' chairs, bookshelves rose all the way to the high ceiling, bearing about half of Wilson's law library. Hands laced behind his head, he scanned the top row of heavy books as though looking for something, though he was not. After a moment he tightened his lips and leaned forward again and made the call he had been postponing.

He had the number by heart already because it had once been his own, the Nashville law firm where he'd formerly worked. In those days Sharon Morgan would likely have answered the phone herself, but they used her more as a researcher now, and had hired a different receptionist. She was good at the work, and with the two children there was no doubt the better pay made a difference. Still studying for her own law degree, part time; Pax had never liked that much. Wilson asked for her and waited till she came on the line, her voice brisk, as he remembered it. It had been some months since they had spoken and the first few exchanges passed in pleasantries, inquiries about each other's children and the like. Then, a pause.

"Well, you never called just to pass the time," Sharon said. "Not if I know you."

Wilson hesitated, thinking, What would she look like now? The same. Phone pinched between her chin and shoulder, a tail of her longish dark hair involved with the cord some way. Chances were she'd be doing something on her desk while she waited for him to continue, brown eyes sharp on some document, wasting no time.

"Right," he said. "Have you heard anything of Pax lately?"

"And don't care to," she said, her tone still easy. "Why would you ask?"

The chair spring squeaked as Wilson shifted position. The distant sound of a typewriter came to him over the line. He flicked his pencil with a fingernail and watched its bevels turning over the lines of the yellow pad. "And not the hospital either, I don't suppose."

"Oh-*ho*," Sharon said. He could hear her voice tightening down, homing in. She took the same grim satisfaction in any discovery, no matter its purport, which was part of what made her good at her job. "Is that what it is?"

"I'm afraid," Wilson said, "they're letting him out, if they haven't already."

"And never even let me know. There ought to be a law..."

"...but there doesn't appear to be one," Wilson said. He picked up the hospital form and read off to her its most salient details. A stall, he thought, even before he was through with it. "The morning mail," he said. "No date, and I don't even know who sent it."

"Then what are you thinking to do?" she said.

"I've been calling the hospital," Wilson said. "If I ever get through to the right doctor, maybe I can convince them to hold him, if he's not already gone."

"*If*," Sharon said sharply. "All up to them, is it?"

"I would call it a case for persuasion," Wilson said. "So, did you have any plans for the weekend? I should be able to get in touch..."

"I'm taking the children out to the lake."

Wilson plucked another cigarette from his breast pocket and began to tamp it rhythmically on the old green desktop blotter. "I don't know," he said. "Why not go to your brother's, say? Instead."

"What would we want to do that for?"

"Look, Sharon," he said. "You know, it's to hell and gone from anywhere, that house on the lake. And nobody even out there this time of year."

"I will *not* run from that—" She interrupted herself, but he thought the calm of her voice was artificial when she went on. "The kids are packed for it. They're counting on it. I don't see any reason to change our plans."

"You don't, do you?" Wilson said without sarcasm, and put a match to his cigarette. He supposed he'd been expecting this, or something a whole lot like it.

"Why don't you get a peace bond on him?" Sharon said. "If he really is out, I mean. Something. Because it ought to be *his* problem. Not mine."

"I could do that," Wilson said. "Try to, anyway. You know what good it'll do, too. You know it better than I do."

There was silence in the receiver; the phantom typewriter had stopped. Pax Morgan had been under a restraining order that night back before the divorce decree when he'd appeared at the house in Nashville he and Sharon had shared and smashed out all the ground-floor windows with the butt end of his deer rifle; he'd made it all the way around the hosue before the police arrived.

"Well, devil take the hindmost," Wilson said. "I'll let you know what I can find out. And you take care."

"Thanks for letting me know."

"Take care, Sharon," Wilson said, but she had already hung up, so he did too.

Shifting the cigarette to his left hand, he picked up the pencil and began jotting a list at the foot of the pad with the blunted tip. Often he did his thinking with the pencil point; he'd discovered that sometimes a solution would appear in the interstices of what he wrote. There were only two items on the list.

    —Judge Oldfield   injunction P.M.
    —Dr. Meagrum   Central State

He added a third.

    —call back S.M.

The pencil doodled away from the last initial. The list was obvious and complete, and after he acted on it nothing would be solved. A long ash was sprouting from his cigarette, but he didn't notice until the spark crawled far enough to burn his knuckle.

For the rest of the morning, he worked abstractedly on the will with imperfect concentration. Every twenty minutes or so he interrupted himself to make some fruitless call. Dr. Meagrum was perpetually "on rounds" or "in consultation." Judge Oldfield was spending his morning on the bench. Wilson's own phone rang occasionally, but always over something trivial. When he called Oldfield's chambers again around noon, he found that the judge was gone to lunch. He tightened his tie, got his seersucker suit coat down from the hat rack and, with a word or two to Mrs. Veech, went out himself.

Circling the square counterclockwise, he passed the Standard Farm Store, the bank and the courthouse steps, where one man or another raised a broad flat palm to greet him. It was warm out, an Indian summer heat wave, though it was late October and the leaves had already turned. A new asphalt path on the southbound street felt tacky on his shoes as he crossed. A couple of blocks west of the square he was already verging on the edge of time; beyond the long low roof of Dotson's Restaurant there were woods, turned fired-clay red patched with sere yellow, with a few deep greed cedars standing anomalously among the other trees.

The fans were on inside the restaurant, revolving on tall poles, fluttering the corners of the checked oilcloths on the small square tables. Judge Oldfield sat toward the rear—alone, for a wonder—behind a plate of fried catfish, hush-puppies and boiled greens. As Wilson approached he put down his newspaper and smiled. "What wind blows you here, young fellow my lad?"

"An ill one, I'd say." Wilson sat down on a ladder-back chair. "Do you remember Sharon Morgan? A Lawrence, she was, before she married."

"Married that crazy fellow, didn't she?"

"That's the one." Wilson ordered an iced tea from the waitress who'd appeared at his elbow, and turned back to the judge. "They're letting him out of Central State, at least that's what it looks like." He ran down the brief of the morning's activity while Oldfield grazed on his catfish and nodded.

"It worrying you personally?" the judge said when he was done. "For yourself, I mean?"

"Oh, no," Wilson said. "Not hardly. It wasn't me he said he'd kill, was it? I doubt he'd remember much about me. I never knew him any too well. Even while the divorce was going on it was just her he was mad at."

"So it's the wife—ex-wife, I mean. She's the one with the worry."

"She's the one." Wilson frowned down at his hands. There was a small watery blister where the cigarette had burned him, surprisingly painful for its size. He turned the cold curve of the iced tea glass against it. "She asked me to get an injunction on him. That's why I came hunting you."

Oldfield took off his fragile rimless glasses, rubbed them with a handkerchief and put them back on. "That's tricky, old son," he said, "when you don't know for sure if he's loose or not."

"Hard to get good information out of that place, don't you know?" Wilson said. "Seems like a lot of them are crazy, doctors and patients alike."

"Must be that's why they call it a madhouse," Oldfield said with a faint smile. "Well. She does live in the county now? Full time?"

"She moved here right after the divorce," Wilson said.

"Just to oblige you, now," Oldfield said, "I could sign you a paper. You draw it up. It happens he *is* out, you let me know and we'll sign it and serve it right away. It won't be much of a help to her, though."

"Don't I know it," Wilson said. "But what else do you do?"

"Not a whole lot that you *can*," said Oldfield. "You really think she's got call to worry? Not just fretful, is she?"

"Not her," Wilson said. "I'm the one fretting. I'm wondering, how can I get a deputy to watch over them for a couple of days?"

"You know you can't set them on her," Oldfield said. "Not without she asks for it herself."

"She won't."

"She was a pretty thing, as I recall," Oldfield said irrelevantly. He took off his glasses and rubbed at the bridge of his nose. "And knew her own mind, or seemed to."

"You mean she's stubborn."

"Yes, that's right."

Wilson stood up. "I thank you," he said.

Oldfield smiled myopically up at him, his eyes a light watery blue. "You ought to stay and try the catfish."

"Well, I believe not," Wilson said. "Not much of an appetite today."

"A young man like you?" The judge shook his head. "Must be this heat."

"Your wife called," Mrs. Veech reported. "She'll call you back. And that man from Central State, he called. Dr. Meagrum."

"He would have, wouldn't he?" Wilson said, shrugging out of his jacket. "Wait till I was gone, I mean."

Mrs. Veech sniffed. "In a tearing-down hurry, too," she said. "He was right cross to find you not here."

"He'll get over it," Wilson said. "All right, then, would you make sure for me that Pax Morgan still has his house in Brentwood? We might want to serve a paper on him a little later in the day."

In the inner office it was a little too warm, though not quite oppressive. He put his coat on the hat rack, cracked the single window and paced for a moment at the far side of his desk. It was a shallow room and the high wall of dark bookbindings seemed uncomfortably close. With a sigh he went back to his seat, lit a cigarette, picked up the will, put it down, lifted a list of the other items on his immediate agenda and then let that drop too.

The urge to pick at the blister seemed irresistible. He tore loose an edge of it, reviewing, in spite of himself, what little he really knew about Pax Morgan. They'd gone to the same high school, but two years apart; Wilson was the younger. Pax had played football—he remembered that—indifferently, in the line. Later on he had inherited money and started dabbling in real estate, or insurance, neither making nor losing much at whatever it might have been. Grown, he was a loud bluff fellow with a ruddy face and crinkly, almost yellow hair. At the large parties where Wilson would occasionally run into him, he was known for drinking too much and becoming not just mush-mouthed but crazily incoherent. The drinking was said to be a factor in his later, more serious breakdowns.

Wilson had gone to Sharon's wedding but he couldn't think if it was before or after it that he'd had the one brush with Pax he remembered with real clarity. Another party, undoubtedly some Christmas gathering, for Pax was wearing an incongruous Santa Claus tie and had managed to get quite drunk on eggnog. Shuffled together by the crowd, they somehow became embroiled in an argument over deer hunting. Wilson shot duck and dove, rabbit and squirrel, and on his father's farm he might shoot what he had to, to protect the livestock, but he had not taste for shooting deer, which now appeared to be Pax's ruling passion. Wilson was trying to get off the subject, but Pax wouldn't let it drop.

"You've never been blooded," he said thickly. "That's your trouble, you've never been *blooded*." He grapsed Wilson's lapel and twisted it, drawing himself unpleasantly near, and Wilson was a little startled by what he himself did next, a trick someone had showed him in the Army. He took hold of Pax's thumb and squeezed the joints of it together, so that the sudden sharp pain made Pax flinch and let go. Reflexively, Wilson took a step backward, jostling someone behind him in the crowded room, but Pax's face went from surprise to a total blank, like a television switched to an empty channel, and so the whole episode was amputated.

Real craziness there, or an early sign of it. Wilson pulled the dead skin back from the blister, creating a small red-rimmed sore. By the time of the divorce, there were many worse examples, enough to fill a dossier. Wilson had nver cared for divorce work much, but Sharon was both a colleague and a sort of distant friend, and also it was in the first thin stage of his independent practice. But once it was over he swore off friends' divorces altogether, no matter how bad he might need the work. It had been an easy case in the sense that the outcome was not in real doubt, but it was angry and ugly on Pax's side, and there'd been some bitter squabbling over property. Sharon had held out for the house on the lake—impractically, as Wilson thought—surrendering the Nashville residence to Pax, who'd later sold it. Reaching for the phone to call the hospital one more time, he wished again she hadn't done that.

His game of telephone tag with Central State went on for a couple more hours, unpromisingly. When the phone finally rang back around two-thirty, it was his wife.

"Not interrupting, I hope," she said. "Is it busy?"

"Not so you'd notice," he said. "It's been pretty quiet."

"Well, we need a gallon of milk," she said, "and cornmeal. Would you stop on the way home?"

"I'll do it," Wilson said, scribbling on the pad. "Lisa driving you crazy today?" Their daughter was four years old, and frantic.

"How should I describe it?" she said, and laughed. "This time next year she'll be in school... I'll miss her, though."

"That's the spirit," Wilson said. The light on his phone began to flash and Mrs. Veech called down the hall, "It's that Dr. Meagrum!"

"I've got to take this call," Wilson said. "I'll be home on time, I think..." He pushed the button.

Dr. Meagrum seemed to be already *in medias res*. "—there's an issue of doctor-patient confidentiality here, Mr., uh, Wilson. I don't know who could have sent you that form but they did so without my authorization."

"Did they?" Wilson said, catching his breath. "As you may know, I represent Mr. Morgan's ex-wife, and given the circumstances of the case, it seems to me appropriate that *both* of us should have been informed."

"I can't agree with you there," Dr. Meagrum snapped.

"All due respect to your point of view," Wilson said, trying to collect himself. The conversation had taken an adversarial turn too soon. "I take it that Mr. Morgan *has*, in fact, been released from your, ah, custodial care."

"My records show that Mr. Morgan has been responding favorably to a course of medication and was transferred to outpatient status two days ago."

"I see," Wilson said. "What medication, may I ask?"

"I'm sorry, but that's confidential."

"And what assurance do we have that he will actually *take* this medication?"

"He's in our outpatient program now, and we'll be monitoring him on a biweekly basis."

"Biweekly, you say. That's *every two weeks?*" Wilson creaked back in his chair, gazing up at the join of his bookcase and the ceiling. "Dr. Meagrum, I would like you to consider"—he paused, thinking over the jargon as if fumbling for a key—"consider returning Mr. Morgan to *inpatient status*. Temporarily, shall we say. In the interests of the safety of his ex-wife and family."

"Our file shows that any such step would be contraindicated," the doctor said. "Not in the patient's best interests."

A white flash of light, something like heat lightning, burst over Wilson's mental horizon, obscuring his view of the bookcases. He found he was clenching the receiver in a strangle grip and talking much louder than before. "Sir, you are describing a *piece of paper* to me, and I am talking to you about a man who has threatened to kill his wife, not once but many times—"

Dr. Meagrum harrumphed. "Yes, someone with this type of pathology might make such a threat, but I wouldn't suggest that you take it too seriously..."

"He came to her house with a thirty-ought-six rifle," Wilson said. "A *loaded* rifle—I'm now referring to the police report. They found him and the gun and they found her barricaded in an upstairs bedroom. With her two children, I should say. The boy is six now, Dr. Meagrum, and the little girl is seven. Your *outpatient* has threatened to kill them too."

Dr. Meagrum resorted to the imperial "we": "We have no record that this patient is violent. We see no reason to alter the treatment program at this time."

With a mighty effort, Wilson established a greater degree of control over his voice. "Very well," he said frostily. "I do sincerely hope you'll see no reason to regret the course you've taken."

* * *

By dumb luck his next call caught Judge Oldfield in his chambers, between cases, on the fly.

"I'm asking the impossible now," Wilson said. "Let's have him picked up. An APB. Lock him up and have a look at him. Just for a day or so."

"You're right," Oldfield said. "That's impossible. I couldn't do it if I wanted to. This is Williamson County. We haven't got a police state here."

"It's a free country, isn't it," Wilson said. "Well, I had to ask."

"I wonder if you did, at that," Oldfield said. "You're acting mighty worked up about this, old son. Don't you think you might be making a little much of it all? He's been out two days already, so you say, and what happened? Nothing. The lady didn't even know until you called her. Simmer down some, think it over. Go home early. It's Friday, after all."

"All right," Wilson said. "Might give it a try."

"You get me that injunction and I'll pass it on to the sheriff direct," Oldfield said. "I can't do any more than that."

"I know," Wilson said. "Not until something happens. Well, I appreciate it."

He hung up and dialed Sharon Morgan at the office but she was gone, gone for the weekend, had left half an hour before to pick up the children from school. He plopped down the phone and tried, forcibly, to relax. Try it. Judge Oldfield was no fool, after all. Wilson picked up the pencil with a fleeting idea of listing off what he was thinking, feeling, but that was a ridiculous notion; probably that was how they spent their time at Central State. Possibly nothing would happen anyway. Possibly. He looked up Sharon's home number and dialed it, but there was no answer, though it rang twenty times.

In ten minutes he had scratched out the requisite injunction and handed it to Mrs. Veech with instructions to type it and walk it over to the courthouse when she was done. After she had gone out, he sat doing nothing but covering the phone, which didn't ring. The jingle of Mrs. Veech's return moved him to at least pretend to work. But he'd had it with the will for the day, though it still wasn't quite finished. He scraped his agenda toward him across the desk and ran his pencil point down item by item. There were two boundary disputes and a zoning complaint. A piece of frivolous litigation to do with somebody's unleashed dog. There was a murder case where the defendant would plead, draw two-to-ten and count himself lucky. A foregone conclusion, Wilson thought in his present skeptical mood, though matters had not yet reached that stage. At the foot of the list was a patent case that would make him and his client rich if he could win it. This one was the most remote, no court date even set for it yet, but at the same time the most intriguing, as much for its intricacy as its promise. He swiveled and dug in the cabinet for the file.

At four he called Sharon Morgan at the lake and got no answer. For another half hour he studied the patent case, though he was losing interest at an exponential rate. When he next called there was still no answer, and he was out of the chair and snatching his coat down from its peg before he even knew he meant to leave. On the highway bound for Keyhole Lake he began to feel a little foolish. He'd been presuming, counting the time from three o'clock, when school let out. It was not more than an hour from Nashville to the lake house, but he hadn't considered that she might have stopped to shop on the way, or taken the children to a movie or simply for a drive. Now it appeared to him that his every move that day had been an error. It was unlike him to have lost his temper with that doctor. Patience had always been his strength; he left it to his opponents to make mistakes in anger. Then too, that last call to Judge Oldfield was something he'd have to live down, and on top of all that he had wasted the day, and would need to come back in Saturday morning to recover the lost time.

All foolishness, and yet the thought did not comfort him. He drove carefully, a hair under the speed limit, sighting through the windshield across the burn mark on his knuckle. For no reason he could think of, he let the car roll past the Morgan mailbox and coast to a stop on the shoulder, where he got softly out. There was a little lip to climb before he could see down the driveway to the steeply pitched roof of the A-frame house and the blue lake distantly visible out past it. It was cooler here; the weather was turning, or else it was a chill coming off the water.

Below him, the drive was matted with fallen leaves. A staining fall of sunset light came slanting through the tree trunks on either side as the wind rose and combed the red leaves back, bringing a few more falling from the branches. Except for the wind it was utterly still; only across the lake the dogs in Jackson's kennel were barking, their voices echoing off the flat expanse of the water. But probably they were barking all the time. That was not the problem. What was wrong was that the passenger door of Sharon's orange Volkswagen had been left hanging open, sticking out stiffly like a broken arm. The car was pulled around parallel to the back porch, and over its roof he saw that the sliding glass door to the house had been left open too.

He walked to the dangling door and stopped. Just past the edge of the drive, not more than three yards from him, there lay a child's blue tennis shoe, a Ked, with maple leaves spread around it like the prints of a large hand. Some twenty paces farther on he found the second shoe and then the little boy, barefoot, lying face down in a pile of sloppily raked leaves. Wilson thought that his name had been Billy, but he couldn't be quite certain of it, which bothered him unreasonably. The child had been shot in the base of the neck; the entry wound was rather small. Beyond the leaf pile a wide swath of dun lawn swept down to the lake shore where a canoe, tethered to a little dock, rocked softly on the water.

A strip of almost total darkness fit into the gap of the glass door. The porch floor moaned as Wilson crossed it, and glancing down he saw a brass shell casing caught in a crack between two boards. He bent to pick it up, then stopped himself and put both hands in his pockets. Through the door was a large living room with no ceiling, only the peaked roof and the rafters. At this time of day it was very dim within and it took Wilson's eyes a moment to adjust. The daughter (he was almost sure her name was Jill) was sprawled on a high-backed wicker chair as if flung there by some strong force. There was a single wound in her chest. Her mouth was open slightly and her eyes showed a little white. Wilson thought it more than likely that Pax had shot her from a standing position on the porch.

It took him only a quarter turn of his head to locate Sharon's body at the far end of the long room, lying across a wide flight of steps that rose to the kitchen and dining area. Pax might well have shot her from the doorway; he was a marksman, the proof was plain, and efficient with his shells. Wilson crossed the room to the steps and paused. He couldn't tell just where she'd been hit, though she'd bled very heavily. She lay crooked, twisted over at the waist, the fingers of one hand folded over the overhang of a step. Her hair had fallen full over her face, and Wilson was grateful for that, but her position looked so uncomfortable that he was tempted to turn and straighten her. His hands were still jammed in his pockets, however, and he left them there.

He went up the steps almost on tiptoe, careful to avoid bloodying his shoes, and made a turn to the left that brought him up against the metal kitchen cabinets. His breath was coming very short, each intake arrested as though by a punch in the midsection. He was aware of the tick of his wristwatch, and that was all. There was a telephone on the kitchen counter, and presently he detached a paper towel from a roll neatly suspended beneath the line of cabinets, wrapped it around the receiver and called the sheriff's office.

At the opposite end of the kitchen, a smaller set of sliding doors opened onto a deck overlooking the lawn and the lake. With the help of another paper towel, he slid back the door and went out and sat on a bench to wait. The lake's surface had a painful metallic glitter, with the sunset colors spreading across it like corrosion. He had left his sunglasses in the car, and being in no mood to retrieve them, he simply shut his eyes. In Korea, where the Army had sent him, he had *seen some action*, as they say, but afterward he had thought very little about what he had seen. In some quietly ticking corner of his mind a speculation was going forward as to how the bodies had come to be positioned as they were, and now it came to him that after they were all inside the house the boy must have missed his shoes and gone back to the car— He opened his eyes with a jerk and looked up. A solitary, premature firefly detached itself from the treetops on one side of the yard and floated dreamily across and into the treetops on the other.

It was twilight by the time he had parked his car behind the square, and for some reason he bypassed his office and walked on down Main Street as far as Saint Paul's Episcopal Church. More leaves had carpeted the white stone steps, and Wilson stood looking at them, one hand curved around a spear of the iron fence, and then turned back. The sidewalk was empty but for him, and he could hear the dry leaves crisping under his every footfall.

The street lights were coming on by the time he had returned to the square. The windows of his office were dark, but he could hear the telephone ringing as he came up the steps. Mrs. Veech had, of course, locked up before she left, and while he was searching out his key the phone stopped ringing. He went inside and pressed the light switch. Again the phone began to jangle, and he reached across Mrs. Veech's typewriter to pick it up.

"Mr. Wilson? It's Sam Trimble here. I had your paper to serve on Paxton Morgan?"

"Yes," Wilson said.

The deputy cleared his throat. "I thought you might like to know we picked him up. He'd gone straight back to his own house, you know, like they do."

"Yes," Wilson said again.

"We got him cold, if it's any comfort," Trimble said. "The gun still warm and blood on his shoes."

"That's all right," Wilson said. "He'll plead insanity."

He was not often here at night, and the overhead fixture was harsh and bright, bouncing blurred reflections from the flat black of the window panes, making his inner office look too much like a cell. But if he used only the desk lamp, the shadows reached toward him so. And yet he was still afraid to go home! He shouldn't have said what he had to Trimble, though at the moment he could hardly bring himself to feel regret for it. And he was late by now; he'd better call.

"Daddy, you're late," Lisa said.

"That's right, kiddo," Wilson said. "Where's your mother?"

"She's outside," Lisa said. "We were, both of us. I'll go call her."

"No, you don't need to," Wilson said. "Just tell her I'll be home shortly. Say I still have to stop by the store, though." Hanging up, he glanced at his watch. A fine evening like this, his wife would certainly spend outdoors, not bothering to watch the evening news.

Flushed with relief, he pictured their long curving yard, thick with fireflies, as it would be now, green pinpoints flashing and hovering in the dark. The lights of the house glowed warm behind the calm silhouettes of his wife and his daughter, and inside, the kitchen steamed with the scent of supper waiting. Upstairs, beside his bedside lamp, lay the copy of *War and Peace* he'd been rereading this fall; at a half hour or so a night, it would last him to Christmas or longer. He thought now of Prince Andrey lying wounded on the battlefield, looking up into the reaches of the sky, that radical change in his perspective.

Still, he was not quite ready to leave. He picked up his pencil and tapped the butt of the dried eraser on the pad. At home, tonight or tomorrow or whenever he finally had to tell the story there, then the murders would be absolutely realized and the alternative of their somehow not having happened would be permanently shut off. Above, the fluorescent fixture made a sort of whining sound; Wilson thought that he could feel it in his teeth.

He turned the pencil over in his hand and set the point on the pad, but there was nothing much to write. The yellow paper was down at the bottom of a long pale shaft, stroked with faint parallel lines which signified nothing. If he could note down all the ingredients of the episode, then they could be comprehended, wrapped in a parcel of law and so managed. Wilson was a believer in due process. Without meaning to, he had become a bystander in this case.

It was only dizziness because he had skipped lunch, undoubtedly, and when he remembered that, the pad came floating back up toward him and the desk flattened and held still. There were some scratch marks on the paper, as if during his vertigo he had been trying unsuccessfully to draw a picture. Now he wondered if he had *known* what would happen, and if he had *known*, what then? He had left no legitimate measure untried but still he could picture himself crossing the lip above the lake house with a gun in his own hand, seeing the Volkswagen door still closed, the glass door of the house pulled to and Pax Morgan outlined against the glimmer of the lake like a paper silhouette.

The pencil slipped from his fingers and hit the desk with a clacking report that broke the fantasy. Pax was alive and the others were dead. His freedom was better protected than their safety—that would be one way of putting it. Simple. It was time to go home. Wilson turned off the desk lamp, stood up and pulled his coat down from the hat rack. Safer and better to have no freedom maybe, but no, you wouldn't say that. The humming stopped when he flicked the light switch by the door. No, you wouldn't say that, would you? In the dark of the hall he could not see his way; he went toward the vague light of the front window with one hand on the wall. No, you wouldn't, but what would you say?

Earthly Justice

E.S. GOLDMAN

AT FIRST THE WORDS were in the wrong sequence to be heard, for death is slight news until a familiar name is in it. "Killed...Pittsburgh...*Sherroder!*"

Try it yourself. How much do you really care about people starving in Africa or sleeping on the sidewalks of Boston or being shot in their garages in Pittsburgh? You care, yes. You're human, and nothing is alien et cetera. But as if they were your own flesh and blood? No aunt of yours is in any of those fixes; not that you know of. Nothing happens that you care all that much about until you hear a name.

I was reading *The Black Arrow* and half-listening to KDKA on the shortwave. I didn't hear anything until I heard the name of my father's sister.

Killed...Pittsburgh...Sherroder! *Aunt Leora!*

I held onto the book as to a brother in a scary place while the newscaster put it in order again for late-arriving minds (the way they used to before jobs were filled by people with no memory of how things should be done. Now they write for radio as if you were tuned from the first word, as if you had nothing to do but sit there and hear them tell the story from A to Z. If you miss the name of the country where the airplane went down in the first sentence, they never tell you again.)

"The dead woman's husband, Dr Myron Sherroder, a well-known Pittsburgh physician, was at home at the time—"

The young don't often play a part as large as being the first to know. I burst out of my room and went down the stairs shouting, "Aunt Leora's been killed! She was shot!"

Leora was very close to us. She and Mother had been best friends since middle school. She often came down from Dedham to stay with us at the shore, and after she married and moved to Pittsburgh, the visiting went on as before. Uncle Myron was part of it. The only regret about Myron was that he was a golfer and not a fisherman as we were in our family; but he was accommodating and could be jollied into wading in for smallmouth on a gray day.

Mother was choked and bewildered and kept saying in an unearthly groaning voice I had never heard before, "What do you mean? Leora? What do you mean? What do you mean? Leora?"

It seemed to me that she was angry with me, which was unreasonable. I had interrupted her kind of sewing that is done on a small linen drumhead. She thrust the tambourine, her fingers extended as if to take me by the shoulder to shake out the nonsense as she had when I was younger. I wasn't sure she would remember the needle. I flinched and looked to Dad.

When my father clenches his jaw, the muscles become bone, his lips bulge as if they have under them the pads a dentist slips in to take up saliva. He has never been a slack man in mind or body and does not appreciate it in others. He assessed the possibility of error in a twelve-year-old boy.

He held a finger up toward Mother to ask her to hold back and asked me to say again what I had heard. He went to the phone.

Instead of calling Uncle Myron as I expected, he asked for Pittsburgh information, and then the number of the police station nearest the Sherroder address.

The questions he asked the police desk and the way he hung up said enough. Separating the more-or-less-known from the said-to-be-known, the police were able to say that they had received a report by telephone at 9:47 P.M. from a man stating that he was the husband of the deceased. The witness at the scene stated that he had found Mrs Sherroder on the floor of the garage, apparently dead, apparently as a consequence of multiple wounds, apparently from shotgun fire. It had happened a little more than an hour ago and the investigation was just beginning. Dad made this report piecemeal in a halting voice while he held Mother.

"I'd better call Myron," he said, gently letting her go.

Myron hadn't realized it was already on the radio. The detectives were there taking pictures and asking questions, and he had been waiting for an opportunity to break away and make the call. After they spoke awhile Dad said, "Life is long, Myron. Take every day one at a time. I'll be there on an early plane," and hung up.

Mother had her voice under control. "What did he say?"

"He doesn't know much more than we do. Leora went to an evening meeting of the Handicapped Services board. He had the television on to a wildlife documentary and didn't hear a thing. When it was past the time Leora usually got home he walked out and saw the garage door open. She was lying beside the car. She was shot. They haven't found a gun."

While Mother made the family phone calls, Dad went to the window and stood fully ten minutes with his hands behind his back, staring through the dark at the few stars of houses on the far side of the bay. Mother left Grandma Dewaine for him. He could have waited until morning and seen Grandma on his way to the airport, but it would have been awful if she heard it first from a reporter calling to ask if she had a photograph of her daughter. He told her that Leora had died in an accident without suffering and that he would stop by in the morning. Being prepared in this way she could be relied on to get through the night. Dewaines managed. She was a Dewaine by assimilation.

Mother was also that much a Dewaine, but only that much. She took the phone and asked Grandma if she would like somebody to spend the night with her. She would be glad to come herself. Would she like Dad to be with her. Would she like her good friend Betty Morse to be called. Mother listened to the timbre of Grandma saying No, that was unnecessary, she would be all right; and was satisfied. It was left as before that her son would stop there early on his way to the airport.

Although Dad had anyhow decided to take the Pittsburgh flight in order to be with Myron on the first difficult day, our family assumed that burial would be in the Dewaine plot in Brewster. When he called to give Myron his flight number, he learned that the service and burial would be in Pittsburgh.

"I don't understand such a decision," Mother said. "Leora has no family in Pittsburgh. They have been married so few years. Myron's family is out West. Your mother is only a two-hour ride from Brewster. It is inconsiderate to bury Leora in Pittsburgh. She ought to be in your family plot. Did you say that to him?"

"I made the case. It's Myron's decision to make. I can understand that he would want her nearby."

"There are others to think about."

"They have many friends in Pittsburgh."

"Friends are not family. Friends do not come to visit your grave site. It is a strange decision."

"It may be arbitrary but it isn't strange. It's his decision to make. It isn't easy to argue at a time like this."

"When is a good time? After the burial?" I seldom heard Mother that sharp with Dad.

"He and Leora chose the site with care. In his view, he is accommodating her wishes."

"In his view."

We all went to Pittsburgh for the funeral.

When people have lived their years it is possible to take satisfaction in memory, and even for levity to soften grief, and after long illness it is possible to speak of relief, but this was a day of harsh, unrelieved mourning, the most solemn day of my life. In the chapel, Uncle Myron sat between his brother Andrew and my father, and beside Father was Grandma Dewaine. Then Uncle Tom Dewaine, then Mother. They sat by bloodline. Except around a dinner table I had never before, at an occasion, seen Father not sit beside Mother. Because of the nature of the wound the casket was closed.

Very little was said among us. When Grandma shook with hidden sobs, Dad took her hand. I did the same to my sister, at first awkwardly; then, when she clutched it to show how glad she was to have it, with (I suppose the right word is) pride.

After the cemetery Mother took Marnie and me directly to the plane. She did not want to stay over. She said tomorrow was a school day and we should be back. My father spent the rest of the day in Pittsburgh with Myron, talking to the police and the district attorney. They posted a reward.

2

You may have forgotten the story by now or may have it confused with the celebrated case of the Cleveland doctor's wife. The death of Leora Dewaine Sherroder was much less a story than the Cleveland story but it was closely followed in Pittsburgh and on Cape Cod where there are three columns of Dewaines in the phone book. You call a Dewaine to put on a roof, survey your land, pick up your rubbish, send you a nurse. To fish out of Rock

Harbor, you sign on the *Cape Corsair*, Cap'n Pres Dewaine. You bank with Leo at Samoset 5¢ Savings. To cater a wedding you call Carolyn.

Dewaines hidden by marriage under other names must be many columns more. The only big rich Dewaines I know of are Ananders, through Cousin Peg. Delbert Anander knew what land to buy and how long to hold it, and how to run a bank and when to sell it. My father was the fourth Dewaine with the hardware and heating store, the first with the oil trucks.

The story in the newspaper about the will gave me an uncomfortable insight that others might not see Aunt Leora's death as I did. It didn't say anything that wasn't already known in the family: except for named bequests, everything was left to Uncle Myron as remainderman. They had no children. Simply stating in the newspaper that Myron was Leora Dewaine's heir seemed to imply something.

In follow-up stories, Leora became the heiress of the Dewaine fortune, the Dewaines became Mayflower descendants. The family had oil interests. A reporter discovered that a brother of Leora's great-grandfather had been a governor of Massachusetts; the family became politically influential. Myron was a kidney specialist; he had been consulted by a Mellon; he was a member of a country club; he became a socialite doctor. They had no children. The socialite doctor was the sole heir.

With such people, in such an environment, all things are possible. You don't have to go beyond your own mind.

Uncle Myron was my friend who took me to the zoo; and to the museum to see the dinosaurs xylophony stretching down the hall ("From *zonnng* on his nose"—Myron had impressive range—"to *tinnngggg*"); and to Three Rivers Stadium to see a big-league baseball game.

We sat in a box behind first base. A high foul went up and I saw that if it did not go up forever it would come down sometime later that day right where I was. Everybody around me stood up. I thought if I could get my hands on that ball I could hold it.

The day was chilly, and the men wore gloves, but I was a boy and of course hadn't thought I needed gloves. While my head followed the nearly vertical rise of the ball Uncle Myron grasped my left hand. "Here's a glove to take the sting out." He raised his voice to the crowd around us. "Give the kid a shot at it."

They cleared a space. I don't think any crowd today would stand back to give a kid a shot. I followed the ball higher than I had ever seen a ball go, while I worked the bunching out of the palm of the glove and displayed the floppy fingers as a target.

I was sure I was under it, but misjudged the angle of the fall, backed into the men and finally fell backward into the seats; and the ball, ignoring the chance to make a stylish landing in a gray suede glove, dropped beyond my farthest reach. My failure that day—despite the cooperation of the entire world to help me succeed—is not yet forgotten. It enhances the memory of Myron Sherroder, my friend, who the newspaper said without saying it might have been the one who killed Aunt Leora.

I began then to understand how words say things that aren't in them. Words reach for meanings that are already inside the hearer. In a card trick the magician fans out the cards and says, "Pick one." Psych the cards as hard as you want, you can't psych a ten of diamonds out of a tarot deck. You have to take a card that's there. I wanted it another way, but the statement that the husband of the murdered woman was the beneficiary of her will picked up the card from my standard human deck.

I began then to read about the case as others would. One day at school I took a question from a friend—"How is your uncle coming with that murder case?" It said to me that when they spoke of Leora Sherroder's murder in their home, they assumed that her husband, the socialite doctor who had inherited her money, was probably complicit in some way. And I could not help but think it too.

I was troubled. I didn't tell my father how I felt, but I put a question in a form that betrayed me. "What if—?"

Before responding, my father laid his narrow eyes on me. "That's the way people are. In this house we do not think like that. My sister was a good judge of character. She chose your Uncle Myron. As far as we know they had a good marriage."

Why "As far as we know...?"

I remembered too that when Dad called Myron that first night he hadn't said to him that he thought he was innocent. I wondered if Myron had noticed that.

I never heard my father say anything about innocence. What I understood him to say was that we had to wait respectfully, withholding judgment, as long as the process took; forever, if necessary. We had a stake in the values of organized society.

We were right to wait. In a few weeks the Pittsburgh police let it out that they were looking for a white man about forty years old with a butch haircut driving a late Plymouth white two-door who had been seen several times in the neighborhood in the week of the murder and nobody knew who he was. They found what they believed was the gun in the Allegheny River about five miles from the house and began to trace it. The gun was a Winchester twelve. There are a lot of them around. We have one in our house.

That got the newspapers going again.

Dad went to Pittsburgh. He saw Uncle Myron. He talked to the district attorney and to Detective Gertner, who had the case from the beginning. Gertner said privately they weren't getting anywhere looking for the man in the Plymouth. There weren't any fingerprints on the gun; they hadn't been able to trace it.

The detective told Dad something else. He did not look at Mother as he reported it.

"They are talking to a woman they say Myron had been seeing before—" It's not easy to say *Before my sister was murdered.* "I have to say that bothers me."

"What did Myron say to that?" Mother asked.

"He's where he was. He knows they're looking into a lot of things."

"Did he say he knew what they were looking into?"

"He mentioned the gun and the man who had been seen in the neighborhood."

"That's all been in the papers. He didn't say anything about the woman?"

"He said 'and the usual gossip you can expect.'"

"Did he say what that was?"

"No, and I didn't ask him. He is a smart man. He can guess what comes to me."

It reinforced my impression that Myron was guilty. I was not so convinced that I would have been unable to be a fair juror; but I thought it probable, and I was sure I was not alone in our house to think it—not since Father's "as far as we know . . ."—not since Mother's refusal to stay in Pittsburgh after the funeral, and the clipped severity of her manner when Myron's name came up. I was in a conspiracy not to acknowledge that a guest had made a bad smell and there was no dog to look at.

3

Uncle Myron was indicted for first-degree homicide—I don't know why the language needs another word for murder.

"That must mean he's pretty guilty," I said.

Expressing judgment in an important matter made me feel important. I didn't know that before the law you are either guilty or not, there is no pretty to it.

My father stiffened his lips. "I don't want that said again in my hearing. A trial is to find that out. We have the adversarial system in this country as the best way to get at the truth. There is nothing like two sides putting up the best argument they know how. You may think you know Uncle Myron's defense, but you don't till you hear it argued. I don't want you to forget that.

Dad went to the trial to hear the woman for himself for the two days she was a witness. She testified that she had carried the gun from the garage when Uncle Myron told her to and had thrown it in the river. Uncle Myron's lawyer brought out that she was seeking revenge because Myron had started to see other women. He brought out that she was an alcoholic. She and a former boyfriend were involved in a larceny, and the district attorney had made a deal to let her off a perjury charge in exchange for her testimony in the Sherroder case. She could even have been the one who committed the murder. Myron's lawyer brought all that out.

"She didn't make a very good witness," my father said. "Myron's lawyer doesn't think she will be convincing to the jury."

But there wasn't any doubt that Myron had something going with her—she knew too much about his life for it to be otherwise.

Myron said she only knew enough to make up the rest in order to get the reward. "I'm sorry all this comes out in this way that must seem sordid to you," he said. "I can't blame you for what you must think."

"Of course he can't blame you," Mother said. "What are you supposed to think? Leora was your sister. Did he still pretend he hadn't been going out with other women?"

"He said he had done what a lot of men do and he apologized for it. He said Leora would have understood why he saw other women had she known, even if she might not necessarily have condoned it."

"Not necessarily. I should think."

Myron had said, "I am not asking you to tell me what you now think about this. I only want you to hear me when I say I had nothing to do with it. I am entirely innocent."

"What *do* you think?" Mother asked.

My father's jaw muscles became bone. "I wasn't hired to be God," he said.

The afternoon the case went to the jury it was expected that deliberations probably wouldn't start until the next day. I was in bed with the lights out and the radio button in my ear when a bulletin came on that the jurors had decided to convene to test their sentiment. They found they had a verdict right away. The judge was coming in to hear it.

I got up and told Mother and Dad. We sat in the library and waited.

None of us made a guess what the verdict would be. It wasn't a ball game or somebody else's family or anything that doesn't count and you can show how smart or how dumb you are. When something is close to you, you don't look at it in the same way as if you're separated from it. In traffic the car ahead of you can be in the middle and won't get out of the way and you get mad. When you're in position to go around, you see it's somebody you know well and you cool off. You wave. Anything that is close to you is different.

The verdict was "Not Guilty."

To tell the truth, I didn't feel the relief you would expect from knowing that my uncle wouldn't have to spend the rest of his life in jail or be electrocuted. I certainly wouldn't have taken any joy from a guilty verdict, but it would have been more fitting and satisfying to human nature.

I suppose I am saying that my Aunt Leora, of my father's blood and therefore of mine, had been murdered, and that the way we are made requires that somebody be accountable. Almost any somebody rather than nobody. I'm the first to agree that for the sake of civilization we must respect the verdict of a court; still it isn't necessarily satisfactory to our natural sense of what is just.

I sensed that my mother felt the same, and for a moment that my father did too, but he said abruptly, "That's the verdict. The reward stands. We are going to look that much harder."

He called Uncle Myron and told him he knew the experience had been hard but he hoped he could get on with his life. He invited him to do some fishing. They arranged a weekend. Mother said, "You invited him *here*? I would just as soon you hadn't."

"I don't want to lose touch."

"I will never be comfortable with Myron. But it's up to you. I suppose men understand these things better." I supposed that wasn't what she thought.

4

Uncle Myron was grateful that we made him one of us. The truth is that without Leora he was a foreign substance. He could not attach himself by shaking my hand and telling me I grew an inch a week; by swinging my sister in the air; by trying to find a place to kiss on Mother's averted cheek. Dad hurried him through the greetings and got him to the stairs of the tower room overlooking the bay. He and Leora always had that room.

Next day was raw and drizzly, an ordinary April day. A good breeze came across the northeast and the tide went out all morning. The open bay wouldn't be very comfortable. I thought they would fish Drum Pond, but Dad said, "Myron, have you ever fished Shelf Lake with me?" Uncle Myron couldn't remember that they had.

I don't think Myron ever fished before he married Leora. As often as not when they visited, he would go over and play Great Dune while the rest of us went to a bass pond. Dad certainly wasn't going to play golf and he didn't offer any choices.

"We'll go over there. We'll get some shelter from the wind. I have a new suit of Red Ball waders you can break in for me. I'll wear my old one."

They loaded rods, boots, waders, parkas, slickers, boxes of lures, leaders, spare lines and tools, and a lunch. They were ready for bass or trout all day in any weather. They dropped me at Everbloom Nursery where I had a Saturday-morning job.

Bob Everbloom and I were moving azaleas from the back field to front beds, beginning in a drizzle we knew would get heavier, and when it did Bob decided we had enough of outside work. I could have worked under glass but I didn't come to do that. I liked to be outside on weekends. I said I would skip it, they didn't need me in the greenhouse. I borrowed Bob's bike and headed for Shelf Lake. They were carrying enough extra tackle to outfit me.

All this country around here, all of Cape Cod, is the tailings left after the great glacier thawed and backed off to Canada. It's all rock brought down by the ice and melted out, pockets of sandy soil from old oceans washing over, and a skin of topsoil from decay. Those big stands of trees are in sand not too far down, then rock. The only clay is wherever you happen to dig your foundation; you can't get drainage, I never saw it fail.

After the margin sand Shelf Lake is a basin of underwater boulders and tables of rock fed by springs and the runoff from Spark's Hill. The surrounding land is in conservation. What falls they let lie. The bones of old downed trees lie around the rim. Those spines of big fish stuck in the ground are dead cedars. A couple of paths lead in through heavy woods.

It was too raw a day for people to come for wilderness walks, and most of the fishermen around here are either commercial and need the quantities they get in saltwater or they want the fast action of bay fishing. Our Jeep was the only vehicle parked at NO VEHICLES PERMITTED BEYOND THIS SIGN. On a busy day there might be two. I locked the bike to the Jeep's bumper and went down the woods path.

Nearing the bottom I heard my father call, "Left, farther left, toward the cove."

Through the trees I glimpsed that they were both in hip-deep, Uncle Myron a hundred or so yards west and working farther. Rain dimpled the water. Away from the lea of the hill, fans of wind patterned the surface like shoaling fish. I was troubled by something but didn't concentrate my attention on what it might be as I was busy picking through catbrier that snatched into the path.

"Another ten yards. They're in there," my father called out.

Then I realized what troubled me. Myron was on the edge of the shelf that gave the lake its name. It fell off without any warning into a deep hole. I took a running step and opened my mouth to shout but it hardly got out when he let out a bellow and pitched down.

My mind churned with what could be done and what I had to do. I could get around to the shoreline nearer to him, and dive in and help him out of his gear. I could—

But I didn't move because more dumbfounding to me than the accident itself was that my father acted as though it wasn't happening. He heard Myron and saw him flail to stay afloat and go under in seconds. He knew as I did that Myron, under the roiled water, fought to get out of his parka and sweater, then out of the waders that were filling and turning into anchors; and my father turned away and cast.

I was locked on dead center. Dad began to reel in. His rod bent. He had a bass fighting and flopping like a sand-filled stocking. Working light tackle, he had to give and take carefully not to lose it. The ripples settled out of the water where Myron had been—it was erased!—and my father was unslipping the net with his free hand and playing the bass with the other.

I was terrified—not frightened, terrified—as much for my father as for myself. He had deliberately led my uncle to be drowned. I tried to make it happen differently in my mind, but I could not doubt what I had seen and heard.

When at last I found the will to move, it was not toward him but back up the trail, to be away and alone long enough to get my bearings before I had to face him.

I rode the bike in the rain to the nursery and put it in the tool-shed. Nobody was around. I didn't have to talk to anybody.

Behind the mall down the road from Everbloom's the receiving platforms stood on iron legs, backed against the cement block, the cheap side of the stores. Weather swept over the blacktop, pooling where the graders hadn't got it right. On raw bulldozed ground beyond the blacktop, weeds and a few stringy locusts tried to start a forest again. A tree line the bulldozers wouldn't get to for a few years failed into the mist at the end of this world. Nobody ever came back there unless a truck was unloading. I hunched under a dock.

As the evidence against Uncle Myron had become stronger and weaker and stronger again in the year that had passed since Aunt Leora's death, I had felt in myself many times the sufficient certainty that he had killed her so that I could imagine myself doing to him as my father had.

I had imagined aiming the gun—the same gun, the twelve-gauge, to make the justice more shapely—and firing. I could do that, I had told myself.

Under the shelter of the platform, I knew I had only been telling myself a story. I could have put my finger on the trigger but not pulled. I might have led him to step off the shelf, but duty as I understood it, as I had learned it from my father, would have compelled me to save a drowning man even if I had been the one who put him in peril.

I had had the chance and not used it. I had not burst out of the trees shouting. I had not waded in. I had watched; then run to get the bike.

My father had pulled the trigger and turned away as if it were nothing.

I drowned in questions. Why had I done nothing? Was it because I was young and not much was expected of me? Was it because it had happened in the presence of my father, and it was not my place to put myself forward where he did not? Was I bound to silence forever? What would happen if he were suspected? And stories were in the paper?

And he went on trial?

Would I come forward to witness for him to say that his account of the event was whatever he said it was? Would I be able to stick with a lie like that—for my father, who had made lying a hard thing for me to do?

What if somebody in one of the cars that had passed on the road recognized me? What if it was reported and I was taken to the police station and asked what I knew and why I had not volunteered it before?

What was expected of me? I had nobody to ask.

The rain drew off. I would have to go home. I took with me the simplest of stories to account for myself. I had biked to Nickerson Park, in the direction of Shelf Lake, and when the rain began had got under the cover of a firewood shed.

A diver found Uncle Myron bundled at the foot of the shelf in forty feet of water. It was never discussed after my father explained that Myron had been warned, that he must have lost track of where he was while my father had been inattentive. Anybody who knew that water and how you could become engrossed working a five-pound bass on a three-pound line understood how easily it happened.

Myron's brother came to the Cape to make arrangements to ship the body to Pittsburgh for burial alongside Aunt Leora. He was Uncle Andrew to me, although we never knew that family very well. They were westerners, we were easterners, we met only at anniversary parties, weddings, funerals.

He said Myron had been a good brother and he would miss him. I suppose in some way he felt that my father had a degree of responsibility as the accident had happened in our territory, so to speak, but he didn't indicate it.

The circumstances were such that the card of suspicion never turned over in anybody's head. Nobody who knew Ben Dewaine would have thought it for an instant.

5

I lived difficult years with my father after that, although all the difficulties were within me. On the surface our close relationship was undisturbed. We fished and hunted together as before, and I took many problems to him for a viewpoint.

As I had declared against going into the family business it was thought that I might become a lawyer. I have an orderly mind and some ability to express myself and therefore thought it too. I was well along in college before I decided to do other work. In those early years, the years in which we allow ourselves to think abstractly, I often reflected about justice, but I never allowed myself to discuss it with my father, fearing that one word would take me to another until I reached one that I would regret.

I came to have considerable respect for Pilate. I thought how much more difficult Pilate's problem may have been than the press reported. I would want to know more about what kind of man Pilate was before I concluded that he had a worn-out conscience or that he had settled for an epigram.

Nine years later the man with the brush haircut turned himself in.

He couldn't live with it. It happens all the time. They see the victim's face at night and think of what a life is and what it is to destroy one, and they get disgusted with themselves. They begin to think there may be Eternal Judgment after all and they will be accountable. They show up at police stations and have to convince desk officers that they aren't nuts. They call up reporters and meet them in diners. They ask priests to be go-betweens. They hire lawyers to get them the best deal.

The man's name was Rome Hurdicke.

Again it was a story in the papers. He had parked, looking for opportunity as he had on other nights, and this night a dark place beside the lane beyond the Sherroder house had been the cover that attracted him. He had followed Aunt Leora into the garage intending to bluff her with the gun. She had been slow to respond. He thought she was about to call for help. He panicked and shot her and then thought only about getting away. The most singular event in two lives, and it was from beginning to end so ordinary that it could have been set in type like a slogan to be called up with a keystroke.

The newspapers rehashed it and added the strange fate that befell so many people associated with the crime. Four of the jurors were dead. The judge had been killed in a private plane accident. The woman who claimed to be the well-known socialite doctor's mistress committed suicide. The husband of the murdered heiress drowned in a fishing accident on Cape Cod.

There could be no doubt Hurdicke was the man. He told them where and when he had bought the gun, and they verified the numbers. They found the Plymouth still in service, three owners forward and a coat of white paint two coats down. It was an old case, and as he had turned himself in he got twenty years and was eligible for parole in twelve.

And so, Uncle Myron's life had been taken without cause.

I think somebody—perhaps his brother Andrew—may care for Myron as we cared for Aunt Leora, and if he knew the circumstances of his death would yearn for human justice as my father did. I don't know. I can't deal with how Uncle Andrew might feel. My father is my flesh and blood and he is a good man.

I can't deal with my own guilt. If I had responded on the instant that I saw Uncle Myron pitch into the water could I have saved him?

I don't know. I will never get over not making the attempt, but confession offers me no way out, for it would be to witness against my father. I am tribal enough to say that my duty is to him, to keep the secret. In some matters it is true that what is not known does not exist. It exists for us who know it.

After Hurdicke confessed I watched my father closely. I trembled that he might turn himself in or even take his own life in remorse. I didn't know if he would be more likely to do it if he knew that I knew his secret, or if he thought he alone knew what had happened at Shelf Lake. As a son who had become also a father I knew that some fragment of his life he intended to be an object lesson for me, but I couldn't know how much.

His manner, naturally reserved, became wintry. He gave up his places on church and hospital boards, and reduced his responsibilities at the company. Time passing without incident did not lull me to suppose that he had made his peace with Uncle Myron's ghost, any more than Hurdicke had made his with Aunt Leora's. Nevertheless, he went on with his life in a normal way, at a lowered tone, into his retirement years.

He entered then a remission in which he seems to have regained his appetite for a more active life. Mother said the other day, "He had a new garden turned over. He is talking about going west in the fall to hunt ram. He rejoined his skeet club. I think he is coming into good years."

That may be, but I have marked my calendar.

I don't know how Father accepts that the sentence of the man who killed his sister has been commuted to time served. Hurdicke will be released next week. I can hope only that my father has had enough of dealing out justice on earth.

1900–1950

The Most Outrageous Consequences

JAMES REID PARKER

MR. DEVORE ALMOST NEVER lost a client except through the regrettable but inescapable eventuality—in his own restful phrase—of death. It was unthinkable that he should lose the Wolverine Commercial Car Corporation, which presumably wasn't susceptible to death and whose affairs at the New York end were as profitable to the law firm of Forbes, Hathaway, Bryan & Devore as those of any business they looked after. And yet this very catastrophe, Mr. Devore told himself, might occur if he continued to suffer reversals in court, as he had been doing lately. Suppose this latest difficulty, *Drucker* v. *Wolverine Comm. Car Corp.*, a rather minor case in its own way, proved to be the breaking point? Mr. Devore, who was about to go over and have a scheduled talk with Mr. Hibben, Wolverine's vice-president in charge of the New York office, was thoroughly downcast. There could be no doubt that Drucker, a taxi-driver who had been driving a Wolverine-built cab for the Sun-Lite system at the time of his accident, had a legal precedent for action. In the State of New York, at least. It was really a horrible precedent, handed down by a judge for whom Mr. Devore entertained bitter loathing, but in Mr. Hibben's eyes this would not excuse defeat, as Mr. Devore knew very well.

Perhaps what grieved the old lawyer most was that his sympathies were with Wolverine, for basically there was something about a Comm. Car Corp. that appealed to him. He loved

Wolverine. Nor was his devotion altogether that of a pensioner; he felt toward Wolverine much as a dog might feel toward a lifelong, if at times unreasonable, master. Mr. Devore put on his derby, selected Ames and Smith's "Law of Torts" from his bookcase, and gloomily started for the Wolverine offices. His first job, clearly, was to mollify Mr. Hibben, if such a thing could be accomplished.

Mr. Hibben greeted him with the barest civility and at once asked the question that Mr. Devore least wanted to hear.

"Well, what chance have we got?"

Before replying, Mr. Devore seated himself very solemnly, although the vice-president had not suggested that he do so, placed the tort collection on the desk in an impressively deliberate manner, and tried to look as much as possible like Mr. Chief Justice Stone on a Monday afternoon.

"The first thing we must consider," he said slowly, caressing the torts as if to put himself under the protection of all the great adjudicators of the past, "is the historic attitude of the courts toward liability."

Mr. Hibben failed to assume the attentive expression of one about to enjoy a scholarly excursion into legal history. "That's not answering my question," he said.

Recklessly, Mr. Devore evaded the issue. "When a somewhat similar case was decided in the Court of the Exchequer in 1842, our American courts lost no time in adopting the decision as a precedent for this country. I'm happy to say that it was a complete and triumphant vindication of the defendant."

"And you say America adopted the same law intact?" Mr. Hibben asked eagerly.

"America accepted the precedent," Mr. Devore acknowledged, wondering how on earth to proceed from this point. It had perhaps been bad strategy to appease Mr. Hibben at the very beginning. The vice-president was nodding with satisfaction and saying, "Fine! Good thing Americans knew enough to tell right from wrong in those days. They don't seem to any more." If Mr. Hibben would only refrain from asking whether the precedent had every been set aside!

"Is this law still O.K.?" Mr. Hibben asked. "You're sure the judges all know about it?"

"Oh, yes, they all know about it," said Mr. Devore soothingly and with perfect truth. "The case that set the precedent was really very much like the Drucker affair. I'd like to tell you about it."

Mr. Hibben now seemed more disposed toward a little excursion into the annals of the Court of the Exchequer. He offered his counsellor a cigar.

"It involved a chattel-maker's liability, or to be more exact, a chattel *vendor's* liability, to a third person," said Mr. Devore, making a heroic effort to be elementary. "The defendant Wright had contracted to supply mailcoaches to the Postmaster General, who had in turn contracted with a man named Atkinson and his business associates for a regular supply of horses and coachmen. Atkinson engaged the plaintiff Winterbottom to drive a coach between Hartford and Holyhead. In other words, A contracted with B, who contracted with C, who contracted with D. One day, most unfortunately, Winterbottom's mailcoach broke down because of a latent defect in its manufacture and he became lamed for life. Seeking damages, D sued not C, his employer, nor B, the Postmaster General, but the original A, with whom D had entered into no contract of any sort whatever."

After digesting these complications, Mr. Hibben said, "If D was hired by C, I think C was the one D should have picked to sue."

Mr. Devore agreed that this would have been a more usual procedure, but added that A was probably a wealthier firm and therefore a more tempting victim against whom to secure a judgment. The analogy was at once apparent to Mr. Hibben, who grunted in a shocked manner. Matters were progressing smoothly at the moment, but it meant only temporary relief for Mr. Devore. Nevertheless, he opened his Ames and Smith with convincing equanimity and turned to *Winterbottom* v. *Wright.*

"I'm sure you'll agree with me that Lord Abinger, the Chief Baron, expressed the whole issue very satisfactorily when he said, 'If the plaintiff can sue, every passenger, or even every person passing along the road, who was injured by the upsetting of the coach, might bring similar action. Unless we confine the operations of such contracts as this to the parties who entered into them, the most absurd and outrageous consequences, to which I can see no limit, would ensue.'"

"Exactly!" said Mr. Hibben. "That's almost word for word what I told our legal adviser in Flint when I talked to him on the phone several days ago. It looks as if you've found a loophole all right, Devore." Mr. Hibben beamed at him. "I've always *said* it wouldn't pay Wolverine to maintain a full-sized legal department when we've got Forbes, Hathaway to take care of us. Frankly, Devore, the fellows out in Flint have been a little disappointed with your work lately, but they'll be tickled to death about *this*."

Mr. Devore tried to smile but wasn't quite able to manage it. Something told him that the fellows in Flint weren't going to do any elaborate rejoicing. And if Wolverine were suddenly to install a full-sized legal department, what would happen to Forbes, Hathaway, Bryan & Devore? What, especially, would happen to Devore?

"I certainly like what he says about confining the operations of such contract," said Mr. Hibben. "Let's hear that part again."

" 'Unless we confine the operation of such contracts to the parties who entered into them'?"

"That's it!" Mr. Hibben said. "That's telling 'em! Why, we never had any dealings at all with Drucker. What we did was sell a cab to the Sun-Lite people, and Drucker was hired by Sun-Lite. Furthermore, it was a defective steering column that broke, and we don't even make steering columns. We buy them from Collins & Kemper!"

His exuberance was a terrible spectacle to Mr. Devore, who didn't quite know how to cut it short.

"Every passer-by," Mr. Hibben said, "every Tom, Dick, and Harry under the sun would start suing. They'd say they were suffering from mental shock or something as a result of being on the scene when the accident happened. Who is this man Abinger, anyway? I'd like to meet him."

"You're forgetting when the case was decided," Mr. Devore reminded him gently. "It was decided back in 1842."

He turned to another section of his Ames and Smith and, marshalling such courage as he had left, prepared to explain why Wolverine, and not Sun-Lite, would be required by law to yield to the plaintiff.

"In recent years," he began, "the most malign forces imaginable have been at work in this country. They have penetrated our government and—much as I dislike confessing the fact—our bar and our bench as well."

A look of surprise crossed Mr. Hibben's face. "You don't have to tell me that!" he snapped.

The unhappy counsellor not only had to tell him but had to tell him without any further postponement.

"You'd be amazed at something that happened once in the

Court of Appeals right here in New York," Mr. Devore said lightly. "It was the really unusual case of MacPherson against the Buick Motor Company—I mean the old Buick company, not the General Motors subsidiary. What happened was that the manufacturer sold one of its cars to a retail dealer, who in turn sold it to this man MacPherson. While MacPherson was driving the car, one of the wheels suddenly collapsed. He was thrown out and injured. The wheel had been made of faulty wood. The wheel wasn't made by Buick; it was bought from another manufacturer, just as you buy your steering columns from Collins & Kemper. The Court decided there was evidence, however, that the defects could have been discovered by reasonable inspection, and that inspection was omitted."

"Certainly inspection was omitted," said Mr. Hibben. "They probably bought their wheels from a reputable firm, and they certainly couldn't go around inspecting hundreds of thousands of wheels just on the chance that maybe they'd find one that wasn't exactly uniform. Why, in our case the steering column on Drucker's cab was the first defective column we'd every heard about."

"I rather imagined that you'd see a similarity between the Drucker case and MacPherson against Buick."

"Of course I see a similarity," said Mr. Hibben.

Mr. Devore took a deep breath and jumped into the flames.

"I think you'll be interested in hearing what one of the judges said about it." The vice-president nodded, evidently retaining great faith in the book from which Mr. Devore had produced the fascinating mailcoach decision. "The judge held that 'if the nature of a thing is such that it is reasonably certain to place life and limb in peril when negligently made, it is then a thing of danger. Its nature gives warning of the consequences to be expected. If to the element of danger there is added knowledge that the thing will be used by persons other than the purchaser, and used without new tests, then, irrespective of contract, the manufacturer of this thing of danger is under a duty to make it carefully.' " He coughed nervously as he neared the most diagreeable part of the whole wretched decision. " 'We are dealing now with the manufacturer of the finished product, who puts it on the market to be used without inspection by his customers. If he is negligent where danger is to be foreseen, a liability will follow.' "

"Wait a minute," said Mr. Hibben. "That line about 'the manufacturer of the finished product' would apply to Collins & Kemper. Drucker could sue *them* if he wanted to. Why don't you write him a letter and tell him about it?"

Mr. Devore shook his head and went on hastily. " 'We think the defendant was not absolved from a duty of inspection because it bought the wheels from a reputable manufacturer.' " Here Mr. Hibben opened his mouth in horrified astonishment but made no comment. " 'It was not merely a dealer in automobiles. It was a manufacturer of automobiles. It was responsible for the finished product. It was not at liberty to put the finished product on the market without subjecting the component parts to ordinary and simple tests.' "

"You mean to say he's blaming the automobile manufacturers even though it was someone else who made the defective wheel?" asked Mr. Hibben. "You mean they'd be just as likely to blame *us*?"

But Mr. Devore, now that his great step had been taken, was unable to stop reading. " 'The defendant knew the danger. It knew also that the car would be used by persons other than the buyer.' "

"Why, it might be a *child* talking," Mr. Hibben gasped.

" 'Precedents drawn from the days of travel by stagecoach do not fit the conditions of travel today,' " Mr. Devore quoted, reading as quickly as possible. " 'The principle that the danger must be imminent does not change, but the things subject to the principle do change. They are whatever the needs of life in a developing civilization require them to be.' " He closed the book with an abrupt gesture. His own patience had worn quite as thin as the vice-president's.

There was a long silence before Mr. Hibben said wearily, "Where did you say this terrible thing happened? Here in New York?"

"Yes. In 1916."

"Couldn't we take it to the Supreme Court? They may have *some* sense of honor and decency left."

Mr. Devore lighted one of his own cigars and closed his eyes. "That opinion was written by Benjamin Cardozo. No court in the United States would reverse a Cardozo ruling, even if it wanted to. Not in times like these."

"I see what you mean," murmured the vice-president. "Good God!" There was infinite worry in the way he spoke the words.

"Well, there you are, Hibben," said Mr. Devore presently. He waited for the storm to break. And then, even as he waited, the realization came to him that everything was going to be all right.

It had been Cardozo, and not he, who had jumped into the flames. If Mr. Hibben entertained any feeling toward him, it was the sympathetic feeling that the same malign forces were in league against them both. Wolverine still loved him, and if he played his cards carefully, it would continue to do so. He leaned back and for the first time really tasted the flavor of his cigar.

The Colonel's Foundation

Louis Auchincloss

R UTHERFORD TOWER, ALTHOUGH A partner, was not the Tower of Tower, Tilney & Webb. It sometimes seemed to him that the better part of his life went into explaining this fact or at least into anticipating the humiliation of having it explained by others. The Tower had been his late Uncle Reginald, the famous Attorney General and leader of the New York bar, and the one substantial hope in Rutherford's legal career. For Rutherford, despite an almost morbid fear of clerks and courts, and a tendency to hide away from the actual clients behind their wills and estates, had even managed to slip into a junior partnership before Uncle Reginald, in his abrupt, downtown fashion, died at his desk. But it was as far as Rutherford seemed likely to go. There was nothing in the least avuncular about Uncle Reginald's successor, Clitus Tilney. A large, violent, self-made man, Tilney had a chip on his shoulder about families like the Towers and a disconcerting habit of checking the firm's books to see if Rutherford's "social-register practice," as he slightingly called it, paid off. The junior Tower, he would remark to the cashier after each such inspection, had evidently been made a partner for only three reasons: because of his name, because of his relatives, and because he was there.

And, of course, Tilney was right. He was always right. Rutherford's practice didn't pay off. The Tower cousins, it was true, were in and out of his office all day, as were the Hallecks, the Rutherfords, the Tremaines, and all the other interconnecting links of his widespread family, but they expected, every last grabbing one

162

of them, no more than a nominal bill. Aunt Mildred, Uncle Reginald's widow, was the worst of all, an opinionated and litigious lady who professed to care not for the money but for the principle of things and was forever embroiled with landlords, travel agencies, and shops. However hard her nephew worked for her, he could never feel more than a substitute. It was Clitus Tilney alone whose advice she respected. Rutherford sometimes wondered, running his long nervous fingers over his pale brow and through his prematurely gray hair, if there was any quality more respected by the timid remnants of an older New York society, even by the flattest-heeled and most velvet-gowned old maid, than naked aggression. What use did they really have for anyone whom they had known, like Rutherford, from his childhood? He was "one of us," wasn't he—too soft for a modern world?

The final blow came when Aunt Margaretta Halleck, the only Tower who had married what Clitus Tilney called "real money," and for whom Rutherford had drawn some dozen wills without fee, died leaving her affairs, including the management of her estate, in the hands of an uptown practitioner who had persuaded her that Wall Street lawyers were a pack of wolves. The next morning, when Rutherford happened to meet the senior partner in the subway, Mr. Tilney clapped a heavy but insincere hand on his shrinking shoulder.

"Tell me, Tower," he boomed over the roar of the train. "Have you ever thought of turning yourself into a securities lawyer? We could use another hand on this Smilax deal."

"Well, it's not a field I know much about," Rutherford said miserably.

"But, man, you're not forty yet! You can learn. Quite frankly, that Halleck fiasco is the last straw. I'm not saying it's anyone's fault, but this family business isn't carrying its share of the load. Think it over, Tower."

Rutherford sat later in his office, staring out the window at a dark brick wall six feet away, and thought gloomily of working night and day on one of Tilney's securities "teams," with bright, intolerant younger men who had been on the *Harvard Law Review*. The telephone rang, startling him. He picked it up. "What is it?" he snapped.

It was the receptionist. "There's a Colonel Hubert here," she said. "He wants to see Mr. Tower. Do you know him, or shall I see if Mr. Tilney can see him?"

It was not unusual for prospective clients to ask for "Mr. Tower," assuming that they were asking for the senior partner. Rutherford, however, was too jostled to answer with his usual self-depreciation. "If I were the receptionist," he said with an edge to his voice, "and somebody asked for Mr. Tower, I think I'd send him to Mr. Tower. But then, I suppose, I have a simple mind."

There was a surprised silence. "I'm sorry, Mr. Tower. I only meant—"

"I know," he said firmly. "It's quite all right. Tell Colonel Hubert I'll be glad to see him."

Sitting back in his chair, Rutherford immediately felt better. *That* was the way to deal with people. And, looking around, he tried to picture his room as it might appear to a client. It was the smallest of the partners' offices, true, but it was not entirely hopeless. If his uncle's best things, including the Sheraton desk, had been taken over by Mr. Tilney, he at least had a couple of relics of that more solid past: the large framed photograph of old Judge Webb in robes, and his uncle's safe, a mammoth green box on wheels with "Reginald Tower" painted on the door in thick gold letters. The safe, of course, would have been more of an asset if Tilney had not insisted that it be used for keeping real-estate papers and if young men from that department were not always bursting into Rutherford's office to bang it open and shut. Sometimes they even left papers unceremoniously on his desk, marked simply "For Safe." Still, he felt, it gave his room some of the flavor of an old-fashioned office, just a touch of Ephraim Tutt.

An office boy appeared at the doorway, saying "This way, sir," and a handsome, sporty old gentleman of certainly more than eighty years walked briskly into the office.

"Mr. Tower?"

Rutherford jumped to his feet to get him a chair, and the old man nodded vigorously as he took his seat. "Thank you, sir. Thank you, indeed," he said.

He was really magnificent, Rutherford decided as he sat down again and looked him over. He had thick white hair and long white mustaches, a straight, large, firm, aristocratic nose, and eyes that at least tried to be piercing. His dark, sharply pressed suit covered a figure whose only fault was a small, neat protruding stomach, and he wore a carnation in his buttonhole and a red tie with a huge knot.

"You are in the business of making wills?" the Colonel asked.

"That is my claim."

"Good. Then I want you to make me one."

There was a pause while the Colonel stared at him expectantly. Rutherford wondered if he was supposed to make the will up then and there, like a sandwich.

"Well, I guess I'd better ask a few questions," he said with a small professional smile. "Do you have a will now, sir?"

"Tore it up," the Colonel said. "Tore them all up. I'm changing my counsel, young man. That's why I'm here."

Rutherford decided not to press the point. "We might start with your family, then. Do you have a wife, sir? Or children?"

"My wife is dead, God bless her. No children. She had a couple of nieces, but they're provided for."

"And you, sir?"

"Oh, I have some grandnephews." He shrugged. "Nice young chaps. You know the sort—married, live in the suburbs, have two children, television. No point in leaving them any money. Real money, I mean. Scare them to death. Prevent their keeping down to the Joneses. Fifty thousand apiece will be plenty."

Rutherford's mouth began to feel pleasantly dry as he leaned forward to pick up a pencil. He quite agreed with the Colonel about the suburbs. "And what did you have in mind, sir, as to the main disposition of your estate?"

"I don't care so much as long as it's spent!" the Colonel exclaimed, slapping the desk. "Money should be spent, damn it! When I was a young man, I knew Ward McAllister. I was a friend of Harry Lehr's, too. Newport. It was something then! Mrs. Fish. The Vanderbilts. Oh, I know, people sneer at them now. They say they were vulgar, aping Europe, playing at being dukes and duchesses, but, by God, they had something to show for their money! Why, do you know, I can remember a ball at the Breakers when they had a footman in livery on every step on the grand stairway! Every step!"

"I guess you wouldn't see that today," Rutherford said, impressed. "Not even in Texas."

"Today!" The Colonel gave a snort. "Today they eat creamed chicken and peas at charity dinners at the Waldorf and listen to do-gooders. No, no, the color's quite gone, young man. The color's entirely gone."

At this, the Colonel sank into a reverie so profound that Rutherford began to worry that he had already lost interest in his will. "Perhaps some charity might interest you?" he suggested cautiously. "Or a foundation? I understand they do considerable spending."

The Colonel shrugged. "Only way to keep the money out of the hands of those rascals in Washington, I suppose. Republicans, Democrats—they're all alike. Grab, grab." He nodded decisively. "All right, young man. Make me a foundation."

Rutherford scratched his head. "What sort of a foundation, sir?"

"What sort? Don't they have to be for world peace or some damn-fool thing? Isn't that the tax angle?"

"Well, not altogether," Rutherford said, repressing a smile. "Your foundation could be a medical one, for example. Research. Grants to hospitals. That sort of thing."

"Good. Make me a medical foundation. But, mind you, I'm no Rockefeller or Carnegie. We're not talking about more than twelve or fifteen million."

Rutherford's head swam. "What—what about your board?" he stammered. "The board of this foundation. Who would you want on that?"

The Colonel looked down at the floor a moment, his lips pursed. When he looked up, he smiled charmingly. "Well, what about you, young man? You seem like a competent fellow. I'd be glad to have you as chairman."

"Me?"

"Why not? And pick your own board. If I want a man to do a job, I believe in letting him do it in his own way."

Rutherford's heart gradually sank. One simply didn't walk in off the street and give one's fortune to a total stranger—not if one was sane. It was like the day, as a child at his grandmother's table, when she suddenly gave him a gold saltcellar in the form of a naked mermaid with a rounded, smooth figure that he had loved to stroke, only to be told by his mother, that it was all in fun, that "Granny didn't mean it." It had been his introduction to senility. Projects like the Colonel's, he had heard, were common in Wall Street. It was a natural place for the demented to live out their fantasies. Nevertheless, as the old Colonel's imagined gold dissolved like the castle of the gods in Valhalla, he felt cheated and bitter. Abruptly, he stood up. "It's a most interesting scheme, Colonel," he said dryly. "I'd like a few days to think it over, if you don't mind. Why don't you leave me your name and address, and I can call you?"

The Colonel seemed surprised. "You mean that's all? For now?"

"If you please, sir. I'm afraid I have an appointment.

After the old man had placed his card on the desk, Rutherford relentlessly ushered him out to the foyer, where he waited until the elevator doors had safely closed between them. Returning, he told the receptionist that he would not be "in" again to Colonel Hubert.

That night, Rutherford tried to salvage what he could out of his disappointment by making a good story of it to his wife as she sat knitting in the living room of their apartment. Phyllis Tower was one of those plain, tall, angular women who are apt to be tense and sharp before marriage and almost stonily contented thereafter. It never seemed to occur to her that she didn't have everything in the world that a well-brought-up girl could possibly want. Limited, unrapturous, but of an even disposition, she made of New York a respectable small town and believed completely that her husband had inherited an excellent law practice.

She followed his story without any particular show of interest. "Hubert," she repeated when he had finished. "You don't suppose it was old Colonel Bill Hubert, do you? He's not really mad, you know. Eccentric, but not mad.

Rutherford felt his heart sink for the second time as he thought of the card left on his desk—"William Lyon Hubert." He watched her placid knitting with a sudden stab of resentment, but closed his lips tightly. After all, to be made ridiculous was worse than *anything.* Then he said guardedly, "This man's name was Frank. Who is Colonel Bill?"

"Oh, you know, dear. He's that old diner-out who married Grandma's friend Mrs. Jack Tyson. Everyone said she was mad for him right up to the day she died."

Again his mouth was dry. It was too much, in one day. "And did she leave him that—that *fortune?*"

"Well, I don't suppose she left him all of it," she said, breaking a strand of yarn. "There were the Tysons, you know. But he still keeps up the house on Fifth Avenue. And *that* takes something."

"Yes," he murmured, a vast impression of masonry clouding his mind. "Yes, I suppose it must."

"What's the matter, dear?" she asked. "You look funny. You don't suppose you could have been wrong about the name, do you? Are you sure it was Frank?"

"Quite sure."

Buried in the evening newspaper, he pondered his discovery. And then, in a flash, he remembered. Of course! Mrs. Jack Tyson has become Mrs. W. L. Hubert! What devil was it that made him forget these things, which Phyllis remembered so effortlessly? And fifteen million—wasn't that just the slice of forty that a grateful widow might have left him?

The next morning, after a restless night, Rutherford looked up Colonel Hubert's number and tried to reach him on the telephone, but this, it turned out, was far from easy. The atmosphere of the great house, as conveyed to him over the line, was, to say the least, confused. Three times he called, and three times a mild, patient, uncoöperative voice, surely that of an ancient butler, discreetly answered. Rutherford was obliged to spell and re-spell his name. He was then switched to an extension and to a maid who evidently regarded the ring of the telephone as a personal affront. While they argued, a third voice, far away and faintly querulous, was intermittently heard, and finally, on the third attempt, an old man called into the telephone "What? What?" very loudly. Then, abruptly, someone hung up and Rutherford heard again the baffling dial tone. He decided to go up to the house.

When he got out of the cab, he took in with renewed pleasure the great façade. He knew it, of course. Everyone who ever walked on the east side of Central Park knew the eclectic architecture of the old Tyson house, rising from a Medicean basement through stories of solemnified French Renaissance to its distinguishing feature, a top-floor balcony in the form of the Porch of the Maidens. To Rutherford, it was simply the kind of house that one built if one was rich. He would have been only too happy to be able to do the same.

Fortunately, it proved as easy to see Colonel Hubert as it was difficult to get him on the telephone. The old butler who opened the massive grilled doors, and whose voice Rutherford immediately recognized, led him without further questions, when he heard he was actually dealing with the Colonel's lawyer, up the gray marble stairway that glimmered in the dark hall and down a long corridor to the Colonel's study. This was Italian; Rutherford had a vague impression of red damask and tapestry as he went up to the long black table at which an old man was sitting, reading a typewritten sheet. He sighed in relief. It *was* the right colonel.

"Good morning, Colonel. I'm Tower. Rutherford Tower. Do you remember me? About your will?"

The Colonel looked up with an expression of faint puzzlement, but smiled politely. "My dear fellow, of course. Pray be seated."

"I wanted to tell you that I've thought it over, and that I'm all set to start," Rutherford went on quickly, taking a seat opposite the Colonel. "There are a few points, however, I'd like to straighten out."

The Colonel nodded several times. "Ah, yes, my will," he said. "Exactly. Very good of you."

"I want to get the names of your grandnephews. I think it is advisable to leave them more substantial legacies in view of the fact that the residue is going to your foundation. And then there's the question of executors..." He paused, wondering if the Colonel was following him. The old man was now playing with a large bronze turtle—the repository of stamps and paper clips—raising and lowering its shell. "That's a handsome bronze you have there," Rutherford said uncertainly.

"Isn't it?" the Colonel said, holding it up. "I'd like Sophie to have it. She always used to admire it. You might take her name down. Sophie Winters, my wife's niece. Or did she take back her own name after her last divorce?" He looked blankly at Rutherford. "Anyway, she's living in Biarritz. Unless she sold that house that Millie left her. Did she, do you know?"

Rutherford took a deep breath. Whatever happened, he must not be impatient again. "If I might suggest, sir, we could take care of the specific items more easily in a letter. A letter to be left with your will."

The Colonel smiled his charming smile. "I'd like to do it the simple way myself, of course. But would it be binding? Isn't that the point? Would it be binding?"

"Well, not exactly," Rutherford admitted, "but, after all, such a request is hardly going to be ignored—"

"How can we be sure? Do you see?" the Colonel said, smiling again. "Now, I tell you what we'll do. I'll ring for my man, Tomkins, and we'll get some luggage tags to tie to the objects marked for the different relatives."

Rutherford sat helpless as the Colonel rang, and told Tomkins what he wanted. When the butler returned with the tags, he gave them to the Colonel and then took each one silently from him as the old man wrote a name on it. He then proceeded gravely to tie it to a lamp or a chair or to stick it with Scotch Tape to the frame of a picture or some other object. Both he and the Colonel seemed quite engrossed in their task and entirely unmindful of Rutherford, who followed them about the study, halfheartedly writing down the name of the fortunate niece who was to receive the Luther Terry "Peasant Girl" or the happy cousin who was to get the John Rogers group. By lunchtime, the study looked like a naval vessel airing its signal flags. The Colonel surveyed the whole with satisfaction.

"Well!" he exclaimed, turning to Rutherford. "I guess that's that for today! All work and no play, you know. Come back tomorrow, my dear young man, and we'll do the music room."

Rutherford, his pockets rustling with useless notes, walked down Fifth Avenue, too overwrought to go immediately back to the office. He stopped at his club and had an early drink in the almost empty bar, calculating how long at this rate it would take them to do the whole house. And what about the one on Long Island? And how did he know there mightn't be another in Florida? It was suddenly grimly clear that unless he managed to get the Colonel out of this distressing new mood of particulars and back to his more sweeping attitudes of the day before, there might never be any will at all. And, looking at his own pale face in the mirror behind the bar, he drew himself up and ordered another drink. What was it that Clitus Tilney always said was the mark of a good lawyer—creative imagination?

At his office, after lunch, he went to work with a determination that he had not shown since the Benzedrine weekend, fifteen years before, when he took his bar examinations. He kept his office door closed, and snapped "Keep out, please!" to each startled young man who banged it open to get to the real-estate safe. He even had the courage to seize one of them, a Mr. Baitsell, and demand his services. When Baitsell protested, Rutherford asserted himself as he had not done since his uncle's death. "I'm sorry. This is emergency," he said.

Once obtained, Baitsell was efficient. He dug out of the files a precedent for a simple foundation for medical purposes and, using it as a guide, drafted that part of the will himself while

Rutherford worked out the legacies for the grandnephews. This was a tricky business, for the bequests had to be large enough to induce the young Huberts not to contest the will. There were moments, but only brief ones, when he stopped to ponder the morality of what he was doing. Was it *his* responsibility to pass on the Colonel's soundness of mind? Did he *know* it to be unsound? And whom, after all, was he gypping? If the old man died without a will, the grandnephews would take everything, to be sure, but everything minus taxes. All he was really doing with his foundation was shifting the tax money from the government, which would waste it, to a charity, which wouldn't. If that wasn't "creative imagination," he wanted to know what was! And did anyone think for a single, solitary second that in his position Clitus Tilney would not have done what he was doing? Why, *he* would probably have made himself residuary legatee! With this thought, Rutherford, after swallowing two or three times, pencilled his own name in the blank space for "executor" on the mimeographed form he was using.

The following morning at ten, Rutherford went uptown with his secretary and Mr. Baitsell to take the Colonel, as he now knew was the only way, by storm. While the other two waited in the hall, he followed the butler up the stairs and down the corridor to the study. Entering briskly, he placed a typed copy of the will on the desk before the astonished old gentleman.

"I've been working all night, Colonel," he said, in a voice so nervous that he didn't quite recognize himself, "and I've decided that it doesn't pay to be too much smarter than one's client—particularly when that client happens to be Colonel Hubert. All of which means, sir, that you were right the first time. My scheme of including in the will all those bequests of objets d'art just isn't feasible. We'll accomplish the same thing in a letter. And in the meanwhile here's your will as you originally wanted it. Clean as a whistle."

The Colonel watched him, nodding vaguely, and fingered the pages of the will. "You think it's all right?"

"Right as Tower, Tilney & Webb can make it," Rutherford said, with the smile and wink that he had seen Clitus Tilney use.

"And you think I should sign it now?"

"No time like the present." Rutherford, who had been too nervous to sit, walked to the window, to conceal his heavy breathing. "If you'll just ring for Tonkins and ask him to tell the young lady and gentleman in the hall to come up, we'll have the necessary witnesses."

"Is Tomkins covered all right?" the Colonel asked as he touched the bell beside him.

"He's covered with the other servants," Rutherford said hastily. "In my opinion, sir, you've been more than generous."

The witnesses came up, and the Colonel behaved better than Rutherford had dared hope. He joked with Baitsell about the formalities, laughed at the red ribbon attached to the will, told a couple of anecdotes about old Newport and Harry Lehr's will, and finally signed his name in a great, flourishing hand. When Rutherford's secretary walked up to the table to sign her name after his, he rose and made her a courtly bow. It was all like a scene from the memoirs of Saint-Simon.

In the taxi afterward, speeding downtown, Rutherford turned to the others. "The Colonel's a bit funny about his private affairs," he told them. "As a matter of fact, I haven't even met his family. So I'd rather you didn't mention this will business. Outside the office *or* in."

Baitsell looked very young and impressed as he gave him his solemn assurance. He then asked, "But if the Colonel should die, sir, who would notify us? And how would the family know about the will?"

"Never mind about that," Rutherford said, with a small smile, handing him the will. "I don't think the Colonel is apt to do very much dying without my hearing of it. When we get to the office, you stick that will in the vault and forget it."

It was risky to warn them, of course, but riskier not to. He couldn't afford to have them talk. There was too much that was phony in the whole picture. He had no guaranty, after all, that the Colonel had either the money or the power to will it. It was the kind of situation where one had to lie low, at least until the old man was dead, and even after that, until it was clear that one had the final and valid will. How would he look, for example, rushing into court to probate the document now under Baitsell's arm if the family produced a later will, or even a judicial ruling that the old man was incompetent to make one? Would he not seem ridiculous and grabby? Or worse? And Clitus Tilney! What would *he* say if his firm was dragged into so humiliating a failure! But no, no, he wouldn't even think of it. He could burn the will secretly, if necessary; nobody need know unless—well, unless he won! And his heart bounded as he thought of the panelled office that Tilney would have to assign to the director of the Hubert Foundation.

A new office was only the first of many imaginative flights in which he riotously indulged. He saw himself dispensing grants to the most important men downtown, called on, solicited, profusely thanked. He calculated and recalculated his executor's commissions on increasingly optimistic estimates of the Colonel's estate. In fact, his concept of the old man's wealth and his own control of it, the apotheosis of Rutherford Tower to the position of benefactor of the city, *the* Tower at long last of Tower, Tilney & Webb, began, in the ensuing months, to edge out the more real prospect of disappointment. The fantasy had become too important not to be deliberately indulged in. When he turned at breakfast to the obituary page, he would close his eyes and actually pray that he would not find the name there, so that he would have another day in which to dream.

When the Colonel did die, it was Phyllis, of course, who spotted it. "I see that old Colonel Bill is dead," she said at breakfast one morning, without looking up from her newspaper. "Eighty-seven. Didn't you say he'd been in to see you?"

For a moment, Rutherford sat utterly still. "Where did he die?" he asked.

"In some lawyer's office in Miami. So convenient, I should imagine. They probably had all his papers ready. Why, Rutherford, where are you going?"

He didn't trust himself to wait, and hurried out. In the street, he bought copies of all the newspapers and went to a Central Park bench to read them. There was little more in any of the obituaries than the headlines—"Former Army Officer Stricken" or "Husband of Mrs. J. L. Tyson Succumbs." He could find nothing else about the lawyer. After all, he reasoned desperately as he got up and walked through the Mall, wasn't it only natural for the Colonel to have Florida counsel? Didn't he spend part of the year there? But, for all his arguments, it was almost lunch-time before he gathered courage to call his office. His secretary, however, had to report only that Aunt Mildred Tower had called twice and wanted him to call back.

"Tell her I'm tied up," he said irritably. "Tell her I've gone to the partners' lunch."

For, indeed, it was Monday, the day of their weekly lunch. When he got to the private room of the downtown club where they met, he found some twenty of them at the table, listening to Clitus Tilney. Rutherford assumed, as he slipped into a chair at the lower end of the table, that the senior partner was telling one of his usual stories to illustrate the greatness of Clitus and the confounding of his rivals. But this story, as he listened to it with a growing void in his stomach, appeared to be something else.

"No, it's true, I'm not exaggerating," Tilney was saying, with a rumbling laugh. "There are twenty-five wills that they know of already, and they're not all in by a long shot. Sam Kennecott, at Standard Trust, told me it was a mania with the old boy. And the killing thing is, they're all the same. Except for one that has forty-five pages of specific bequests, they all set up some crazy foundation under the control of—guess who—the little shyster who drew the will! Sam says you've never seen such an accumulation of greed in your life! In my opinion, they ought to be disbarred, the lot of them, for taking advantage of the poor old dodo. Except the joke's on them—that's the beauty of it!"

Rutherford did not have to ask one of his neighbors the name of the deceased, but, feeling dazed, he did. The neighbor told him.

"Did any of the big firms get hooked?" someone asked.

"Good Lord, we have *some* ethics, I hope!" Tilney answered. "Though there's a rumor that one did. Harrison & Lambert, someone said. Wouldn't it be wonderful?" Tilney's large jowls positively shook with pleasure. "What wouldn't I give to see old Cy Lambert caught like a monkey with his fist in the bottle!"

Rutherford spoke up suddenly. His voice was so high that everyone turned and looked at him. "But what about the man with the *last* will?" he called down the table to Mr. Tilney. "Why is it a joke on him?"

"You mean the man in Miami?" Tilney said, flashing at Rutherford the fixed smile of his dislike. "Because the old guy didn't have that sort of money. Not foundation money. The big stuff was all in trust, of course, and goes to the Tysons, where it should go."

Rutherford concentrated on eating a single course. It would look odd, after his interruption, to leave at once. When he had emptied his plate, he wiped his mouth carefully, excused himself to his neighbors, and walked slowly from the room.

Back at the office, however, he almost dashed to Baitsell's room.

Closing the door behind him, he faced the startled young man with wild eyes. "Look, Baitsell, about that will of Colonel Hubert's—you remember?" Baitsell nodded quickly. "Well, he died, you see."

"Yes, sir. I read about it."

"Apparently, he's written some subsequent wills. I think we'd better do nothing about filing ours for the time being. And if I were you I wouldn't mention this around the office. It might—"

"But it's already filed, sir!"

"It's *what?*"

"Yes, sir. I filed it."

"How could you?" Rutherford's voice was almost a scream. "You haven't had time to prepare a petition, let alone get it signed!"

"Oh, I don't mean that I filed it for probate, Mr. Tower. I mean I filed it for safekeeping in the Surrogate's Court. *Before* he died. The same day he signed it."

Rutherford, looking into the young man's clear, honest eyes, knew now that he faced the unwitting agent of his own devil. "Why did you do that?" he asked in a low, almost curious tone. "We never do that with wills. We keep them in our vault."

"Oh, I know that, sir," Baitsell answered proudly. "But you told me you didn't know the relatives. I thought if the old gentleman died and you didn't hear about it at once, they might rush in with another will. Now they'll find ours sitting up there in the courthouse, staring them right in the face. Yes, sir, Mr. Tower, you'll have to be given notice of every will that's offered! Public notice!"

Rutherford looked at the triumphant young man for a moment and then returned without a word to his own office. There he leaned against Uncle Reginald's safe and thought in a stunned, stupid way of Cy Lambert laughing, even shouting, at Clitus Tilney. Then he shook his head. It was too much—too much to take in. He wondered, in a sudden new mood of detachment, if it wasn't rather distinguished to be hounded so personally by the furies. Orestes. Orestes Rutherford Tower. His telephone rang.

"Rutherford? Is it you?" a voice asked.

"Yes, Aunt Mildred," he said quietly.

"Well, I'm glad to get you at last. I don't know what your uncle would have said about the hours young lawyers keep today. And people talk about the pressure of modern life! Talk is all it is. But look, Rutherford. That blackguard of a landlord of mine is acting up again. He now claims that my apartment lease doesn't include an extra maid's room in the basement. I want you to come right up and talk to him. This afternoon. You can, can't you?"

"Yes, Aunt Mildred," he said again. "I'm practically on my way."

Justice Is Blind

THOMAS WOLFE

T HERE USED TO BE—perhaps there still exists—a purveyor of *belles lettres* in the older, gentler vein who wrote a weekly essay in one of the nation's genteeler literary publications, under the whimsical *nom de plume* of Old Sir Kenelm. Old Sir Kenelm, who had quite a devoted literary following that esteemed him as a perfect master of delightful letters, was a leisurely essayist of the Lambsian school. He was always prowling around in out-of-the-way corners and turning up with something quaint and unexpected that made his readers gasp and say, "Why, I've passed that place a thousand times and I never *dreamed* of anything like that!"

In the rush, the glare, the fury of modern life many curious things, alas, get overlooked by most of us; but leave it to Old Sir Kenelm, he would always smell them out. He had a nose for it. He was a kind of enthusiastic rubber-up of tarnished brasses, and assiduous ferreter-out of grimy cornerstones. The elevated might roar above him, and the subway underneath him, and a hurricane of machinery all about him, while ten thousand strident tones passed and swarmed and dinned in his ears—above all this raucous tumult Old Sir Kenelm rose serene: if there was a battered inscription anywhere about, caked over with some fifty years of city dirt, he would be sure to find it, and no amount of paint of scaly rust could deceive his falcon eye for Revolutionary brick.

The result of it was, Old Sir Kenelm wandered all around through the highways and byways of Manhattan, Brooklyn, and the Bronx discovering Dickens everywhere; moreover, as he assured his readers constantly, anyone with half an eye could do the same. Whimsical characters in the vein of Pickwick simply abounded in the most unexpected places—in filling stations, automats, and the corner stores of the United Cigar Company. More than this, seen properly, the automat was just as delightful and quaint a place as an old inn, and a corner cigar store as delightfully musty and redolent of good cheer as a tavern in Cheapside. Old Sir Kenelm was at his best when describing the customs and whimsical waterfront life of Hoboken, which he immortalized in a delightful little essay as "Old Hobie"; but he really reached the heights when he applied his talents to the noon-time rush hour at the soda counter of the corner pharmacy. His description of the quaint shopgirls who foregathered at the counter, the swift repartee and the Elizabethan jesting of the soda jerkers, together with his mouth-watering descriptions of such Lucullan delicacies as steamed spaghetti and sandwiches of pimento cheese, were enough to make the ghosts of the late William Hazlitt and Charles Lamb roll over in their shrouds and weep for joy.

It is therefore a great pity that Old Sir Kenelm never got a chance to apply his elfin talent to a description of the celebrated partnership that bore the name of Paget and Page. Here, assuredly if ever, was grist for his mill, or in somewhat more modern phrase, here was a subject right down his alley. Since this yearning subject has somehow escaped the Master's hand, we are left to supply the lack as best we can by the exercise of our own modest talents.

The offices of the celebrated firm of Paget and Page were on the thirty-seventh floor of one of the loftier skyscrapers, a building that differed in no considerable respect from a hundred others: unpromising enough, it would seem, for purposes of Dickensian exploration and discovery. But one who has been brought up in the hardy disciplines of Old Sir Kenelm's school is not easily dismayed. If one can find Charles Lamb at soda fountains, why should one not find Charles Dickens on the thirty-seventh floor?

One's introduction to this celebrated firm was swift, and from an eighteenth century point of view perhaps a bit unpromising. One entered the great marble corridor of the building from Manhattan's swarming streets, advanced through marble halls and passed the newspaper and tobacco stand, and halted before a double row of shining elevators. As one entered and to the charioteer spoke the magic syllables, "Paget and Page," the doors slid to and one was imprisoned in a cage of shining splendor; a lever was pulled back, there was a rushing sound, punctuated now and then by small clicking noises—the whole thing was done quite hermetically, and with no sense of movement save for a slight numbness in the ears, very much, no doubt, as a trip to the moon in a projectile would be—until at length, with the same magic instancy, the cage halted, the doors slid open, and one stepped out upon the polished marble of the thirty-seventh floor feeling dazed, bewildered, and very much alone, and wondering how one got there. One turned right along the corridor, and then left, past rows of glazed-glass offices, formidable names, and the clattering cachinnations of a regiment of typewriters, and almost before one knew it, there squarely to the front, at the very dead end of the hall, one stood before another glazed-glass door in all respects identical with the others except for these words:

PAGET AND PAGE
Counselors at Law

This was all—these simple functions of the alphabet in orderly arrangement—but to anyone who has ever broached that portal, what memories they convey!

Within, the immediate signs of things to come were also unremarkable. There was an outer office, some filing cases, a safe, a desk, a small telephone switchboard, and two reasonably young ladies seated busily at typewriters. Opening from this general vestibule were the other offices of the suite. First one passed a rather small office with a flat desk, behind which sat a quiet and timid-looking little gentleman of some sixty years, with a white mustache, and a habit of peering shyly and quickly at each new visitor over the edges of the papers with which he was usually involved, and a general facial resemblance to the little man who has become well known in the drawings of a newspaper cartoonist as Caspar Milquetoast. This was the senior clerk, a sort of good man Friday to this celebrated firm. Beyond his cubicle a corridor led to the private offices of the senior members of the firm.

As one went down this corridor in the direction of Mr. Page— for it is with him that we shall be principally concerned—one passed the office of Mr. Paget. Lucius Page Paget, as he had been christened, could generally be seen sitting at his desk as one went by. He, too, was an elderly gentleman with silvery hair, a fine white mustache, and gentle patrician features. Beyond was the office of Mr. Page.

Leonidas Paget Page was a few years younger than his partner, and in appearance considerably more robust. As he was sometimes fond of saying, for Mr. Page enjoyed his little joke as well as any man, he was "the kid member of the firm." He was a man of average height and of somewhat stocky build. He was bald, save for a surrounding fringe of iron-gray hair, he wore a short-cropped mustache, and his features, which were round and solid and fresh-colored, still had something of the chunky plumpness of a boy. At any rate, one got a very clear impression of what Mr. Page must have looked like as a child. His solid, healthy-looking face, and a kind of animal drive and quickness in his stocky figure, suggested that he was a man who liked sports and out-of-doors.

This was true. Upon the walls were several remarkable photographs portraying Mr. Page in pursuit of his favorite hobby, which was ballooning. One saw him, for example, in a splendid exhibit marked "Milwaukee, 1908," helmeted and begoggled, peering somewhat roguishly over the edges of the wicker basket of an enormous balloon which was apparently just about to take off. There were other pictures showing Mr. Page in similar attitudes, marked "St. Louis," or "Chicago," or "New Orleans." There was even one showing him in the proud possession of an enormous silver cup: this was marked "Snodgrass Trophy, 1916."

Elsewhere on the walls, framed and hung, were various other evidences of Mr. Page's profession and his tastes. There was his diploma from the Harvard Law School, his license to practice, and most interesting of all, in a small frame, a rather faded and ancient-looking photograph of a lawyer's shingle upon which, in almost indecipherable letters, was the inscription: "Paget and Page." Below, Mr. Page's own small, fine handwriting informed one that this was evidence of the original partnership, which had been formed in 1838.

Since then, fortunately, there had always been a Paget to carry on partnership with Page, and always a Page so to combine in legal union with Paget. The great tradition had continued in a line of unbroken succession from the time of the original Paget and the original Page, who had been great-grandfathers of the present ones. Now, for the first time in almost one hundred years, that hereditary succession was in danger of extinction; for the present Mr. Page was a bachelor, and there were no others of his name and kin who could carry on. But come!—that prospect is a gloomy one and not to be thought of any longer here.

There exist in modern life, as Spangler was to find out, certain types of identities or people who, except for contemporary manifestations of dress, of domicile, or of furniture, seem to have stepped into the present straight out of the life of a vanished period. This archaism is particularly noticeable among the considerable group of people who follow the curious profession known as the practice of the law. Indeed, as Spangler was now to discover, the archaism is true of that curious profession itself. Justice, he had heard, is blind. Of this he was unable to judge, because in all his varied doings with legal gentlemen he never once had the opportunity of meeting the Lady. If she was related to the law, as he observed it in majestic operation, the relationship was so distant that no one, certainly no lawyer, ever spoke of it.

In his first professional encounter with a member of this learned craft, Spangler was naive enough to mention the Lady right away. He had just finished explaining to Mr. Leonidas Paget Page the reason for his visit, and in the heat of outraged innocence and embattled indignation he had concluded:

"But good Lord! They can't do a thing like this! There's no Justice in it!"

"Ah, now," replied Mr. Page. "Now you're talking about Justice!"

Spangler, after a somewhat startled pause, admitted that he was.

"Ah, now! Justice—" said Mr. Page, nodding his head reflectively as if somewhere he had heard the word before—"Justice. Hm, now, yes. But my dear boy, that's quite another matter. This problem of yours," said Mr. Page, "is not a matter that involves Justice. It is a matter of the Law." And, having delivered himself of these portentous words, his voice sinking to a note of unctuous piety as he pronounced the holy name of Law, Mr. Page settled back in his chair with a relaxed movement, as if to say: 'There you have it in a nutshell. I hope this makes it clear to you.'

Unhappily it didn't. Spangler, still persisting in his error, struck his hand sharply against the great mass of letters and documents he had brought with him and deposited on Mr. Page's desk—the whole accumulation of the damning evidence that left no doubt whatever about the character and conduct of his antagonist—and burst out excitedly:

"But good God, Mr. Page, the whole thing's here! As soon as I found out what was going on, I simply had to write her as I did, the letter I told you about, the one that brought all this to a head."

"And quite properly," said Mr. Page with an approving nod. "Quite properly. It was the only thing to do. I hope you kept a copy of the letter," he added thriftily.

"Yes," said Spangler. "But see here. Do you understand this thing? The woman's *suing* me! Suing *me!*" The victim went on in an outraged and exasperated tone of voice, as of one who could find no words to express the full enormity of the situation.

"But of course she's suing you," said Mr. Page. "That's just the point. That's why you're here. That's why you've come to see me, isn't it?"

"Yes, sir. But good God, she can't do this!" the client cried in a baffled and exasperated tone. "She's in the wrong and she knows it! The whole thing's here, don't you see that, Mr. Page?" Again Spangler struck the mass of papers with an impatient hand. "It's here, I tell you, and she can't deny it. She can't sue me!"

"But she is," said Mr. Page tranquilly.

"Yes—but dammit!—" in an outraged yell of indignation—"this woman *can't* sue me. I've done nothing to be sued about."

"Ah, now!" Mr. Page, who had been listening intently but with a kind of imperturbable, unrevealing detachment which said plainly, "I hear you but I grant you nothing," now straightened with a jerk and with an air of recognition, and said: "Ah, now I follow you. I get your point. I see what you're driving at. You can't be sued, you say, because you've done nothing to be sued about. My dear boy!" For the first time Mr. Page allowed himself a smile, a smile tinged with a shade of good humor and forgiving tolerance, as one who is able to understand and overlook the fond delusions of youth and immaturity. "My dear boy," Mr. Page repeated, "that has nothing in the world to do with it. Oh, absolutely nothing!" His manner had changed instantly as he spoke these words: he shook his round and solid face quickly, grimly, with a kind of bulldog tenacity that characterized his utterance when he stated an established fact, one that allowed no further discussion or debate. "Absolutely nothing!" cried Mr. Page, and shook his bulldog jaw again. "You say you can't be sued unless you've done something to be sued about. My dear sir!"—here Mr. Page turned in his chair and looked grimly at his client with a kind of bulldog earnestness, pronouncing his words now deliberately and gravely, with the emphasis of a slowly wagging finger, as if he wanted to rivet every syllable and atom of his meaning into his client's brain and memory—"My dear sir," said Mr. Page grimly, "you are laboring under a grave misapprehension if you think you have to do something to be sued about. Do not delude yourself. That has nothing on earth to do with it! Oh, absolutely nothing!" Again he shook his bulldog jaws. "From this time on," as he spoke, his words became more slow and positive, and he hammered each word home with the emphasis of his authoritative finger—"from this time on, sir, I want you to bear this fact in mind and never to forget it for a moment, because it may save you much useless astonishment and chagrin as you go on through life. *Anybody,* Mr. Spangler," Mr. Page's voice rose strong and solid, *"anybody*—can sue—*anybody* about *anything!"* He paused a full moment after he had uttered these words, in order to let their full significance sink in; then he said: "Now have you got that straight? Can you remember it?"

The younger man stared at the attorney with a look of dazed and baffled stupefaction. Presently he moistened his dry lips, and as if he still hoped he had not heard correctly, said: "You—you mean—even if I have not done anything?"

"That has nothing on earth to do with it," said Mr. Page as before. "Absolutely nothing."

"But suppose—suppose, then, that you do not even know the person who is suing you—that you never even heard of such a person—do you mean to tell me—?"

"Absolutely!" cried Mr. Page before his visitor could finish. "It doesn't matter in the slightest whether you've heard of the person or not! That has nothing to do with it!"

"Good Lord, then," the client cried, as the enormous possibilities of legal action were revealed to him, "if what you say is true, then anybody at all—" he exclaimed as the concept burst upon him in its full power, "why you could be sued, then, by a one-eyed boy in Bethlehem, Pennsylvania, even if you'd never seen him!"

"Oh, absolutely!" Mr. Page responded instantly. "He could

claim," Mr. Page paused a moment and became almost mystically reflective as the juicy possibilities suggested themselves to his legally fertile mind, "he could claim, for example, that—that, er, one of your books—hm, now, yes!"—briefly and absently he licked his lips with an air of relish, as if he himself were now becoming professionally interested in the case—"he could claim that one of your books was printed in such small type that—that—that the sight of the other eye had been *permanently* impaired!" cried Mr. Page triumphantly. He settled back in his swivel chair and rocked back and forth a moment with a look of such satisfaction that it almost seemed as if he were contemplating the possibility of taking a hand in the case himself. "Yes! By all means!" cried Mr. Page, nodding his head in vigorous affirmation. "He might make a very good case against you on those grounds. While I haven't considered carefully all the merits of such a case, I can see how it might have its points. Hm, now, yes." He cleared his throat reflectively. "It might be very interesting to see what one could do with a case like that."

For a moment the younger man could not speak. He just sat there looking at the lawyer with an air of baffled incredulity. "But—but—" he managed presently to say—"why, there's no Justice in the thing!" he burst out indignantly, in his excitement making use of the discredited word again.

"Ah, Justice," said Mr. Page, nodding. "Yes, I see now what you mean. That's quite another matter. But we're not talking of Justice. We're talking of the Law—which brings us to this case of yours." And, reaching out a pudgy hand, he pulled the mass of papers toward him and began to read them.

Such was our pilgrim's introduction to that strange, fantastic world of twist and weave, that labyrinthine cave at the end of which waits the Minotaur, the Law.

Triumph of Justice

IRWIN SHAW

M IKE PILATO PURPOSEFULLY THREW open the door of Victor's shack. Above him the sign that said, "Lunch, Truckmen Welcome," shook a little, and the pale shadows its red bulbs threw in the twilight waved over the State Road.

"Victor," Mike said, in Italian.

Victor was leaning on the counter, reading Walter Winchell in a spread-out newspaper. He smiled amiably. "Mike," he said, "I am so glad to see you."

Mike slammed the door. "Three hundred dollars, Victor," he said, standing five feet tall, round and solid as a pumpkin against the door. "You owe me three hundred dollars, Victor, and I am here tonight to collect."

Victor shrugged slightly and closed the paper on Walter Winchell.

"As I've been telling you for the past six months," he said, "business is bad. Business is terrible. I work and I work and at the end... " He shrugged again. "Barely enough to feed myself."

Mike's cheeks, farmer-brown, and wrinkled deeply by wind and sun, grew dark with blood. "Victor, you are lying in my face," he said slowly, his voice desperately even. "For six months, each time it comes time to collect the rent you tell me, 'Business is bad.' What do I say? I say 'All right, Victor, don't worry, I know how it is.' "

"Frankly, Mike," Victor said sadly, "there has been no improvement this month."

Mike's face grew darker than ever. He pulled harshly at the ends

185

of his iron-gray mustache, his great hands tense and swollen with anger, repressed but terrible. "For six months, Victor," Mike said, "I believed you. Now I no longer believe you."

"Mike," Victor said reproachfully.

"My friends, my relatives," Mike said, "they prove it to me. Your business is wonderful, ten cars an hour stop at your door; you sell cigarettes to every farmer between here and Chicago; on your slot machine alone..." Mike waved a short thick arm at the machine standing invitingly against a wall, its wheels stopped at two cherries and a lemon. Mike swallowed hard, stood breathing heavily, his deep chest rising and falling sharply against his sheepskin coat. "Three hundred dollars!" he shouted. "Six months at fifty dollars! I built this shack with my own hands for you, Victor. I didn't know what kind of a man you were. You were an Italian, I trusted you! Three hundred dollars or get out tomorrow! Finish! That's my last word."

Victor smoothed his newspaper down delicately on the counter, his hands making a dry brushing sound in the empty lunchroom. "You misunderstand," he said gently.

"I misunderstand nothing!" Mike yelled. "You are on my land in my shack and you owe me three hundred dollars..."

"I don't owe you anything," Victor said, looking coldly at Mike. "That is what you misunderstand. I have paid you every month, the first day of the month, fifty dollars."

"Victor!" Mike whispered, his hands dropping to his sides. "Victor, what are you saying...?"

"I have paid the rent. Please do not bother me any more." Calmly Victor turned his back on Mike and turned two handles on the coffee urn. Steam, in a thin little plume, hissed up for a moment.

Mike looked at Victor's narrow back, with the shoulder blades jutting far out, making limp wings in the white shirt. There was finality in Victor's pose, boredom, easy certainty. Mike shook his head slowly, pulling hard at his mustache. "My wife," Mike said to the disdainful back, "she told me not to trust you. My wife knew what she was talking about, Victor." Then, with a last flare of hope, "Victor, do you really mean it when you said you paid me?"

Victor didn't turn around. He flipped another knob on the coffee urn. "I mean it."

Mike lifted his arm, as though to say something, pronounce

warning. Then he let it drop and walked out of the shack, leaving the door open. Victor came out from behind the counter, looked at Mike moving off with his little rolling limp down the road and across the cornfield. Victor smiled and closed the door and went back and opened the paper to Walter Winchell.

Mike walked slowly among the cornstalks, his feet crunching unevenly in the October earth. Absently he pulled at his mustache. Dolores, his wife, would have a thing or two to say. "No," she had warned him, "do not build a shack for him. Do not permit him onto your land. He travels with bad men; it will turn out badly. I warn you!" Mike was sure she would not forget this conversation and would repeat it to him word for word when he got home. He limped along unhappily. Farming was better than being a landlord. You put seed into the earth and you knew what was coming out. Corn grew from corn, and the duplicity of Nature was expected and natural. Also no documents were signed in the compact with Nature, no leases and agreements necessary, a man was not at a disadvantage if he couldn't read or write. Mike opened the door to his house and sat down heavily in the parlor, without taking his hat off, Rosa came and jumped on his lap, yelling, "Poppa, Poppa, tonight I want to go to the movies, Poppa, take me to the movies!"

Mike pushed her off. "No movies," he said harshly. Rosa stood in a corner and watched him reproachfully.

The door from the kitchen opened and Mike sighed as he saw his wife coming in, wiping her hands on her apron. She stood in front of Mike, round, short, solid as a plow horse, canny, difficult to deceive.

"Why're you sitting in the parlor?" she asked.

"I feel like sitting in the parlor," Mike said.

"Every night you sit in the kitchen," Dolores said. "Suddenly you change."

"I've decided," Mike said loudly, "that it's about time I made some use of this furniture. After all, I paid for it, I might as well sit in it before I die."

"I know why you're sitting in the parlor," Dolores said.

"Good! You know!"

"You didn't get the money from Victor." Dolores wiped the last bit of batter from her hands. "It's as plain as the shoes on your feet."

"I smell something burning," Mike said.

"Nothing is burning. Am I right or wrong?" Dolores sat in the upright chair opposite Mike. She sat straight, her hands neatly in her lap, her head forward and cocked a little to one side, her eyes staring directly and accusingly into his. "Yes or no?"

"Please attend to your own department," Mike said miserably. "I do the farming and attend to the business details."

"Huh!" Dolores said disdainfully.

"Are you starving?" Mike shouted. "Answer me, are you starving?"

Rosa started to cry because her father was shouting.

"Please, for the love of Jesus," Mike screamed at her, "don't cry!"

Dolores enfolded Rosa in her arms.... "Baby, baby," she crooned. "I will not let him harm you."

"Who offered to harm her?" Mike screamed, banging on a table with his fist like a mallet. "Don't lie to her!"

Dolores kissed the top of Rosa's head soothingly. "There, there," she crooned. "There." She looked coldly at Mike. "Well. So he didn't pay."

"He..." Mike started loudly. Then he stopped, spoke in a low, reasonable voice. "So. To be frank with you, he didn't pay. That's the truth."

"What did I tell you?" Dolores said as Mike winced. "I repeat the words. 'Do not permit him onto your land. He travels with bad men; it will turn out badly. I warn you!' Did I tell you?"

"You told me," Mike said wearily.

"We will never see that money again," Dolores said, smoothing Rosa's hair. "I have kissed it good-bye."

"Please," said Mike. "Return to the kitchen. I am hungry for dinner. I have made plans already to recover the money."

Dolores eyed him suspiciously. "Be careful, Mike," she said. "His friends are gangsters and he plays poker every Saturday night with men who carry guns in their pockets."

"I am going to the law," Mike said. "I'm going to sue Victor for the three hundred dollars."

Dolores started to laugh. She pushed Rosa away and stood up and laughed.

"What's so funny?" Mike asked angrily. "I tell you I'm going to sue a man for money he owes me, you find it funny! Tell me the joke."

Dolores stopped laughing. "Have you got any papers? No! You trust him, he trusts you, no papers. Without papers you're lost in a court. You'll make a fool of yourself. They'll charge you for the lawyers. Please, Mike, go back to your farming."

Mike's face set sternly, his wrinkles harsh in his face with the gray stubble he never managed completely to shave. "I want my dinner, Dolores," he said coldly, and Dolores discreetly moved into the kitchen, saying, "It is not my business, my love; truly, I merely offer advice."

Mike walked back and forth in the parlor, limping, rolling a little from side to side, his eyes on the floor, his hands plunged into the pockets of his denims like holstered weapons, his mouth pursed with thought and determination. After a while he stopped and looked at Rosa, who prepared to weep once more.

"Rosa, baby," he said, sitting down and taking her gently on his lap. "Forgive me."

Rosa snuggled to him. They sat that way in the dimly lit parlor.

"Poppa," Rosa said finally.

"Yes," Mike said.

"Will you take me to the movies tonight, Poppa?"

"All right," Mike said. "I'll take you to the movies."

The next day Mike went into town, dressed in his neat black broadcloth suit and his black soft hat and his high brown shoes. He came back to the farm like a businessman in the movies, busily, preoccupied, sober, but satisfied.

"Well?" Dolores asked him, in the kitchen.

He kissed her briskly, kissed Rosa, sat down, took his shoes off, rubbed his feet luxuriously, said paternally to his son who was reading *Esquire* near the window, "That's right, Anthony, study."

"Well?" asked Dolores.

"I saw Dominic in town," Mike said, watching his toes wiggling. "They're having another baby."

"Well," asked Dolores. "The case? The action?"

"All right," Mike said. "What is there for dinner?"

"Veal," Dolores said. "What do you mean 'all right'?"

"I've spoken to Judge Collins. He is filling out the necessary papers for me and he will write me a letter when I am to appear in court. Rosa, have you been a good girl?"

Dolores threw up her hands. "Lawyers. We'll throw away a fortune on lawyers. Good money after bad. We could put in an electric pump with the money."

"Lawyers will cost us nothing." Mike stuffed his pipe elaborately.

"I have different plans. Myself. I will take care of the case myself."
He lit up, puffed deliberately.

Dolores sat down across the table from him, spoke slowly,
carefully. "Remember, Mike," she said. "This is in English. They
conduct the court in English."

"I know," said Mike. "I am right. Justice is on my side. Why
should I pay a lawyer fifty, seventy-five dollars to collect my own
money? There is one time you need lawyers—when you are
wrong. I am not wrong. I will be my own lawyer."

"What do you know about the law?" Dolores challenged him.

"I know Victor owes me three hundred dollars." Mike puffed
three times, quickly, on his pipe. "That's all I need to know."

"You can hardly speak English, you can't even read or write,
nobody will be able to understand you. They'll all laugh at you,
Mike."

"Nobody will laugh at me. I can speak English fine."

"When did you learn?" Dolores asked. "Today?"

"Dolores!" Mike shouted. "I tell you my English is all right."

"Say Thursday," Dolores said.

"I don't want to say it," Mike said, banging the table. "I have
no interest in saying it."

"Aha," Dolores crowed. "See? He wants to be a lawyer in an
American court, he can't even say Thursday."

"I can," Mike said. "Keep quiet, Dolores."

"Say Thursday." Dolores put her head to one side, spoke co-
quettishly, slyly, like a girl asking her lover to say he loved her.

"Stirday," Mike said, as he always said. "There!"

Dolores laughed, waving her hand. "And he wants to conduct
a law case! Holy Mother! They will laugh at you!"

"Let them laugh!" Mike shouted. "I will conduct the case! Now
I want to eat dinner! Anthony!" he yelled. "Throw away that trash
and come to the table."

On the day of the trial, Mike shaved closely, dressed carefully
in his black suit, put his black hat squarely on his head, and with
Dolores seated grimly beside him drove early into town in the
1933 family Dodge.

Dolores said nothing all the way into town. Only after the car
was parked and they were entering the courthouse, Mike's shoes
clattering bravely on the legal marble, did Dolores speak. "Behave
yourself," she said. Then she pinched his arm. Mike smiled at
her, braced his yoke-like shoulders, took off his hat. His rough

gray hair sprang up like steel wool when his hat was off, and Mike ran his hand through it as he opened the door to the courtroom. There was a proud, important smile on his face as he sat down next to his wife in the first row and patiently waited for his case to be called.

When Victor came, Mike glared at him, but Victor, after a quick look, riveted his attention on the American flag behind the Judge's head.

"See," Mike whispered to Dolores. "I have him frightened. He doesn't dare to look at me. Here he will have to tell the truth."

"Shhh!" hissed Dolores. "This is a court of law."

"Michael Pilato," the clerk called, "versus Victor Fraschi."

"Me!" Mike said loudly, standing up.

"Shhh," said Dolores.

Mike put his hat in Dolores' lap, moved lightly to the little gate that separated the spectators from the principals in the proceedings. Politely, with a deep ironic smile, he held the gate open for Victor and his lawyer. Victor passed through without looking up.

"Who's representing you, Mr. Pilato?" the Judge asked when they were all seated. "Where's your lawyer?"

Mike stood up and spoke in a clear voice. "I represent myself. I am my lawyer."

"You ought to have a lawyer," the Judge said.

"I do not need a lawyer," Mike said loudly. "I am not trying to cheat anybody." There were about forty people in the courtroom and they all laughed. Mike turned and looked at them, puzzled. "What did I say?"

The Judge rapped with his gavel and the case was opened. Victor took the stand, while Mike stared, coldly accusing, at him. Victor's lawyer, a young man in a blue pinstripe suit and a starched tan shirt, questioned him. Yes, Victor said, he had paid each month. No, there were no receipts, Mr. Pilato could neither read nor write and they had dispensed with all formalities of that kind. No, he did not understand on what Mr. Pilato based his claim. Mike looked incredulously at Victor, lying under solemn oath, risking Hell for three hundred dollars.

Victor's lawyer stepped down and waved to Mike gracefully. "Your witness."

Mike walked dazedly past the lawyer and up to the witness stand, round, neat, his bull neck, deep red-brown and wrinkled, over his pure white collar, his large scrubbed hands politely but awkwardly held at his sides. He stood in front of Victor, leaning over a little toward him, his face close to Victor's.

"Victor," he said, his voice ringing through the courtroom, "tell the truth, did you pay me the money?"

"Yes," said Victor.

Mike leaned closer to him. "Look in my eye, Victor," Mike said, his voice clear and patient, "and answer me. Did you pay me the money?"

Victor lifted his head and looked unflinchingly into Mike's eyes. "I paid you the money."

Mike leaned even closer. His forehead almost touched Victor's now. "Look me *straight* in the eye, Victor."

Victor looked bravely into Mike's eyes, less than a foot away now.

"Now, Victor," Mike said, his eyes narrowed, cold, the light in them small and flashing and gray, "DID YOU PAY ME THE MONEY?"

Victor breathed deeply. "Yes," he said.

Mike took half a step back, almost staggering, as though he had been hit. He stared incredulously into the perjurer's eyes, as a man might stare at a son who has just admitted he has killed his mother, beyond pity, beyond understanding, outside all the known usage of human life. Mike's face worked harshly as the tides of anger and despair and vengeance rolled up in him.

"You're a godam liar, Victor!" Mike shouted terribly. He leapt down from the witness platform, seized a heavy oak armchair, raised it murderously above Victor's head.

"Mike, oh, Mike!" Dolores' wail floated above the noise of the courtroom.

"Tell the truth, Victor!" Mike shouted, his face brick red, his teeth white behind his curled lips, almost senseless with rage, for the first time in his life threatening a fellow-creature with violence. "Tell it fast!"

He stood, the figure of Justice, armed with the chair, the veins pulsing in his huge wrists, the chair quivering high above Victor's head in his huge gnarled hands, his tremendous arms tight and bulging in their broadcloth sleeves. "Immediately, Victor!"

"Pilato!" shouted the Judge. "Put that chair down!"

Victor sat stonily, his eyes lifted in dumb horror to the chair above his head.

"Pilato," the Judge shouted, "you can be sent to jail for this!"

He banged sternly but helplessly on his desk. "Remember, this is a court of law!"

"Victor?" Mike asked, unmoved, unmoving. "Victor? Immediately, please."

"No," Victor screamed, cringing in his seat, his hands now held in feeble defense before his eyes. "I didn't pay! I didn't!"

"Pilato," screamed the Judge, "this is not evidence!"

"You were lying?" Mike said inexorably, the chair still held, ax-like, above him.

"Mike, oh, Mike," wailed Dolores.

"It was not my idea," Victor babbled. "As God is my judge, I didn't think it up. Alfred Lotti, he suggested it, and Johnny Nolan. I am under the influence of corrupt men. Mike, for the love of God, please don't kill me. Mike, it would never have occurred to me myself, forgive me, forgive me..."

"Guiness!" the Judge called to the court policeman. "Are you going to stand there and let this go on? Why don't you do something?"

"I can shoot him," Guiness said. "Do you want me to shoot the plaintiff?"

"Shut up," the Judge said.

Guiness shrugged and turned his head toward the witness stand, smiling a little.

"You were lying?" Mike asked, his voice low, patient.

"I was lying," Victor cried.

Slowly, with magnificent calm, Mike put the chair down neatly in its place. With a wide smile he turned to the Judge. "There," he said.

"Do you know any good reason," the Judge shouted, "why I shouldn't have you locked up?"

Victor was crying with relief on the witness stand, wiping the tears away with his sleeve.

"There is no possible excuse," the Judge said, "for me to admit this confession as evidence. We are a court of law in the State of Illinois, in the United States. We are not conducting the Spanish Inquisition, Mr. Pilato."

"Huh?" Mike asked, cocking his head.

"There are certain rules," the Judge went on, quickly, his voice high, "which it is customary to observe. It is not the usual thing, Mr. Pilato," he said harshly, "to arrive at evidence by bodily threatening to brain witnesses with a chair."

"He wouldn't tell the truth," Mike said simply.

"At the very least, Mr. Pilato," the Judge said, "you should get thirty days."

"Oh, Mike," wept Dolores.

"Mr. Fraschi," the Judge said, "I promise you that you will be protected. That nobody will harm you."

"I did it," sobbed Victor, his hands shaking uncontrollably in a mixture of fear, repentance, religion, joy at delivery from death. "I did it. I will not tell a lie. I'm a weak man and influenced by loafers. I owe him three hundred dollars. Forgive me, Mike, forgive me..."

"He will not harm you," the Judge said patiently. "I guarantee it. You can tell the truth without any danger. Do you owe Mr. Pilato three hundred dollars?"

"I owe Mr. Pilato three hundred dollars," Victor said, swallowing four times in a row.

The young lawyer put three sheets of paper into his briefcase and snapped the lock.

The Judge sighed and wiped his brow with a handkerchief as he looked at Mike. "I don't approve of the way you conducted this trial, Mr. Pilato," he said. "It is only because you're a working man who has many duties to attend to on his land that I don't take you and put you away for a month to teach you more respect for the processes of law."

"Yes, sir," Mike said faintly.

"Hereafter," the Judge said, "kindly engage an attorney when you appear before me in this court."

"Yes, sir," Mike said.

"Mr. Pilato," the Judge said, "it is up to you to decide when and how he is to pay you."

Mike turned and walked back to Victor. Victor shrank into his chair. "Tomorrow morning, Victor," Mike said, waving his finger under Victor's nose, "at eight-thirty o'clock, I am coming into your store. The money will be there."

"Yes," said Victor.

"Is that all right?" Mike asked the Judge.

"Yes," said the Judge.

Mike strode over to the young lawyer. "And you," he said, standing with his hands on his hips in front of the young man with the pinstripe suit. "Mr. Lawyer. You knew he didn't pay me. A boy with an education. You should be ashamed of yourself."

He turned to the Judge, smiled broadly, bowed. "Thank you," he said. "Good morning." Then, triumphantly, smiling broadly, rolling like a sea captain as he walked, he went through the little gate. Dolores was waiting with his hat. He took the hat, put Dolores' arm through his, marched down the aisle, nodding, beaming to the spectators. Someone applauded and by the time he and Dolores got to the door all the spectators were applauding.

He waited until he got outside, in the bright morning sunshine down the steps of the courthouse, before he said anything to Dolores. He put his hat on carefully, turned to her, grinning. "Well," he said, "did you observe what I did?"

"Yes," she said. "I was never so ashamed in my whole life!"

"Dolores!" Mike was shocked. "I got the money. I won the case."

"Acting like that in a court of law!" Dolores started bitterly toward the car. "What are you, a red Indian?"

Dolores got into the car and slammed the door and Mike limped slowly around and got into the other side. He started the car without a word and shaking his head from time to time, drove slowly toward home.

The Paradise of Bachelors

HERMAN MELVILLE

I T LIES NOT FAR FROM TEMPLE BAR.
Going to it, by the usual way, is like stealing from a heated plain into some cool, deep glen, shady among harboring hills.

Sick with the din and soiled with the mud of Fleet Street—where the Benedick tradesmen are hurrying by, with ledgerlines ruled along their brows, thinking upon rise of bread and fall of babies—you adroitly turn a mystic corner—not a street—glide down a dim, monastic way, flanked by dark, sedate, and solemn piles, and still wending on, give the whole care-worn world the slip, and, disentangled, stand beneath the quiet cloisters of the Paradise of Bachelors.

Sweet are the oases in Sahara: charming the isle-groves of August prairies; delectable pure faith amidst a thousand perfidies; but sweeter, still more charming, most delectable, the dreamy Paradise of Bachelors, found in the stony heart of stunning London.

In mild meditation pace the cloisters; take your pleasure, sip your leisure, in the garden waterward; go linger in the ancient library; go worship in the sculptured chapel; but little have you seen, just nothing do you know, not the sweet kernel have you tasted, till you dine among the banded Bachelors, and see their convivial eyes and glasses sparkle. Not dine in bustling commons, during term-time, in the hall, but tranquilly, by private hint, at a private table; some fine Templar's hospitably invited guest.

199

Templar? That's a romantic name. Let me see. Brian de Bois-Guilbert was a Templar, I believe. Do we understand you to insinuate that those famous Templars still survive in modern London? May the ring of their armed heels be heard, and the rattle of their shields, as in mailed prayer the monk-knights kneel before the consecrated Host? Surely a monk-knight were a curious sight picking his way along the Strand, his gleaming corselet and snowy surcoat spattered by an omnibus. Long-bearded, too, according to his order's rule; his face fuzzy as a pard's; how would the grim ghost look among the crop-haired, close-shaven citizens? We know indeed—sad history recounts it—that a moral blight tainted at last this sacred Brotherhood. Though no sworded foe might outskill them in the fence, yet the worm of luxury crawled beneath their guard, gnawing the core of knightly troth, nibbling the monastic vow, till at last the monk's austerity relaxed to wassailing, and the sworn knights-bachelors grew to be but hypocrites and rakes.

But for all this, quite unprepared were we to learn that Knights-Templars (if at all in being) were so entirely secularized as to be reduced from carving our immortal fame in glorious battling for the Holy Land, to the carving of roast-mutton at a dinner-board. Like Anacreon, do these degenerate Templars now think it sweeter far to fall in banquet than in war? Or, indeed, how can there be any survival of that famous order? Templars in modern London! Templars in their red-cross mantles smoking cigars at the Divan! Templars crowded in a railway train, till, stacked with steel helmet, spear, and shield, the whole train looks like one elongated locomotive!

No. The genuine Templar is long since departed. Go view the wondrous tombs in the Temple Church; see there the rigidly-haughty forms stretched out, with crossed arms upon their stilly hearts, in everlasting and undreaming rest. Like the years before the flood, the bold Knights-Templars are no more. Nevertheless, the name remains, and the nominal society, and the ancient grounds, and some of the ancient edifices. But the iron heel is changed to a boot of patent leather; the long two-handed sword to a one-handed quill; the monk-giver of gratuitous ghostly counsel now counsels for a fee; the defender of the sarcophagus (if in good practice with his weapon) now has more than one case to defend, the vowed opener and clearer of all highways leading to the Holy Sepulchre, now has it in particular charge to check, to clog, to hinder, and embarrass all the courts and avenues of Law; the knight-combatant of the Saracen, breasting spear-points at Acre, now fights law-points in Westminster Hall. The helmet is a wig. Struck by Time's enchanter's wand, the Templar is today a Lawyer.

But, like many others tumbled from proud glory's height—like the apple, hard on the bough but mellow on the ground—the Templar's fall has but made him all the finer fellow.

I dare say those old warrior-priests were but gruff and grouty at the best; cased in Birmingham hardware, how could their crimped arms give yours or mine a hearty shake? Their proud, ambitious, monkish souls clasped shut, like horn-book missals; their very faces clapped in bomb-shells; what sort of genial men were these? But best of comrades, most affable of hosts, capital diner is the modern Templar. His wit and wine are both of sparkling brands.

The church and cloisters, courts and vaults, lanes and passages, banquet-halls, refectories, libraries, terraces, gardens, broad walks, domiciles, and dessert-rooms, covering a very large space of ground, and all grouped in central neighborhood and quite sequestered from the old city's surrounding din; and everything about the place being kept in most bachelor-like particularity, no part of London offers to a quiet wight so agreeable a refuge.

The Temple is, indeed, a city by itself. A city with all the best appurtenances, as the above enumeration shows. A city with a park to it, and flower beds, and a riverside—the Thames flowing by as openly, in one part, as by Eden's primal garden flowed the mild Euphrates. In what is now the Temple Garden, the old Crusaders used to exercise their steeds and lances; the modern Templars now lounge on the benches beneath the trees, and, switching their patent-leather boots, in gay discourse exercise at repartee.

Long lines of stately portraits in the banquet-halls, show what great men of mark—famous nobles, judges, and Lord Chancellors—have in their time been Templars. But all Templars are not known to universal fame; though, if the having warm hearts and warmer welcomes, full minds and fuller cellars, and giving good advice and glorious dinners, spiced with rare divertisements of fun and fancy, merit immortal mention, set down, ye muses, the names of R. F. C. and his imperial brother.

Though to be a Templar, in the one true sense, you must needs be a lawyer, or a student at the law, and be ceremoniously enrolled as member of the order, yet as many such, though Templars, do not reside within the Temple's precincts, though they may have their offices there, just so, on the other hand, there are many residents of the hoary old domiciles who are not admitted Templars. If being, say, a lounging gentleman and bachelor, or a quiet, unmarried, literary man, charmed with the soft seclusion of the spot, you much desire to pitch your shady tent among the rest in this serene encampment, then you must make some special friend among the order, and procure him to rent, in his name but at your charge, whatever vacant chamber you may find to suit.

Thus, I suppose, did Dr. Johnson, that nominal Benedick and widower but virtual bachelor, when for a space he resided here. So, too, did that undoubted bachelor and rare good soul, Charles Lamb. And hundreds more, of sterling spirits, Brethren of the Order of Celibacy, from time to time have dined, and slept, and tabernacled here. Indeed, the place is all a honey-comb of offices and domiciles. Like any cheese, it is quite perforated through and through in all directions with the snug cells of bachelors. Dear, delightful spot! Ah! when I bethink me of the sweet hours there passed, enjoying such genial hospitalities beneath those time-honored roofs, my heart only finds due utterance through poetry; and, with a sigh, I softly sing, "Carry me back to old Virginny!"

Such then, at large, is the Paradise of Bachelors. And such I found it one pleasant afternoon in the smiling month of May, when, sallying from my hotel in Trafalgar Square, I went to keep my dinner appointment with that fine Barrister, Bachelor, and Bencher, R. F. C. (he *is* the first and second, and *should be* the third; I hereby nominate him), whose card I kept fast pinched between my gloved forefinger and thumb, and every now and then snatched still another look at the pleasant address inscribed beneath the name, "No. —, Elm Court, Temple."

At the core he was a right bluff, care-free, right comfortable, and most companionable Englishman. If on a first acquaintance he seemed reserved, quite icy in his air—patience; this Champagne will thaw. And if it never do, better frozen Champagne than liquid vinegar.

There were nine gentlemen, all bachelors, at the dinner. One was from "No. —, King's Beach Walk, Temple"; a second, third, and fourth, and fifth, from various courts or passages christened with some similarly rich resounding syllables. It was, indeed, a sort of Senate of the Bachelors, sent to this dinner from widely scattered districts, to represent the general celibacy of the Temple. Nay, it was, by representation, a Grand Parliament of the best Bachelors in universal London; several of those present being from distant quarters of the town, noted immemorial seats of lawyers and unmarried men—Lincoln's Inn, Furnival's Inn; and one gentleman, upon whom I looked with a sort of collateral awe, hailed from the spot where Lord Verulam once abode a bachelor—Gray's Inn.

The apartment was well up toward heaven. I know not how many strange old stairs I climbed to get to it. But a good dinner, with famous company, should be well earned. No doubt our host had his dining room so high with a view to secure the prior exercise necessary to the due relishing and digesting of it.

The furniture was wonderfully unpretending, old, and snug. No new shining mahogany, sticky with undried varnish; no uncomfortably luxurious ottomans, and sofas too fine to use, vexed you in this sedate apartment. It is a thing which every sensible American should learn from every sensible Englishman, that glare and glitter, gim-cracks and gewgaws, are not indispensable to domestic solacement. The American Benedick snatches, downtown, a tough chop in a gilded showbox; the English bachelor leisurely dines at home on that incomparable South Down of his, off a plain deal board.

The ceiling of the room was low. Who wants to dine under the dome of St. Peter's? High ceilings! If that is your demand, and the higher the better, and you be so very tall, then go dine out with the topping giraffe in the open air.

In good time the nine gentlemen sat down to nine covers, and soon were fairly under way.

If I remember right, ox-tail soup inaugurated the affair. Of a rich russet hue, its agreeable flavor dissipated my first confounding of its main ingredient with teamsters' gads and the raw-hides of ushers. (By way of interlude, we here drank a little claret.) Neptune's was the next tribute rendered—turbot coming second; snow-white, flaky, and just gelatinous enough, not too turtleish in its unctuousness.

(At this point we refreshed ourselves with a glass of sherry.) After these light skirmishers had vanished, the heavy artillery of the feast marched in, led by that well-known English generalissimo, roast beef. For aides-de-camp we had a saddle of mutton, a fat turkey, a chicken-pie, and endless other savory things; while for avant-couriers came nine silver flagons of humming ale. This heavy ordnance having departed on the track of the light skirmishers, a picked brigade of game-fowl encamped upon the board, their camp-fires lit by the ruddiest of decanters.

Tarts and puddings followed, with innumerable niceties; then cheese and crackers. (By way of ceremony, simply, only to keep up good old fashions, we here each drank a glass of good old port.)

The cloth was now removed; and, like Blucher's army coming in at the death on the field of Waterloo, in marched a fresh detachment of bottles, dusty with their hurried march.

All these manœuvrings of the forces were superintended by a surprising old field-marshal (I can not school myself to call him by the inglorious name of waiter), with snowy hair and napkin, and a head like Socrates. Amidst all the hilarity of the feast, intent on important business, he disdained to smile. Venerable man!

I have above endeavored to give some slight schedule of the general plan of operations. But any one knows that a good, genial dinner is a sort of pell-mell, indiscriminate affair, quite baffling to detail in all particulars. Thus, I spoke of taking a glass of claret, and a glass of sherry, and a glass of port, and a mug of ale—all at certain specific periods and times. But those were merely the state bumpers, so to speak. Innumerable impromptu glasses were drained between the periods of those grand imposing ones.

The nine bachelors seemed to have the most tender concern for each other's health. All the time, in flowing wine, they most earnestly expressed their sincerest wishes for the entire well-being and lasting hygiene of the gentleman on the right and on the left. I noticed that when one of these kind bachelors desired a litle more wine (just for his stomach's sake, like Timothy), he would not help himself to it unless some other bachelor would join him. It seemed held something indelicate, selfish, and unfraternal, to be seen taking a lonely, unparticipated glass. Meantime, as the wine ran apace, the spirits of the company grew more and more to perfect genialness and unconstraint. They related all sorts of pleasant stories. Choice experiences in their private lives were now brought out, like choice brands of Moselle or Rhenish, only kept for particular company. One told us how mellowly he lived when a student at Oxford; with various spicy anecdotes of most frank-hearted noble lords, his liberal companions. Another bachelor, a gray-headed man, with a sunny face, who, by his own account, embraced every opportunity of leisure to cross over into the Low Countries, on sudden tours of inspection of the fine old Flemish architecture there—this learned, white-haired, sunny-faced old bachelor excelled in his descriptions of the elaborate splendors of those old guild-halls, town-halls, and stadthold-houses, to be seen in the land of the ancient Flemings. A third was a great frequenter of the British Museum, and knew all about scores of wonderful antiquities, of Oriental manuscripts, and costly books without a duplicate. A fourth had lately returned from a trip to Old Granada, and, of course, was full of Saracenic scenery. A fifth had a funny case in law to tell. A sixth was erudite in wines. A seventh had a strange characteristic anecdote of the private life of the Iron Duke, never printed, and never before announced in any public or private company. An eighth had lately been amusing his evenings, now and then, with translating a comic poem of Pulci's. He quoted for us the more amusing passages.

And so the evening slipped along, the hours told, not by a water-clock, like King Alfred's, but a wine-chronometer. Meantime the table seemed a sort of Epsom Heath; a regular ring, where the decanters galloped round. For fear one decanter should not with sufficient speed reach his destination, another was sent express after him to hurry him; and then a third to hurry the second; and so on with a fourth and fifth. And throughout all this nothing loud, nothing unmannerly, nothing turbulent. I am quite sure, from the scrupulous gravity and austerity of his air, that had Socrates, the field-marshal, perceived aught of indecorum in the company he served, he would have forthwith departed without giving warning. I afterward learned that, during the repast, an invalid bachelor in an adjoining chamber enjoyed his first sound refreshing slumber in three long, weary weeks.

It was the very perfection of quiet absorption of good living, good drinking, good feeling, and good talk. We were a band of brothers. Comfort—fraternal, household comfort, was the grand trait of the affair. Also, you could plainly see that these easy-hearted men had no wives or children to give an anxious thought. Almost all of them were travelers, too; for bachelors alone can travel freely, and without any twinges of their consciences touching desertion of the fireside.

The thing called pain, the bugbear styled trouble—those two legends seemed preposterous to their bachelor imaginations. How could men of liberal sense, ripe scholarship in the world, and capacious philosophical and convivial understandings—how could they suffer themselves to be imposed upon by such monkish fables? Pain! Trouble! As well talk of Catholic miracles. No such thing.—Pass the sherry, sir.—Pooh, pooh! Can't be!—The port, sir, if you please. Nonsense; don't tell me so.—The decanter stops with you, sir, I believe.

And so it went.

Not long after the cloth was drawn our host glanced significantly upon Socrates, who, solemnly stepping to a stand, returned with an immense convolved horn, a regular Jericho horn, mounted with polished silver, and otherwise chased and curiously enriched; not omitting two life-like goats' heads, with four more horns of solid silver, projecting from opposite sides of the mouth of the noble main horn.

Not having heard that our host was a performer on the bugle, I was surprised to see him lift this horn from the table, as if he were about to blow an inspiring blast. But I was relieved from this, and set quite right as touching the purposes of the horn, by his now inserting his thumb and forefinger into its mouth; whereupon a slight aroma was stirred up, and my nostrils were greeted with the smell of some choice Rappee. It was a mull of snuff. It went to the rounds. Capital idea this, thought I, of taking snuff about this juncture. This goodly fashion must be introduced among my countrymen at home, further ruminated I.

The remarkable decorum of the nine bachelors—a decorum not to be affected by any quantity of wine—a decorum unassailable by any degree of mirthfulness—this was again set in a forcible light to me, by now observing that, though they took snuff very freely, yet not a man so far violated the proprieties, or so far molested the invalid bachelor in the adjoining room as to indulge himself in a sneeze. The snuff was snuffed silently, as if it had been some fine innoxious powder brushed off the wings of butterflies.

But fine though they be, bachelors' dinners, like bachelors' lives, can not endure forever. The time came for breaking up. One by one the bachelors took their hats, and two by two, and arm-in-arm, they descended, still conversing, to the flagging of the court; some going to their neighboring chambers to turn over the *Decameron* ere retiring for the night; some to smoke a cigar, promenading in the garden on the cool river-side; some to make for the street, call a hack, and be driven snugly to their distant lodgings.

I was the last lingerer.

"Well," said my smiling host, "what do you think of the Temple here, and the sort of life we bachelors make out to live in it?"

"Sir," said I, with a burst of admiring candor—"Sir, this is the very Paradise of Bachelors!"

The Web of Circumstance

CHARLES W. CHESNUTT

I

WITHIN A LOW CLAPBOARDED HUT, with an open front, a forge was glowing. In front a blacksmith was shoeing a horse, a sleek, well-kept animal with the signs of good blood and breeding. A young mulatto stood by and handed the blacksmith such tools as he needed from time to time. A group of negroes were sitting around, some in the shadow of the shop, one in the full glare of the sunlight. A gentleman was seated in a buggy a few yards away, in the shade of a spreading elm. The horse had loosened a shoe, and Colonel Thornton, who was a lover of fine horseflesh, and careful of it, had stopped at Ben Davis's blacksmith shop, as soon as he discovered the loose shoe, to have it fastened on.

"All right, Kunnel," the blacksmith called out. "Tom," he said, addressing the young man, "he'p me hitch up."

Colonel Thornton alighted from the buggy, looked at the shoe, signified his approval of the job, and stood looking on while the blacksmith and his assistant harnessed the horse to the buggy.

"Dat's a mighty fine whip yer got dere, Kunnel," said Ben, while the young man was tightening the straps of the harness on the opposite side of the horse. "I wush I had one like it. Where kin yer git dem whips?"

"My brother brought me this from New York," said the Colonel. "You can't buy them down here."

The whip in question was a handsome one. The handle was wrapped with interlacing threads of variegated colors, forming an elaborate pattern, the lash being dark green. An octagonal

208

ornament of glass was set in the end of the handle. "It cert'n'y is fine," said Ben; "I wish I had one like it." He looked at the whip longingly as Colonel Thornton drove away.

" 'Pears ter me Ben gittin' mighty blooded," said one of the bystanders, "drivin' a hoss an' buggy, an' wantin' a whip like Colonel Thornton's."

"What's de reason I can't hab a hoss an' buggy an' a whip like Kunnel Tho'nton's, ef I pay fer 'em?" asked Ben. "We colored folks never had no chance ter git nothin' befo' de wah, but ef eve'y nigger in dis town had a tuck keer er his money sence de wah, like I has, an' bought as much lan' as I has, de niggers might 'a' got half de lan' by dis time," he went on, giving a finishing blow to a horseshoe, and throwing it on the ground to cool.

Carried away by his own eloquence, he did not notice the approach of two white men who came up the street from behind him.

"An' ef you niggers," he continued, raking the coals together over a fresh bar of iron, "would stop wastin' yo' money on 'scursions to put money in w'ite folks' pockets, an' stop buildin' fine chu'ches, an' buil' houses fer yo'se'ves, you'd git along much faster."

"You're talkin' sense, Ben," said one of the white men. "Yo'r people will never be respected till they've got property."

The conversation took another turn. The white men transacted their business and went away. The whistle of a neighboring steam sawmill blew a raucous blast for the hour of noon, and the loafers shuffled away in different directions.

"You kin go ter dinner, Tom," said the blacksmith. "An' stop at de gate w'en yer go by my house, and tell Nancy I'll be dere in 'bout twenty minutes. I got ter finish dis yer plough p'int fus'. "

The young man walked away. One would have supposed, from the rapidity with which he walked, that he was very hungry. A quarter of an hour later the blacksmith dropped his hammer, pulled off his leather apron, shut the front door of the shop, and went home to dinner. He came into the house out of the fervent heat, and, throwing off his straw hat, wiped his brow vigorously with a red cotton handkerchief.

"Dem collards smells good," he said, sniffing the odor that came in through the kitchen door, as his good-looking yellow wife opened it to enter the room where he was. "I've got a monst'us good appetite ter-day. I feels good, too. I paid Majah Ransom de intrus' on de mortgage dis mawnin' an' a hund'ed dollahs besides, an' I spec's ter hab de balance ready by de fust of nex' Jiniwary; an' den we won't owe nobody a cent. I tell yer dere ain' nothin' like propputy ter make a pusson feel like a man. But w'at's de matter wid yer, Nancy? Is sump'n' skeered yer?"

The woman did seem excited and ill at ease. There was a heaving of the full bust, a quickened breathing, that betokened suppressed excitement.

"I—I—jes' seen a rattlesnake out in de gyahden," she stammered.

The blacksmith ran to the door. "Which way? Whar wuz he?" he cried.

He heard a rustling in the bushes at one side of the garden, and the sound of a breaking twig, and, seizing a hoe which stood by the door, he sprang toward the point from which the sound came.

"No, no," said the woman hurriedly, "it wuz over here," and she directed her husband's attention to the other side of the garden.

The blacksmith, with the uplifted hoe, its sharp blade gleaming in the sunlight, peered cautiously among the collards and tomato plants, listening all the while for the ominous rattle, but found nothing.

"I reckon he's got away," he said, as he set the hoe up again by the door. "Whar's de chillen?" he asked with some anxiety. "Is dey playin' in de woods?"

"No," answered his wife, "dey've gone ter de spring."

The spring was on the opposite side of the garden from that on which the snake was said to have been seen, so the blacksmith sat down and fanned himself with a palm-leaf fan until the dinner was served.

"Yer ain't quite on time ter-day, Nancy," he said, glancing up at the clock on the mantel, after the edge of his appetite had been taken off. "Got ter make time ef yer wanter make money. Didn't Tom tell yer I'd be heah in twenty minutes?"

"No," she said; "I seen him goin' pas'; he didn' say nothin'."

"I dunno w'at's de matter wid dat boy," mused the blacksmith over his apple dumpling. "He's gittin' mighty keerless heah lately; mus' hab sump'n' on 'is min',—some gal, I reckon."

The children had come in while he was speaking,—a slender, shapely boy, yellow like his mother, a girl several years younger, dark like her father: both bright-looking children and neatly dressed.

"I seen cousin Tom down by de spring," said the little girl, as she lifted off the pail of water that had been balanced on her head. "He come out er de woods just ez we wuz fillin' our buckets."

"Yas," insisted the blacksmith, "he's got some gal on his min'."

II

The case of the State of North Carolina *vs.* Ben Davis was called. The accused was led into court, and took his seat in the prisoner's dock.

"Prisoner at the bar, stand up."

The prisoner, pale and anxious, stood up. The clerk read the indictment, in which it was charged that the defendant by force and arms had entered the barn of one G. W. Thornton, and feloniously taken therefrom one whip, of the value of fifteen dollars.

"Are you guilty or not guilty?" asked the judge.

"Not guilty, yo' Honah; not guilty, Jedge. I never tuck de whip."

The State's attorney opened the case. He was young and zealous. Recently elected to the office, this was his first batch of cases, and he was anxious to make as good a record as possible. He had no doubt of the prisoner's guilt. There had been a great deal of petty thieving in the county, and several gentlemen had suggested to him the necessity for greater severity in punishing it. The jury were all white men. The prosecuting attorney stated the case.

"We expect to show, gentlemen of the jury, the facts set out in the indictment,—not altogether by direct proof, but by a chain of circumstantial evidence which is stronger even than the testimony of eyewitnesses. Men might lie, but circumstances cannot. We expect to show that the defendant is a man of dangerous character, a surly, impudent fellow; a man whose views of property are prejudicial to the welfare of society, and who has been heard to assert that half the property which is owned in this county has been stolen, and that, if justice were done, the white people ought to divide up the land with the negroes; in other words, a negro nihilist, a communist, a secret devotee of Tom Paine and Voltaire, a pupil of the anarchist propaganda, which, if not checked by the stern hand of the law, will fasten its insidious fangs on our social system, and drag it down to ruin."

"We object, may it please your Honor," said the defendant's attorney. "The prosecutor should defer his argument until the testimony is in."

"Confine yourself to the facts, Major," said the court mildly.

The prisoner sat with half-open mouth overwhelmed by this flood of eloquence. He had never heard of Tom Paine or Voltaire. He had no conception of what a nihilist or an anarchist might be, and could not have told the difference between a propaganda and a potato.

"We expect to show, may it please the court, that the prisoner had been employed by Colonel Thornton to shoe a horse; that the horse was taken to the prisoner's blacksmith shop by a servant of Colonel Thornton's; that, this servant expressing a desire to go somewhere on an errand before the horse had been shod, the prisoner volunteered to return the horse to Colonel Thornton's stable; that he did so, and the following morning the whip in question was missing; that, from circumstances, suspicion naturally fell upon the prisoner, and a search was made of his shop, where the whip was found secreted; that the prisoner denied that the whip was there, but when confronted with the evidence of his crime, showed by his confusion that he was guilty beyond a peradventure."

The prisoner looked more anxious; so much eloquence could not but be effective with the jury.

The attorney for the defendant answered briefly, denying the defendant's guilt, dwelling upon his previous good character for honesty, and begging the jury not to pre-judge the case, but to remember that the law is merciful, and that the benefit of the doubt should be given to the prisoner.

The prisoner glanced nervously at the jury. There was nothing in their faces to indicate the effect upon them of the opening statements. It seemed to the disinterested listeners as if the defendant's attorney had little confidence in his client's cause.

Colonel Thornton took the stand and testified to his ownership of the whip, the place where it was kept, its value, and the fact that it had disappeared. The whip was produced in court and identified by the witness. He also testified to the conversation at the blacksmith shop in the course of which the prisoner had expressed a desire to possess a similar whip. The cross-examination was brief, and no attempt was made to shake the Colonel's testimony.

The next witness was the constable who had gone with a warrant to search Ben's shop. He testified to the circumstances under which the whip was found.

"He wuz brazen as a mule at fust, an' wanted ter git mad about it. But when we begun ter turn over that pile er truck in the cawner, he kinder begun ter trimble; when the whip-handle stuck out, his eyes commenced ter grow big, an' when we hauled the whip out he turned pale ez ashes, an' begun to swear he did n' take the whip an' did n' know how it got thar."

"You may cross-examine," said the prosecuting attorney triumphantly.

The prisoner felt the weight of the testimony, and glanced furtively at the jury, and then appealingly at his lawyer.

"You say that Ben denied that he had stolen the whip," said the prisoner's attorney, on cross-examination. "Did it not occur to you that what you took for brazen impudence might have been but the evidence of conscious innocence?"

The witness grinned incredulously, revealing thereby a few blackened fragments of teeth.

"I've tuck up more'n a hundred niggers fer stealin', Kurnel, an' I never seed one yit that did n' 'ny it ter the las'."

"Answer my question. Might not the witness's indignation have been a manifestation of conscious innocence? Yes or no?"

"Yes, it mought, an' the moon mought fall—but it don't."

Further cross-examination did not weaken the witness's testimony, which was very damaging, and every one in the court room felt instinctively that a strong defense would be required to break down the State's case.

"The State rests," said the prosecuting attorney, with a ring in his voice which spoke of certain victory.

There was a temporary lull in the proceedings, during which a bailiff passed a pitcher of water and a glass along the line of jurymen. The defense was then begun.

The law in its wisdom did not permit the defendant to testify in his own behalf. There were no witnesses to the facts, but several were called to testify to Ben's good character. The colored witnesses made him out possessed of all the virtues. One or two white men testified that they had never known anything against his reputation for honesty.

The defendant rested his case, and the State called its witnesses in rebuttal. They were entirely on the point of character. One testified that he had heard the prisoner say that, if the negroes had their rights, they would own at least half the property. Another testified that he had heard the defendant say that the negroes spent too much money on churches, and that they cared a good deal more for God than God had ever seemed to care for them.

Ben Davis listened to this testimony with half-open mouth and staring eyes. Now and then he would lean forward and speak perhaps a word, when his attorney would shake a warning finger at him, and he would fall back helplessly, as if abandoning himself to fate; but for a moment only, when he would resume his puzzled look.

The arguments followed. The prosecuting attorney briefly summed up the evidence, and characterized it as almost a mathematical proof of the prisoner's guilt. He reserved his eloquence for the closing argument.

The defendant's attorney had a headache, and secretly believed his client guilty. His address sounded more like an appeal for mercy than a demand for justice. Then the State's attorney delivered the maiden argument of his office, the speech that made his reputation as an orator, and opened up to him a successful political career.

The judge's charge to the jury was a plain, simple statement of the law as applied to circumstantial evidence, and the mere statement of the law foreshadowed the verdict.

The eyes of the prisoner were glued to the jury-box, and he looked more and more like a hunted animal. In the rear of the crowd of blacks who filled the back part of the room, partly concealed by the projecting angle of the fireplace, stood Tom, the blacksmith's assistant. If the face is the mirror of the soul, then this man's soul, taken off its guard in this moment of excitement, was full of lust and envy and all evil passions.

The jury filed out of their box, and into the jury room behind the judge's stand. There was a moment of relaxation in the court room. The lawyers fell into conversation across the table. The judge beckoned to Colonel Thornton, who stepped forward, and they conversed together a few moments. The prisoner was all eyes and ears in this moment of waiting, and from an involuntary gesture on the part of the judge he divined that they were speaking of him. It is a pity he could not hear what was said.

"How do you feel about the case, Colonel?" asked the judge.

"Let him off easy," replied Colonel Thornton. "He's the best blacksmith in the county."

The business of the court seemed to have halted by tacit consent, in anticipation of a quick verdict. The suspense did not last long. Scarcely ten minutes had elapsed when there was a rap on the door, the officer opened it, and the jury came out.

The prisoner, his soul in his eyes, sought their faces, but met no reassuring glance; they were all looking away from him.

"Gentlemen of the jury, have you agreed upon a verdict?"

"We have," responded the foreman. The clerk of the court stepped forward and took the fateful slip from the foreman's hand.

The clerk read the verdict: "We, the jury impaneled and sworn to try the issues in this cause, do find the prisoner guilty as charged in the indictment."

There was a moment of breathless silence. Then a wild burst of grief from the prisoner's wife, to which his two children, not understanding it all, but vaguely conscious of some calamity, added their voices in two long, discordant wails, which would have been ludicrous had they not been heart-rending.

The face of the young man in the back of the room expressed relief and badly concealed satisfaction. The prisoner fell back upon the seat from which he had half risen in his anxiety, and his dark face assumed an ashen hue. What he thought could only be surmised. Perhaps, knowing his innocence, he had not believed conviction possible; perhaps, conscious of guilt, he dreaded the punishment, the extent of which was optional with the judge, within very wide limits. Only one other person present knew whether or not he was guilty, and that other had slunk furtively from the court room.

Some of the spectators wondered why there should be so much ado about convicting a negro of stealing a buggy-whip. They had forgotten their own interest of the moment before. They did not realize out of what trifles grow the tragedies of life.

It was four o'clock in the afternoon, the hour for adjournment, when the verdict was returned. The judge nodded to the bailiff.

"Oyez, oyez! this court is now adjourned until ten o'clock tomorrow morning," cried the bailiff in a singsong voice. The judge left the bench, the jury filed out of the box, and a buzz of conversation filled the court room.

"Brace up, Ben, brace up, my boy," said the defendant's lawyer, half apologetically. "I did what I could for you, but you can never tell what a jury will do. You won't be sentenced till to-morrow morning. In the meantime I'll speak to the judge and try to get him to be easy with you. He may let you off with a light fine."

The negro pulled himself together, and by an effort listened.

"Thanky, Majah," was all he said. He seemed to be thinking of something far away.

He barely spoke to his wife when she frantically threw herself on him, and clung to his neck, as he passed through the side room on his way to jail. He kissed his children mechanically, and did not reply to the soothing remarks made by the jailer.

III

There was a good deal of excitement in town the next morning. Two white men stood by the post office talking.

"Did yer hear the news?"

"No, what wuz it?"

"Ben Davis tried ter break jail las' night."

"You don't say so! What a fool! He ain't be'n sentenced yit."

"Well, now," said the other, "I've knowed Ben a long time, an' he wuz a right good nigger. I kinder found it hard ter b'lieve he did steal that whip. But what's a man's feelin's ag'in' the proof?"

They spoke on awhile, using the past tense as if they were speaking of a dead man.

"Ef I know Jedge Hart, Ben 'll wish he had slep' las' night, 'stidder tryin' ter break out'n jail."

At ten o'clock the prisoner was brought into court. He walked with shambling gait, bent at the shoulders, hopelessly, with downcast eyes, and took his seat with several other prisoners who had been brought in for sentence. His wife, accompanied by the children, waited behind him, and a number of his friends were gathered in the court room.

The first prisoner sentenced was a young white man, convicted several days before of manslaughter. The deed was done in the heat of passion, under circumstances of great provocation, during a quarrel about a woman. The prisoner was admonished of the sanctity of human life, and sentenced to one year in the penitentiary.

The next case was that of a young clerk, eighteen or nineteen years of age, who had committed a forgery in order to procure the means to buy lottery tickets. He was well connected, and the case would not have been prosecuted if the judge had not refused to allow it to be nolled, and, once brought to trial, a conviction could not have been avoided.

"You are a young man," said the judge gravely, yet not unkindly, "and your life is yet before you. I regret that you should have been led into evil courses by the lust for speculation, so dangerous in its tendencies, so fruitful of crime and misery. I am led to believe that you are sincerely penitent, and that, after such punishment as the law cannot remit without bringing itself into contempt, you will see the error of your ways and follow the strict path of rectitude. Your fault has entailed distress not only upon yourself, but upon your relatives, people of good name and good family, who suffer as keenly from your disgrace as you yourself. Partly out of consideration for their feelings, and partly because I feel that, under the circumstances, the law will be satisfied by the penalty I shall inflict, I sentence you to imprisonment in the county jail for six months, and a fine of one hundred dollars and the costs of this action."

"The jedge talks well, don't he?" whispered one spectator to another.

"Yes, and kinder likes ter hear hisse'f talk," answered the other.

"Ben Davis, stand up," ordered the judge.

He might have said "Ben Davis, wake up," for the jailer had to touch the prisoner on the shoulder to rouse him from his stupor. He stood up, and something of the hunted look came again into his eyes, which shifted under the stern glance of the judge.

"Ben Davis, you have been convicted of larceny, after a fair trial before twelve good men of this county. Under the testimony, there can be no doubt of your guilt. The case is an aggravated one. You are not an ignorant, shiftless fellow, but a man of more than ordinary intelligence among your people, and one who ought to know better. You have not even the poor excuse of having stolen to satisfy hunger or a physical appetite. Your conduct is wholly without excuse, and I can only regard your crime as the result of a tendency to offenses of this nature, a tendency which is only too common among your people; a tendency which is a menace to civilization, a menace to society itself, for society rests upon the sacred right of property. Your opinions, too, have been given a wrong turn; you have been heard to utter sentiments which, if disseminated among an ignorant people, would breed discontent, and give rise to strained relations between them and their best friends, their old masters, who understand their real nature and their real needs, and to whose justice and enlightened guidance they can safely trust. Have you anything to say why sentence should not be passed upon you?"

"Nothin', suh, cep'n dat I did n' take de whip."

"The law, largely, I think, in view of the peculiar circumstances of your unfortunate race, has vested a large discretion in courts as to the extent of the punishment for offenses of this kind. Taking your case as a whole, I am convinced that it is one which, for the sake of the example, deserves a severe punishment. Nevertheless, I do not feel disposed to give you the full extent of the law, which would be twenty years in the penitentiary,[1] but, considering the fact that you have a family, and have heretofore borne a good reputation in the community, I will impose upon you the light sentence of imprisonment for five years in the penitentiary at hard labor. And I hope that this will be a warning to you and others who may be similarly disposed, and that after your sentence has expired you may lead the life of a law-abiding citizen."

"O Ben! O my husband! O God!" moaned the poor wife, and tried to press forward to her husband's side.

"Keep back, Nancy, keep back," said the jailer. "You can see him in jail."

Several people were looking at Ben's face. There was one flash of despair, and then nothing but a stony blank, behind which he masked his real feelings, whatever they were.

Human character is a compound of tendencies inherited and habits acquired. In the anxiety, the fear of disgrace, spoke the nineteenth century civilization with which Ben Davis had been more or less closely in touch during twenty years of slavery and fifteen years of freedom. In the stolidity with which he received this sentence for a crime which he had not committed, spoke who knows what trait of inherited savagery? For stoicism is a savage virtue.

---

1. There are no degrees of larceny in North Carolina, and the penalty for any offense lies in the discretion of the judge, to the limit of twenty years.

IV

One morning in June, five years later, a black man limped slowly along the old Lumberton plank road; a tall man, whose bowed shoulders made him seem shorter than he was, and a face from which it was difficult to guess his years, for in it the wrinkles and flabbiness of age were found side by side with firm white teeth, and eyes not sunken,—eyes bloodshot, and burning with something, either fever or passion. Though he limped painfully with one foot, the other hit the ground impatiently, like the good horse in a poorly matched team. As he walked along, he was talking to himself:—

"I wonder what dey'll do w'en I git back? I wonder how Nancy's s'ported the fambly all dese years? Tuck in washin', I s'ppose,— she was a monst'us good washer an' ironer. I wonder ef de chillen 'll be too proud ter reco'nize deir daddy come back f'um de penetenchy? I 'spec' Billy must be a big boy by dis time. He won' b'lieve his daddy ever stole anything. I'm gwine ter slip roun' an' s'prise 'em."

Five minutes later a face peered cautiously into the window of what had once been Ben Davis's cabin,—at first an eager face, its coarseness lit up with the fire of hope; a moment later a puzzled face; then an anxious, fearful face as the man stepped away from the window and rapped at the door.

"Is Mis' Davis home?" he asked of the woman who opened the door.

"Mis' Davis don' live here. You er mistook in de house."

"Whose house is dis?"

"It b'longs ter my husban', Mr. Smith,—Primus Smith."

" 'Scuse me, but I knowed de house some years ago, w'en I wuz here oncet on a visit, an' it b'longed ter a man name' Ben Davis."

"Ben Davis—Ben Davis?—oh yes, I 'member now. Dat wuz de gen'man w'at wuz sent ter de penitenchy fer sump'n er nuther, —sheep-stealin', I b'lieve. Primus," she called, "w'at wuz Ben Davis, w'at useter own dis yer house, sent ter de penitenchy fer?"

"Hoss-stealin'," came back the reply in sleepy accents, from the man seated by the fireplace.

The traveler went on to the next house. A neat-looking yellow woman came to the door when he rattled the gate, and stood looking suspiciously at him.

"W'at you want?" she asked.

"Please, ma'am, will you tell me whether a man name' Ben Davis useter live in dis neighborhood?"

"Useter live in de nex' house; wuz sent ter de penitenchy fer killin' a man."

"Kin yer tell me w'at went wid Mis' Davis?"

"Umph! I's a 'spectable 'oman, I is, en don' mix wid dem kind er people. She wuz 'n' no better'n her husban'. She tuk up wid a man dat useter wuk fer Ben, an' dey're livin' down by de ole wagon-ya'd, where no 'spectable 'oman ever puts her foot."

"An' de chillen?"

"De gal's dead. Wuz'n no better'n she oughter be'n. She fell in de crick an' got drown'; some folks say she wuz'n' sober w'en it happen'. De boy tuck atter his pappy. He wuz 'rested las' week fer shootin' a w'ite man, an' wuz lynch' de same night. Dey wa'n't none of 'em no 'count after deir pappy went ter de penitenchy."

"What went wid de proputty?"

"Hit wuz sol' fer de mortgage, er de taxes, er de lawyer, er sump'n,—I don' know w'at. A w'ite man got it."

The man with the bundle went on until he came to a creek that crossed the road. He descended the sloping bank, and, sitting on a stone in the shade of a water-oak, took off his coarse brogans, unwound the rags that served him in lieu of stockings, and laved in the cool water the feet that were chafed with many a weary mile of travel.

After five years of unrequited toil, and unspeakable hardship in convict camps,—five years of slaving by the side of human brutes, and of nightly herding with them in vermin-haunted huts, —Ben Davis had become like them. For a while he had received occasional letters from home, but in the shifting life of the convict camp they had long since ceased to reach him, if indeed they had been written. For a year or two, the consciousness of his innocence had helped to make him resist the debasing influences that surrounded him. The hope of shortening his sentence by good behavior, too, had worked a similar end. But the transfer from one contractor to another, each interested in keeping as long as possible a good worker, had speedily dissipated any such hope. When hope took flight, its place was not long vacant. Despair followed, and black hatred of all mankind, hatred especially of the man to whom he attributed all his misfortunes. One who is suffering unjustly is not apt to indulge in fine abstractions, nor to balance probabilities. By long brooding over his wrongs, his mind became, if not unsettled, at least warped, and he imagined that Colonel Thornton had deliberately set a trap into which he had fallen. The Colonel, he convinced himself, had disapproved of his prosperity, and had schemed to destroy it. He reasoned himself into the belief that he represented in his person the accumulated wrongs of a whole race, and Colonel Thornton the race who had oppressed them. A burning desire for revenge sprang up in him, and he nursed it until his sentence expired and he was set at liberty. What he had learned since reaching home had changed his desire into a deadly purpose.

When he had again bandaged his feet and slipped them into his shoes, he looked around him, and selected a stout sapling from among the undergrowth that covered the bank of the stream. Taking from his pocket a huge clasp-knife, he cut off the length of an ordinary walking stick and trimmed it. The result was an ugly-looking bludgeon, a dangerous weapon when in the grasp of a strong man.

With the stick in his hand, he went on down the road until he approached a large white house standing some distance back from the street. The grounds were filled with a profusion of shrubbery. The negro entered the gate and secreted himself in the bushes, at a point where he could hear any one that might approach.

It was near midday, and he had not eaten. He had walked all night, and had not slept. The hope of meeting his loved ones had been meat and drink and rest for him. But as he sat waiting, outraged nature asserted itself, and he fell asleep, with his head on the rising root of a tree, and his face upturned.

And as he slept, he dreamed of his childhood; of an old black mammy taking care of him in the daytime, and of a younger face, with soft eyes, which bent over him sometimes at night, and a pair of arms which clasped him closely. He dreamed of his past, —of his young wife, of his bright children. Somehow his dreams all ran to pleasant themes for a while.

Then they changed again. He dreamed that he was in the convict camp, and, by an easy transition, that he was in hell, consumed with hunger, burning with thirst. Suddenly the grinning devil who stood over him wtih a barbed whip faded away, and a little white angel came and handed him a drink of water. As he raised it to his lips the glass slipped, and he struggled back to consciousness.

"Poo' man! Poo' man sick, an' sleepy. Dolly b'ing f'owers to cover poo' man up. Poo' man mus' be hungry. W'en Dolly get him covered up, she go b'ing poo' man some cake."

A sweet little child, as beautiful as a cherub escaped from Paradise, was standing over him. At first he scarcely comprehended the words the baby babbled out. But as they became clear to him, a novel feeling crept slowly over his heart. It had been so long since he had heard anything but curses and stern words of command, or the ribald songs of obscene merriment, that the clear tones of this voice from heaven cooled his calloused heart as the water of the brook had soothed his blistered feet. It was so strange, so unwonted a thing, that he lay there with half-closed eyes while the child brought leaves and flowers and laid them on his face and on his breast, and arranged them with little caressing taps.

She moved away, and plucked a flower. And then she spied another farther on, and then another, and, as she gathered them, kept increasing the distance between herself and the man lying there, until she was several rods away.

Ben Davis watched her through eyes over which had come an unfamiliar softness. Under the lingering spell of his dream, her golden hair, which fell in rippling curls, seemed like a halo of purity and innocence and peace, irradiating the atmosphere around her. It is true the thought occurred to Ben, vaguely, that through harm to her he might inflict the greatest punishment upon her father; but the idea came like a dark shape that faded away and vanished into nothingness as soon as it came within the nimbus that surrounded the child's person.

The child was moving on to pluck still another flower, when there came a sound of hoof-beats, and Ben was aware that a horseman, visible through the shrubbery, was coming along the curved path that led from the gate to the house. It must be the man he was waiting for, and now was the time to wreak his vengeance. He sprang to his feet, grasped his club, and stood for a moment irresolute. But either the instinct of the convict, beaten, driven, and debased, or the influence of the child, which was still strong upon him, impelled him, after the first momentary pause, to flee as though seeking safety.

His flight led him toward the little girl, whom he must pass in order to make his escape, and as Colonel Thornton turned the corner of the path he saw a desperate-looking negro, clad in filthy rags, and carrying in his hand a murderous bludgeon, running toward the child, who, startled by the sound of footsteps, had turned and was looking toward the approaching man with wondering eyes. A sickening fear came over the father's heart, and drawing the ever-ready revolver, which according to the Southern custom he carried always upon his person, he fired with unerring aim. Ben Davis ran a few yards farther, faltered, threw out his hands, and fell dead at the child's feet.

Some time, we are told, when the cycle of years has rolled around, there is to be another golden age, when all men will dwell together in love and harmony, and when peace and righteousness shall prevail for a thousand years. God speed the day, and let not the shining thread of hope become so enmeshed in the web of circumstance that we lose sight of it; but give us here and there, and now and then, some little foretaste of this golden age, that we may the more patiently and hopefully await its coming!

Bartleby, The Scrivener

$$\boxed{\textit{Herman Melville}}$$

I AM A RATHER ELDERLY MAN. The nature of my avocations, for the last thirty years, has brought me into more than ordinary contact with what would seem an interesting and somewhat singular set of men, of whom, as yet, nothing, that I know of, has ever been written—I mean, the law-copyists, or scriveners. I have known very many of them, professionally and privately, and, if I pleased, could relate divers histories, at which good-natured gentlemen might smile, and sentimental souls might weep. But I waive the biographies of all other scriveners, for a few passages in the life of Bartleby, who was a scrivener, the strangest I ever saw, or heard of. While, of other law-copyists, I might write the complete life, of Bartleby nothing of that sort can be done. I believe that no materials exist, for a full and satisfactory biography of this man. It is an irreparable loss to literature. Bartleby was one of those beings of whom nothing is ascertainable, except from the original sources, and, in his case, those are very small. What my own astonished eyes saw of Bartleby, *that* is all I know of him, except, indeed, one vague report, which will appear in the sequel.

Ere introducing the scrivener, as he first appeared to me, it is fit I make some mention of myself, my *employés*, my business, my chambers, and general surroundings; because some such description is indispensable to an adequate understanding of the chief character about to be presented. Imprimis: I am a man who, from his youth upwards, has been filled with a profound conviction that the easiest way of life is the best. Hence, though I belong to a profession proverbially energetic and nervous, even to turbulence, at times, yet nothing of that sort have I ever suffered to invade my peace. I am one of those unambitious lawyers who never addresses a jury, or in any way draws down public applause; but, in the cool tranquillity of a snug retreat, do a snug business among rich men's bonds, and mortgages, and titledeeds. All who know me, consider me an eminently *safe* man. The late John Jacob Astor, a personage little given to poetic enthusiasm, had no hesitation in pronouncing my first grand point to be prudence; my next, method. I do not speak it in vanity, but simply record the fact, that I was not unemployed in my profession by the late John Jacob Astor; a name which, I admit, I love to repeat; for it hath a rounded and orbicular sound to it, and rings like unto bullion. I will freely add, that I was not insensible to the late John Jacob Astor's good opinion.

Some time prior to the period of which this little history begins, my avocations had been largely increased. The good old office, now extinct in the State of New York, of a Master in Chancery, had been conferred upon me. It was not a very arduous office, but very pleasantly remunerative. I seldom lose my temper; much more seldom indulge in dangerous indignation at wrongs and outrages; but, I must be permitted to be rash here, and declare, that I consider the sudden and violent abrogation of the office of Master in Chancery, by the new Constitution, as a—premature act; inasmuch as I had counted upon a life-lease of the profits, whereas I only received those of a few short years. But this is by the way.

My chambers were up stairs, at No. — Wall Street. At one end, they looked upon the white wall of the interior of a spacious skylight shaft, penetrating the building from top to bottom.

This view might have been considered rather tame than otherwise, deficient in what landscape painters call "life." But, if so, the view from the other end of my chambers offered, at least, a contrast, if nothing more. In that direction, my windows commanded an unobstructed view of a lofty brick wall, black by age and everlasting shade; which wall required no spy-glass to bring out its lurking beauties, but, for the benefit of all near-sighted spectators, was pushed up to within ten feet of my window panes. Owing to the great height of the surrounding buildings, and my chambers being on the second floor, the interval between this wall and mine not a little resembled a huge square cistern.

At the period just preceding the advent of Bartleby, I had two persons as copyists in my employment, and a promising lad as an office-boy. First, Turkey; second, Nippers; third, Ginger Nut. These may seem names, the like of which are not usually found in the Directory. In truth, they were nicknames, mutually conferred upon each other by my three clerks, and were deemed expressive of their respective persons or characters. Turkey was a short, pursy Englishman, of about my own age—that is, somewhere not far from sixty. In the morning, one might say, his face was of a fine florid hue, but after twelve o'clock, meridian—his dinner hour—it blazed like a grate full of Christmas coals; and continued blazing—but, as it were, with a gradual wane—till six o'clock, P.M., or thereabouts; after which, I saw no more of the proprietor of the face, which, gaining its meridian with the sun, seemed to set with it, to rise, culminate, and decline the following day, with the like regularity and undiminished glory. There are many singular coincidences I have known in the course of my life, not the least among which was the fact, that, exactly when Turkey displayed his fullest beams from his red and radiant countenance, just then, too, at that critical moment, began the daily period when I considered his business capacities as seriously disturbed for the remainder of the twenty-four hours. Not that he was absolutely idle, or averse to business, then; far from it. The difficulty was, he was apt to be altogether too energetic. There was a strange, inflamed, flurried, flighty recklessness of activity about him. He would be incautious in dipping his pen into his inkstand. All his blots upon my documents were dropped there after twelve o'clock, meridian. Indeed, not only would he be reckless, and sadly given to making blots in the afternoon, but, some days, he went further, and was rather noisy. At such times, too, his face flamed with augmented blazonry, as if cannel coal had been heaped on anthracite. He made an unpleasant racket with his chair; spilled his sand-box; in mending his pens, impatiently split them all to pieces, and threw them on the floor in a sudden passion; stood up, and leaned over his table, boxing his papers about in a most indecorous manner, very sad to behold in an elderly man like him. Nevertheless, as he was in many ways a most valuable person to me, and all the time before twelve o'clock, meridian, was the quickest, steadiest creature, too, accomplishing a great deal of work in a style not easily to be matched— for these reasons, I was willing to overlook his eccentricities, though, indeed, occasionally, I remonstrated with him. I did this very gently, however, because, though the civilest, nay, the blandest and most reverential of men in the morning, yet, in the afternoon, he was disposed, upon provocation, to be slightly rash with his tongue—in fact, insolent. Now, valuing his morning services as I did, and resolved not to lose them—yet, at the same time, made uncomfortable by his inflamed ways after twelve o'clock—and being a man of peace, unwilling by my admonitions to call forth unseemly retorts from him, I took upon me, one Saturday noon (he was always worse on Saturdays) to hint to him, very kindly, that, perhaps, now that he was growing old, it might be well to abridge his labors; in short, he need not come to my chambers after twelve o'clock, but, dinner over, had best go home to his lodgings, and rest himself till tea-time. But no; he insisted upon his afternoon devotions. His countenance became intolerably fervid, as he oratorically assured me—gesticulating with a long ruler at the other end of the room—that if his services in the morning were useful, how indispensable, then, in the afternoon?

"With submission, sir," said Turkey, on this occasion, "I consider myself your right-hand man. In the morning I but marshal and deploy my columns; but in the afternoon I put myself at their head, and gallantly charge the foe, thus"—and he made a violent thrust with the ruler.

"But the blots, Turkey," intimated I.

"True; but, with submission, sir, behold these hairs! I am getting old. Surely, sir, a blot or two of a warm afternoon is not to be severely urged against gray hairs. Old age—even if it blot the page—is honorable. With submission, sir, we *both* are getting old."

This appeal to my fellow-feeling was hardly to be resisted. At all events I saw that go he would not. So, I made up my mind to let him stay, resolving, nevertheless, to see to it that, during the afternoon, he had to do with my less important papers.

Nippers, the second on my list, was a whiskered, sallow, and, upon the whole, rather piratical-looking young man, of about five and twenty. I always deemed him the victim of two evil powers—ambition and indigestion. The ambition was evinced by a certain impatience of the duties of a mere copyist, an unwarrantable usurpation of strictly professional affairs, such as the original drawing up of legal documents. The indigestion seemed betoken in an occasional nervous testiness and grinning irrita-

bility, causing the teeth to audibly grind together over mistakes
committed in copying; unnecessary maledictions, hissed, rather
than spoken, in the heat of business; and especially by a continual discontent with the height of the table where he worked.
Though of a very ingenious mechanical turn, Nippers could never
get this table to suit him. He put chips under it, blocks of various
sorts, bits of pasteboard, and at last went so far as to attempt an
exquisite adjustment, by final pieces of folded blotting-paper. But
no invention would answer. If, for the sake of easing his back,
he brought the table lid at a sharp angle well up towards his chin,
and wrote there like a man using the steep roof of a Dutch house
for his desk, then he declared that it stopped the circulation in
his arms. If now he lowered the table to his waistbands, and
stooped over it in writing, then there was a sore aching in his
back. In short, the truth of the matter was, Nippers knew not
what he wanted. Or, if he wanted anything, it was to be rid of
a scrivener's table altogether. Among the manifestations of his
diseased ambition was a fondness he had for receiving visits from
certain ambiguous-looking fellows in seedy coats, whom he called
his clients. Indeed, I was aware that not only was he, at times,
considerable of a ward-politician, but he occasionally did a little
business at the Justices' courts, and was not unknown on the
steps of the Tombs. I have good reason to believe, however, that
one individual who called upon him at my chambers, and who,
with a grand air, he insisted was his client, was no other than
a dun, and the alleged title-deed, a bill. But, with all his failings,
and the annoyances he caused me, Nippers, like his compatriot
Turkey, was a very useful man to me; wrote a neat, swift hand;
and, when he chose, was not deficient in a gentlemanly sort of
way; and so, incidentally, reflected credit upon my chambers.
Whereas, with respect to Turkey, I had much ado to keep him
from being a reproach to me. His clothes were apt to look oily,
and smell of eating-houses. He wore his pantaloons very loose
and baggy in summer. His coats were execrable; his hat not to
be handled. But while the hat was a thing of indifference to me,
inasmuch as his natural civility and deference, as a dependent
Englishman, always led him to doff it the moment he entered
the room, yet his coat was another matter. Concerning his coats,
I reasoned with him; but with no effect. The truth was, I suppose, that a man with so small an income could not afford to
sport such a lustrous face and a lustrous coat at one and the same

time. As Nippers once observed, Turkey's money went chiefly for red ink. One winter day, I presented Turkey with a highly respectable-looking coat of my own—a padded gray coat, of a most comfortable warmth, and which buttoned straight up from the knee to the neck. I thought Turkey would appreciate the favor, and abate his rashness and obstreperousness of afternoons. But no; I verily believe that buttoning himself up in so downy and blanket-like a coat had a pernicious effect upon him—upon the same principle that too much oats are bad for horses. In fact, precisely as a rash, restive horse is said to feel his oats, so Turkey felt his coat. It made him insolent. He was a man whom prosperity harmed.

Though, concerning the self-indulgent habits of Turkey, I had my own private surmises, yet, touching Nippers, I was well persuaded that, whatever might be his faults in other respects, he was, at least, a temperate young man. But, indeed, nature herself seemed to have been his vintner, and, at his birth, charged him so thoroughly with an irritable, brandy-like disposition, that all subsequent potations were needless. When I consider how, amid the stillness of my chambers, Nippers would sometimes impatiently rise from his seat, and stooping over his table, spread his arms wide apart, seize the whole desk, and move it, and jerk it, with a grim, grinding motion on the floor, as if the table were a perverse voluntary agent, intent on thwarting and vexing him, I plainly perceive that, for Nippers, brandy-and-water were altogether superfluous.

It was fortunate for me that, owing to its peculiar cause—indigestion—the irritability and consequent nervousness of Nippers were mainly observable in the morning, while in the afternoon he was comparatively mild. So that, Turkey's paroxysms only coming on about twelve o'clock, I never had to do with their eccentricities at one time. Their fits relieved each other, like guards. When Nipper's was on, Turkey's was off; and *vice versa*. This was a good natural arrangement, under the circumstances.

Ginger Nut, the third on my list, was a lad, some twelve years old. His father was a car-man, ambitious of seeing his son on the bench instead of a cart, before he died. So he sent him to my office, as student at law, errand-boy, cleaner and sweeper, at the rate of one dollar a week. He had a little desk to himself, but he did not use it much. Upon inspection, the drawer exhibited a great array of the shells of various sorts of nuts. Indeed, to this quick-witted youth, the whole noble science of the law was contained in a nut-shell. Not the least among the employments of Ginger Nut, as well as one which he discharged with the most alacrity, was his duty as cake and apple purveyor for Turkey and Nippers. Copying law-papers being proverbially a dry, husky sort of business, my two scriveners were fain to moisten their mouths very often with Spitzenbergs, to be had at the numerous stalls nigh the Custom House and Post Office. Also, they sent Ginger Nut very frequently for that peculiar cake—small, flat, round, and very spicy—after which he had been named by them. Of a cold morning, when business was but dull, Turkey would gobble up scores of these cakes, as if they were mere wafers— indeed, they sell them at the rate of six or eight for a penny—the scrape of his pen blending with the crunching of the crisp particles in his mouth. Of all the fiery afternoon blunders and flurried rashnesses of Turkey, was his once moistening a ginger-cake between his lips, and clapping it on to a mortgage, for a seal. I came within an ace of dismissing him then. But he mollified me by making an oriental bow, and saying—

"With submission, sir, it was generous of me to find you in stationery on my own account."

Now my original business—that of a conveyancer and title hunter, and drawer-up of recondite documents of all sorts—was considerably increased by receiving the master's office. There was now great work for scriveners. Not only must I push the clerks already with me, but I must have additional help.

In answer to my advertisement, a motionless young man one morning stood upon my office threshold, the door being open, for it was summer. I can see that figure now—pallidly neat, pitiably respectable, incurably forlorn! It was Bartleby.

After a few words touching his qualifications, I engaged him, glad to have among my corps of copyists a man of so singularly sedate an aspect, which I thought might operate beneficially upon the flighty temper of Turkey, and the fiery one of Nippers.

I should have stated before that ground glass folding-doors divided my premises into two parts, one of which was occupied by my scriveners, the other by myself. According to my humor, I threw open these doors, or closed them. I resolved to assign Bartleby a corner by the folding-doors, but on my side of them, so as to have this quiet man within easy call, in case any trifling thing was to be done. I placed his desk close up to a small side-window in that part of the room, a window which originally had afforded a lateral view of certain grimy back-yards and bricks, but which, owing to subsequent erections, commanded at present no view at all, though it gave some light. Within three feet of the panes was a wall, and the light came down from far above, between two lofty buildings, as from a very small opening in a dome. Still further to a satisfactory arrangement, I procured a high green folding screen, which might entirely isolate Bartleby from my sight, though not remove him from my voice. And thus, in a manner, privacy and society were conjoined.

At first, Bartleby did an extraordinary quantity of writing. As if long famishing for something to copy, he seemed to gorge himself on my documents. There was no pause for digestion. He ran a day and night line, copying by sun-light and by candle-light. I should have been quite delighted with his application, had he been cheerfully industrious. But he wrote on silently, palely, mechanically.

It is, of course, an indispensable part of a scrivener's business to verify the accuracy of his copy, word by word. Where there are two or more scriveners in an office, they assist each other in this examination, one reading from the copy, the other holding the original. It is a very dull, wearisome, and lethargic affair. I can readily imagine that, to some sanguine temperaments, it would be altogether intolerable. For example, I cannot credit that the mettlesome poet, Byron, would have contentedly sat down with Bartleby to examine a law document of say five hundred pages, closely written in a crimpy hand.

Now and then, in the haste of business, it had been my habit to assist in comparing some brief document myself, calling Turkey or Nippers for this purpose. One object I had, in placing Bartleby so handy to me behind the screen, was, to avail myself of his services on such trivial occasions. It was on the third day, I think, of his being with me, and before any necessity had arisen for having his own writing examined, that, being much hurried to complete a small affair I had in hand, I abruptly called to Bartleby. In my haste and natural expectancy of instant compliance, I sat with my head bent over the original on my desk, and my right hand sideways, and somewhat nervously extended with the copy, so that, immediately upon emerging from his retreat, Bartleby might snatch it and proceed to business without the least delay.

In this very attitude did I sit when I called to him, rapidly stating what it was I wanted him to do—namely, to examine a small paper with me. Imagine my surprise, nay, my consternation, when, without moving from his privacy, Bartleby, in a singularly mild, firm voice, replied, "I would prefer not to."

I sat awhile in perfect silence, rallying my stunned faculties. Immediately it occurred to me that my ears had deceived me, or Bartleby had entirely misunderstood my meaning. I repeated my request in the clearest tone I could assume; but in quite as clear a one came the previous reply, "I would prefer not to."

"Prefer not to," echoed I, rising in high excitement, and crossing the room with a stride. "What do you mean? Are you moonstruck? I want you to help me compare this sheet here—take it," and I thrust it towards him.

"I would prefer not to," said he.

I looked at him steadfastly. His face was leanly composed his gray eye dimly calm. Not a wrinkle of agitation rippled him. Had there been the least uneasiness, anger, impatience or impertinence in his manner; in other words, had there been any thing ordinarily human about him, doubtless I should have violently dismissed him from the premises. But as it was, I should have as soon thought of turning my pale plaster-of-paris bust of Cicero out of doors. I stood gazing at him awhile, as he went on with his own writing, and then reseated myself at my desk. This is very strange, thought I. What had one best do? But my business hurried me. I concluded to forget the matter for the present, reserving it for my future leisure. So calling Nippers from the other room, the paper was speedily examined.

A few days after this, Bartleby concluded four lengthy documents, being quadruplicates of a week's testimony taken before me in my High Court of Chancery. It became necessary to examine them. It was an important suit, and great accuracy was imperative. Having all things arranged, I called Turkey, Nippers, and Ginger Nut, from the next room, meaning to place the four copies in the hands of my four clerks, while I should read from the original. Accordingly, Turkey, Nippers, and Ginger Nut had taken their seats in a row, each with his document in his hand, when I called to Bartleby to join this interesting group.

"Bartleby! quick, I am waiting."

I heard a slow scrape of his chair legs on the uncarpeted floor, and soon he appeared standing at the entrance of his hermitage.

"What is wanted?" said he, mildly.

"The copies, the copies," said I hurriedly. "We are going to examine them. There"—and I held towards him the fourth quadruplicate.

"I would prefer not to," he said, and gently disappeared behind the screen.

For a few moments I was turned into a pillar of salt, standing at the head of my seated column of clerks. Recovering myself, I advanced towards the screen, and demanded the reason for such extraordinary conduct.

"*Why* do you refuse?"

"I would prefer not to."

With any other man I should have flown outright into a dreadful passion, scorned all further words, and thrust him ignominiously from my presence. But there was something about Bartleby that not only strangely disarmed me, but, in a wonderful manner, touched and disconcerted me. I began to reason with him.

"These are your own copies we are about to examine. It is labor saving to you, because one examination will answer for your four papers. It is common usage. Every copyist is bound to help examine his copy. Is it not so? Will you not speak? Answer!"

"I prefer not to," he replied in a flutelike tone. It seemed to me that, while I had been addressing him, he carefully revolved every statement that I made; fully comprehended the meaning; could not gainsay the irresistible conclusion; but, at the same time, some paramount consideration prevailed with him to reply as he did.

"You are decided, then, not to comply with my request—a request made according to common usage and common sense?"

He briefly gave me to understand, that on that point my judgment was sound. Yes: his decision was irreversible.

It is not seldom the case that, when a man is browbeaten in some unprecedented and violently unreasonable way, he begins to stagger in his own plainest faith. He begins, as it were, vaguely to surmise that, wonderful as it may be, all the justice and all the reason is on the other side. Accordingly, if any disinterested persons are present, he turns to them for some reinforcement of his own faltering mind.

"Turkey," said I, "what do you think of this? Am I not right?"

"With submission, sir," said Turkey, in his blandest tone, "I think that you are."

"Nippers," said I, "what do *you* think of it?"

"I think I should kick him out of the office.

(The reader, of nice perceptions, will here perceive that, it being morning, Turkey's answer is couched in polite and tranquil terms, but Nippers replies in ill-tempered ones. Or, to repeat a previous sentence, Nippers's ugly mood was on duty, and Turkey's off.)

"Ginger Nut," said I, willing to enlist the smallest suffrage in my behalf, "what do *you* think of it?"

"I think, sir, he's a little *luny*," replied Ginger Nut, with a grin.

"You hear what they say," said I, turning towards the screen, "come forth and do your duty."

But he vouchsafed no reply. I pondered a moment in sore perplexity. But once more business hurried me. I determined again to postpone the consideration of this dilemma to my future leisure. With a little trouble we made out to examine the papers without Bartleby, though at every page or two Turkey deferentially dropped his opinion, that this proceeding was quite out of the common; while Nippers, twitching in his chair with a dyspeptic nervousness, ground out, between his set teeth, occasional hissing maledictions against the stubborn oaf behind the screen. And for his (Nippers's) part, this was the first and the last time he would do another man's business without pay.

Meanwhile Bartleby sat in his hermitage, oblivious to everything but his own peculiar business there.

Some days passed, the scrivener being employed upon another lengthy work. His late remarkable conduct led me to regard his ways narrowly. I observed that he never went to dinner; indeed, that he never went anywhere. As yet I had never, of my personal knowledge, known him to be outside of my office. He was a perpetual sentry in the corner. At about eleven o'clock though, in the morning, I noticed that Ginger Nut would advance toward the opening in Bartleby's screen, as if silently beckoned thither by a gesture invisible to me where I sat. The boy would then leave the office, jingling a few pence, and reappear with a handful of ginger-nuts, which he delivered in the hermitage, receiving two of the cakes for his trouble.

He lives, then, on ginger-nuts, thought I; never eats a dinner, properly speaking; he must be a vegetarian, then; but no! he never eats even vegetables, he eats nothing but ginger-nuts. My mind then ran on in reveries concerning the probable effects upon the human constitution of living entirely on ginger-nuts. Ginger-nuts are so called, because they contain ginger as one of their peculiar constituents, and the final flavoring one. Now, what was ginger? A hot, spicy thing. Was Bartleby hot and spicy? Not at all. Ginger, then, had no effect upon Bartleby. Probably he preferred it should have none.

Nothing so aggravates an earnest person as a passive resistance. If the individual so resisted be of a not inhumane temper, and the resisting one perfectly harmless in his passivity, then, in the better moods of the former, he will endeavor charitably to construe to his imagination what proves impossible to be solved by his judgment. Even so, for the most part, I regarded Bartleby and his ways. Poor fellow! thought I, he means no mischief; it is plain he intends no insolence; his aspect sufficiently evinces that his eccentricities are involuntary. He is useful to me. I can get along with him. If I turn him away, the chances are he will fall in with some less-indulgent employer, and then he will be rudely treated, and perhaps driven forth miserably to starve. Yes. Here I can cheaply purchase a delicious self-approval. To befriend Bartleby; to humor him in his strange willfulness, will cost me little or nothing, while I lay up in my soul what will eventually prove a sweet morsel for my conscience. But this mood was not invariable with me. The passiveness of Bartleby sometimes irritated me. I felt strangely goaded on to encounter him in new opposition—to elicit some angry spark from him answerable to my own. But, indeed, I might as well have essayed to strike fire with my knuckles against a bit of Windsor soap. But one afternoon the evil impulse in me mastered me, and the following little scene ensued:

"Bartleby," said I, "when those papers are all copied, I will compare them with you."

"I would prefer not to."

"How? Surely you do not mean to perist in that mulish vagary?"

No answer.

I threw open the folding-doors near by, and, turning upon Turkey and Nippers, exclaimed:

"Bartleby a second time says, he won't examine his papers. What do you think of it, Turkey?"

It was afternoon, be it remembered. Turkey sat glowing like a brass boiler; his bald head steaming; his hands reeling among his blotted papers.

"Think of it?" roared Turkey; "I think I'll just step behind his screen, and black his eyes for him!"

So saying, Turkey rose to his feet and threw his arms into a

pugilistic position. He was hurrying away to make good his promise, when I detained him, alarmed at the effect of incautiously
rousing Turkey's combativeness after dinner.

"Sit down, Turkey," said I, "and hear what Nippers has to say.
What do you think of it, Nippers? Would I not be justified in
immediately dismissing Bartleby?"

"Excuse me, that is for you to decide, sir. I think his conduct
quite unusual, and, indeed, unjust, as regards Turkey and myself.
But it may only be a passing whim."

"Ah," exclaimed I, "you have strangely changed your mind,
then—you speak very gently of him now."

"All beer," cried Turkey; "gentleness is effects of beer—Nippers
and I dined together to-day. You see how gentle *I* am, sir. Shall
I go and black his eyes?"

"You refer to Bartleby, I suppose. No, not to-day, Turkey," I
replied; "pray, put up your fists."

I closed the doors, and again advanced towards Bartleby. I felt
additional incentives tempting me to my fate. I burned to be
rebelled against again. I remembered that Bartleby never left the
office.

"Bartleby," said I, "Ginger Nut is away; just step around to the
Post Office, won't you? (it was but a three minutes' walk), and
see if there is anything for me."

"I would prefer not to."

"You *will* not?"

"I *prefer* not."

I staggered to my desk, and sat there in a deep study. My blind
inveteracy returned. Was there any other thing in which I could
procure myself to be ignominiously repulsed by this lean, penni-
less wight?—my hired clerk? What added thing is there, perfectly
reasonable, that he will be sure to refuse to do?

"Bartleby!"

No answer.

"Bartleby," in a louder tone.

No answer.

"Bartleby," I roared.

Like a very ghost, agreeable to the laws of magical invocation, at
the third summons, he appeared at the entrance of his hermitage.

"Go to the next room, and tell Nippers to come to me."

"I prefer not to," he respectfully and slowly said, and mildly
disappeared.

"Very good, Bartleby," said I, in a quiet sort of serenely-severe self-possessed tone, intimating the unalterable purpose of some terrible retribution very close at hand. At the moment I half intended something of the kind. But upon the whole, as it was drawing towards my dinner-hour, I thought it best to put on my hat and walk home for the day, suffering much from perplexity and distress of mind.

Shall I acknowledge it? The conclusion of this whole business was, that it soon became a fixed fact of my chambers, that a pale young scrivener, by the name of Bartleby, had a desk there; that he copied for me at the usual rate of four cents a folio (one hundred words); but he was permanently exempt from examining the work done by him, that duty being transferred to Turkey and Nippers, out of compliment, doubtless, to their superior acuteness; moreover, said Bartleby was never, on any account, to be dispatched on the most trivial errand of any sort; and that even if entreated to take upon him such a matter, it was generally understood that he would "prefer not to"—in other words, that he would refuse point-blank.

As days passed on, I became considerably reconciled to Bartleby. His steadiness, his freedom from all dissipation, his incessant industry (except when he chose to throw himself into a standing revery behind his screen), his great stillness, his unalterableness of demeanor under all circumstances, made him a valuable acquisition. One prime thing was this—*he was always there*—first in the morning, continually through the day, and the last at night. I had a singular confidence in his honesty. I felt my most precious papers perfectly safe in his hands. Sometimes, to be sure, I could not, for the very soul of me, avoid falling into sudden spasmodic passions with him. For it was exceeding difficult to bear in mind all the time those strange peculiarities, privileges, and unheard of exemptions, forming the tacit stipulations on Bartleby's part under which he remained in my office. Now and then, in the eagerness of dispatching pressing business, I would inadvertently summon Bartleby, in a short, rapid tone, to put his finger, say, on the incipient tie of a bit of red tape with which I was about compressing some papers. Of course, from behind the screen the usual answer, "I prefer not to," was sure to come; and then, how could a human creature, with the common infirmities of our nature, refrain from bitterly exclaiming upon such perverseness— such unreasonableness. However, every added repulse of this

sort which I received only tended to lessen the probability of my
repeating the inadvertence.

Here it must be said, that according to the custom of most
legal gentlemen occupying chambers in densely-populated law
buildings, there were several keys to my door. One was kept by
a woman residing in the attic, which person weekly scrubbed
and daily swept and dusted my apartments. Another was kept
by Turkey for convenience sake. The third I sometimes carried
in my own pocket. The fourth I knew not who had.

Now, one Sunday morning I happened to go to Trinity Church,
to hear a celebrated preacher, and finding myself rather early on
the ground I thought I would walk around to my chambers for
a while. Luckily, I had my key with me; but upon applying it
to the lock, I found it resisted by something inserted from the
inside. Quite surprised, I called out; when to my consternation
a key was turned from within; and thrusting his lean visage at
me, and holding the door ajar, the apparition of Bartleby appeared, in his shirt sleeves, and otherwise in a strangely tattered
deshabille, saying quietly that he was sorry, but he was deeply
engaged just then, and—preferred not admitting me at present.
In a brief word or two, he moreover added, that perhaps I had
better walk around the block two or three times, and by that time
he would probably have concluded his affairs.

Now, the utterly unsurmised appearance of Bartleby, tenanting
my law-chambers of a Sunday morning, with his cadaverously
gentlemanly *nonchalance*, yet withal firm and self-possessed, had
such a strange effect upon me, that incontinently I slunk away
from my own door, and did as desired. But not without sundry
twinges of impotent rebellion against the mild effrontery of this
unaccountable scrivener. Indeed, it was his wonderful mildness
chiefly, which not only disarmed me, but unmanned me as it
were. For I consider that one, for the time, is a sort of unmanned
when he tranquilly permits his hired clerk to dictate to him, and
order him away from his own premises. Furthermore, I was full
of uneasiness as to what Bartleby could possibly be doing in my
office in his shirt sleeves, and in an otherwise dismantled condition of a Sunday morning. Was anything amiss going on? Nay,
that was out of the question. It was not to be thought of for a
moment that Bartleby was an immoral person. But what could
he be doing there?—copying? Nay again, whatever might be his
eccentricities, Bartleby was an eminently decorous person. He

would be the last man to sit down to his desk in any state approaching to nudity. Besides, it was Sunday; and there was something about Bartleby that forbade the supposition that he would by any secular occupation violate the properties of the day.

Nevertheless, my mind was not pacified; and full of a restless curiosity, at last I returned to the door. Without hindrance I inserted my key, opened it, and entered. Bartleby was not to be seen. I looked round anxiously, peeped behind his screen; but it was very plain that he was gone. Upon more closely examining the place, I surmised that for an indefinite period Bartleby must have ate, dressed, and slept in my office, and that, too without plate, mirror, or bed. The cushioned seat of a rickety old sofa in one corner bore the faint impress of a lean, reclining form. Rolled away under his desk, I found a blanket; under the empty grate, a blacking box and brush; on a chair, a tin basin, with soap and a ragged towel; in a newspaper a few crumbs of ginger-nuts and a morsel of cheese. Yes, thought I, it is evident enough that Bartleby has been making his home here, keeping bachelor's hall all by himself. Immediately then the thought came sweeping across me, what miserable friendlessness and loneliness are here revealed! His poverty is great; but his solitude, how horrible! Think of it. Of a Sunday, Wall Street is deserted as Petra; and every night of every day it is an emptiness. This building, too, which of weekdays hums with industry and life, at nightfall echoes with sheer vacancy, and all through Sunday is forlorn. And here Bartleby makes his home; sole spectator of a solitude which he has seen all populous—a sort of innocent and transformed Marius brooding among the ruins of Carthage!

For the first time in my life a feeling of over-powering stinging melancholy seized me. Before, I had never experienced aught but a not unpleasing sadness. The bond of a common humanity now drew me irresistibly to gloom. A fraternal melancholy! For both I and Bartleby were sons of Adam. I remembered the bright silks and sparkling faces I had seen that day, in gala trim, swanlike sailing down the Mississippi of Broadway; and I contrasted them with the pallid copyist, and thought to myself, Ah, happiness courts the light, so we deem the world is gay; but misery hides aloof, so we deem that misery there is none. These sad fancyings—chimeras, doubtless, of a sick and silly brain—led on to other and more special thoughts, concerning the eccentricities of Bartleby. Presentiments of strange discoveries hovered round me. The scrivener's pale form appeared to me laid out, among uncaring strangers, in its shivering winding sheet.

Suddenly I was attracted by Bartleby's closed desk, the key in open sight left in the lock.

I mean no mischief, seek the gratification of no heartless curiosity, thought I; besides, the desk is mine, and its contents, too, so I will make bold to look within. Everything was methodically arranged, the papers smoothly placed. The pigeon holes were deep, and removing the files of documents, I groped into their recesses. Presently I felt something there, and dragged it out. It was an old bandanna handkerchief, heavy and knotted. I opened it, and saw it was a savings bank.

I now recalled all the quiet mysteries which I had noted in the man. I remembered that he never spoke but to answer; that, though at intervals he had considerable time to himself, yet I had never seen him reading—no, not even a newspaper; that for long periods he would stand looking out, at his pale window behind the screen, upon the dead brick wall; I was quite sure he never visited any refectory or eating house; while his pale face clearly indicated that he never drank beer like Turkey, or tea and coffee even, like other men; that he never went anywhere in particular that I could learn; never went out for a walk, unless, indeed, that was the case at present; that he had declined telling who he was, or whence he came, or whether he had any relatives in the world; that though so thin and pale, he never complained of ill health. And more than all, I remembered a certain unconscious air of pallid—how shall I call it?—of pallid haughtiness, say, or rather an austere reserve about him, which had positively awed me into my tame compliance with his eccentricities, when I had feared to ask him to do the slightest incidental thing for me, even though I might know, from his long-continued motionlessness, that behind his screen he must be standing in one of those dead-wall reveries of his.

Revolving all these things, and coupling them with the recently discovered fact, that he made my office his constant abiding place and home, and not forgetful of his morbid moodiness; revolving all these things, a prudential feeling began to steal over me. My first emotions had been those of pure melancholy and sincerest pity; but just in proportion as the forlornness of Bartleby grew and grew to my imagination, did that same melancholy merge into fear, that pity into repulsion. So true it is, and so terrible, too, that up to a certain point the thought or sight of misery enlists our best affections; but, in certain special cases, beyond that point it does not. They err who would assert that invariably this is owing to the inherent selfishness of the human heart. It rather proceeds from a certain hopelessness of remedying excessive and organic ill. To a sensitive being, pity is not seldom pain. And when at last it is perceived that such pity cannot lead to effectual succor, common sense bids the soul be rid of it. What I saw that morning persuaded me that the scrivener was the victim of innate and incurable disorder. I might give alms to his body; but his body did not pain him; it was his soul that suffered, and his soul I could not reach.

I did not accomplish the purpose of going to Trinity Church that morning. Somehow, the things I had seen disqualified me for the time from church-going. I walked homeward, thinking what I would do with Bartleby. Finally, I resolved upon this—I would put certain calm questions to him the next morning, touching his history, etc., and if he declined to answer them openly and unreservedly (and I supposed he would prefer not), then to give him a twenty dollar bill over and above whatever I might owe him, and tell him his services were no longer required; but that if in any other way I could assist him, I would be happy to do so, especially if he desired to return to his native place, wherever that might be, I would willingly help to defray the expenses. Moreover, if, after reaching home, he found himself at any time in want of aid, a letter from him would be sure of a reply.

The next morning came.

"Bartleby," said I, gently calling to him behind his screen.

No reply.

"Bartleby," said I, in a still gentler tone, "come here; I am not going to ask you to do anything you would prefer not to do—I simply wish to speak to you."

Upon this he noiselessly slid into view.

"Will you tell me, Bartleby, where you were born?"

"I would prefer not to."

"Will you tell me *anything* about yourself?"

"I would prefer not to."

"But what reasonable objection can you have to speak to me? I feel friendly towards you."

He did not look at me while I spoke, but kept his glance fixed upon my bust of Cicero, which, as I then sat, was directly behind me, some six inches above my head.

"What is your answer, Bartleby," said I, after waiting a considerable time for a reply, during which his countenance remained immovable, only there was the faintest conceivable tremor of the white attenuated mouth.

"At present I prefer to give no answer," he said, and retired into his hermitage.

It was rather weak in me I confess, but his manner, on this occasion, nettled me. Not only did there seem to lurk in it a certain calm disdain, but his perverseness seemed ungrateful, considering the undeniable good usage and indulgence he had received from me.

Again I sat ruminating what I should do. Mortified as I was at his behavior, and resolved as I had been to dismiss him when I entered my office, nevertheless I strangely felt something superstitious knocking at my heart, and forbidding me to carry out my purpose, and denouncing me for a villain if I dared to breathe one bitter word against this forlornest of mankind. At last, familiarly drawing my chair behind his screen, I sat down and said: "Bartleby, never mind, then, about revealing your history; but let me entreat you, as a friend, to comply as far as may be with the usages of this office. Say now, you will help to examine papers to-morrow or next day: in short, say now, that in a day or two you will begin to be a little reasonable:—say so, Bartleby."

"At present I would prefer not to be a little reasonable," was his mildly cadaverous reply.

Just then the folding-doors opened, and Nippers approached. He seemed suffering from an unusually bad night's rest, induced by severer indigestion than common. He overheard those final words of Bartleby.

"*Prefer not*, eh?" gritted Nippers—"I'd *prefer* him, if I were you, sir," addressing me—"I'd *prefer* him; I'd give him, preferences, the stubborn mule! What is it, sir, pray, that he *prefers* not to do now?"

Bartleby moved not a limb.

"Mr. Nippers," said I, "I'd prefer that you withdraw for the present."

Somehow, of late, I had got into the way of involuntarily using this word "prefer" upon all sorts of not exactly suitable occasions. And I trembled to think that my contact with the scrivener had already and seriously affected me in a mental way. And what further and deeper aberration might it not yet produce? This apprehension had not been without efficacy in determining me to summary measures.

As Nippers, looking very sour and sulky, was departing, Turkey blandly and deferentially approached.

"With submission, sir," said he, "yesterday I was thinking about Bartleby here, and I think that if he would but prefer to take a quart of good ale every day, it would do much towards mending him, and enabling him to assist in examining his papers."

"So you have got the word, too," said I slightly excited.

"With submission, what word, sir," asked Turkey, respectfully crowding himself into the contracted space behind the screen, and by so doing, making me jostle the scrivener. "What word, sir?"

"I would prefer to be left alone here," said Bartleby, as if offended at being mobbed in his privacy.

"*That's* the word, Turkey," said I—"*that's* it."

"Oh, *prefer*? oh yes—queer word. I never use it myself. But, sir, as I was saying, if he would but prefer—"

"Turkey," interrupted I, "you will please withdraw."

"Oh, certainly, sir, if you prefer that I should."

As he opened the folding-door to retire, Nippers at his desk caught a glimpse of me, and asked whether I would prefer to have a certain paper copied on blue paper or white. He did not in the least roguishly accent the word prefer. It was plain that it involuntarily rolled from his tongue. I thought to myself, surely I must get rid of a demented man, who already has in some degree turned the tongues, if not the heads of myself and clerks. But I thought it prudent not to break the dismission at once.

The next day I noticed that Bartleby did nothing but stand at his window in his dead-wall revery. Upon asking him why he did not write, he said that he had decided upon doing no more writing.

"Why, how now? what next?" exclaimed I, "do no more writing?"

"No more."

"And what is the reason?"

"Do you not see the reason for yourself," he indifferently replied.

I looked steadfastly at him, and perceived that his eyes looked dull and glazed. Instantly it occurred to me, that his unexampled diligence in copying by his dim window for the first few weeks of his stay with me might have temporarily impaired his vision.

I was touched. I said something in condolence with him. I hinted that of course he did wisely in abstaining from writing for a while; and urged him to embrace the opportunity of taking wholesome exercise in the open air. This, however, he did not do. A few days after this, my other clerks being absent, and being in a great hurry to dispatch certain letters by the mail, I thought that, having nothing else earthly to do, Bartleby would surely be less inflexible than usual, and carry these letters to the post-office. But he blankly declined. So, much to my inconvenience, I went myself.

Still added days went by. Whether Bartleby's eyes improved or not, I could not say. To all appearance, I thought they did. But when I asked him if they did, he vouchsafed no answer. At all events, he would do no copying. At last, in reply to my urgings, he informed me that he had permanently given up copying.

"What!" exclaimed I; "suppose your eyes should get entirely well—better than ever before—would you not copy then?"

"I have given up copying," he answered, and slid aside.

He remained as ever, a fixture in my chamber. Nay—if that were possible—he became still more of a fixture than before. What was to be done? He would do nothing in the office; why should he stay there? In plain fact, he had now become a millstone to me, not only useless as a necklace, but afflictive to bear. Yet I was sorry for him. I speak less than truth when I say that, on his own account, he occasioned me uneasiness. If he would but have named a single relative or friend, I would instantly have written, and urged their taking the poor fellow away to some convenient retreat. But he seemed alone, absolutely alone in the universe. A bit of wreck in the mid Atlantic. At length, necessities connected with my business tyrannized over all other considerations. Decently as I could, I told Bartleby that in six days time he must unconditionally leave the office. I warned him to take measures, in the interval, for procuring some other abode. I offered to assist him in this endeavor, if he himself would but take the first step towards a removal. "And when you finally quit me, Bartleby," added I, "I shall see that you go not away entirely unprovided. Six days from this hour, remember."

At the expiration of that period, I peeped behind the screen, and lo! Bartleby was there.

I buttoned up my coat, balanced myself; advanced slowly toward him, touched his shoulder, and said, "The time has come; you must quit this place; I am sorry for you; here is money; but you must go."

"I would prefer not," he replied, with his back still toward me.

"You *must.*"

He remained silent.

Now I had an unbounded confidence in this man's common honesty. He had frequently restored to me sixpences and shillings carelessly dropped upon the floor, for I am apt to be very reckless in such shirt-button affairs. The proceeding, then, which followed will not be deemed extraordinary.

"Bartleby," said I, "I owe you twelve dollars on account; here are thirty-two; the odd twenty are yours—Will you take it?" and I handed the bills towards him.

But he made no motion.

"I will leave them here, then," putting them under a weight on the table. Then taking my hat and cane and going to the door, I tranquilly turned and added—"After you have removed your things from these offices, Bartleby, you will of course lock the door—since every one is now gone for the day but you—and if you please, slip your key underneath the mat, so that I may have it in the morning. I shall not see you again; so good-by to you. If, hereafter, in your new place of abode, I can be of any service to you, do not fail to advise me by letter. Good-by, Bartleby, and fare you well."

But he answered not a word; like the last column of some ruined temple, he remained standing mute and solitary in the middle of the otherwise deserted room.

As I walked home in a pensive mood, my vanity got the better of my pity. I could not but highly plume myself on my masterly management in getting rid of Bartleby. Masterly I call it, and such it must appear to any dispassionate thinker. The beauty of my procedure seemed to consist in its perfect quietness. There was no vulgar bullying, no bravado of any sort, no choleric hectoring, and striding to and fro across the apartment, jerking out vehement commands for Bartleby to bundle himself off with his beggarly traps. Nothing of the kind. Without loudly bidding Bartleby depart—as an inferior genius might have done—I *assumed* the ground that depart he must; and upon that assumption built all I had to say. The more I thought over my procedure, the more I was charmed with it. Nevertheless, next morning, upon awakening, I had my doubts—I had somehow slept off the fumes of vanity. One of the coolest and wisest hours a man has, is just after he awakes in the morning. My procedure seemed as sagacious as ever—but only in theory. How it would prove in practice—there was the rub. It was truly a beautiful thought to have assumed Bartleby's departure; but, after all, that assumption was simply my own, and none of Bartleby's. The great point was, not whether I had assumed that he would quit me, but whether he would prefer so to do. He was more a man of preferences than assumptions.

After breakfast, I walked down town, arguing the probabilities *pro* and *con*. One moment I thought it would prove a miserable failure, and Bartleby would be found all alive at my office as usual; the next moment it seemed certain that I should find his chair empty. And so I kept veering about. At the corner of Broadway and Canal Street, I saw quite an excited group of people standing in earnest conversation.

"I'll take odds he doesn't," said a voice as I passed.

"Doesn't go?—done!" said I, "put up your money."

I was instinctively putting my hand in my pocket to produce my own, when I remembered that this was an election day. The words I had overheard bore no reference to Bartleby, but to the success or non-success of some candidate for the mayoralty. In my intent frame of mind, I had, as it were, imagined that all Broadway shared in my excitement, and were debating the same question with me. I passed on, very thankful that the uproar of the street screened my momentary absent-mindedness.

As I had intended, I was earlier than usual at my office door. I stood listening for a moment. All was still. He must be gone. I tried the knob. The door was locked. Yes, my procedure had worked to a charm; he indeed must be vanished. Yet a certain melancholy mixed with this: I was almost sorry for my brilliant success. I was fumbling under the door mat for the key, which Bartleby was to have left there for me, when accidentally my knee knocked against a panel, producing a summoning sound, and in response a voice came to me from within—"Not yet; I am occupied."

It was Bartleby.

I was thunderstruck. For an instant I stood like the man who, pipe in mouth, was killed one cloudless afternoon long ago in

Virginia, by summer lightning; at his own warm open window he was killed, and remained leaning out there upon the dreamy afternoon, till some one touched him, when he fell.

"Not gone!" I murmured at last. But again obeying that wondrous ascendancy which the inscrutable scrivener had over me, and from which ascendancy, for all my chafing, I could not completely escape, I slowly went down stairs and out into the street, and while walking round the block, considered what I should next do in this unheard-of perplexity. Turn the man out by an actual thrusting I could not; to drive him away by calling him hard names would not do; calling in the police was an unpleasant idea; and yet, permit him to enjoy his cadaverous triumph over me—this, too, I could not think of. What was to be done? or, if nothing could be done, was there anything further that I could *assume* in the matter? Yes, as before I had prospectively assumed that Bartleby would depart, so now I might retrospectively assume that departed he was. In the legitimate carrying out of this assumption, I might enter my office in a great hurry, and pretending not to see Bartleby at all, walk straight against him as if he were air. Such a proceeding would in a singular degree have the appearance of a home-thrust. It was hardly possible that Bartleby could withstand such an application of the doctrine of assumptions. But upon second thoughts the success of the plan seemed rather dubious. I resolved to argue the matter over with him again.

"Bartleby," said I, entering the office, with a quietly severe expression, "I am seriously displeased. I am pained, Bartleby. I had thought better of you. I had imagined you of such a gentlemanly organization, that in any delicate dilemma a slight hint would suffice—in short, an assumption. But it appears I am deceived. Why," I added, unaffectedly starting, "you have not even touched that money yet," pointing to it, just where I had left it the evening previous.

He answered nothing.

"Will you, or will you not, quit me?" I now demanded in a sudden passion, advancing close to him.

"I would prefer *not* to quit you," he replied, gently emphasizing the *not*.

"What earthly right have you to stay here? Do you pay any rent? Do you pay my taxes? Or is this property yours?"

He answered nothing.

"Are you ready to go on and write now? Are your eyes recovered? Could you copy a small paper for me this morning? or help examine a few lines? or step round to the post-office? In a word, will you do anything at all, to give a coloring to your refusal to depart the premises?"

He silently retired into his hermitage.

I was now in such a state of nervous resentment that I thought it but prudent to check myself at present from further demonstrations. Bartleby and I were alone. I remembered the tragedy of the unfortunate Adams and the still more unfortunate Colt in the solitary office of the latter; and how poor Colt, being dreadfully incensed by Adams, and imprudently permitting himself to get wildly excited, was at unawares hurried into his fatal act—an act which certainly no man could possibly deplore more than the actor himself. Often it had occurred to me in my pondering upon the subject, that had that altercation taken place in the public street, or at a private residence, it would not have terminated as it did. It was the circumstance of being alone in a solitary office, up stairs, of a building entirely unhallowed by humanizing domestic associations—an uncarpeted office, doubtless, of a dusty, haggard sort of appearance—this it must have been, which greatly helped to enhance the irritable desperation of the hapless Colt.

But when this old Adam of resentment rose in me and tempted me concerning Bartleby, I grappled him and threw him. How? Why, simply by recalling the divine injunction: "A new commandment give I unto you, that ye love one another." Yes, this it was that saved me. Aside from higher considerations, charity often operates as a vastly wise and prudent principle—a great safeguard to its possessor. Men have committed murder for jealousy's sake, and anger's sake, and hatred's sake, and selfishness' sake, and spiritual pride's sake; but no man, that ever I heard of, ever committed a diabolical murder for sweet charity's sake. Mere self-interest, then, if no better motive can be enlisted, should, especially with high-tempered men, prompt all beings to charity and philanthropy. At any rate, upon the occasion in question, I strove to drown my exasperated feelings towards the scrivener by benevolently construing his conduct. Poor fellow, poor fellow! thought I, he don't mean anything; and besides, he has seen hard times, and ought to be indulged.

I endeavored, also, immediately to occupy myself, and at the same time to comfort my despondency. I tried to fancy, that in the course of the morning, at such time as might prove agreeable to him, Bartleby, of his own free accord, would emerge from his hermitage and take up some decided line of march in the direction of the door. But no. Half-past twelve o'clock came; Turkey began to glow in the face, overturn his inkstand, and become generally obstreperous; Nippers abated down into quietude and courtesy; Ginger Nut munched his noon apple; and Bartleby remained standing at his window in one of his profoundest dead-wall reveries. Will it be credited? Ought I to acknowledge it? That afternoon I left the office without saying one further word to him.

Some days now passed, during which, at leisure intervals I looked a little into "Edwards on the Will," and "Priestly on Necessity." Under the circumstances, those books induced a salutary feeling. Gradually I slid into the persuasion that these troubles of mine, touching the scrivener, had been all predestinated from eternity, and Bartleby was billeted upon me for some mysterious purpose of an allwise Providence, which it was not for a mere mortal like me to fathom. Yes, Bartleby, stay there behind your screen, thought I; I shall persecute you no more; you are harmless and noiseless as any of these old chairs; in short, I never feel so private as when I know you are here. At last I see it, I feel it; I penetrate to the predestinated purpose of my life. I am content. Others may have loftier parts to enact; but my mission in this world, Bartleby, is to furnish you with office-room for such period as you may see fit to remain.

I believe that this wise and blessed frame of mind would have continued with me, had it not been for the unsolicited and uncharitable remarks obtruded upon me by my professional friends who visited the rooms. But thus it often is, that the constant friction of illiberal minds wears out at last the best resolves of the more generous. Though to be sure, when I reflected upon it, it was not strange that people entering my office should be struck by the peculiar aspect of the unaccountable Bartleby, and so be tempted to throw out some sinister observations concerning him. Sometimes an attorney, having business with me, and calling at my office, and finding no one but the scrivener there, would undertake to obtain some sort of precise information from him touching my whereabouts; but without heeding his idle talk, Bartleby would remain standing immovable in the middle of the room. So after contemplating him in that position for a time, the attorney would depart, no wiser than he came.

Also, when a reference was going on, and the room full of

lawyers and witnesses, and business driving fast, some deeply-occupied legal gentleman present, seeing Bartleby wholly un-employed, would request him to run round to his (the legal gentleman's) office and fetch some papers for him. Thereupon, Bartleby would tranquilly decline, and yet remain idle as before. Then the lawyer would give a great stare, and turn to me. And what could I say? At last I was made aware that all through the circle of my professional acquaintance, a whisper of wonder was running round, having references to the strange creature I kept at my office. This worried me very much. And as the idea came upon me of his possibly turning out a long-lived man, and keep occupying my chambers, and denying my authority; and perplexing my visitors; and scandalizing my professional reputation; and casting a general gloom over the premises; keeping soul and body together to the last upon his savings (for doubtless he spent but half a dime a day), and in the end perhaps outlive me, and claim possession of my office by right of his perpetual occupancy: as all these dark anticipations crowded upon me more and more, and my friends continually intruded their relentless remarks upon the apparition in my room; a great change was wrought in me. I resolved to gather all my faculties together, and forever rid me of this intolerable incubus.

Ere revolving any complicated project, however, adapted to this end, I first simply suggested to Bartleby the propriety of his permanent departure. In a calm and serious tone, I commended the idea to his careful and mature consideration. but, having taken three days to meditate upon it, he apprised me, that his original determination remained the same; in short, that he still preferred to abide with me.

What shall I do? I now said to myself, buttoning up my coat to the last button. What shall I do? what ought I to do? what does conscience say I *should* do with this man, or, rather, ghost. Rid myself of him, I must; go, he shall. But how? You will not thrust him, the poor, pale, passive mortal—you will not thrust such a helpless creature out of your door? you will not dishonor yourself by such cruelty? No, I will not, I cannot do that, Rather would I let him live and die here, and then mason up his remains in the wall. What, then, will you do? For all your coaxing, he will not budge. Bribes he leaves under your own paper-weight on your table; in short, it is quite plain that he prefers to cling to you.

Then something severe, something unusual must be done.

What! surely you will not have him collared by a constable, and commit his innocent pallor to the common jail? And upon what ground could you procure such a thing to be done?—a vagrant, is he? What! he a vagrant, a wanderer, who refuses to budge? It is because he will *not* be a vagrant, then, that you seek to count him *as* a vagrant. That is too absurd. No visible means of support: there I have him. Wrong again: for indubitably he *does* support himself, and that is the only unanswerable proof that any man can show of his possessing the means so to do. No more, then. Since he will not quit me, I must quit him. I will change my offices; I will move elsewhere, and give him fair notice, that if I find him on my new premises I will then proceed against him as a common trespasser.

Acting accordingly, next day I thus addressed him: "I find these chambers too far from the City Hall; the air is unwholesome. In a word, I propose to remove my offices next week, and shall no longer require your services. I tell you this now, in order that you may seek another place."

He made no reply, and nothing more was said.

On the appointed day I engaged carts and men, proceeded to my chambers, and, having but little furniture, everything was removed in a few hours. Throughout, the scrivener remained standing behind the screen, which I directed to be removed the last thing. It was withdrawn; and, being folded up like a huge folio, left him the motionless occupant of a naked room. I stood in the entry watching him a moment, while something from within me upbraided me.

I re-entered, with my hand in my pocket—and—and my heart in my mouth.

"Good-by, Bartleby; I am going—good-by, and God some way bless you; and take that," slipping something in his hand. But it dropped upon the floor, and then—strange to say—I tore myself from him whom I had so longed to be rid of.

Established in my new quarters, for a day or two I kept the door locked, and started at every footfall in the passages. When I returned to my rooms, after any little absence, I would pause at the threshold for an instant, and attentively listen, ere applying my key. But these fears were needless. Bartleby never came nigh me.

I thought all was going well, when a perturbed-looking stranger visited me, inquiring whether I was the person who had recently occupied rooms at No.— Wall Street.

Full of forebodings, I replied that I was.

"Then, sir," said the stranger, who proved a lawyer, "you are responsible for the man you left there. He refuses to do any copying; he refuses to do anything; he says he prefers not to; and he refuses to quit the premises."

"I am very sorry, sir," said I, with assumed tranquillity, but an inward tremor, "but, really, the man you allude to is nothing to me—he is no relation or apprentice of mine, that you should hold me responsible for him."

"In mercy's name, who is he?"

"I certainly cannot inform you. I know nothing about him. Formerly I employed him as a copyist; but he has done nothing for me now for some time past."

"I shall settle him, then—good morning, sir."

Several days passed, and I heard nothing more; and, though I often felt a charitable prompting to call at the place and see poor Bartleby, yet a certain squeamishness, of I know not what, withheld me.

All is over with him, by this time, thought I, at last, when, through another week, no further intelligence reached me. But, coming to my room the day after, I found several persons waiting at my door in a high state of nervous excitement.

"That's the man—here he comes," cried the foremost one, whom I recognized as the lawyer who had previously called upon me alone.

"You must take him away, sir, at once," cried a portly person among them, advancing upon me, and whom I knew to be the landlord of No.— Wall Street. "These gentlemen, my tenants, cannot stand it any longer; Mr. B—," pointing to the lawyer, "has turned him out of his room, and he now persists in haunting the building generally, sitting upon the banisters of the stairs by day, and sleeping in the entry by night. Everybody is concerned; clients are leaving the offices; some fears are entertained of a mob; something you must do, and that without delay."

Aghast at this torrent, I fell back before it, and would fain have locked myself in my new quarters. In vain I persisted that Bartleby was nothing to me—no more than to any one else. In vain—I was the last person known to have anything to do with him, and they held me to the terrible account. Fearful, then, of being exposed in the papers (as one person present obscurely threatened), I considered the matter, and, at length, said, that if the lawyer would give me a confidential interview with the scrivener, in his (the lawyer's) own room, I would, that afternoon, strive my best to rid them of the nuisance they complained of.

Going up stairs to my old haunt, there was Bartleby silently sitting upon the banister at the landing.

"What are you doing here, Bartleby?" said I.

"Sitting upon the banister," he mildly replied.

I motioned him into the lawyer's room, who then left us.

"Bartleby," said I, "are you aware that you are the cause of great tribulation to me, by persisting in occupying the entry after being dismissed from the office?"

No answer.

"Now one of two things must take place. Either you must do something, or something must be done to you. Now what sort of business would you like to engage in? Would you like to re-engage in copying for some one?"

"No; I would prefer not to make any change."

"Would you like a clerkship in a dry-goods store?"

"There is too much confinement about that. No, I would not like a clerkship; but I am not particular."

"Too much confinement," I cried, "why you keep yourself confined all the time!"

"I would prefer not to take a clerkship," he rejoined, as if to settle that little item at once.

"How would a bar-tender's business suit you? There is no trying of the eye-sight in that."

"I would not like it at all; though, as I said before, I am not particular."

His unwonted wordiness inspirited me. I returned to the charge.

"Well, then, would you like to travel through the country collecting bills for the merchants? That would improve your health."

"No, I would prefer to be doing something else."

"How, then, would going as a companion to Europe, to entertain some young gentleman with your conversation—how would that suit you?"

"Not at all. It does not strike me that there is anything definite about that. I like to be stationary. But I am not particular."

"Stationary you shall be, then," I cried, now losing all patience, and, for the first time in all my exasperating connection with him, fairly flying into a passion. "If you do not go away from these premises before night, I shall feel bound—indeed, I *am* bound—

to—to—to quit the premises myself!" I rather absurdly concluded, knowing not with what possible threat to try to frighten his immobility into compliance. Despairing of all further efforts, I was precipitately leaving him, when a final thought occurred to me—one which had not been wholly unindulged before.

"Bartleby," said I, in the kindest tone I could assume under such exciting circumstances, "will you go home with me now—not to my office, but my dwelling—and remain there till we can conclude upon some convenient arrangement for you at our leisure? Come, let us start now, right away."

"No: at present I would prefer not to make any change at all."

I answered nothing; but, effectually dodging every one by the suddenness and rapidity of my flight, rushed from the building, ran up Wall Street towards Broadway, and jumping into the first omnibus, was soon removed from pursuit. As soon as tranquillity returned, I distinctly perceived that I had now done all that I possibly could, both in respect to the demands of the landlord and his tenants, and with regard to my own desire and sense of duty, to benefit Bartleby, and shield him from rude persecution. I now strove to be entirely care-free and quiescent; and my conscience justified me in the attempt; though, indeed, it was not so successful as I could have wished. So fearful was I of being again hunted out by the incensed landlord and his exasperated tenants, that, surrendering my business to Nippers, for a few days, I drove about the upper part of the town and through the suburbs, in my rockaway; crossed over to Jersey City and Hoboken, and paid fugitive visits to Manhattanville and Astoria. In fact, I almost lived in my rockaway for the time.

When again I entered my office, lo, a note from the landlord lay upon the desk. I opened it with trembling hands. It informed me that the writer had sent to the police, and had Bartleby removed to the Tombs as a vagrant. Moreover, since I knew more about him than any one else, he wished me to appear at that place, and make a suitable statement of the facts. These tidings had a conflicting effect upon me. At first I was indignant; but, at last, almost approved. The landlord's energetic, summary disposition, had led him to adopt a procedure which I do not think I would have decided upon myself; and yet, as a last resort, under such peculiar circumstances, it seemed the only plan.

As I afterwards learned, the poor scrivener, when told that he must be conducted to the Tombs, offered not the slightest obstacle, but, in his pale, unmoving way, silently acquiesced.

Some of the compassionate and curious bystanders joined the party; and headed by one of the constables arm in arm with Bartleby, the silent procession filed its way through all the noise, and heat, and joy of the roaring thoroughfares at noon.

The same day I received the note, I went to the Tombs, or, to speak more properly, the Halls of Justice. Seeking the right officer, I stated the purpose of my call, and was informed that the individual I described was, indeed, within. I then assured the functionary that Bartleby was a perfectly honest man, and greatly to be compassionated, however, unaccountably eccentric. I narrated all I knew, and closed by suggesting the idea of letting him remain in as indulgent confinement as possible, till something less harsh might be done—though, indeed, I hardly knew what. At all events, if nothing else could be decided upon, the alms-house must receive him. I then begged to have an interview.

Being under no disgraceful charge, and quite serene and harmless in all his ways, they had permitted him freely to wander about the prison, and, especially, in the inclosed grass-platted yards thereof. And so I found him there, standing all alone in the quietest of the yards, his face towards a high wall, while all around, from the narrow slits of the jail windows, I thought I saw peering out upon him the eyes of murderers and thieves.

"Bartleby!"

"I know you," he said, without looking round—"and I want nothing to say to you."

"It was not I that brought you here, Bartleby," said I, keenly pained at his implied suspicion. "And to you, this should not be so vile a place. Nothing reproachful attaches to you by being here. And see, it is not so sad a place as one might think. Look, there is the sky, and here is the grass."

"I know where I am," he replied, but would say nothing more, and so I left him.

As I entered the corridor again, a broad meat-like man, in an apron, accosted me, and, jerking his thumb over his shoulder, said—"Is that your friend?"

"Yes."

"Does he want to starve? If he does, let him live on the prison fare, that's all."

"Who are you?" asked I, not knowing what to make of such an unofficially speaking person in such a place.

"I am the grub-man. Such gentlemen as have friends here, hire me to provide them with something good to eat."

"Is this so?" said I, turning to the turnkey.

He said it was.

"Well, then," said I, slipping some silver into the grub-man's hands (for so they called him), "I want you to give particular attention to my friend there; let him have the best dinner you can get. And you must be as polite to him as possible."

"Introduce me, will you?" said the grub-man, looking at me with an expression which seemed to say he was all impatience for an opportunity to give a specimen of his breeding.

Thinking it would prove of benefit to the scrivener, I acquiesced; and, asking the grub-man his name, went up with him to Bartleby.

"Bartleby, this is a friend; you will find him very useful to you."

"Your sarvant, sir, your sarvant," said the grub-man, making a low salutation behind his apron. "Hope you find it pleasant her, sir; nice grounds—cool apartments—hope you'll stay with us sometime—try to make it agreeable. What will you have for dinner to-day?"

"I prefer not to dine to-day," said Bartleby, turning away. "It would disagree with me; I am unused to dinners." So saying, he slowly moved to the other side of the inclosure, and took up a position fronting the dead-wall.

"How's this?" said the grub-man, addressing me with a stare of astonishment. "He's odd, ain't he?"

"I think he is a little deranged," said I, sadly.

"Deranged? deranged is it? Well, now, upon my word, I thought that friend of yourn was a gentleman forger; they are always pale and genteel-like, them forgers. I can't help pity 'em—can't help it, sir. Did you know Monroe Edwards?" he added, touchingly, and paused. Then, laying his hand piteously on my shoulder, sighed, "he died of consumption at Sing-Sing. So you weren't acquainted with Monroe?"

"No, I was never socially acquainted with any forgers. But I cannot stop longer. Look to my friend yonder. You will not lose by it. I will see you again."

Some few days after this, I again obtained admission to the

Tombs, and went through the corridors in quest of Bartleby; but without finding him.

"I saw him coming from his cell not long ago," said a turnkey, "may be he's gone to loiter in the yards."

So I went in that direction.

"Are you looking for the silent man?" said another turnkey, passing me. "Yonder he lies—sleeping in the yard there. 'Tis not twenty minutes since I saw him lie down."

The yard was entirely quiet. It was not accessible to the common prisoners. The surrounding walls, of amazing thickness, kept off all sounds behind them. The Egyptian character of the masonry weighed upon me with its gloom. But a soft imprisoned turf grew under foot. The heart of the eternal pyramids, it seemed, wherein, by some strange magic, through the clefts, grass-seed, dropped by birds, had sprung.

Strangely huddled at the base of the wall, his knees drawn up, and lying on his side, his head touching the cold stones, I saw the wasted Bartleby. But nothing stirred. I paused; then went close up to him; stooped over, and saw that his dim eyes were open; otherwise he seemed profoundly sleeping. Something prompted me to touch him. I felt his hand, when a tingling shiver ran up my arm and down my spine to my feet.

The round face of the grub-man peered upon me now. "His dinner is ready. Won't he dine to-day, either? Or does he live without dining?"

"Lives without dining," said I, and closed the eyes.

"Eh!—He's asleep, ain't he?"

"With kings and counselors," murmured I.

There would seem little need for proceeding further in this history. Imagination will readily supply the meagre recital of poor Bartleby's interment. But, ere parting with the reader, let me say, that if this little narrative has sufficiently interested him, to awaken curiosity as to who Bartleby was, and what manner of life he led prior to the present narrator's making his acquaintance, I can only reply, that in such curiosity I fully share, but am wholly unable to gratify it. Yet here I hardly know whether I should divulge one little item of rumor, which came to my ear a few months after the scrivener's decease. Upon what basis it rested, I could never ascertain; and hence, how true it is I cannot now tell. But, in-asmuch as this vague report has not been without a certain suggestive interest to me, however sad, it may prove the same with some others; and so I will briefly mention it. The report was this: that Bartleby had been a subordinate clerk in the Dead Letter Office at Washington, from which he had been suddenly removed by a change in the administration. When I think over this rumor, hardly can I express the emotions which seize me. Dead letters! does it not sound like dead men? Conceive a man by nature and misfortune prone to a pallid hopelessness, can any business seem more fitted to heighten it than that of continually handling these dead letters, and assorting them for the flames? For by the cart-load they are annually burned. Sometimes from out the folded paper the pale clerk takes a ring—the finger it was meant for, perhaps, moulders in the grave; a bank-note sent in swiftest charity—he whom it would relieve, nor eats nor hungers any more; pardon for those who died despairing; hope for those who died unhoping; good tidings for those who died stifled by unrelieved calamities. On errands of life, these letters speed to death.

Ah, Bartleby! Ah, humanity!

HUMOR

Congress in Crisis: The Proximity Bill

GARRISON KEILLOR

T HE NINETY-THIRD CONGRESS CONVENED in January in very poor light, overshadowed as it was by the President's initiatives abroad and beset by dark omens of declining power, if not actual impotence. Among members of both parties, there was general agreement that Congress must act soon to reassert itself as a separate and equal branch of the national government, especially since congressmen found, upon opening their January pay envelopes, that an additional $25.75 had been deducted under "Misc." Calls to the Treasury Department failed to clear up the matter, largely because telephone service is so poor on the Hill. Most members have been put on party lines by a recent presidential directive aimed at curbing inflation, and telephone static is very heavy on cold days and whenever it rains.

Nowhere is the disparity of power between executive and legislative branches more evident, however, than in the area of personal inviolability. While the Presidency is whisked away to Camp David without an unfriendly eye laid on it, it isn't uncommon to see the legislative branch late at night pacing the Capitol sidewalk and calling into the darkness for a cab. The Presidency's path is cleared by squadrons of dark brown suits that carefully secure the area against perturbed or irked individuals. *Nobody*

261

says "Hey! You!" within earshot of the Presidency. Congress walks crowded hallways and waits for elevators like the rest of us. Sometimes individuals laugh right in Congress's face. Sometimes a person yells, "Whaddaya mean, this is *your* cab? Bark off, bozo!" and almost slams the door on Congress's fingers. And every time it is jostled or its shoulder grabbed or its fingers almost pinched, a little bit of power is drained away.

The fact of legislative vulnerability was borne out dramatically on February 6, when a young man accosted Representative Frank L. Riemer (R–Cal.) in the foyer of the Rayburn Building and announced that he wanted to talk about the expanding economy and its dangerous effects on the life cycle. Rep. Riemer, whose record on environmental issues is quite good, smiled and welcomed the visitor to Washington, whereupon the youth grasped him in a bear hug and wouldn't let go. "We are one," the youth said calmly. "We embrace. We participate. We are part of each other. If one creature suffers, it must be felt by all. It is time to communicate that. It is time to go that extra mile."

With Rep. Riemer protesting strenuously, the young man then carried him outdoors, across the lawn, up the Capitol steps, and all the way to the door of the House chamber before the congressman got the attention of a guard and was let go.

Congress was naturally concerned about the incident, and a few weeks later it saw the need for new and stricter legislation when the youth was acquitted of the charge of obstructing a federal official in the performance of his duties. Defense counsel argued successfully that the accused had not obstructed the lawmaker but in fact had transported him to his place of work—a theory supported by testimony from the guard, who had heard the congressman's cry of "How dare you!" (or so Riemer testified) as a call for "More bearers!" Furthermore, defense argued, the act was not hostile but an act of love and commitment; the youth was a seminarian and presumably knew what he was doing. "His sole intent," defense stated, "was to indicate—and certainly any reasonable person would agree—that it was high time for the legislative branch to get cracking."

In directing acquittal, the trial judge complained of vagueness in the obstruction statute. "It is difficult for us under the present law as written to distinguish between actual obstruction and the perseverance of a citizen exercising his right to petition," he said, and he called on Congress to provide clearer guidelines.

The following Monday, a House Internal Security subcommittee took the matter under investigation and, to nobody's surprise, uncovered numerous instances of congressmen grasped and handled by dissident individuals. Several had been set upon by persons who, citing some moral imperative, had bound the lawmakers to themselves with twine or thread. Added to the twinings were scores of bumpings, hand-holdings, sleeve-tuggings, chest-pokings, and extremely proximitous starings and breathings. Forty-three congressmen testified or submitted affidavits, including one who recounted this episode:

> On leaving the floor to return to my office, I was aware of being followed at a close distance by a woman who seemed extremely upset. When I turned around to get a good look at her, she displayed an outstretched forefinger in a threatening manner. She closed in as we came to a group of tourists. I was then fairly certain that she intended to goose me.... I was caught in the crowd and couldn't get away. As I struggled across the Rotunda...

Thus the legislation that came to be known as the Proximity Bill began to take shape. In its first draft, it read as follows:

> (1) It is the finding of Congress that Members of Congress are subject to licentious, unwarranted, and vexatious acts upon or near their persons without their consent, and that such acts do hinder, distract, or otherwise obstruct said Members from the performance of their duties.
> (2) Therefore, it shall be unlawful, and punishable by a fine of not more than $1000, or imprisonment for not more than a year, or both, for any person or persons to cross state lines, or wear, display, or employ any article of clothing or any other object that has crossed state lines, to approach a Member of Congress with the thought, idea, or intention of performing said acts, including embracing, the holding of hands or other extremities, grasping of clothing, poking, pushing, lifting, or carrying, shouting at a distance of less than fifty feet, likewise singing or humming at a distance of less than ten feet, or the expulsion of breath upon said Member, or any sort of prolonged and unconsented-to proximity, whether for the purpose of portraying, communicating, or

dramatizing ethical, spiritual, moral, or political principles, theories, or beliefs, or any other purpose.

Though the bill has yet to be reported out of committee, many congressmen are thought to have expressed support for it, and passage by both houses is considered not unlikely. It is felt, however, that the use of the interstate-commerce clause of the Constitution may need to be reconsidered—that the bill, as now written, leaves room for residents of the District of Columbia to perform such acts in the nude. Rep. Riemer has said that the bill should also prohibit obscene, vulgar, offensive, or "inappropriate" sounds or speech. And some congressmen are said to believe that similar protection should be granted to all citizens.

It is known that in its deliberations the subcommittee has been looking very closely at *N.Y. Rangers* v. *Flint*, 484 F.2d 143 (11th Cir. 1971), cert. den. 415 U.S. 703 (1972). In this case, the Eleventh Circuit Court of Appeals found that noises made by the defendant in the direction of the Ranger goalie were both intentional and vulgar, and, as such, tended to have a chilling effect on his fulfillment of contractual obligations. Setting aside the long-standing "what-kind-of-country" principle—as stated in the well-known *U.S.* v. *Heins*, 319 U.S. 626 (1943); viz., "What kind of country is this if a man can't say what he wants?"—the court upheld the conviction. Speaking for the majority, Judge Whirter wrote, "Nobody has the right to act like a God-damned idiot, or to treat other people like dirt, or to tear down all the time without having something better to replace it with, and then come around and ask us for favors."

Szyrk v. Village
of Tatamount et al.

WILLIAM GADDIS

IN THE UNITED STATES DISTRICT COURT,
SOUTHERN DISTRICT OF VIRGINIA,
NO. 105-87

OPINION OF THE COURT
CREASE, *Judge*

T HE FACTS ARE NOT in dispute. On the morning of September 30th while running at large in the Village a dog identified as Spot entered under and therewith became entrapped in the lower reaches of a towering steel sculpture known as "Cyclone 7" which dominates the plaza overlooking and adjoining the depot of the Norfolk & Pee Dee Railroad. Searching for his charge, the dog's master James B. who is seven years old was alerted by its whines and yelps to discover its plights, whereupon his own vain efforts to deliver it attracted those of a passerby soon joined by others whose combined attempts to wheedle, cajole, and intimidate the unfortunate animal forth served rather to compound its predicament, driving it deeper into the structure. These futile activities soon assembled a good cross-section of the local population, from the usual idlers and senior citizens to members of the Village Board, the Sheriff's office, the Fire Department, and, not surprisingly, the victim's own kind, until by nightfall word having spread to neighboring hamlets attracted not only them in numbers sufficient to cause an extensive traffic jam but members of the local press and an enterprising television crew. Notwithstanding means successfully devised to assuage the dog's pangs of hunger, those of its confinement continued well into the following day when the decision was taken by the full Village Board to engage the Fire Department to enter the structure employing acetylene torches to effect its safe delivery, without considering the good likelihood of precipitating an action for damages by the creator of "Cyclone 7" Mr. Szyrk, a sculptor of some wide reputation in artistic circles.

Alerted by the media to the threat posed to his creation, Mr. Szyrk moved promptly from his SoHo studio in New York to file for a temporary restraining order "on a summary showing of its necessity to prevent immediate and irreparable injury" to his sculptural work, which was issued ex parte even as the torches of deliverance were being kindled. All this occurred four days ago.

Given the widespread response provoked by this confrontation in the media at large and echoing as far distant as the deeper South and even Arkansas but more immediately at the site itself, where energies generated by opposing sympathies further aroused by the police presence and that of the Fire Department in full array, the floodlights, vans, and other paraphernalia incident to a fiercely competitive television environment bringing in its train the inevitable placards and displays of the American flag, the venders of food and novelty items, all enhanced by the barks and cries of the victim's own local acquaintance, having erupted in shoving matches, fistfights, and related hostilities with distinctly racial overtones (the dog's master James B. and his family are black), and finally in rocks and beer cans hurled at the sculpture "Cyclone 7" itself, the court finds sufficient urgency in the main action of this proceeding to reject defendants' assertions and cross-motions for the reasons set forth below and grants summary judgment to plaintiff on the issue of his motion for a preliminary injunction to supersede the temporary restraining order now in place.

To grant summary judgment, as explicated by Judge Stanton in *Steinberg v. Columbia Pictures et. al.*, Fed. R. Civ. P. 56 requires a court to find that "there is no genuine issue as to any material fact and that the moving party is entitled to a judgment as a matter of law." In reaching its decision the court must "assess whether there are any factual issues to be tried, while resolving ambiguities and drawing reasonable inferences against the moving party"

(*Knight v. U.S. Fire Ins. Co.*, 804 F.2d 9, 11, 2d Cir., 1986 citing *Anderson v. Liberty Lobby,* 106 S.Ct. 2505 2509]11, 1986). In plaintiff's filing for a restraining order his complaint alleges, by counts, courses of action to which defendants have filed answers and cross-claims opposing motion for a preliminary injunction. The voluminous submissions accompanying these cross-motions leave no factual issues concerning which further evidence is likely to be presented at a trial. Moreover, the factual determinations necessary to this decision do not involve conflicts in testimony that would depend for their resolution on an assessment of witness credibility as cited infra. The interests of judicial economy being served by deciding the case at its present stage, summary judgment is therefore appropriate.

Naming as defendants the Village Board, the dog's master James B. through his guardian ad litem, "and such other parties and entities as may emerge in the course of this proceeding," Mr. Szyrk first alleges animal trespass, summoning in support of this charge a citation from early law holding that "where my beasts of their own wrong without my will and knowledge break another's close I shall be punished, for I am the trespasser with my beasts" (*12 Henry VII, Kielwey 3b*), which exhibit the court, finding no clear parallel in the laws of this Commonwealth, dismisses as ornamental. Concerning plaintiff's further exhibit of Village Code 21 para. 6b (known as "the leash law"), we take judicial notice of defendants' response alleging that, however specific in wording and intent, this ordinance appears more honored in the breach, in that on any pleasant day well-known members of the local dog community are to be served in all their disparity of size, breed, and other particulars ambling in the raffish camaraderie of sailors down the Village main street and thence wherever habit and appetite may take them undeterred by any citizen or arm of the law. Spot, so named for the liver-colored marking prominent on his loin, is described as of mixed breed wherein, from his reduced stature, silken coat, and "soulful" eyes, that of spaniel appears to prevail. His age is found to be under one year. Whereas in distinguishing between animals as either mansuetae or ferae naturae Spot is clearly to be discovered among the former "by custom devoted to the service of mankind at the time and in the place in which it is kept" and thus granted the indulgence customarily accorded such domestic pets, and further whereas as in the instant case scienter is not required (*Weaver v. National Biscuit Co.*, 125 F.2d 463, 7th Cir., 1942; *Parsons v. Manser*, 119 Iowa 88, 93 N.W. 86, 1903), such indulgence is indicative of the courts' retreat over the past century from strict liability for trespass (*Sanders v. Teape & Swan*, 51 L.T. 263, 1884; *Olson v. Pederson*, 206 Minn. 415, 288 N.W. 856, 1939), we find plaintiff's allegation on this count without merit (citation omitted).

On the related charge of damages brought by plaintiff the standard for preliminary relief must first be addressed. Were it to be found for plaintiff that irreparable harm has indeed been inflicted upon his creation, and that adequate remedy at law should suffice in the form of money damages, in such event the court takes judicial notice in directing such claim to be made against the Village Board and the dog's master in tandem, since as in the question posed by the Merchant of Venice (I, iii, 122) "Hath a dog money?" the answer must be that it does not. However, as regards the claim that the dog Spot, endowed with little more than milk teeth however sharp, and however extreme the throes of his despair, can have wreaked irreparable harm upon his steel confines this appears to be without foundation. Further to this charge, defendants respond, and the court concurs, citing plaintiff's original artistic intentions, that these steel surfaces have become pitted and acquired a heavy patina of rust following plaintiff's stated provision that his creation stand freely exposed to the mercy or lack thereof of natural forces, wherewith we may observe that a dog is not a boy, much less a fireman brandishing an acetylene torch, but nearer in its indifferent ignorance to those very forces embraced in the pathetic fallacy and so to be numbered among them. We have finally no more than a presumption of damage due to the inaccessibility of this inadvertent captive's immediate vicinity, and failing such evidentiary facts we find that the standards for preliminary relief have not been met and hold this point moot.

Here we take judicial notice of counterclaims filed on behalf of defendant James B. seeking to have this court hold both plaintiff and the Village and other parties thereto liable for willfully creating, installing, and maintaining an attractive nuisance which by its very nature and freedom of access constitutes an allurement to trespass, thus enticing the dog into its present allegedly dangerous predicament. Here plaintiff demurs, the Village joining in his demurrer, offering in exhibit similar structures of which

"Cyclone 7" is one of a series occupying sites elsewhere in the land, wherein among the four and on only one occasion a similar event occurred at a Long Island, New York, site in the form of a boy similarly entrapped and provoking a similar outcry until a proffered ten-dollar bill brought him forth little the worse. However a boy is not a dog, and whereas in the instant case "Cyclone 7" posed initially a kind of ornate "jungle gym" to assorted younger members of the community, we may find on the part of Spot absent his testimony neither a perception of challenge to his prowess at climbing nor any aesthetic sensibility luring him into harm's way requiring a capacity to distinguish "Cyclone 7" as a work of art from his usual environs in the junk yard presided over by defendant James B.'s father and guardian ad litem, where the progeny of man's inventiveness embraces three acres of rusting testimony thereto, and that hence his trespass was entirely inadvertent and in good likelihood dictated by a mere call of nature as abounding evidence of similar casual missions on the part of other members of the local dog community in the sculpture's immediate vicinity attest.

In taking judicial notice of defendant's counterclaim charging allurement we hold this charge to be one of ordinary negligency liability, already found to be without merit in this proceeding; however, we extend this judicial notice to embrace that section of plaintiff's response to the related charge of dangerous nuisance wherein plaintiff alleges damage from the strong hence derogatory implication that his sculptural creation, with a particular view to its internal components, was designed and executed not merely to suggest but to actually convey menace, whereto he exhibits extensive dated and annotated sketches, drawings, and notes made, revised, and witnessed in correspondence, demonstrating that at no time was the work, in any way or ways as a whole or in any component part or parts or combinations thereof including but not limited to sharp planes, spirals, and serrated steel limbs bearing distinct resemblances to teeth, ever in any manner conceived or carried out with intent of entrapment and consequent physical torment, but to the contrary that its creation was inspired and dictated in its entirety by wholly artistic considerations embracing its component parts in an aesthetic synergy wherein the sum of these sharp planes, jagged edges, and tooth-like projections aforementioned stand as mere depictions and symbols being in the aggregate greater than the sum of the parts taken individually to serve the work as, here quoting the catalogue distributed at its unveiling, "A testimony to man's indiminable [*sic*] spirit."

We have in other words plaintiff claiming to act as an instrument of higher authority, namely "art," wherewith we may first cite its dictionary definition as "(1) Human effort to imitate, supplement, alter, or counteract the work of nature." Notwithstanding that "Cyclone 7" clearly answers this description especially in its last emphasis, there remain certain fine distinctions posing some little difficulty for the average lay observer persuaded from habit and even education to regard sculptural art as beauty synonymous with truth in expressing harmony as visibly incarnate in the lineaments of Donatello's "David," or as the very essence of the sublime manifest in the "Milos Aphrodite," leaving him in the present instance quite unprepared to discriminate between sharp steel teeth as sharp steel teeth, and sharp steel teeth as artistic expressions of sharp steel teeth, obliging us for the purpose of this proceeding to confront the theory that in having become self-referential art is in itself theory without which it has no more substance than Sir Arthur Eddington's famous step "on a swarm of flies," here present in further exhibits by plaintiff drawn from prestigious art publications and highly esteemed critics in the lay press, where they make their livings, recommending his sculptural creation in terms of slope, tangent, acceleration, force, energy, and similar abstract extravagancies serving only a corresponding self-referential confrontation of language with language and thereby, in reducing language itself to theory, rendering it a mere plaything, which exhibits the court finds frivolous. Having here in effect thrown the bathwater out with the baby, in the clear absence of any evidentiary facts to support defendants' countercharge "dangerous nuisance," we find it without merit.

We next turn to a related complaint contained in defendant James B.'s cross-claim filed in rem "Cyclone 7" charging plaintiff, the Village, "and other parties and entities as their interests may appear" with erecting and maintaining a public nuisance in the form of "an obstruction making use of passage inconvenient and unreasonably burdensome upon the general public" (*Fugate v. Carter*, 151 Va. 108, 144 S.E. 483, 1928; *Regester v. Lincoln Oil Ref. Co.*, 95 Ind.App. 425, 183 N.E. 693, 1933). As specified in this complaint, "Cyclone 7" stands 24 feet 8 inches high with an irregular base circumference of approximately 74 feet and weighs 24 tons, and in support of his allegation of public nuisance defendant cites a basic tenet of early English law defining such nuisance as that "which obstructs or causes inconvenience or damage to the public in the exercise of rights common to all Her Majesty's subjects," further citing such nuisance as that which "injuriously affects the safety, health or morals of the public, or works some substantial annoyance, inconvenience or injury to the public" (*Commonwealth v. South Covington & Cincinnati Street Railway Co.*, 181 Ky. 459, 463, 205 S.W. 581, 583, 6 A.L.R. 118, 1918). Depositions taken from selected Village residents and submitted in rem "Cyclone 7" include: "We'd used to be this nice peaceable town before this foreigner come in here putting up this [expletive] piece of [obscenity] brings in every [expletive] kind of riffraff, even see some out-of-state plates;" "Since that [expletive] thing went up there I have to park my pickup way down by Ott's and walk all hell and gone just for a hoagie;" "Let's just see you try and catch a train where you can't hardly see nothing for the rain and sleet and you got to detour way round that heap of [obscenity] to the depot to get there;" "I just always used the men's room up there to the depot but now there's times when I don't hardly make it;" "They want to throw away that kind of money I mean they'd have just better went and put us up another [expletive] church."

Clearly from this and similar eloquent testimony certain members of the community have been subjected to annoyance and serious inconvenience in the pursuit of private errands of some urgency; however recalling to mind that vain and desperate effort to prevent construction of a subway kiosk in Cambridge, Massachusetts, enshrined decades ago in the news headline "PRESIDENT LOWELL FIGHTS ERECTION IN HARVARD SQUARE," by definition the interest of the general public must not be confused with that of one or even several individuals (*People v. Brooklyn & Queens Transit Corp.*, 258 App.Div. 753, 15 N.Y.S. 2d 295, 1939, affirmed 283 N.Y. 484, 28 N.E.2d 925, 1940); furthermore the obstruction is not so substantial as to preclude access (*Holland v. Grant County*, 208 Or. 50, 298 P.2d 832, 1956; *Ayers v. Stidham*, 260 Ala. 390, 71 So.2d 95, 1954), and in finding the former freedom of access to have been provided by mere default where no delineated path or thoroughfare was ever ordained or even contemplated this claim is denied.

On a lesser count charging private nuisance, H. R. Suggs, Jr., joins himself to this proceeding via intervention naming all parties thereto in his complaint on grounds of harboring a dog "which makes the night hideous with its howls" which the court severs from this action nonetheless taking judicial notice of intervener's right inseparable from ownership of the property bordering directly thereupon, to its undisturbed enjoyment thereof (Restatement of the Law, Second, Torts 2d, 822c), and remands to trial. Similarly, whereas none of the parties to this action has sought relief on behalf of the well-being and indeed survival of the sculpture's unwilling resident, and whereas a life-support system of sorts has been devised pro tem thereto, this matter is not at issue before the court, which nonetheless, taking judicial notice thereof should it arise in subsequent litigation, leaves it for adjudication to the courts of this local jurisdiction.

We have now cleared away the brambles and may proceed to the main action as set forth in plaintiff's petition for a preliminary injunction seeking to hold inviolable the artistic and actual integrity of his sculptural creation "Cyclone 7" in situ against assault, invasion, alteration, or destruction or removal or any act posing irreparable harm by any person or persons or agencies thereof under any authority or no authority assembled for such purpose or purposes for any reason or for none, under threat of recovery for damages consonant with but not limited to its original costs. While proof of ownership is not at issue in this proceeding, parties agree that these costs, including those incident to its installation, in the neighborhood of fourteen million dollars, were borne by contributions from various private patrons and underwritten by such corporate entities as Martin Oil, Incidental Oil, Bush AFG Corp., Anco Steel, Norfolk & Pee Dee Railroad, Frito-Cola Bottling Co., and the Tobacco Council, further supported with cooperation from the National Arts Endowment and both state and regional Arts Councils. The site, theretofore a weed-infested rubble-strewn area service for casual parking of vehicles and as an occasional dumping ground by day and trysting place by night, was donated under arrangements worked out between its proprietor Miller Feed Co. and the Village in consideration of taxes unpaid and accrued thereon over the preceding thirty-eight years. In re the selection of this specific site plaintiff exhibits drawings, photographs, notes, and other pertinent materials accompanying his original applications to and discussions with the interested parties aforementioned singling out the said site as "epitomizing that unique American environment of moral torpor and spiritual vacuity" requisite to his artistic enterprise, together with correspondence validating his intentions and applauding their results. Here we refer to plaintiff's exhibits drawn from contemporary accounts in the press of ceremonies inaugurating the installation of "Cyclone 7" wherein it was envisioned as a compelling tourist attraction though not, in the light of current events, for the reasons it enjoys today. Quoted therein, plaintiff cites, among numerous contemporary expressions of local exuberance, comments by then presiding Village Board member J. Harret Ruth at the ribbon cutting and reception held at nearby Mel's Kandy Kitchen with glowing photographic coverage, quoting therefrom "the time, the place, and the dedication of all you assembled here from far and wide, the common people and captains of industry and the arts rubbing elbows in tribute to the patriotic ideals rising right here before our eyes in this great work of sculptural art."

Responding to plaintiff's exhibits on this count, those of defendant appear drawn well after the fact up to and including the present day and provoked (here the court infers) by the prevailing emotional climate expressed in, and elicited by, the print and television media, appending thereto recently published statements by former Village official J. Harret Ruth in his current pursuit of a seat on the federal judiciary referring to the sculptural work at the center of this action as "a rusting travesty of our great nation's vision of itself" and while we may pause to marvel at his adroitness in ascertaining the direction of the parade before leaping in front to lead it we dismiss this and supporting testimony supra as contradictory and frivolous, and find plaintiff's exhibits in evidence conclusive.

Another count in plaintiff's action naming defendants both within and beyond this jurisdiction seeks remedy for defamation and consequent incalculable damage to his career and earning power derived therefrom (*Reiman v. Pacific Development Soc.*, 132 Or. 82, 284 P. 575, 1930; *Brauer v. Globe Newspaper Co.*, 351 Mass. 53, 217 N.E.2d 736, 1966). It is undisputed that plaintiff and his work, as here represented by the steel sculpture "Cyclone 7," have been held up to public ridicule both locally and, given the wide-ranging magic of the media, throughout the land, as witnessed in a cartoon published in the *South Georgia Pilot* crudely depicting a small dog pinioned under a junk heap comprising old bed-springs, chamber pots, and other household debris, and from the *Arkansas Family Visitor* an editorial denouncing plaintiff's country of origin as prominent in the Soviet bloc, thereby distinctly implying his mission among us to be one of atheistic subversion of our moral values as a Christian nation, whereas materials readily available elsewhere show plaintiff to have departed his birthplace at age three with his family who were in fact fleeing the then newly installed Communist regime. We take judicial notice of this exhibit as defamatory communication and libellous per se, tending "to lower him in the estimation of the community or to deter third persons from associating or dealing with him" (Restatement of the Law, Second, Torts 2d, 559), but it remains for plaintiff to seek relief in the courts of those jurisdictions.

Similarly, where plaintiff alleges defamation in this and far wider jurisdictions through radio and television broadcast we are plunged still deeper into the morass of legal distinctions embracing libel and slander that have plagued the common law since the turn of the seventeenth century. As slander was gradually wrested from the jurisdiction of the ecclesiastical courts through tort actions seeking redress for temporal damage rather than spiritual offense, slander became actionable only with proof or the reasonable assumption of special damage of a pecuniary character. Throughout, slander retained its identity as spoken defamation, while with the rise of the printing press it became libel in the written or printed word, a distinction afflicting our own time in radio and television broadcasting wherein defamation has been held as libel if read from a script by the broadcaster (*Hartmann v. Winchell*, 296 N.Y. 296, N.E.2d 30, 1947; *Hryhorijiv v. Winchell*, 1943, 180 Misc. 574, 45 N.Y.S 2d 31, affirmed, 267 App.Div. 817, 47 N.Y.S.2d 102, 1944) but as slander if it is not. But see Restatement of the Law, Second, Torts 2d, showing libel as "broadcasting of defamatory matter by means of radio or television, whether or not it is read from a manuscript" (#568A). Along this tortuous route, our only landmark in this proceeding is the aforementioned proof or reasonable assumption of special damage of a pecuniary character and, plaintiff failing in these provisions, this remedy is denied.

In reaching these conclusions, the court acts from the conviction that risk of ridicule, or attracting defamatory attentions from his colleagues and even raucous demonstrations by an outraged public have ever been and remain the foreseeable lot of the serious artist, recalling among the most egregious examples Ruskin accusing Whistler of throwing a paint pot in the public's face, the initial scorn showered upon the Impressionists and, once they were digested, upon the Cubists, the derision greeting Bizet's musical innovations credited with bringing about his death of a broken heart, the public riots occasioned by the first performance of Stravinsky's "Rite of Spring," and from the day Aristophanes labelled Euripides "a maker of ragamuffin manniquins" the avalanche of disdain heaped upon writers; the press sending the author of "Ode on a Grecian Urn" "back to plasters, pills, and ointment boxes," finding Ibsen's "Ghosts" "a loathsome sore unbandaged, a dirty act done publicly" and Tolstoy's "Anna Karenina" "sentimental rubbish," and in our own land the contempt accorded each succeeding work of Herman Melville, culminating in "Moby Dick" as "a huge dose of hyperbolical slang, maudlin sentimentalism and tragic-comic bubble and squeak," and since Melville's time upon writers too numerous to mention. All this must most arguably in deed and intent affect the sales of their books and the reputations whereon rest their hopes of advances and future royalties, yet to the court's knowledge none of this opprobrium however enviously and maliciously conceived and however stupid, careless, and ill-informed in its publication has ever yet proved grounds for a successful action resulting in recovery from the marplot. In short, the artist is fair game and his cause is turmoil. To echo the words of Horace, *Pictoribus atque poetis quidlibet audendi semper fuit aequa potestas,"* in this daring invention the artist comes among us not as the bearer of *idées reçus* embracing art as decoration or of the comfort of churchly beliefs enshrined in greeting-card sentiments but rather in the aesthetic equivalent of one who comes on earth "not to send peace, but a sword."

The foregoing notwithstanding, before finding for plaintiff on the main action before the court set forth in his motion for a preliminary injunction barring interference of any sort by any means by any party or parties with the sculptural creation "Cyclone 7" the court is compelled to address whether, following such a deliberate invasion for whatever purpose however merciful in intent, the work can be restored to its original look in keeping with the artist's unique talents and accomplishment or will suffer irreparable harm therefrom. Bowing to the familiar adage *"Cuilibet in arte sua perito est credendum,"* we hold the latter result to be an inevitable consequence of such invasion and such subsequent attempt at reconstitution at the hands of those assembled for such purposes in the form of members of the local Fire Department, whose training and talents such as they may be must be found to lie elsewhere, much in the manner of that obituary upon our finest poet of the century wherein one of his purest lines was reconstituted as "I do not think they will sing to me" by a journalist trained to eliminate on sight the superfluous "that."

For the reasons set out above, summary judgment is granted to plaintiff as to preliminary injunction.

Coyote v. Acme

IAN FRAZIER

IN THE UNITED STATES DISTRICT COURT,
SOUTHWESTERN DISTRICT, TEMPE, ARIZONA
CASE NO. B19294, JUDGE JOAN KUJAVA, PRESIDING

WILE E. COYOTE, Plaintiff
-v.-
ACME COMPANY, Defendant

OPENING STATEMENT OF Mr. Harold Schoff, attorney for Mr. Coyote: My client, Mr. Wile E. Coyote, a resident of Arizona and contiguous states, does hereby bring suit for damages against the Acme Company, manufacturer and retail distributor of assorted merchandise, incorporated in Delaware and doing business in every state, district, and territory. Mr. Coyote seeks compensation for personal injuries, loss of business income, and mental suffering caused as a direct result of the actions and/or gross negligence of said company, under Title 15 of the United States Code, Chapter 47, section 2072, subsection (a), relating to product liability.

Mr. Coyote states that on eighty-five separate occasions he has purchased of the Acme Company (hereinafter, "Defendant"), through that company's mail-order department, certain products which did cause him bodily injury due to defects in manufacture or improper cautionary labelling. Sales slips made out to Mr. Coyote as proof of purchase are at present in the possession of the Court, marked Exhibit A. Such injuries sustained by Mr. Coyote have temporarily restricted his ability to make a living in his profession of predator. Mr. Coyote is self-employed and thus not eligible for Workmen's Compensation.

Mr. Coyote states that on December 13th he received of Defendant via parcel post one Acme Rocket Sled. The intention of Mr. Coyote was to use the Rocket Sled to aid him in pursuit of his prey. Upon receipt of the Rocket Sled Mr. Coyote removed it from its wooden shipping crate and, sighting his prey in the distance, activated the ignition. As Mr. Coyote gripped the handlebars, the Rocket Sled accelerated with such sudden and precipitate force as to stretch Mr. Coyote's forelimbs to a length of fifty feet. Subsequently, the rest of Mr. Coyote's body shot forward with a violent jolt, causing severe strain to his back and neck and placing him unexpectedly astride the Rocket Sled. Disappearing over the horizon at such speed as to leave a diminishing jet trail along its path, the Rocket Sled soon brought Mr. Coyote abreast of his prey. At that moment the animal he was pursuing veered sharply to the right. Mr. Coyote vigorously attempted to follow this maneuver but was unable to, due to poorly designed steering on the Rocket Sled and a faulty or nonexistent braking system. Shortly thereafter, the unchecked progress of the Rocket Sled brought it and Mr. Coyote into collision with the side of a mesa.

Paragraph One of the Report of Attending Physician (Exhibit B), prepared by Dr. Ernest Grosscup, M.D., D.O., details the multiple fractures, contusions, and tissue damage suffered by Mr. Coyote as a result of this collision. Repair of the injuries required a full bandage around the head (excluding the ears), a neck brace, and full or partial casts on all four legs.

Hampered by these injuries, Mr. Coyote was nevertheless obliged to support himself. With this in mind, he purchased of Defendant as an aid to mobility one pair of Acme Rocket Skates. When he attempted to use this product, however, he became involved in an accident remarkably similar to that which occurred with the Rocket Sled. Again, Defendant sold over the counter, without caveat, a product which attached powerful jet engines (in this case, two) to inadequate vehicles, with little or no provision for passenger safety. Encumbered by his heavy casts, Mr. Coyote lost control of the Rocket Skates soon after strapping them on, and collided with a roadside billboard so violently as to leave a hole in the shape of his full silhouette.

Mr. Coyote states that on occasions too numerous to list in this document he has suffered mishaps with explosives purchased of Defendant: the Acme "Little Giant" Firecracker, the Acme Self-Guided Aerial Bomb, etc. (For a full listing, see the Acme Mail Order Explosives Catalogue and attached deposition, entered in evidence as Exhibit C.) Indeed, it is safe to say that not once has an explosive purchased of Defendant by Mr. Coyote performed in an expected manner. To cite just one example: At the expense of much time and personal effort, Mr. Coyote constructed around the outer rim of a butte a wooden trough beginning at the top of the butte and spiralling downward around it to some few feet above a black X painted on the desert floor. The trough was designed in such a way that a spherical explosive of the type sold by Defendant would roll easily and swiftly down to the point of detonation indicated by the X. Mr. Coyote placed a generous pile of birdseed directly on the X, and then, carrying the spherical Acme Bomb (Catalogue # 78-832), climbed to the top of the butte. Mr. Coyote's prey, seeing the birdseed, approached, and Mr. Coyote proceeded to light the fuse. In an instant, the fuse burned down to the stem, causing the bomb to detonate.

In addition to reducing all Mr. Coyote's careful preparations to naught, the premature detonation of Defendant's product resulted in the following disfigurements to Mr. Coyote:

1. Severe singeing of the hair on the head, neck, and muzzle.

2. Sooty discoloration.

3. Fracture of the left ear at the stem, causing the ear to dangle in the aftershock with a creaking noise.

4. Full or partial combustion of whiskers, producing kinking, frazzling, and ashy disintegration.

5. Radical widening of the eyes, due to brow and lid charring.

We come now to the Acme Spring-Powered Shoes. The remains of a pair of these purchased by Mr. Coyote on June 23rd are Plaintiff's Exhibit D. Selected fragments have been shipped to the metallurgical laboratories of the University of California at Santa Barbara for analysis, but to date no explanation has been found for this product's sudden and extreme malfunction. As advertised by Defendant, this product is simplicity itself: two wood-and-metal sandals, each attached to milled-steel springs of high tensile strength and compressed in a tightly coiled position by a cocking device with a lanyard release. Mr. Coyote believed that this product would enable him to pounce upon his prey in the initial moments of the chase, when swift reflexes are at a premium.

To increase the shoes' thrusting power still further, Mr. Coyote affixed them by their bottoms to the side of a large boulder.

Adjacent to the boulder was a path which Mr. Coyote's prey was known to frequent. Mr. Coyote put his hind feet in the wood-and-metal sandals and crouched in readiness, his right forepaw holding firmly to the lanyard release. Within a short time Mr. Coyote's prey did indeed appear on the path coming toward him. Unsuspecting, the prey stopped near Mr. Coyote, well within range of the springs at full extension. Mr. Coyote gauged the distance with care and proceeded to pull the lanyard release.

At this point, Defendant's product should have thrust Mr. Coyote forward and away from the boulder. Instead, for reasons yet unknown, the Acme Spring-Powered Shoes thrust the boulder away from Mr. Coyote. As the intended prey looked on un-harmed, Mr. Coyote hung suspended in air. Then the twin springs recoiled, bringing Mr. Coyote to a violent feet-first colli-sion with the boulder, the full weight of his head and forequarters falling upon his lower extremities.

The force of this impact then caused the springs to rebound, whereupon Mr. Coyote was thrust skyward. A second recoil and collision followed. The boulder, meanwhile, which was roughly ovoid in shape, had begun to bounce down a hillside, the coiling and recoiling of the springs adding to its velocity. At each bounce, Mr. Coyote came into contact with the boulder, or the boulder came into contact with Mr. Coyote, or both came into contact with the ground. As the grade was a long one, this process continued for some time.

The sequence of collisions resulted in systemic physical damage to Mr. Coyote, viz., flattening of the cranium, sideways displace-ment of the tongue, reduction of length of legs and upper body, and compression of vertebrae from base of tail to head. Repeti-tion of blows along a vertical axis produced a series of regular horizontal folds in Mr. Coyote's body tissues—a rare and painful condition which caused Mr. Coyote to expand upward and con-tract downward alternately as he walked, and to emit an off-key, accordionlike wheezing with every step. The distracting and embarrassing nature of this symptom has been a major impedi-ment to Mr. Coyote's pursuit of a normal social life.

As the Court is no doubt aware, Defendant has a virtual monopoly of manufacture and sale of goods required by Mr. Coyote's work. It is our contention that Defendant has used its market advantage to the detriment of the consumer of such specialized products as itching powder, giant kites, Burmese tiger traps, anvils, and two-hundred-foot-long rubber bands. Much as he has come to mistrust Defendant's products, Mr. Coyote has no other domestic source of supply to which to turn. One can only wonder what our trading partners in Western Europe and Japan would make of such a situation, where a giant company is allowed to victimize the consumer in the most reckless and wrongful manner over and over again.

Mr. Coyote respectfully requests that the Court regard these larger economic implications and assess punitive damages in the amount of seventeen million dollars. In addition, Mr. Coyote seeks actual damages (missed meals, medical expenses, days lost from professional occupation) of one million dollars; general damages (mental suffering, injury to reputation) of twenty million dollars; and attorney's fees of seven hundred and fifty thousand dollars. Total damages: thirty-eight million seven hundred and fifty thousand dollars. By awarding Mr. Coyote the full amount, this Court will censure Defendant, its directors, officers, share-holders, successors, and assigns, in the only language they understand, and reaffirm the right of the individual predator to equal protection under the law.

OTHER VOICES
OTHER COUNTRIES

Before the Law

FRANZ KAFKA

BEFORE THE LAW stands a doorkeeper. To this doorkeeper there comes a man from the country and prays for admittance to the Law. But the doorkeeper says that he cannot grant admittance at the moment. The man thinks it over and then asks if he will be allowed in later. "It is possible," says the doorkeeper, "but not at the moment." Since the gate stands open, as usual, and the doorkeeper steps to one side, the man stoops to peer through the gateway into the interior. Observing that, the doorkeeper laughs and says: "If you are so drawn to it, just try to go in despite my veto. But take note: I am powerful. And I am only the least of the doorkeepers. From hall to hall there is one doorkeeper after another, each more powerful than the last. The third doorkeeper is already so terrible that even I cannot bear to look at him." These are difficulties the man from the country has not expected; the Law, he thinks, should surely be accessible at all times and to everyone, but as he now takes a closer look at the doorkeeper in his fur coat, with his big sharp nose and long, thin, black Tartar beard, he decides that it is better to wait until he gets permission to enter. The doorkeeper gives him a stool and lets him sit down at one side of the door. There he sits for days and years. He makes many attempts to be admitted, and wearies the doorkeeper by his importunity. The doorkeeper frequently has little interviews with him, asking him questions about his home and many other things, but the questions are put indifferently, as great lords put them, and always finish with the statement that he cannot be let in yet. The man, who has furnished himself with many things for his journey, sacrifices all he has, however valuable, to bribe the doorkeeper. The doorkeeper accepts everything, but always with the remark: "I am only taking it to keep you from thinking you may have omitted anything." During these many years the man fixes his attention almost continuously on the doorkeeper. He forgets the other doorkeepers, and this first one seems to him the sole obstacle preventing access to the Law. He curses his bad luck, in his early years boldly and loudly; later, as he grows old, he only grumbles to himself. He becomes childish, and since in his yearlong contemplation of the doorkeeper he has come to know even the fleas in his fur collar, he begs the fleas as well to help him and to change the doorkeeper's mind. At length his eyesight begins to fail, and he does not know whether the world is really darker or whether his eyes are only deceiving him. Yet in his darkness he is now aware of a radiance that streams inextinguishably from the gateway of the Law. Now he has not very long to live. Before he dies, all his experiences in these long years gather themselves in his head to one point, a question he has not yet asked the doorkeeper. He waves him nearer, since he can no longer raise his stiffening body. The doorkeeper has to bend low toward him, for the difference in height between them has altered much to the man's disadvantage. "What do you want to know now?" asks the doorkeeper; "you are insatiable." "Everyone strives to reach the Law," says the man, "so how does it happen that for all these many years no one but myself has ever begged for admittance?" The doorkeeper recognizes that the man has reached his end, and, to let his failing senses catch the words, roars in his ear: "No one else could ever be admitted here, since this gate was made only for you. I am now going to shut it."

Translated by Willa and Edwin Muir

The Litigants

$$\boxed{\text{ISAAC BASHEVIS SINGER}}$$

T HERE WAS TALK ABOUT LAWSUITS, and old Genendl, a distant relative of ours, a woman learned, as they say, in the small letters, was saying, "There are people who like this kind of legal wrangling. Even among us Jews there are those who at any opportunity will run to the rabbi for a *din torah*. In olden times, duels and trials were a madness among the Polish squires. Not far from our town there were two squires, Zbigniew Piorun and Adam Lech, small landowners, not like the Radziwills or the Zamoyskis. Piorun had a few hundred serfs. It was before the peasants were freed. He owned fields, forests, and a stable with race horses. In his younger years he was a hunter and a rider, and he used to attend all the races. There was still the Sejm in Warsaw and Piorun attended its sessions every year. It was in the constitution of Poland that when the nobles tried to vote for a certain law or impose a tax, if only one delegate vetoed it, the whole project came to nothing. This was called *vetum separatum*. They could never come to any decision. Because of this wild situation Poland was finally torn to pieces. Piorun was almost always among those who used the veto. He loved making long speeches and made mincemeat of all the programs anyone introduced. At home, every few weeks he challenged someone to a duel. He had a court Jew named Reb Getz, who was in charge of the whole estate and, among other things, of milking the cows. It was Piorun's permanent ambition to prove to Reb Getz that Jesus was the real Messiah. Once, when Piorun began a debate with Reb Getz which lasted until evening, Reb Getz said, 'Your

Excellency, whoever the Messiah is or will be, he is not going to milk your cows.'

"Piorun and his wife had sons and daughters. They were all good-looking and they married into the high aristocracy. Every year he gave a ball and people of high rank came from the whole of Poland. The other squire, Adam Lech, was small and black like a gypsy, with no wife or children. He had a neglected little estate with some hundred serfs. He had no court Jew. He managed everything himself. He was an angry man, and when a peasant did something he didn't like, he whipped him with his own hands. There was an old enmity between Zbigniew Piorun and Adam Lech. Their estates had a common boundary and for many years they quarreled about a piece of land which Lech claimed as his property. Piorun had included it in his territory and had fenced it in. The dispute came to a trial, and like all trials in Poland it went on for many years. One judge issued one verdict, another judge a different verdict. Each petition had to have costly tax stamps affixed. All the clerks had to be bribed with money or gifts. Piorun could afford all this, but not Lech. How does the saying go? 'Before the fat one turns lean, the lean one dies.' Neighboring squires tried to effect a compromise. Both sides remained stubborn. In time Lech lost everything. His hair became prematurely white. From too much grief and perhaps from drinking he became emaciated as if he had consumption. Gradually he sold all his fields, his forest, and even his serfs. People expected him to die any day, but some power kept him alive. Adam Lech was supposed to have said he could not leave this world until the courts gave him back what Piorun had stolen, since the truth must come out like oil over water.

"One day both squires, Piorun and Lech, received notice from Warsaw that on a future date they had to appear before the highest tribunal, where a final verdict would be handed down. Piorun didn't care anymore about the whole business. His wife had died, his children had dispersed. He barely remembered all the details of the litigation, but since the Sejm would be convening in Warsaw, Piorun had the desire once more to set forth his veto. He had an old carriage and an old coachman by the name of Wojciech. Piorun's old-maid servant gave the squire provisions for his trip, as well as a few bottles of vodka. The carriage had traveled only a short distance when suddenly it stopped. 'Hey, Wojciech, why have you stopped?' Piorun asked, and Wojciech said, 'Adam Lech is standing in the middle of the road and doesn't let me pass.' 'What? Lech, that old corpse!' Piorun said. At once he understood why. Lech had threatened many times to shoot Piorun like a dog, and now he was about to do it. 'It's good that I haven't forgotten my pistol,' Piorun said. The sun had set and it was twilight, as Piorun began to shoot his rusty pistol. He barely saw where he was aiming. His hand trembled. Wojciech alighted from the coachman's seat and began to scream, 'Your Excellency, Adam Lech is without weapons. He is waving his empty hands.'

" 'No weapons, what kind of duel is this?' Piorun shouted.

"Why drag the story out? Lech had also received a notice to come to Warsaw, but had neither carriage nor horses and, after long brooding, had decided to ask his longtime enemy to take him to Warsaw.

"You're laughing, huh?" Genendl asked. "This is what really happened. What does a squire do who is called to a trial and has no horse and carriage? Lech came up to Piorun's carriage and began to bow and scrape, to stutter and beg Piorun to do him a favor and take him to Warsaw.

"When Piorun heard these words and saw his archenemy bent down, wrinkled, and shriveled like a skeleton, dressed in an old worn coat, with a bag on his shoulders like a beggar, he forgot all their conflicts. He began to laugh and cry, and said, 'My dear neighbor, my friend, why didn't you come to me first? By a hair I almost shot you. It is true that we were once enemies, but we are Poles, brothers of one nation, and I will not let you go to Warsaw on foot. Come in, sir, to my carriage.' The two squires seized each other and began to kiss and embrace like old chums. Piorun took out a bottle of vodka and they drank each other's health and good-humoredly drank toasts to each other's success in the trial. Then Piorun said, 'Why do I need your piece of land? To whom will I leave it? My heirs are all richer than I am. All one needs at our age is a grave.' Lech spoke in the same manner. 'The whole war between us was nothing but a mistake, a caprice, a silly ambition,' Lech said. 'Perhaps the Devil himself, who always lurks behind God's children and tries to befuddle their spirits, has corrupted us. Your Excellency, why do I need the land? I don't even have anyone to take care of my flower pots.'

"Both squires traveled together to Warsaw, talking about old times, making fun of the Polish courts, their lawyers, their accusers, the false witnesses each litigant had hired, the court language written in a Latin no one could understand. Lech said, 'My friend, I don't believe anymore that the Warsaw parasites and vampires are about to come out with a final verdict. No litigant in Poland has ever lived long enough for a trial to be finished. The end comes to the litigants, not to the trials.'

"Adam Lech was right. In Warsaw both litigants learned that the court was far from ready to hand down a final verdict. They were asked to hire land surveyors once again to measure the land, which over the years had become overgrown with weeds and teeming with snakes, field mice, porcupines, and all kinds of vermin. These measurements were going to cost a lot of money. They were to be compared with other measurements in archives, which only God knew if they still existed. Both Piorun and Lech scolded the court officials and called them thieves, plate lickers, rats, and scavengers. Then together they went to a tavern to drink.

"There was a lot of talk about this extraordinary settlement in the corridors of the Sejm, and when both squires came to the session in the Sejm, they received an ovation from all the benches. In honor of this peacemaking, Piorun did not use his veto on this occasion. For the first time in his life, he agreed with the other lawmakers as a sign that the Poles should from then on act like a united people.

"Too late! Not long after, the Kings of Austria, Russia, and Prussia divided Poland among themselves. Piorun and Lech died, and were buried not far from each other. For many years afterward the tale of these two friendly litigants was told among the squires and landowners all over Poland."

Translated by the author and Lester Goran

Crimes of Conscience

NADINE GORDIMER

APPARENTLY THEY NOTICED EACH OTHER at the same moment, coming down the steps of the Supreme Court on the third day of the trial. By then casual spectators who come for a look at the accused—to see for themselves who will risk prison walls round their bodies for ideas in their heads—have satisfied curiosity; only those who have some special interest attend day after day. He could have been a journalist; or an aide to the representative of one of the Western powers who 'observe' political trials in countries problematic for foreign policy and subject to human rights lobbying back in Western Europe and America. He wore a corduroy suit of unfamiliar cut. But when he spoke it was clear he was, like her, someone at home—he had the accent, and the casual, colloquial turn of phrase. 'What a session! I don't know... After two hours of that... feel like I'm caught in a roll of sticky tape... unreal...'

There was no mistaking her. She was a young woman whose cultivated gentleness of expression and shabby homespun style of dress, in the context in which she was encountered, suggested not transcendental mediation centre or environmental concern group or design studio, but a sign of identification with the humanity of those who had nothing and risked themselves. Her only adornment, a necklace of ostrich-shell discs stacked along a thread, moved tight at the base of her throat tendons as she smiled and agreed. 'Lawyers work like that... I've noticed. The first few days, it's a matter of people trying each to confuse the other side.'

291

Later in the week, they had coffee together during the court's lunch adjournment. He expressed some naïve impressions of the trial, but as if fully aware of gullibility. Why did the State call witnesses who came right out and said the regime oppressed their spirits and frustrated their normal ambitions? Surely that kind of testimony favoured the Defence, when the issue was a crime of conscience? She shook fine hair, ripply as a mohair rug. 'Just wait. Just wait. That's to establish credibility. To prove their involvement with the accused, their intimate knowledge of what the accused said and did, to *inculpate* the accused in what the Defence's going to deny. Don't you see?'

'Now I see.' He smiled to himself. 'When I was here before, I didn't take much interest in political things...activist politics, I suppose you'd call it? It's only since I've been back from overseas...'

She asked conversationally what was expected of her: how long had he been away?

'Nearly five years. Advertising then computers...' The dying-out of the sentence suggested the lack of interest in which these careers had petered. 'Two years ago I just felt I wanted to come back. I couldn't give myself a real reason. I've been doing the same sort of work here—actually, I ran a course at the business school of a university, this year—and I'm slowly beginning to find out *why* I wanted to. To come back. It seems it's something to do with things like *this*.'

She had a face that showed her mind following another's; eyebrows and mouth expressed quiet understanding.

'I imagine all this sounds rather feeble to you. I don't suppose you're someone who stands on the sidelines.'

Her thin, knobbly little hands were like tools laid upon the formica counter of the coffee bar. In a moment of absence from their capability, they fiddled with the sugar sachets while she answered. 'What makes you think that.'

'You seem to know so much. As if you'd been through it yourself...Or maybe...you're a law student?'

'Me? Good lord, no.' After one or two swallows of coffee, she offered a friendly response. 'I work for a correspondence college.'

'Teacher.'

Smiling again: 'Teaching people I never see.'

'That doesn't fit too well. You look the kind of person who's more involved.'

For the first time, polite interest changed, warmed. 'That's what you missed, in London? Not being involved...?'

At that meeting he gave her a name, and she told him hers.

The name was Derek Felterman. It was his real name. He *had* spent five years in London; he *had* worked in an advertising company and then studied computer science at an appropriate institution, and it was in London that he was recruited by someone from the Embassy who wasn't a diplomat but a representative of the internal security section of State security in his native country. Nobody knows how secret police recognize likely candidates; it is as mysterious as sexing chickens. But if the definitive characteristic sought is there to be recognized, the recruiting agent will see it, no matter how deeply the individual may hide his likely candidacy from himself.

He was not employed to infiltrate refugee circles plotting abroad. It was decided that he would come home 'clean', and begin work in the political backwater of a coastal town, on a university campus. Then he was sent north to the mining and industrial centre of the country, told to get himself an ordinary commercial job without campus connections, and, as a new face, seek contacts wherever the information his employers wanted was likely to be let slip—left-wing cultural gatherings, poster-waving protest groups, the public gallery at political trials. His employers trusted him to know how to ingratiate himself; that was one of the qualities he had been fancied for, as a woman might fancy him for some other characteristic over which he had no volition—the way one corner of his mouth curled when he smiled, or the brown gloss of his eyes.

He, in turn, had quickly recognized her—first as a type, and then, the third day, when he went away from the court for verification of her in police files, as the girl who had gone secretly to visit a woman friend who was under House Arrest, and subsequently had served a three-month jail sentence for refusing to testify in a case brought against the woman for breaking her isolation ban. Aly, she had called herself. Alison Jane Ross. There was no direct connection to be found between Alison Jane Ross's interest in the present trial and the individuals on trial; but from the point of view of his avocation this did not exclude her possible involvement with a master organization or back-up group involved in continuing action of the subversive kind the charges named.

Felterman literally moved in to friendship with her, carrying a heavy case of books and a portable grill. He had asked if she would come to see a play with him on Saturday night. Alas, she was moving house that Saturday; perhaps he'd like to come and help, instead? The suggestion was added, tongue-in-cheek at her own presumption. He was there on time. Her family of friends, introduced by diminutives of their names, provided a combined service of old combi, springless station-wagon, take-away food and affectionate energy to fuel and accomplish the move from a flat to a tiny house with an ancient palm tree filling a square of garden, grating its dried fronds in the wind with the sound of a giant insect rubbing its legs together. To the night-song of that creature they made love for the first time a month later. Although all the Robs, Jimbos and Ricks, as well as the Jojos, Bets and Lils, kissed and hugged their friend Aly, there seemed to be no lover about who had therefore been supplanted. On the particular, delicate path of intimacy along which she drew him or that he laid out before her, there was room only for the two of them. At the beginning of ease between them, even before they were lovers, she had come of herself to the stage of mentioning that experience of going to prison, but she talked of it always in banal surface terms—how the blankets smelled of disinfectant and the Chief Wardress's cat used to do the inspection round with its mistress. Now she did not ask him about other women, although he was moved, occasionally, in some involuntary warm welling-up complementary to that other tide—of sexual pleasure spent—to confess by the indirection of an anecdote, past affairs, women who had had their time and place. When the right moment came naturally to her, she told without shame, resentment or vanity that she had just spent a year 'on her own' as something she felt she needed after living for three years with someone who, in the end, went back to his wife. Lately there had been one or two brief affairs—'Sometimes—don't you find—an old friend suddenly becomes something else...just for a little while, as if a face is turned to another angle...? And next day, it's the same old one again. Nothing's changed.'

'Friends are the most important thing for you, aren't they? I mean, everybody has friends, but you... You'd really do *anything*. For your friends. Wouldn't you?

There seemed to come from her reaction rather than his words a reference to the three months she had spent in prison. She lifted the curly pelmet of hair from her forehead and the freckles faded against a flush colouring beneath: 'And they for me.'

'It's not just a matter of friendship, either—of course, I see that. Comrades—a band of brothers...'

She saw him as a child staring through a window at others playing. She leant over and took up his hand, kissed him with the kind of caress they had not exchanged before, on each eyelid.

Nevertheless her friends were a little neglected in favour of him. He would have liked to have been taken into the group more closely, but it is normal for two people involved in a passionate love affair to draw apart from others for a while. It would have looked unnatural to press to behave otherwise. It was also understood between them that Felterman didn't have much more than acquaintances to neglect; five years abroad and then two in the coastal town accounted for that. He revived for her pleasures she had left behind as a schoolgirl: took her water-skiing and climbing. They went to see indigenous people's theatre together, part of a course in the politics of culture she was giving him not by correspondence, without being aware of what she was doing and without giving it any such pompous name. She was not to be persuaded to go to a discothèque, but one of the valuable contacts he did have with her group of friends of different races and colours was an assumption that he would be with her at their parties, where she out-danced him, having been taught by blacks how to use her body to music. She was wild and nearly lovely, in this transformation, from where he drank and watched her and her associates at play. Every now and then she would come back to him: an offering, along with the food and drink she carried. As months went by, he was beginning to distinguish certain patterns in her friendships; these were extended beyond his life with her into proscribed places and among people restricted by law from contact, like the woman for whom she had gone to prison. Slowly she gained the confidence to introduce him to risk, never discussing but evidently always sensitively trying to gauge how much he really wanted to find out if 'why he wanted to come back' had to do with 'things like this.'

It was more and more difficult to leave her, even for one night, going out late, alone under the dry, chill agitation of the old palm tree, rustling through its files. But although he knew his place had been made for him to live in the cottage with her, he had to go back to his flat that was hardly more than an office, now, unoccupied except for the chair and dusty table at which he sat down to write his reports: he could hardly write them in the house he shared with her.

She spoke often of her time in prison. She herself was the one to find openings for the subject. But even now, when they lay in one another's arms, out of reach, undiscoverable to any investigation, out of scrutiny, she did not seem able to tell of the experience what there really was in her being, necessary to be told: why she risked, for whom and what she was committed. She seemed to be waiting passionately to be given the words, the key. From him.

It was a password he did not have. It was a code that was not supplied him.

And then one night it came to him; he found a code of his own; that night he had to speak. 'I've been spying on you.'

Her face drew into a moment of concentration akin to the animal world, where a threatened creature can turn into a ball of spikes or take on a fearsome aspect of blown-up muscle and defensive garishness.

The moment left her face instantly as it had taken her. He had turned away before it as a man does with a gun in his back.

She shuffled across the bed on her haunches and took his head in her hands, holding him.

A Few Selected Sentences

B.S. JOHNSON

S OMEONE HAS TO KEEP THE RECORDS . . .

The Cacao is a fruite little lesse then Almonds, yet more fat, the which being roasted hath no ill taste. The chief use of this Cacao is in a drinke which they call Chocholate, whereof they make great accompt in that Country, foolishly, and without reason; for it is loathsome to such as are not acquainted with it, having a skum or froth that is very unpleasant to taste, if they be not very well conceited thereof. Yet it is a drinke very much esteemed among the Indians, wherewith they feast Noble men as they passe through their Country.

What are hands for, if not to hide the eyes?

Le Soixante-neuf est Interdit dans les Couloirs.

Eight years' penal servitude.

As a lorry driven by Corxley left the scene, the sound of a hunting horn was heard. Was it a warning? The police found the body of a stag in the bracken, still warm. Later, police came across Croxley, Ryman and Straker standing by the lorry at the place where the stag had been. Croxley said he was birdwatching, Ryman said his hobby was photography, and Straker, who was carrying a crossbow, said: "I am interested in all forms of medieval weaponry." In the lorry police found a quiver full of arrows, a

297

pair of binoculars, two pairs of Sherwood Green tights, and five sheath knives. A broken arrowshaft corresponded to an arrow-head embedded in the dead stag. All three men said they were committee members of Bowmen for Britain, had been out seeking small vermin, and had been on a public footpath. Straker said: 'I saw a squirrel and fired at it but the stag which I did not know was there ran into it.'

A child left to himself bringeth his mother to shame.

I love anecdotes. I fancy mankind may come in time to write all aphoristically, except in narrative; grow weary of preparation and connection and illustration, and all those arts by which a big book is made.

The man had long white hands which he clasped tightly behind his back when not using them to eat several helpings of jellied eels. Most customers looked thoughtful.

One year, suspended.

All afternoon the girl threatened to jump. She said her husband had become converted to a religious sect which forbade her the use of her television. When she had wished to listen to the Queen's Xmas broadcast she had had to go into the bathroom. It was her radio. Because she used makeup her husband likened her to Jezebel, the painted woman of the Scriptures. It was ac-cepted that he was sincere. As soon as they brought a priest to talk to her, she jumped.

Permission to laugh?

Have you heard what Cynon sang?
Beware of drunkards—
Drink unlocks the human heart.

The father appealed for witnesses to his son's death to come for-ward, not expecting to be overwhelmed by numbers. What had happened as far as they knew was that on Furse Bend he had crossed the inner edge on to the central reserve and in the resulting spill (which was not particularly dangerous in itself) the point of the clutch lever had entered his brain by way of the base of the skull. The father wished to know how designers of safety helmets had not taken this possibility into account. His colleagues said he should have had a ball on it.

But I am trying to be benign.

A rusty charlatan stated dogmatically that a discussion was an agument in which no one was particularly interested. He was reminded that every good deed is followed by the punishment of God. But, he insisted, one must have a proper regard for the ordinary.

The continuous process of recognizing that what is possible is not achievable.

A man taking pictures of a man taking pictures: there must be something in that.

At a wedding reception everyone was drunk, including the children. Indeed, one of the children became so affected as to seem ill, and it was considered advisable to take him to a hospital to have him seen to, stomach-pumped if necessary. They chose the receptor who seemed least drunk to drive the child, quickly. On the way the car was stopped by a policeman on a horse, who invited the driver to puff breath into a plastic bag. Crystals in the tube attached to this bag turned a certain colour which convinced the policeman that the driver was under the influence of alcohol and he informed him that he would be charged with an offence. 'Oh no,' said the driver, 'Your bags must be faulty. Perhaps indeed you have a batch of faulty bags. Why don't we test them by trying one out on this innocent child?'

A bard's land shall be free. He shall have a horse when he follows the king and a gold ring from the queen and the harp he shall never part with.

Do I want that to be the truth?

The Vice-Chancellor was killed when inspecting the progress of the building of Senate House. A technician was pushing a loaded wheel-barrow across a plank spanning a liftshaft. He saved himself, but the wheelbarrow was lost. The Vice-Chancellor was standing at the bottom of the liftshaft. Accommodate that mess.

Most of the time they look for things to want, schoolfriends.

Miceal and I would play snooker. He would generally win. His was always the same remark when he sank the green or the brown which would put him beyond being caught unless he gave away an unlikely number of penalty points: 'Now you haven't got enough balls. You'll have to put your own up.' I cannot say I laughed more than the first and second times, despite tradition. And 'No points for hard luck' was another saying of his that stuck.

—Who was there?
—The usual mess, of course. Baldies, hairies, collapsed faces, fallen women, who would you think?

Life.

———

Someone has to keep records. I may even be thanked, in time.

Heart of a Judge

R. SARIF EASMON

S IR GEOFFREY ROBIN HAD HAD A good day, his second in
Sunia. Sitting at dinner, taken a little late at nine o'clock,
with his wife Cynthia facing him across the beautiful
mahogany table, he felt sure he was going to have an even better
night. Life felt good. It always did if Cynthia was a part of it.
Her golden hair, falling down to her shoulders, wavy always
without art, was as lovely as it was ten years before when, against
many who in his heart he admitted were better-qualified suitors,
he had won her heart and married her.

He refilled his glass with port.

"You know, Cynthia," he said, waving his hand around the
dining room, toward the elegant sitting room, "this is yet another
manifestation of the younger Pliny's dictum: *Ex Africa semper
aliquid novi.*"

"You're too old-fashioned, Geoffrey," laughed the beautiful
blonde. "Too old-fashioned for a man, for a judge, for the modern
world—"

"Not for a husband, I hope!" he laughed back.

"No, dear. But Latin is becoming a stranger even in Oxford.
You must forget your double first and stop quoting Latin at your
wife: especially over port and a crab salad. By the way, you'd
better go easy with both."

"Western civilization has made an alien of Latin," he grumbled.
"That only means something's gone seriously wrong with the
world. Pliny's apothegm is still as valid today as it was nineteen
hundred years ago."

301

"You old-fashioned thing!" his wife reproved him again. "Nobody, just nobody, says 'apothegm' these days. Why not maxim? From the day we landed in Africa you've been drilling Pliny in my ear: *'There's always something new out of Africa'!'*"

"Well," he grinned, "look around and admit it's very apposite for the time and place in which we find ourselves this week."

She looked around the room. In the light of the kerosene pressure lamp, the dark cream paint of the walls looked lovely. The parquet floor continued into the sitting area. Electric lamps with beautiful shades had been installed in the ceiling and on the walls. But each room was lit with the white lights of a pressure lamp, awaiting the completion of the power station six months from that date. The six dining chairs were upholstered in red. Their servant—the steward they had brought up on "trek"—stood by the mahogany sideboard to one side of the dining room. Another servant, not visible, was pulling the cord of the punkah which sent cooling currents of air down from the ceiling over the diners.

"It's almost incredible, Geoffrey," Lady Robin admitted. (Her husband had been knighted when he became chief justice of Luawaland the year before.) "It doesn't seem possible all this should be happening in this wild African bush. And yet they're always running us British down! But you know, seeing for myself what's happening here in this backward Sunia District, I feel proud to be British. I'm even prouder of you, Geoffrey."

"Who's old-fashioned *and* jingoistic now?" he laughed at her. But at that moment he was proud, too, to be so appreciated. Few men were heroes to their wives. But even at that moment his happiness was spoiled by jealousy. She was so young and beautiful that he felt guilty to be fifteen years older. Always he was jealous and afraid she might be having affairs with younger men. There was Mike Hendrick; Edward Charteris, Henry—He had never had any proof of her infidelity. In secret despair he would tell himself it was because she was too clever for him.

In truth, though, he wronged her. Looking across the table, she thought he looked as always handsome, and his hair, more gray now than black, added to his air of distinction. He looked born to be chief justice anywhere in the world. His nose was large. But that was not noticeably under the high, noble forehead. Eyes black and very brilliant. She had loved him most for his lips. They were almost girlish, exquisitely shaped. She was a little worried about his complexion. It was becoming slightly florid in the last year.

As he picked up the port bottle again she said, with great firmness, "*No*, Geoffrey. You'd finished the white wine before the crab."

"Then I'll have a little more of your excellent crab salad."

"You've had enough, dear. I shouldn't think port goes so well with—"

"*Please.*"

"Oh, very well."

The steward served coffee and brandy. After which the Robins retired to their bedroom.

There were three bedrooms in the large bungalow. Each one had a bathroom. In the main bedroom, there was a magnificent mahogany double bed. The servant had let down the mosquito net around it. The moon shone through the lace curtains in the large, barred windows.

The couple soon changed for the night.

Lady Robin went to bed straightaway.

Sir Geoffrey slipped his old blue silk dressing gown over his pajama suit.

"Hadn't you better come to bed, Geoffrey?" his lady asked rather crossly. "I know the Vamboi case is very important. But you must have gone over the records of the lower court a dozen times."

"But there are peculiar circumstances in the case, Cynthia. Anyway, this is the very last time I'm reading the records. I'll soon turn in."

He took the records out of his briefcase. He sat down by the dressing table to read them. He was studying them for almost an hour.

That was perhaps a mistake. While he assimilated all the salient facts of the case, it also enabled the atmosphere of Sunia to get him. The two days of court sittings he had dealt with ease with the cases of larceny, rape, etc.: the usual humdrum type to be found on a judge's up-country list. Nevertheless, this case of *Regina* versus *James Vamboi* still worried him. But after the last reading of the transcript he was convinced he could cope. The method of murder was new in the annals of crime. But he would have no need as a judge to bring in the panoply of the occult to explain the features of the case, though these were macabre enough, to be sure.

"It seems a straightforward case to me," he told himself, putting the typescript away in his briefcase and stifling a yawn. He reached out his hand to the pressure lamp on its stand between the dressing table and the wardrobe. He turned the knob preparatory to turning in for the night. "A straightforward case, and I shall so deal with it."

The air began to hiss out of the reservoir of the pressure lamp. But before the judge could take his fingers off the milled head of the knob, a lot of strange things began to happen.

First he was conscious that the door opened. At the same time a coldness entered the room. It was not an uncomfortable coldness, though. On the contrary, it had been a hot night. Now the room felt as if it was air-conditioned.

But why had the door opened? Was it in fact open? Judge Robin's back was turned to it. In spite of this, he was as sure as if he was looking at the panels that the door had opened. To settle the point he turned; or rather, attempted to turn to face into the room.

But he could not move. He could not move his hand from the lamp. Something soft and gently was holding his fingers to the milled head. Whatever influence it was, though gentle, it seemed to have all the power in the universe behind it.

Then, against his own will, the judge felt his right hand twist, so that he tightened the knob again. But much of the air had escaped from the reservoir. By now the light in the mantle was trembling between a pallid whiteness and the threat of going out altogether. Nevertheless, against all the rules it continued to flicker, and seemed capable of flickering throughout eternity without going out.

"A straightforward case, eh, Robin? What asses we judges are."

Judge Robin started at the sound of the voice. His fingers broke contact with the lamp. That voice again! He knew it very well. But he knew it only in the long ago. At a time blurred by sorrow and a funeral. How in the name of goodness could a voice challenge Time and the grave to be so natural? How— But just as the force in the room had willed his hand on the knob of the lamp, so now he felt it bending his mind away from the past. He could have sworn that something willed him to remember that his wife had been an actress, and would sometimes play superb tricks of mimicry on him. He smiled to himself. Without surprise to himself, he found himself gliding toward the bed. He was not conscious of limbs, of muscles, of balance.

The lamp continued to flicker behind him. The moonlight blazed through the curtains, splashing the bed with silver.

Sir Geoffrey saw his lady lying on the far side of the bed. She lay on her side. Her hair was scattered like a skein of gold over the pillow. She was fast asleep. Then the judge experienced a slight shock, not unpleasant. It was at seeing *himself* lying in the bed beside his wife. He too was fast asleep. He lay on his back, staring at the ceiling, the moonlight reflected from his eyes.

Now the judge's heart began to beat rather fast. Still, though excited, he felt nothing like fear. Furthermore, though he knew he was wide awake—never mind that chunk of inertia disguised as flesh pretending to be *him* in the bed—he was convinced he was awake in a way different from all the other three hundred and sixty-four days in the year. His brain was working as if it had kicked away material limitations. He was Mind incarnate. Thus though he was certain his wife was asleep beside his carcass in the bed, he felt no astonishment whatever to hear her voice coming from behind him. Now that he was able to turn, he saw her standing across the room in her all too familiar housecoat.

"Ernest!" she was saying. "How wonderful to see you again after all these years!"

"Yes indeed, Ernest!" Sir Geoffrey echoed her welcome with pleasure. "But why did you not send us a wire to say you were coming?"

Sir Geoffrey wondered if it was Sir Ernest who had come through the door with the coldness. He did not look a cold figure as he stood in the middle of the room between him and Cynthia. He was a tall African with a long, very handsome face. (The ladykiller of the bar he was called in his young days.) He wore a full-bottomed judge's wig and crimson robe and looked immensely distinguished.

He smiled with affability as husband and wife converged on him in the middle of the room. Though they greeted him with such warmth, they did not shake hands. Nor did it strike the Robins as odd that their visitor should walk into their bedroom in full judge's regalia while they were in their night attire. Somehow Sir Ernest's smile and carriage were able to take care of all that. And when he spoke, his voice, a golden one, was full of solicitude.

"Friendship proves itself when friends can welcome each other whatever the circumstances on either side. I've come as a matter of urgency, Cynthia, because I'm not happy about Geoff. This visit is for him, and is not necessarily a social one."

"I suppose you judges must talk shop," returned Cynthia with a smile. "Will you have your usual Black Label whisky, Ernest?"

"No thank you, my dear."

Lady Robin took the only armchair in the room. Sir Ernest sat on the stool, his back to the dressing table mirror. Sir Geoffrey remained standing.

All the while the room remained cold, the light continued to flicker.

"May I smoke, Cynthia?"

"Certainly, Ernest," returned his hostess. "Is it one of your famous scented cigars?"

"Thanks. Yes, it's the same old brand," Sir Ernest chuckled. Judge Robin did not observe where the gold cigar case came from. But there it was in Sir Ernest's hand. He opened it, took out one cigar. He did not offer his host one. He cut the cylinder with a gold pen-knife. The action looked so natural. Though it was cold, and the light was flickering.

Sir Ernest lit up.

The first mouthful of smoke at once embraced the Robins in nostalgia. For Sir Ernest was the first friend they made when they came to West Africa. And, as Lady Robin so well recalled, that distinguished African, famous as a *bon viveur*, always smoked a special brand of Havana, gloriously scented.

"I've come about that murder case you're to try in the morning, Geoff," said Sir Ernest, sitting on the stool, very affable and quite at home. He blew a cone of smoke toward his friend. "Do be careful. Don't be carried away by circumstantial evidence. That has in its time killed as many innocents as judges' consciences. I had a very similar case in this very Sunia some years ago. The result for me, as you'll recall, was disastrous. It looked a straightforward case. I'm sorry to say my summing up to the jury was wrong in toto. Circumstantial evidence, you see. I hope you will—"

He stopped in the middle of the sentence. His eyes were staring with a frightening intensity through and through Judge Robin.

All the time he had sat on the stool Sir Ernest had looked as large and clear as life. But all at once the color began to fade from his robe. The full-bottomed wig became more lacelike. The flesh appeared to evaporate from the face. Soon, only the outline of wig and face remained: till Sir Geoffrey became aware he was seeing the dressing table through the outline figure of a long-dead judge of the Supreme Court.

In one bound he was across the room. He began to pump the lamp as if his life depended on it.

"Cynthia!"

"Geoffrey!"

The beautiful blond woman leapt up in bed and sought to rush to her husband. She got entangled in the mosquito net—which came tearing down to the floor around her. In frenzy she freed herself and ran across to her husband.

"Geoffrey," she gasped, shuddering, "I—I—I have had the most disturbing dream."

"What was the dream, my dear?"

"I dreamed the late Sir Ernest Williams called on us—"

"Wearing a new judge's robe—"

"With full-bottomed wig—"

They stared at each other, shocked beyond measure at the simultaneous invasion of their collective unconscious.

"And—and—and—" Lady Robin stammered, shivered, "he-he was—smoking—"

She stopped and sniffed the air.

"Have you been smoking, Geoffrey?"

"I'm a pipe man, dear," her husband reminded her. "Besides, with young Geoff at Harrow, I can't afford tobacco *that* expensive."

The room was redolent of scented cigar smoke.

Then he took his lady by the hand and led her to the dressing table.

"Look!" he said softly.

He pointed to the object at one corner of the table. In the brilliant white light of the pressure lamp could be seen cigar ash more than half an inch long, lying on the dressing-table just as the smoker had flicked it off. When Lady Robin touched it it was still warm. It crumbled instantly—and vanished.

"O-O-Oh!"

Sir Geoffrey caught his wife to his chest before she fell to the floor. She had fainted.

Only then as reality exploded on him did his hair stand on end.

But the feeling of terror he had was momentary. The next instant he lifted his wife in his arms and bore her to the bed.

She was not unconscious for long. But it was some time before he was able to calm her fears.

"There must be some *rational* explanation," the judge kept telling himself all through the night.

But if there was an explanation the judge did not find it. Sir Ernest Williams, the chief justice of Luawaland, had died in very mysterious circumstances. It was in that very Sunia, in the very house pulled down to build this beautiful bungalow. It was on the night following the trial of a notorious case of murder. A juju man had been sentenced to death. The prisoner had maintained his innocence to the end. When the judge passed sentence on him, he had told him calmly he, the judge, would die before his unjust sentence was carried out. Sir Ernest had spent his last night in the old rest house. The next morning, he was found lying on his back in bed, staring wide-eyed at the ceiling. He was stone dead. Two palm leaves were crossed on the pillow above his head. A cowrie lay on the center of his forehead. There was no mark of violence on his body. No blood was spilled. And though he was a man reputed never to have had an illness in life, at autopsy no cause of death was found.

The case the chief justice had tried had been one of the most sensational in the country. It was steeped in juju. Some seven years after the juju man was hanged, even more sensational evidence was raked out of the embers of the case. This evidence proved conclusively that the old case had been one of "ritual murder." Several of the "big men" in the district were involved. Eight culprits were hanged. And the poor juju man who had been judicially murdered had had nothing to do with the case.

This and other matters Sir Geoffrey Robin pondered and worried over through the rest of the night. He made his wife take a sleeping tablet. As for himself, barbiturates gave him a hangover worse than insomnia. In any case, he would never take any kind of sedative if he had a case in court next day. Thus though he put the light out, and lay beside his wife in bed, he did not sleep at all.

He watched the new day dawn. It brought no dawn to his spirits. He took breakfast. And though, radiant after a good night's rest, Cynthia fussed over him, his breakfast turned out a meal at which the coffee was without flavor, the bacon like pulped newsprint.

He was not feeling his best when he walked the short distance to the new courthouse. It had been completed not three months before. And that was the first time he was coming up on circuit there.

His orderly accompanied him up to his office. He robed there in his office. At half past eight sharp he walked down the corridor into the court room.

"Court rise!"

The judge walked up to the dais, mounted. He bowed first on one side, then the other, took his seat on the rostrum.

The case *Regina* versus *James Vamboi* was called. Wilful murder. Defense counsel entered a plea of not guilty.

"M'lord, gentlemen of the jury..."

The attorney general rose in the well of the court, standing by the baize-topped table. The voice boomed through the new courthouse and echoed round the mahogany-paneled walls. Proud of having the finest voice of any barrister in West Africa, the A.G. turned toward the sunlit windows beneath which twelve Africans sat on benches of that aggressively uncomfortable kind encountered only in those two places where men, apart from fools and tyrants, admit they are inferior to their institutions: a church and a court of law.

"I doubt if it is possible to describe the malice and low cunning that motivated this murder. More pertinent, gentlemen of the jury, is that yet again something new has come out of Africa. Look in the dock, gentlemen, at the author of this novelty in ghastliness."

On his rostrum Sir Geoffrey drew himself up. His eyes, along with the twelve pairs of the jury, as well as those of the large crowd sitting breathless in court, surveyed what instead of a monster, looked like a very ordinary human male in the dock. Murmurs and movements blended with the subdued sunlight, which, absorbed in part by the wooden panels that lined the walls, managed to tone down the tropical brightness of the morning. The new courtroom also gave an air of gravity, and seriousness appropriate for a murder trial. The policeman standing beside the prisoner coughed. The crowd in the body of the court stirred more nervously. As usher called, "Silence in court."

The judge's face became less impassive as he surveyed the man in the dock.

That young African, in a cheap gray suit, appeared to be the only person in court unconcerned about the trial. As the judge's eyes were fixed on him across the court, the prisoner raised a steel rat trap to the level of his eyes. He winked and whistled to the inmate of the cage. The rat sat up on its haunches and chirped back just like a cricket.

"How are we, Robin?" the prisoner asked the creature in the cage. Thereupon he raised his face and grinned across to the judge.

Robin! That was the judge's own name. It echoed round and round in Sir Geoffrey's head as the prisoner again called to his rodent friend.

From habit, the face under the judge's wig that was now turned to the prisoner became as expressive as a cadaver's. Nevertheless Judge Robin's heart was working like a strange machine in his chest. With an effort he made a mental note that he would not allow the goings-on in the dock, however bizarre, to bolster up a plea of insanity.

"Gentlemen of the jury," the attorney general went on, "the facts of the case are these—"

"Just a minute, Mr. Attorney General," said the judge. Though all in court observed him to be making records in the book before him, he was not in fact writing. His heart was racing away so that it almost choked him.

For neither the prisoner's appearance nor his comportment was conducive to the judge's peace of mind. Nor, for that matter, were his recollections of the incidents of the night. Sitting there on the dais, high above the court, and so isolated, he wanted to be detached from the passions and frailties that prejudice judgment in a court of law. Above all, he desired to perform his work that day with a mind more than ordinarily free from distraction.

But that morning, for the first time in his career on the bench, he did not feel he could give his undivided mind to the case in the jurisdiction of his court. That distressed him in the extreme. A true rationalist, justice was his religion. He was so distressed he felt obliged to take the unusual course of ordering an adjournment even before the case properly opened.

"The court," he announced without preliminary, "is adjourned for fifteen minutes."

An astonished court rose and watched him go toward the side door, on his way to his office.

It was a cream-painted, airy place. He locked the door behind him. As soon as he sat down at the desk his distress passed, and his confidence began to return. The view through the window gave onto a rice field, bordering on the little river. The hills rose in greenery beyond. With the sun shining over the whole, it brought to Sir Geoffrey's mind the assurance of the permanence of Nature and natural laws, the permanence of normality. For that his soul craved that morning.

Besides, this was the first time he was coming on circuit to Sunia District. The region was one of the most backward in West Africa. It had a bad name for juju and witchcraft. Being an Englishman, Judge Robin knew he could rise, as he was expected to rise, above such superstitions. The administration had the greatest confidence in him. And, he admitted with pride, he was deserving of that confidence. He was one of those splendid white men in all the British West African colonies who set up judicial systems equal to what they knew in England. He was determined, too, that this his first major case in Sunia with juju associations would make legal history, and deal a mortal blow to the pernicious superstitions in the country. Such was his resolution when he came down from the capital three days before.

"And that is my resolution *now*," he told himself with firmness, "never mind what happened last night."

In a matter of seconds he recapitulated all the strange things that had happened in the night.

"That is all past," Sir Geoffrey now told himself. "It is morning, I am in court. The case must go on."

However, Sir Ernest's warning of the night stuck like a beacon in his mind.

"I will be wary of circumstantial evidence," he promised himself.

Finding calm in his heart, he took a grip on himself and returned to the court room.

"Gentlemen of the jury," the attorney general's voice rang around the hall, "the facts of the case are as follows. On the morning of the twelfth of June last, the police received the report of the sudden death of one John Lebbie. The prisoner, James Vamboi, reported the death. The manner of his reporting it drew the suspicion of the officer on duty. There was blood on the prisoner's clothes. And he had said"—he turned with a ponderosity meant to impress toward the man in the dock—" 'Cock Robin has killed my Uncle John.' "

The A.G.'s smile gained a tinge of the ominous as he turned

it on the jury, "holding it" long enough for the interpreter to translate his words into Sowanah for some of the jurors not acquainted with English.

"Have you ever heard, gentlemen of the jury, of such callousness, allied with flippancy in the presence of death, as a man going to the police station to accuse Cock Robin of murder? As it turned out, the prisoner rationalized this brutality by stating that Cock Robin was not the bird the British brainwashed us to cry over in our nursery days, but his late uncle's pet rat. Cock Robin a rat? Why not Little Red Riding Hood turned wolf?"

"Your lordship." The defense counsel leapt up like a very agitated jack-in-the-box at the table and bawled up to the bench, "Your lordship, I object."

The A.G. regarded him with a stern ferocity, though he sat down for about a tenth of a second.

"To what," came his cold query, "does my learned friend object, m'lord?"

"My learned friend, my lord, is trying to influence you with European suggestions. This is an *African* murder—an alleged one. It has nothing to do with British wolves, riding hoods or what have you."

"Objection overruled," said the judge.

The defense counsel, a short wizened man with a bloated face, gave a knowing glance at the jury. He left them feeling he kept a host of aces up his sleeve.

"Thank you, m'lord." The A.G.'s smile was all urbanity. "Leaving aside this flimsy attempt at an alibi, gentlemen of the jury, let me give you the outline of what the police found at the scene of the crime.

"The murdered man was found in his bed in his bedroom. According to the prisoner, the body had not been moved. There was no sign of violence on the corpse. The right foot lay in a pool of blood which had soaked through the mattress and congealed on the floor.

We shall call the family doctor of the deceased, gentlemen of the jury, to inform you about his condition of health up to the day of his death. As a result of this, he had no sensation whatever in the toes of his feet. This fact was known to the accused. He himself had admitted it in the lower court. Thus the right great toe of the deceased became, if your lordship will excuse the classical allusion, his Achilles' heel. Through that toe death came to him. In short, he bled to death through a hole in his toe.

"John Lebbie dies in the quiet of the night, in sleep, mercifully without pain. We shall call the pathologist to give expert evidence that the deceased died as the result of the artery in his right great toe being cut across. The wound on the underside of the toe was of a peculiar nature. It was not a cut. It was a gnawed, gouged wound.

"A search of the prisoner's room revealed an old and rusty nail gouge. Rusty, that is, in every part but its business end. This end, contrary to all usage, was not blunt. Oh, no! It was bright as stainless steel, having been filed and honed till it was as sharp as a razor. The width of the gouge fitted perfectly into the furrows left on the underside of the deceased's great toe. The pathologist will inform you, gentlemen, that this instrument could have caused the wound that proved fatal to John Lebbie. My lord, I tender it in evidence."

The court clerk passed the nail gouge turned weapon up to the bench. The judge glanced at it, instructed that it be accepted, entered and labeled as Exhibit A.

With satisfaction, the A.G. observed Exhibit A had produced all the effect he had hoped for on the jury. He continued.

"The instrument was to hand. The opportunity came to the prisoner on the night of June eleven–twelve. At any rate that was the night he seized it. He was alone in the house with his uncle. He himself admits all the doors and windows were locked on the inside. No one had forced an entry. He knew John Lebbie would not feel a wound in his toes if even he was awake. He killed him when he was asleep.

"We have proven instrument of and opportunity for murder. A cast-iron case, gentlemen of the jury. It is not for the prosecution to prove motive in any case. In this case, however, motive is plainer than a pikestaff. James Vamboi was broke. He had just closed his account at Barclay's Bank. He was in debt. Creditors were squeezing him. Very hard. He had been used to a profligate life in the capital. He knew he was his uncle's heir. John Lebbie was a very wealthy farmer. His nephew was happy to pay his own debts with his uncle's life."

Here he made a satisfied as well as dramatic pause. He knew the jury were his to the last doubting Thomas.

The A.G. now pulled himself up to his full six-foot height. He was a striking figure in his wig and gown. And to this grandeur of his peroration—as the jury thought—added further distinction.

"It is not my business, gentlemen, to work on your feelings. The case is stark and brutal enough to have done that in its mere narration. But I have given you only the outline. I shall now call evidence to prove the case.

The police, the pathologist, and the rest of the grim and boring parade took two morning and two afternoon sessions to go to and from the witness box. Every witness was harried and counter-harried by prosecution and defense.

The defense counsel, though he looked so mild and harmless—indeed, slightly if not certifiably insane—gave the pathologist a grueling time in the witness box. Expert witnesses are very often so extremely expert they cease to be sensible. It was one thing for the pathologist to say with that brutal confidence of the forensic expert that Exhibit A *could* have caused the wound that killed John Lebbie. It was quite another to show that it actually *did*. In short, while the expert tried to look over defense with godly disdain, the little man had made him look a fool to the jury. Indeed, he was so clever he succeeded in making the "twelve good men and true" believe he had led only one of the dozens of aces up his sleeve to trump the pathologist.

What these aces of the defense counsel might have been—apart from suggestion, a psychological weapon that often turns out a damp squib—it would have been difficult for any prejudiced observer in court to tell. At any rate, as far as the case had gone up to that point, all the evidence that had been adduced had gone, all along the line, against the prisoner. Admittedly it was circumstantial. Then again the prisoner's levity in the dock, his insouciance later verging on the bizarre, had done nothing to secure him the sympathy of the jury.

It is no matter for surprise, then, that all the jurors leaned forward in their seats to stare in wonder at Vamboi when he elected to give evidence in his own defense. As every lawyer knows, this can be a very dangerous procedure for a criminal. He could easily hang himself. But James Vamboi had no fear. Carrying his rat trap, he moved over from the dock to the witness box.

As he entered the witness box, he flourished the rat trap like a trophy above his head. He set it down on the shelf in front of the box: on top of the Bible, Koran and gris-gris on which witnesses were sworn.

With his long wiry hair standing up all over his head, he looked altogether quite macabre, frightening in his wildness.

Judge Robin fixed his eyes on the rat trap. He went slightly green.

"Is the presence of that rat really necessary in my court?" he asked.

"It's vital for our case, m'lord," defense counsel assured him.

"Very well," Sir Geoffrey conceded, turning greener. "But," he muttered, "I hate the creatures."

As soon as he was sworn—on the Bible—James Vamboi began to spread confusion in court. It was a confusion of tongues. He would speak perfect English, Creole, Sowanah—and then some dialect no one in court understood.

Defense counsel rose to lead his witness.

"Name?"

"James Vamboi."

"Where do you live?"

"At Thirty-five Taranko Road."

"Is that the same address as the deceased?"

"Yes."

"What's your occupation?"

"I'm out of work."

"Did you know the deceased?"

"He was my uncle."

Here defense counsel picked up Exhibit A from the table.

"Do you recognize this nail gouge?"

"Yes. It's mine."

"Did you kill your uncle, John Lebbie, with it?"

The prisoner started. He fixed on his lawyer a look of the gravest indignation. His forehead gathered in a ferocious frown.

"Have you," he asked in fury, "joined the prosecution against me?"

Judge Robin leaned over his desk, above which the punkah was going to and fro, and warned the witness, "Confine your answers to the questions asked."

From the way Vamboi grinned and leered at him Sir Geoffrey was not sure if he had understood him. So he addressed himself to the attorney general.

"Mr. Attorney General, I dread to think what irrelevancies we may be dragged into if we take witness's evidence in the strict, formal way. I suggest we let him tell his story in his own way."

"No objection, m'lord," the A.G. rose to answer. "Only I pray you to keep him tightly in rein."

"Now," defense counsel resumed, turning to the man in the box, "tell the court what you found in your uncle's bedroom that morning you called the police.

James Vamboi first grinned up to the rostrum, as if there was some cabalistic understanding between him and the judge.

"When I went to uncle's room," he began, "I found he was dead. Robin here"—to avoid confusion he pointed to the trap. The judge felt rather squeamish at the implied comparison—as though he were "Robin up there." "Robin here was at the foot of the bed. He—Robin, not my uncle who was already dead—jumped down to the floor as I approached the bed. He left a spoor of blood all along the floor. It was then I saw his fur was all caked with blood."

Robin, he deposed, was his uncle's pet rat. Every night his uncle used to put some dried fish in Robin's cage. He was quite tame. The cage—it was a trap, but of course it was Robin's home, so it could not be a trap to *him*—was in its usual place by the wall in the bedroom. The round door (here Vamboi pointed it out) at the back of the cage was open. He had observed Robin hop back into his cage. He noticed the blood about his uncle's foot. "You know when there's no food about a house at night rats come out of their holes and eat the feet of people sleeping." Robin must have been very hungry, he thought. His uncle must have forgotten to put food in the cage.

"Poor Robin meant no harm. I'm sure he would have preferred dried fish to uncle's toe. I'm sure he meant no harm."

Giving evidence, he looked mad to everyone in court; most of all to the judge.

Nevertheless, from that story plainly told James Vamboi would not budge an inch.

Defense counsel, smiling as if he had laid a booby trap for the prosecution, sat down.

The attorney general tried all his forensic wiles to shake the evidence. But he soon developed the sensation he was battering his head against the Rock of Gibraltar. Finding his sanity confronted with that robust madness from the witness box, the A.G. began to feel he must have become made by induction. At last he was exasperated to the point of losing his temper: a thing no one ever remembered him doing.

"So Robin did it all, eh?" he sneered, his sarcasm firing on all six cylinders, shooting out the most potent nerve poison for witnesses known to the bar. "Pity," he roared so that his voice echoed from the walls, "pity poor Robin can't talk!"

The judge, the jury, the whole court chuckled at that. But the man in the witness box laughed—loud, and diabolically. Then, leaning over the front of the box, grinning hugely, he told the A.G. in a penetrating whisper:

"A-ha! But Robin *can*!"

The judge sat bolt upright. The court stirred like a giant beehive warming in the morning sun. For five whole seconds the A.G.'s mouth remained agape. Then he roared at the witness:

"Robin can *what?*"

"Robin *can* talk," Vamboi assured him with the simplicity born of confidence—or lunacy. He bent with affection over the cage. "Can't you, Robin?"

Robin's answer was a twitter common to all rats. If he could speak the language of Shakespeare, he was keeping it mighty dark: at least, for the moment.

"Let me take him out of his cage," the witness offered.

"You'll do no such thing!" Judge Robin screamed at him. Once, as a toddler he had been bitten by a rat. He had since had a phobia for all rodents. His breath came rasping out of his chest. The sweat began to pour down his face. "Mr. Attorney General," he asked in a shaking voice, "did the government psychiatrist report this man to be *compos mentis?*"

"Who am I, m'lord," the Crown prosecutor returned with his famous sarcasm, "to question the strange ways of experts?"

The judge muttered that psychiatrists were themselves the best fitted subjects for straitjackets.

But that did not help the situation. So the judge wiped off the perspiration running into his eyes. A cold shiver ran down his spine when he turned from the A.G. to the man in the witness box.

"Tell them," that extraordinary young man was saying, as with affection he wagged his finger at the rat in the trap. "*You* killed the old cock, didn't you, Robin?"

Robin ran twice around the cage, twittering.

"Come on, my friend." The prisoner's exhortation to the rodent now held a note of anxiety, like an impresario being let down by his most renowned prima donna. "*You* killed the old cock, didn't you, Robin?"

And now the words were beating like hammer blows within the judge's head. In all his years in Africa he had never witnessed anything so preposterous as the scene unfolding in his court. This surely was juju on the rampage. If science had pronounced this man sane, then he, Geoffrey Robin, was bonkers. But what was sanity? At once he recalled Sir Ernest's warnings about the pitfalls of circumstantial evidence. He saw him as clearly as he had seen him in his dream: as if he had come to his court to keep him up to scratch. Evidence? What was evidence in the quicksands of juju country? What was evidence when science could vouch for Vamboi's sanity? His, Judge Robin's, was already tottering. Sweating, breathing shallowly through his mouth, he felt powerless to control the scene whose madness now began to gather momentum in his court.

Nor was he the only one there so affected. Hardboiled as the A.G. was supposed to be, master of every court situation he had ever found himself in in twenty years, he was gaping in consternation at the man in the witness box. The jurors were sitting forward speechless, still as wax figures on their benches.

The prisoner exhorted the rat, begged, whined. It was as if the rodent had turned into a god the way he prayed to it. Finally, with anguish and terror, and the sweat pouring out of his face, he bent over the cage sobbing:

"*You* killed the old cock, didn't you, Robin?"

At last sanity returned to the judge's mind. In a flash he saw through the whole situation. The prisoner's story hung together. It was the police who were bonkers to have organized a plot too complex for the criminal's understanding. And with all his high intelligence the attorney general had outbonkered all the rest. But then, though he would not have admitted this to anyone connected with the bar, he knew from experience that star forensic skill sometimes spun reason into such a close spiral it could not tell its backside from its front. The rat-kill-man story was all too unfamiliar and unnewsworthy compared with the man-kill-man one. Damn the police and their circumstantial or other evidence.

"Young man," said the judge. The court knew by the tone of his voice where his sympathy and his judgment lay. "Young man, surely you're not expecting sense and coherence out of a mere rat?"

As soon as he said this Judge Robin knew he had undone the knot that held the macabre situation together in his court. Like an actor behind the footlights, every judge in court is sensitive to the "feel" of that court; the meandering of the jury-mind; above all of his control over the proceedings. Now for the first time in his professional life Judge Robin knew what it was to panic and lose control over his court.

For the words were no sooner out of his mouth than Robin the rat spun around to face him through the bars of his cage.

The attitude of the rodent was less significant than that of the prisoner. Vamboi was standing in the witness box staring raptly at the judge. His stance was rigid, cataleptic. Over the cage he held two palm leaves crossed in one hand, in the other a large cowrie.

The knowledge came to the judge with the impact of a psychological blockbuster: Vamboi was using occult means to impose his will on him. Judge Robin trembled with the wrath of outrage. Practice juju on him—on *him*: the choice product of England's premium university; the inheritor of that enlightened sanity European civilization had taken three thousand years to spawn. Juju on *him*!

But outrage is born of resentment, and implies the will to resist. To his horror Judge Robin found he had no will to resist the waves of suggestion impinging on his personality from across the well of the court. It dawned on him in a flash that Vamboi had the means of willing him not so much to *do* whatever he willed, but to see, feel, and think what Vamboi relayed he should. The realization came to him with a terror that was insupportable. The fellow swiftly oozed and squeezed into his personality so that he felt himself to be possessed by the foulness in the witness box that passed for man. It was a kind of possession by an unclean spirit, a demonic combination between man working through the rat as an instrument of destructive psychological power. Something again new—though so old—out of Africa.

Suggestion. That was it. But how could he—*he*, Geoffrey Robin, double first at Oxford, president of the Union, he!—be suggestible by such a source? That was the last flicker of resistance in him, his last controlled thought. Beyond that his mind was not his to control. But how he could *feel!*

He felt some three hundred and more pairs of eyes around the court riveted like nails upon him. He felt most horribly isolated up on his rostrum. He felt and saw the rat stand on his hind legs. It gripped the bars of the cage with its forepaws and began to shake the cage.

No one else in court saw or heard the cage shake and rattle. A last tremor of thought shivered in the judge telling him the thing was not happening; it was only he himself who was being made to feel it was taking place. But the thought would not stick to reality.

Suddenly Judge Robin felt the air around him to be impregnated with the smell and discomfort of juju. In a twinkling the rat had run from the trap. Across the floor. Up on the rostrum. There it was, sitting at the front of his desk. At that diabolical moment when Robin the rat appeared to swell to the size of a bull gorilla the judge *knew* he was not on the desk at all. He knew it was Vamboi inside him, Geoffrey Robin, making him see the rodent there, pouring his soundless thoughts across to him in waves that almost burst his eardrums.

"Of course," Robin the rat roared, "I *can* talk! And of course, it was *I* who killed the old cock. James has an alibi. You dare hang him and you'll go the way of Sir Ernest Williams. James's alibi?" The rat's eyes became incandescent with malice. "You were on circuit the night Uncle Lebbie died. James spent the night with your wife, Lady Cynthia. *Ha-ha-ha! Ha-ha-ha!*"

The laugh reverberated in thunderclaps around the courtroom.

Overwhelmed by a foreboding and a constriction in his chest, Judge Robin clutched at his throat. His wife, beautiful, charming and much younger than himself, had been an actress. Second only to his phobia for rats was his unfounded fear that she was unfaithful to him. And now he knew that the two greatest aversions of his life had joined to disgrace him in his court. Was it possible that that half-mad Vamboi across the court could, by just holding palm leaves and cowrie in his hands, invade, permeate and destroy him from within? At that moment of mental anguish he felt the teeth of the rat tearing into his throat. African juju had done its worst. With a gasp of horror the judge fell foward fainting on the rostrum—

"Geoffrey! Geoffrey!" A woman was shouting into Judge Robin's ear. "Wake up!"

"My God, Cynthia!" Sir Geoffrey gasped, sitting bolt upright on the bed.

The bedroom was flooded with moonlight.

Her blond hair scattered over her shoulders, Lady Robin was standing in her nightdress in the flood of moonlight. She still held her husband by the shoulders.

The judge rubbed his eyes in disbelief. For it was not yet morning. He had not gone to court. The case of *Regina* versus *James Vamboi* was still to be tried.

"What a nightmare I've had, my dear!" he sighed.

"I warned you," said his lovely lady, "to go easy with that crab salad at dinner."

Judge Robin burst into gargantuan laughter.

"Really, Geoffrey," his wife protested, "you're behaving strangely."

Sir Geoffrey was unrepentant in his mirth. He was a double fanatic: of detective novels and bridge. Conan Doyle, Agatha Christie, Erle Stanley Gardner, the lot: he had them all almost by heart. Bridge, however, was the joy of his life. For two of his three years at Oxford he had captained the bridge club against Cambridge.

"Never mind, my dear," he said with a very pleased smile. "I wouldn't have missed the crab salad or the nightmare for a dinner at the Coq d'Or in the West End. I've played the hand of my life: a double, miracle takeout bid against tall detective stories; and the even taller stories that come so frequently out of good old Africa."

Joy and the Law

GIUSEPPE DI LAMPEDUSA

W HEN HE GOT ONTO the bus he irritated everyone. The briefcase crammed with other people's business, the enormous parcel which made his left arm stick out, the grey velvet scarf, the umbrella on the point of opening, all made it difficult for him to produce his return ticket. He was forced to put his parcel on the ticket collector's bench, setting off an avalanche of small coins; as he tried to bend down to pick them up, he provoked protests from those who stood behind him, who feared that because of his dallying their coats would be caught in the automatic doors. At last he managed to squeeze into the row of people clinging to the handles in the gangway. He was slight of build, but his bundles gave him the cubic capacity of a nun in seven habits. As the bus slid through the chaos of the traffic, his inconvenient bulk spread resentment from front to rear of the coach. He stepped on people's feet, they trod on his; he invited rebuke, and when he heard the word *cornuto* from the rear of the bus alluding to his presumed marital disgrace, his sense of honor compelled him to turn his head in that direction and make his exhausted eyes assume what he imagined to be a threatening expression.

The bus, meanwhile, was passing through streets where rustic baroque fronts hid a wretched hinterland which emerged at each street corner in the yellow light of eighty-year-old shops.

At his stop he rang the bell, descended, tripped over the umbrella, and found himself alone at last on his square meter of disconnected footpath. He hastened to make sure that he still

322

had his plastic wallet. And then he was free to relish his bliss.

Enclosed in that wallet were 37,245 lire — the 'thirteenth month-ly salary' received as a Christmas bonus an hour before. This sum meant the removal of several thorns from his flesh: the obliga-tions to his landlord, all the more pressing because his was a controlled rent and he owed two quarters; and to the ever-punctual installment collector for the short lapin coat ('It suits you better than a long coat, my dear — it makes you look slim-mer'); the dirty looks from the fishmonger and the greengrocer. Those four bank notes of high denomination also eased the fear of the next electricity bill, the pained glances at the children's shoes, and the anxious watching of the gas cylinder's flickering flame; they did not represent opulence, certainly, but did give that breathing space in distress which is the true joy of the poor; a couple of thousand lire might survive for a while, before being eaten up in the resplendence of a Christmas dinner.

However, he had known too many 'thirteenths' to attribute the euphoria which now enveloped him to the ephemeral exhilara-tion they could produce. He was filled with a rosy feeling, as rosy as the wrapping on the sweet burden that was making his left arm numb. The feeling sprang from the seven-kilo Christmas cake, the panettone that he had brought home from the office. He had no passion for the mixture — as highly guaranteed as it was questionable — of flour, sugar, dried eggs and raisins. At heart he did not care for it at all. But seven kilos of luxury food all at once! A limited but vast abundance in a household where provisions came in hectograms and half-liters! A famous product in a larder devoted to third-rate items! What a joy for Maria! What a riot for the children who for two weeks would explore the unknown Wild West of an afternoon snack!

These, however, were the joys of others, the material joys of vanilla essence and colored cardboard; of panettone, in sum. His personal joy was different — a spiritual bliss based on pride and loving affection; yes, spiritual!

When, a few hours before, the baronet who was managing director of his firm had distributed pay envelopes and Christmas wishes with the overbearing affability of the pompous old man that he was, he also announced that the seven-kilo panettone, which had come with the compliments of the big firm that pro-duced it, would be awarded to the most deserving employee; and he asked his dear colleagues democratically (that was the word he had actually used) to choose the lucky man then and there.

The panettone had stood on the middle of the desk, heavy, hermetically sealed, 'laden with good omens' as the same baronet, dressed in Fascist uniform, would have said in Mussolini's phrase twenty years before. There was laughing and whispering among the employees; and then everyone, the managing director first, shouted his name. A great satisfaction; a guarantee that he would keep his job — in short, a triumph. Nothing that followed could lessen the tonic effect; neither the three hundred lire that he had to pay in the coffee bar below, treating his friends in the two-fold dusk of a squally sunset and dim neon lights, nor the weight of his trophy, nor the unpleasant comments in the bus — nothing; not even the lightning flash from the depths of his consciousness that it had all been an act of rather condescending pity from his fellow-employees: he was really too poor to permit the weed of pride to sprout where it had no business to appear.

He turned toward home across a decrepit street to which the bombardments of fifteen years previously had given the finishing touches, and finally reached the grim little square in the depths of which the ghostly edifice in which he lived stood tucked away.

He heartily greeted Cosimo, the porter, who despised him because he knew that his salary was lower than his own. Nine steps, three steps, nine steps: the floor where Cavaliere Tizio lived. Pooh! He did have a Fiat 1100, true enough, but he also had an old, ugly and dissolute wife. Nine steps, three steps — a slip almost made him fall — nine steps: young Sempronio's apart-ment; worse still! — a bone-idle lad, mad on Lambrettas and Vespas, whose hall was still unfurnished. Nine steps, three steps, nine steps: his own apartment, the little abode of a beloved, honest and honored man, a prize-winner, a book-keeper beyond compare.

He opened the door and entered the narrow hall, already filled with the heavy smell of onion soup. He placed the weighty parcel, the briefcase loaded with other people's affairs, and his muffler on a little locker the size of a hamper. His voice rang out: 'Maria! Come quickly! Come and see — what a beauty!'

His wife came out of the kitchen in a blue housecoat spotted with grime from saucepans; her little hands, still red from washing up, rested on a belly deformed by pregnancies. The children with their slimy noses crowded around the rose-colored sight and squealed without daring to touch it.

'Oh good! Did you bring your pay back? I haven't a single lira left.'

'Here it is, dear. I'll only keep the small change — 245 lire. But look at this grace of God here!'

Maria had been pretty; until a few years previously she had had a cheeky little face and whimsical eyes. But the wrangles with the shopkeepers had made her voice grow harsh, the poor food had ruined her complexion, the incessant peering into a future clouded with problems had spent the luster of her eyes. Only the soul of a saint survived within her, inflexible and bereft of tenderness; deep-seated virtue expressing itself in rebukes and restrictions; and in addition a repressed but persistent pride of class because she was the granddaughter of a big hatter in one of the main streets, and despised the origins of her Girolamo — whom she adored as a silly but beloved child — because they were inferior to her own.

Indifferently her eyes ran over the gilded cardboard box. 'That's fine. Tomorrow we'll send it to Signor Risma, the solicitor; we're under such an obligation to him!'

Two years previously this solicitor had given him a complicated book-keeping job to do, and over and above paying for it, had invited both of them to lunch in his abstract-and-metal apartment. The clerk had suffered acutely from the shoes bought specially for the occasion. And he and his Maria, his Andrea, his Saverio, his little Josephine were now to give up the only seam of abundance they had hit in many, many years, for that lawyer who had everything.

He ran to the kitchen, grabbed a knife, and rushed to cut the gold string that a deft working girl in Milan had beautifully tied around the wrapping paper; but a reddened hand wearily touched his shoulder. 'Girolamo, don't behave like a child — you know we have to repay Risma's kindness.'

The law had spoken: the law laid down by unblemished hat-shop owners.

'But dear, this is a prize, an award of merit, a token of esteem!'

'Don't say that. Nice people, those colleagues of yours, with their tender feelings! It was alms-giving, Giro, nothing but alms-giving.' She called him by his old pet name, and smiled at him with eyes that only for him still held traces of the old spell. 'Tomorrow I'll buy a little panettone, just big enough for us, and four of those twisted red candles from Standa's — that'll make a fine feast!'

The next day he bought an undistinguished miniature panettone, and not four but two of the astonishing candles; through
a delivery agency, at a cost of another two hundred lire, he for-
warded the mammoth cake to the solicitor Risma.

After Christmas he had to buy a third panettone which, disguised by slicing, he took to his colleagues who were teasing him
because they hadn't been offered a morsel of the sumptuous
trophy.

A smoke screen enveloped the fate of the original cake. He went
to the Lightning Delivery Agency to make enquiries. With disdain he was shown the receipts book which the solicitor's manser-
vant had signed upside down. However, just after Twelfth Night
a visiting card arrived 'with sincerest thanks and best wishes.'

Honor was saved.

Translated by Alfred Alexander

The Condemned Man's Last Night

BENJAMIN PÉRET

"**J**UST LET ME FIX MY HAIR and I'll be right with you."

It was me speaking and I was perched on one of the highest branches of a hundred-year old chestnut tree. It was raining hard. Children were playing at the foot of the tree. Inside the trunk, which was hollow and held together only by its bark, a hen was endlessly laying eggs, breaking each one with sharp pecks as it dropped.

The person I was talking to was smoking a big pipe made of blue glass, which was actually a hollowed-out insulator attached to a reed; he was a young farmer from the area, who took off his goatee and put it in his pocket when he was tired, particularly at night.

I climbed down from my tree and, taking my friend by the arm, went off hunting, although the regulations forbade it at this time of year.

At that moment, the door of my cell clattered open, and an eight-year old child dragging a small pitch black goat entered at the head of a crowd of people I did not know. Among them was my defence lawyer. He was holding a pair of braces which he was staring at obstinately, and his lips were moving, pronouncing words I could not make out. "Hello, Papa," said the child as he pushed the goat under the bed.

One of the men I did not know came up to me and said:

—Benjamin Péret, you know what is happening.

ME. — No.

HIM. — Write what you wish.

ME. — I haven't anything to write.

HIM. — Fine, get dressed.

I dressed, shaved with care, out of habit unplugged my electric lightbulb, read a few verses of the Bible as well as a chapter of Apollinaire's "Eleven Thousand Pricks", and announced that I was ready.

On the way, the conversation never faltered. I told my lawyer about my projects. As soon as I got out of prison, I intended to take up my profession again, since I considered it to be the most beautiful of all. I was planning to rape, and afterwards murder with new and unheard-of forms of torture, a young woman I had met one day on a road near Epinal and who I had followed all the way home — not without declaring that she was the fairest of all, and that if she would allow me to love her, I would be infinitely happy. She smiled slightly and gave me a little bird which had only one leg. I kept it for a long time. It lived in my breast pocket; here, look.

My lawyer was a charming man who knew what life was about and, even as I spoke, I felt him won over to my ideas, my ambitions. Murder, is it not one of the most delicate pleasures given to man?

—You know, I said to him, when I feel a long sharp dagger in my hand and when the dagger plunges into the chest of a young girl or into the face of one of those men who read the evening paper in their shirtsleeves by the window...

I sensed that this life tempted him and, as it would have pleased me if the man who had defended me with so much talent at the Assizes were to continue with me in the work I had undertaken, that is, the popularisation of crime, I developed the arguments which seemed to me the most favourable to my proposition. And so, when we arrived in the prison yard after a period of time which seemed to me very short or very long (it is difficult to appreciate time), he was completely disposed to kill one of the people who was accompanying us so that, he said, we could profit from the confusion and escape.

Once in the prison yard I saw the guillotine and found myself, with no noticeable transition, in a state of astonishing sexual excitement. I think, had I had the opportunity, I could have made love to fifteen women in a row. Nonetheless, I mastered myself and, addressing Mr. Deibler, I asked him for permission to have a word with the head guard of the prison.

I told this fine man how sad I was to leave him and what pleasant memories I held of the friendly relations we had established. As a token of my feelings I told him that I would sow, in the sunniest part of the prison yard, a cherry stone; and I made him promise that he would devote the greatest care to its cultivation. When he gave me this promise, I explained how sweet it was for me to think that in a few years, when the seed had become a tree, he would gather delicious fruit. I asked of him only to give a handful to those who would come, like myself, to expiate their crimes, even though I did not think that my crimes deserved any punishment whatsoever. My lawyer murmured agreement —Dear friend—.

Then it was the priest's turn to tell me that I should not die without asking God's forgiveness for my faults. This time I lost my temper and, straightening my shoulders, I told him squarely that I had no faults to be pardoned. He quickly made the sign of the cross and began telling his rosary silently, which greatly annoyed me.

Mr. Deibler came toward me and, with a politeness which touched me deeply, asked if I was ready. Upon my affirmative answer, he prepared me according to the custom* for a condemned man. Once this was done, I walked forward, supported by Mr. Deibler and my lawyer, toward the guillotine, next to which the aides were standing ready. The three of us were singing "Die Wacht am Rhein." In the distance a mechanical piano was grating out Beethoven's Fifth Symphony.

As I was about to take my place on the rocker* I asked to make a telephone call.

—To whom? asked Mr. Deibler.

—It doesn't matter, I just want to telephone.

He did not want to refuse me. I requested a number. It was that of an admiral who, without giving me time to speak, announced that he was leaving Paris to board his ship. He was to take part in naval manoeuvres in the Mediterranean. I hung up. I was thrown on the rocker. I found myself in the same state of sexual excitement as when I first saw the guillotine. Mr. Deibler noticed and enjoined one of his aides to satisfy me.

—Since he is about to die and there are no women here, he said, you may as well satisfy him.

Never in my life had my fulfilment been so complete: it is true that I was about to die. Indeed, a few minutes later, the blade of the guillotine came down on my head. Justice was done, as the old saying goes...

Legal Aid

FRANK O'CONNOR

D ELIA CARTY CAME OF A very respectable family. It was
going as maid to the O'Grady's of Pouladuff that ruined
her. That whole family was slightly touched. The old
man, a national teacher, was hardly ever at home, and the
daughters weren't much better. When they weren't away visiting,
they had people visiting them, and it was nothing to Delia to
come in late at night and find one of them plastered round some
young fellow on the sofa.

That sort of thing isn't good for any young girl. Like mistress
like maid; inside six months she was smoking, and within a year
she was carrying on with one Tom Flynn, a farmer's son. Her
father, a respectable, hard-working man, knew nothing about it,
for he would have realized that she was no match for one of the
Flynns, and even if Tom's father, Ned, had known, he would
never have thought it possible that any laborer's daughter could
imagine herself a match for Tom.

Not, God knows, that Tom was any great catch. He was a big
uncouth galoot who was certain that love-making, like drink, was
one of the simple pleasures his father tried to deprive him of,
out of spite. He used to call at the house while the O'Grady's
were away, and there would be Delia in one of Eileen O'Grady's
frocks and with Eileen O'Grady's lipstick and powder on, doing
the lady over the tea thing in the parlor. Throwing a glance over
his shoulder in case anyone might spot him, Tom would heave
himself onto the sofa with his boots over the end.

"Begod, I love sofas," he would say with simple pleasure.

"Put a cushion behind you," Delia would say.

"Oh, begod," Tom would say, making himself comfortable, "if ever I have a house of my own 'tis unknown what sofas and cushions I'll have. Them teachers must get great money. What the hell do they go away at all for?"

Delia loved making the tea and handing it out like a real lady, but you couldn't catch Tom out like that.

"Ah, what do I want tay for?" he would say with a doubtful glance at the cup. "Haven't you any whiskey? Ould O'Grady must have gallons of it.... Leave it there on the table. Why the hell don't they have proper mugs with handles a man could get a grip on? Is that taypot silver? Pity I'm not a teacher!"

It was only natural for Delia to show him the bedrooms and the dressing-tables with the three mirrors, the way you could see yourself from all sides, but Tom, his hands under his head, threw himself with incredulous delight on the low double bed and cried: "Springs! Begod, 'tis like a car!"

What the springs gave rise to was entirely the O'Gradys' fault since no one but themselves would have left a house in a lonesome part to a girl of nineteen to mind. The only surprising thing was that it lasted two years without Delia showing any signs of it. It probably took Tom that time to find the right way.

But when he did he got into a terrible state. It was hardly in him to believe that a harmless poor devil like himself whom no one ever bothered his head about could achieve such unprecedented results on one girl, but when he understood it he knew only too well what the result of it would be. His father would first beat hell out of him and then throw him out and leave the farm to his nephews. There being no hope of conciliating his father, Tom turned his attention to God, who, though supposed to share Ned Flynn's views about fellows and girls, had some nature in Him. Tom stopped seeing Delia, to persuade God that he was reforming and to show that anyway it wasn't his fault. Left alone he could be a decent, good-living young fellow, but the Carty girl was a forward, deceitful hussy who had led him on instead of putting him off the way any well-bred girl would do. Between lipstick, sofas, and tay in the parlor, Tom put it up to God that it was a great wonder she hadn't got him into worse trouble.

Delia had to tell her mother, and Mrs. Carty went to Father Corcoran to see could he induce Tom to marry her. Father Corcoran was a tall, testy old man who, even at the age of sixty-five, couldn't make out for the life of him what young fellows saw in girls, but if he didn't know much about lovers he knew a lot about farmers.

"Wisha, Mrs. Carty," he said crankily, "how could I get him to marry her? Wouldn't you have a bit of sense? Some little financial arrangement, maybe, so that she could leave the parish and not be a cause of scandal—I might be able to do that."

He interviewed Ned Flynn, who by this time had got Tom's version of the story and knew financial arrangements were going to be the order of the day unless he could put a stop to them. Ned was a man of over six foot with a bald brow and a smooth unlined face as though he never had a care except his general concern for the welfare of humanity which made him look so abnormally thoughtful. Even Tom's conduct hadn't brought a wrinkle to his brow.

"I don't know, father," he said, stroking his bald brow with a dieaway air, "I don't know what you could do at all."

"Wisha, Mr. Flynn," said the priest who, when it came to the pinch, had more nature than twenty Flynns, "wouldn't you do the handsome thing and let him marry her before it goes any farther?"

"I don't see how much farther it could go, father," said Ned.

"It could become a scandal."

"I'm afraid 'tis that already, father."

"And after all," said Father Corcoran, forcing himself to put in a good word for one of the unfortunate sex whose very existence was a mystery to him, "is she any worse than the rest of the girls that are going? Bad is the best of them, from what I see, and Delia is a great deal better than most."

"That's not my information at all, father," said Ned, looking like "The Heart Bowed Down."

"That's a very serious statement, Mr. Flynn," said Father Corcoran, giving him a challenging look.

"It can be proved, father," said Ned gloomily. "Of course I'm not denying the boy was foolish, but the cleverest can be caught."

"You astonish me, Mr. Flynn," said Father Corcoran who was beginning to realize that he wasn't even going to get a subscription. "Of course I can't contradict you, but 'twill cause a terrible scandal."

"I'm as sorry for that as you are, father," said Ned, "but I have my son's future to think of."

Then, of course, the fun began. Foolish to the last, the O'Gradys wanted to keep Delia on till it was pointed out to them that Mr. O'Grady would be bound to get the blame. After this, her father had to be told. Dick Carty knew exactly what became a devoted father, and he beat Delia till he had to be hauled off her by the neighbors. He was a man who loved to sit in his garden reading his paper; now he felt he owed it to himself not to be seen enjoying himself, so instead he sat over the fire and brooded. The more he brooded the angrier he became. But seeing that, with the best will in the world, he could not beat Delia every time he got angry, he turned his attention to the Flynns. Ned Flynn, that contemptible bosthoon, had slighted one of the Cartys in a parish where they had lived for hundreds of years with unblemished reputations; the Flynns, as everyone knew, being mere upstarts and outsiders without a date on their gravestones before 1850—nobodies!

He brought Delia to see Jackie Canty, the solicitor in town. Jackie was a little jenny-ass of a man with thin lips, a pointed nose, and a pince-nez that wouldn't stop in place, and he listened with grave enjoyment to the story of Delia's misconduct. "And what happened then, please?" he asked in his shrill singsong, looking at the floor and trying hard not to burst out into a giggle of delight. "The devils!" he thought. "The devils!" It was as close as Jackie was ever likely to get to the facts of life, an opportunity not to be missed.

"Anything in writing?" he sang, looking at her over the pince-nez. "Any letters? Any documents?"

"Only a couple of notes I burned," said Delia, who thought him a very queer man, and no wonder.

"Pity!" Jackie said with an admiring smile. "A smart man! Oh, a very smart man!"

"Ah, 'tisn't that at all," said Delia uncomfortably, "only he had no occasion for writing."

"Ah, Miss Carty," cried Jackie in great indignation, looking at her challengingly through the specs while his voice took on a steely ring, "a gentleman in love always finds plenty of occasion for writing. He's a smart man; your father might succeed in an action for seduction, but if 'tis defended 'twill be a dirty case."

"Mr. Canty," said her father solemnly, "I don't mind how dirty it is so long as I get justice." He stood up, a powerful man of six feet, and held up his clenched fist. "Justice is what I want," he said dramatically. "That's the sort I am. I keep myself to myself and mind my own business, but give me a cut, and I'll fight in a bag, tied up."

"Don't forget that Ned Flynn has the money, Dick," wailed Jackie.

"Mr. Canty," said Dick with a dignity verging on pathos, "you know me?"

"I do, Dick, I do."

"I'm living in this neighborhood, man and boy, fifty years, and I owe nobody a ha'penny. If it took me ten years, breaking stones by the road, I'd pay it back, every penny."

"I know, Dick, I know," moaned Jackie. "But there's other things as well. There's your daughter's reputation. Do you know what they'll do? They'll go into court and swear someone else was the father."

"Tom could never say that," Delia cried despairingly. "The tongue would rot in his mouth."

Jackie had no patience at all with this chit of a girl, telling him his business. He sat back with a weary air, his arm over the back of his chair.

"That statement has no foundation," he said icily. "There is no record of any such things happening a witness. If there was, the inhabitants of Ireland would have considerably less to say for themselves. You would be surprised the things respectable people will say in the witness box. Rot in their mouths indeed! Ah, dear me, no. With documents, of course, it would be different, but it is only our word against theirs. Can it be proved that you weren't knocking round with any other man at this time, Miss Carty?"

"Indeed, I was doing nothing of the sort," Delia said indignantly. "I swear to God I wasn't, Mr. Canty. I hardly spoke to a fellow the whole time, only when Tom and myself might have a row and I'd go out with Timmy Martin."

"Timmy Martin!" Canty cried dramatically, pointing an accusing finger at her. "There is their man!"

"But Tom did the same with Betty Daly," cried Delia on the point of tears, "and he only did it to spite me. I swear there was nothing else in it, Mr. Canty, nor he never accused me of it."

"Mark my words," chanted Jackie with a mournful smile, "he'll make up for lost time now."

In this he showed considerably more foresight than Delia gave him credit for. After the baby was born and the action begun,

Tom and his father went to town to see their solicitor, Peter Humphreys. Peter, who knew all he wanted to know about the facts of life, liked the case much less than Jackie. A crosseyed, full-blooded man who had made his money when law was about land, not love, he thought it a terrible comedown. Besides, he didn't think it nice to be listening to such things.

"And so, according to you, Timmy Martin is the father?" he asked Tom.

"Oh, I'm not swearing he is," said Tom earnestly, giving himself a heave in his chair and crossing his legs. "How the hell could I? All I am saying is that I wasn't the only one, and what's more she boasted about it. Boasted about it, begod!" he added with a look of astonishment at such female depravity.

"Before witnesses?" asked Peter, his eyes doing a double cross with hopelessness.

"As to that," replied Tom with great solemnity, looking over his shoulder for an open window he could spit through, "I couldn't swear."

"But you understood her to mean Timmy Martin?"

"I'm not accusing Timmy Martin at all," said Tom in great alarm, seeing how the processes of law were tending to involve him in a row with the Martins, who were a turbulent family with ways of getting their own back unknown to any law. "Timmy Martin is one man she used to be round with. It might be Timmy Martin or it might be someone else, or what's more," he added with the look of a man who has had a sudden revelation, "it might be more than one." He looked from Peter to his father and back again to see what effect the revelation was having, but like other revelations it didn't seem to be going down too well. "Begod," he said giving himself another heave, "it might be any God's number . . . But, as to that," he added cautiously, "I wouldn't like to swear."

"Nor indeed, Tom," said his solicitor with a great effort at politeness, "no one would advise you. You'll want a good counsel."

"Begod, I suppose I will," said Tom with astonished resignation before the idea that there might be people in the world bad enough to doubt his word.

There was great excitement in the village when it became known that the Flynns were having the Roarer Cooper as counsel. Even as a first-class variety turn Cooper could always command attention, and everyone knew that the rights and wrongs of the case would be relegated to their proper position while the little matter of Eileen O'Grady's best frock received the attention it deserved.

On the day of the hearing the court was crowded. Tom and his father were sitting at the back with Peter Humphreys, waiting for Cooper, while Delia and her father were talking to Jackie Canty and their own counsel, Ivers. He was a well-built young man with a high brow, black hair, and half-closed, red-tinged sleepy eyes. He talked in a bland drawl.

"You're not worrying, are you?" he asked Delia kindly. "Don't be a bit afraid...I suppose there's no chance of them settling, Jackie?"

"Musha, what chance would there be?" Canty asked scoldingly. "Don't you know yourself what sort they are?"

"I'll have a word with Cooper myself," said Ivers. "Dan isn't as bad as he looks." He went to talk to a coarse-looking man in wig and gown who had just come in. To say he wasn't as bad as he looked was no great compliment. He had a face that was almost a square, with a big jaw and blue eyes in wicked little slits that made deep dents across his cheekbones.

"What about settling this case of ours, Dan?" Ivers asked gently.

Cooper didn't even return his look; apparently he was not responsive to charm.

"Did you ever know me to settle when I could fight?" he growled.

"Not when you could fight your match," Ivers said, without taking offense. "You don't consider that poor girl your match?"

"We'll soon see what sort of girl she is," replied Cooper complacently as his eyes fell on the Flynns. "Tell me," he whispered, "what did she see in my client?"

"What you saw yourself when you were her age, I suppose," said Ivers. "You don't mean there wasn't a girl in a tobacconist's shop that you thought came down from Heaven with the purpose of consoling you?"

"She had nothing in writing," Cooper replied gravely. "And, unlike your client, I never saw double."

"You don't believe that yarn, do you?"

"That's one of the things I'm going to inquire into."

"I can save you the trouble. She was too fond of him."

"Hah!" snorted Cooper as though this were a good joke. "And I suppose that's why she wants the cash."

"The girl doesn't care if she never got a penny. Don't you know yourself what's behind it? A respectable father. Two respectable fathers! The trouble about marriage in this country, Dan Cooper, is that the fathers always insist on doing the coorting."

"Hah!" grunted Cooper, rather more uncertain of himself. "Show me this paragon of the female sex, Ivers."

"There in the brown hat beside Canty," said Ivers without looking round. "Come on, you old devil, and stop trying to pretend you're Buffalo Bill. It's enough going through what she had to go through. I don't want her to go through any more."

"And why in God's name do you come to me?" Cooper asked in sudden indignation. "What the hell do you take me for? A Society for Protecting Fallen Women? Why didn't the priest make him marry her?"

"When the Catholic Church can make a farmer marry a laborer's daughter the Kingdom of God will be at hand," said Ivers. "I'm surprised at you, Dan Cooper, not knowing better at your age."

"And what are the neighbors doing here if she has nothing to hide?"

"Who said she had nothing to hide?" Ivers asked lightly, throwing in his hand. "Haven't you daughters of your own? You know she played the fine lady in the O'Gradys' frocks. If 'tis any information to you she wore their jewelry as well."

"Ivers, you're a young man of great plausibility," said Cooper, "but you can spare your charm on me. I have my client's interests to consider. Did she sleep with the other fellow?"

"She did not."

"Do you believe that?"

"As I believe my own mother."

"The faith that moves mountains," Cooper said despondently. "How much are ye asking?"

"Two hundred and fifty," replied Ivers, shaky for the first time.

"Merciful God Almighty!" moaned Cooper, turning his eyes to the ceiling. "As if any responsible Irish court would put that price on a girl's virtue. Still, it might be as well. I'll see what I can do."

He moved ponderously across the court and with two big arms outstretched like wings shepherded out the Flynns.

"Two hundred and fifty pounds?" gasped Ned, going white. "Where in God's name would I get that money?"

"My dear Mr. Flynn," Cooper said with coarse amiability, "that's only half the yearly allowance his Lordship makes the young lady that obliges him, and she's not a patch on that girl in court. After a lifetime of experience I can assure you that for two years' fornication with a fine girl like that you won't pay a penny less than five hundred."

Peter Humphreys's eyes almost grew straight with the shock of such reckless slander on a blameless judge. He didn't know what had come over the Roarer. But that wasn't the worst. When the settlement was announced and the Flynns were leaving he went up to them again.

"You can believe me when I say you did the right thing, Mr. Flynn," he said. "I never like cases involving good-looking girls. Gentlemen of his Lordship's age are terribly susceptible. But tell me, why wouldn't your son marry her now as he's about it?"

"Marry her?" echoed Ned, who hadn't yet got over the shock of having to pay two hundred and fifty pounds and costs for a little matter he could have compounded for with Father Corcoran for fifty. "A thing like that!"

"With two hundred and fifty pounds, man?" snarled Cooper. " 'Tisn't every day you'll pick up a daughter-in-law with that ... What do you say to the girl yourself?" he asked Tom.

"Oh, begod, the girl is all right," said Tom.

Tom looked different. It was partly relief that he wouldn't have to perjure himself, partly astonishment at seeing his father so swiftly overthrown. His face said: "The world is wide."

"Ah, Mr. Flynn, Mr. Flynn," whispered Cooper scornfully, "sure you're not such a fool as to let all that good money out of the family?"

Leaving Ned gasping, he went on to where Dick Carty, aglow with pride and malice, was receiving congratulations. There were no congratulations for Delia who was standing near him. She felt a big paw on her arm and looked up to see the Roarer.

"Are you still fond of that boy?" he whispered.

"I have reason to be, haven't I?" she retorted bitterly.

"You have," he replied with no great sympathy. "The best. I got you that money so that you could marry him if you wanted to. Do you want to?"

Her eyes filled with tears as she thought of the poor broken china of an idol that was being offered her now.

"Once a fool, always a fool," she said, sullenly.

"You're no fool at all, girl," he said, giving her arm an encoura-

ging squeeze. "You might make a man of him yet. I don't know
what the law in this country is coming to. Get him away to hell
out of this till I find Michael Ivers and get him to talk to your
father."

The two lawyers made the match themselves at Johnny Des-
mond's pub, and Johnny said it was like nothing in the world
so much as a mission, with the Roarer roaring and threatening
hellfire on all concerned, and Michael Ivers piping away about
the joys of Heaven. Johnny said it was the most instructive evening he ever had. Ivers was always recognized as a weak man
so the marriage did him no great harm, but of course it was a
terrible comedown for a true Roarer, and Cooper's reputation has
never been the same since then.

General Bellomo

PAUL WEST

N|OW, AS THE SUN TOOK up its appointed station in the zenith, aimed at the silken rosette in the center of his military cap, General Bellomo felt glad he was not bareheaded, as he had been all through the trial.

"Please stand here a moment," they had said to him as he emerged blinking into the sunshine, newly found guilty and sentenced to death by rifle fire. They left him alone to ponder, unguarded, unwatched even; indeed, with no one in sight, the massive door into the courtyard wide open, the resplendent avenue beyond it visible and busy.

I am supposed, he thought, to make a break for it and will be shot while attempting to escape. They want butter and jam on it. Shot in the back, like Ciano and all those others, except *they* sat backward in chairs like spectators at their own *auto da fé*. No, Bellomo stays put. A man is entitled to judge the good taste of his would-be liberators. Who wants favors, even life-and-death ones, from people he would not be caught eating pizza with?

There he stood, his mind far away, though locally aimed, wondering about dandruff: why, as you reached a certain age, did it crackle from among your hair like bits of smashed eggshell? Large pieces, curved; not flakes at all. Was there meaning in that? Either I run now, he mused, or I will be shot tomorrow. I must have done something wrong. What can it be? I once saved an Allied airman from the Germans by hiding him in the trunk of my car. That? I once received a decoration for fighting against the Nazis. *That*? Hardly. I am the only avowed anti-Nazi among

341

the surviving postwar generals. The war is over. Italy is Italy again.
In the most technical and insufferable way, we have wom; we
won by losing. And now begins the cleaning out of the Augean
stables. How did the prosecutor's argument go?

"During the war, you opposed our allies, which makes of you
a recent traitor. You opposed Generals Badoglio and Graziani,
the pride of Italy. These two generals have now returned into
the world of *civitas humana* by virtue of the war's end. You,
however, do not make that smooth transition. You opposed Italy,
General. Italy was personified in its generals. You cannot be both
for and against Italy in the same war." General Bellomo's neck
began to tighten. "You seemed to have no idea of who the enemy
was. Feeling a personal aversion to two generals does not entitle
you to dislike Italy too, or to fail it. If you were unqualified to
wage the war, what then of the peace? Whom will you betray
next? In these difficult days, an ambiguous general is more than
we need or can stand. You would be wise to condemn yourself
before the tribunal does. You may have been patriotic, but you
were not loyal."

A Savoia-Marchetti droned over, then a Macchi. Thank goodness his aircraft recognition had not deserted him. All phenomena
were penultimate now — such was the language of the tribunal.
If they wanted to railroad him, why use language about it? Why
not just announce his simultaneous promotion and retirement?
Words again. *With* us, Graziani had said, but not *of* us. Ally but
not comrade, Badoglio had said. Jerkoffs both, commandeering
the peace, getting their names attached to perfectly adequate place
names, beginning with the places of their birth, with "Roma-
Badoglio" soon to come, and "Venezia-Graziani." Milano-Bellomo
would have been too much for them. Why, they had not even
allowed his own attorney to enter the court to save him, appoint-
ing instead that British fathead who waffled away about *res
cogitans* and *res extensa*, whatever that meant. The useless English
lawyer had spoken almost entirely in Latin, like an uncouth
version of Italian, as if the tribunal were in the Vatican.

"*Temptat clausa,*" he said, meaning (for General Bellomo knew
Latin quite well) the accused had sought to open up all secret
places with whatever means he had at hand, exposing both
civilian and military secrets as if to single-handedly admit the
Americans into Italy's highest military councils. "He meddled
with the locks. He banged his fist against the panels. He oiled

the springs. He rubbed pencil lead on the undersides of drawers to make them slide soundlessly. He used binoculars and telescopes upon a world that was already near enough. He uttered the phrase 'Allah's terrible whimsy,' a clear slur on the Duce. He left enigmatic messages written in dust. He denied that the Ethiopians were a militaristic nation intent on European conquest and had tried to purchase jet airplanes from Germany. He had shown strong pro-Anglo-Saxon tendencies."

General Bellomo could not even separate the speeches of defense and prosecution; having understood most of the Latin, he now heard it in Italian and mingled it with the prosecution's own. It had not been very good Latin, he recalled: mostly Caesarian, never Ciceronian, though with stolen tags from Tacitus. The Pope should have judged him instead. Or the trial should have been staged in Esperanto, the language of international hope. There was nothing to be done: escape or stay. Never do as you are told, he said to himself, marvelling at the still open door, his unguarded condition. He was like a cliff-diver poised, bare concrete beneath him. There might have been a loaded Luger in his pocket: one bullet only. Were there no lions to feed him to, like the recumbent sleeper on the desert sand in — whose was that painting? Not a Nazi in sight to bully him. Not even a lawyer. Reaccusing himself, he stood where they had stationed him, a parcel parked for later pick-up. Where was the logic of all this?

Graziani and Badoglio, being Italian generals, and unarrested themselves, were bound to be right.

They were Italian Caesars.

Being treacherous themselves, and experts on treachery, they had the right to point out treachery in others — no one was asking them to solve problems in complex astronomy.

Only a murderer should be a judge to send men to the gallows.

Since Italy *a siempre raggione* — was always right — how could Italian generals be wrong?

Ah, now it came: a general unpopular with the postwar clique was like someone in the class of all classes not members of themselves. A general *perversus*, i.e., twisted and contorted, as the defense lawyer had said in his desperate attempt to blind them with Latin, could not be judged by ordinary standards, was not an ordinary general. So they at once evolved a new law for him that read only thus, having no subject: "must be condemned as being beyond the law." Bellomo was unmentionable, therefore;

and such a *lex extensa perversaque*, as the Generals dubbed it, might be applied without tedious recitals of whoever was accused. If nobody was mentioned, then how could the law fail to apply?

Therefore the final verdict, trimmed and trussed, sounded as follows: "Does not agree with the two presiding judges, Generals Graziani and Badoglio, about his guilt, so is in the minority and hence un-Italian. Condemned as being beyond the law. Of no further use. Take the prisoner down." They had doomed him merely to head a beheaded sentence.

A simulacrum of logic, a caricature of law (which had a healthier incarnation among the peasants of Sicily), his sentence turned out to be an invitation to take his own life. In refusing this final privilege, he had broken the law, predicated as it was on amenable response to civil overture. General Bellomo had spurned his own freedom, had he not, and therefore freedom in the round? He could have fled and been shot. Or fled and shot himself. Or shot himself on the spot. Clearly he wished to put the state to some trouble, like old Xerxes who put the sea to some trouble by thrashing it with rods. The main thing was to get the general circuitously to extinction, even though a British newspaperman, Cyril Ray, had shouted from the body of the court before being bundled out: "This is a kangaroo court. He's not being properly defended. It's another Nazi court. You should be ashamed." General Bellomo bowed and clicked his heels as the bellowing journalist went.

"You could suspend the judgment," General Bellomo said, "as having been shouted down. Inaudible."

He waited for the bullet to tear through him even as he stood, a free man, a supplicant in the fresh air. Nothing happened. They came and escorted him away to a cell no bigger than a sentry-box, at once putting him in mind of the butterfly he used to carry with him in a perforated cigarette box of embossed silver. He liked the creature's colors, the way it flew back to his hand for warmth, but he never presumed to name it.

As well as having a whitewashed cell, he had the use of an open-air *gabinetto*, a narrow roofless hovel of stones with the usual foot-shaped blocks to stand his feet on while squatting. It was from a balcony above him that they shot him, at the squat, right down through the scalp into the chest. Execution from on high, even as he hummed and heaved. He was dead before the ludicrousness of the setting — open-air toilet full of Jove's lambent breezes — came to him. It never came to him. He died with no sense of his own absurdity. They were careful to save him from anything such as that, but no-one has ever explained why a balcony jutted out over a toilet. At least one general had suggested that it was for uncouth revellers to use, aiming from the balcony into the toilet, whether the condemned was already in position below, or not.

The Clairvoyant

KAREL ČAPEK

"**Y**OU KNOW, MR. DA," Mr. Janowitz declared, "I'm not an easy person to fool; after all, I'm not a Jew for nothing, right? But what this fellow does is simply beyond belief. It isn't just graphology, it's—I don't know what. Here's how it works: you give him someone's handwriting in an unsealed envelope; he never even looks at the writing, just pokes his fingers inside the envelope and feels the handwriting, all over; and all the while his face is twisting as if he were in pain. And before very long, he starts telling you about the nature of the writer, but he does it in such a way that—well, you'd be dumbfounded. He pegs the writer perfectly, down to the last detail. I gave him an envelope with a letter from old Weinberg in it; he had Weinberg figured out in no time, diabetes, even his planned bankruptcy. What do you say to that?"

"Nothing," the DA said drily. "Maybe he knows old Weinberg."

"But he never once looked at the handwriting," Mr. Janowitz protested. "He says every person's handwriting has its own aura, and he says that you can feel it, clearly and precisely. He says it's purely a physical phenomenon, like radio. This isn't some kind of swindle, Mr. DA; this Prince Karadagh doesn't make a penny from it. He's supposed to be from a very old family in Baku, according to what this Russian told me. But I'll tell you what, come see for yourself; he'll be here this evening. You must come."

"Listen, Mr. Janowitz," the DA said, "this is all very nice, but I only believe fifty per cent of what foreigners say, especially when I don't know how they make their living; I believe Russians even

346

less, and fakirs less than that; but when on top of everything else the man's a prince, then I don't believe one word of it. Where did you say he learned this? Ah yes, in Persia. Forget it, Mr. Janowitz; the whole Orient's a fraud."

"But Mr. DA," Mr. Janowitz protested, "this young fellow explains it all scientifically; no magic tricks, no mysterious powers, I'm telling you, strictly scientific method."

"Then he's an even bigger phony," the DA admonished him. "Mr. Janowitz, I'm surprised at you; you've managed to live your entire life without strictly scientific methods, and here you are embracing them wholesale. Look, if there were something to it, it would have been known a long time ago, right?"

"Well," Mr. Janowitz replied, a little shaken, "but when I saw with my own eyes how he guessed everything about old Weinberg! Now there's genius for you. I'll tell you what, Mr. DA, come and have a look for yourself; it it's a hoax, you'll know it, that's your specialty, sir; nobody can put one over on you, Mr. DA."

"Hardly," the DA said modestly. "All right, I'll come, Mr. Janowitz, but only to keep an eye on your phenomenon's fingers. It's a shame that people are so gullible. But you mustn't tell him who I am; wait, I'll bring along some handwriting in an envelope for him, something special. Count on it, friend, I'll prove he's a phony."

You should understand that the district attorney (or, more accurately: chief public prosecutor Dr. Klapka) would, in his next court proceeding, be trying the case against Hugo Müller, who was charged with premeditated murder. Mr. Hugo Müller, millionaire industrialist, had been accused of insuring his younger brother Ota for a large sum of money and then drowning him in the lake at a summer resort; in addition to this he also had been under suspicion, during the previous year, of dispatching his lover, but of course that had not been proven. In short, it was a major trial, one to which the district attorney wanted to devote particular attention; and he had labored over the trial documents with all the persistence and acumen that had made him a most formidable prosecutor. The case was not clear; the district attorney would have given God-knows-what for one particle of direct evidence; but as things stood, he would have to rely more on his winning way with words if the jury were to award him a rope for Mr.

Müller; you must understand that, for prosecutors, this is a point of honor.

Mr. Janowitz was a bit flustered that evening. "Dr. Klapka," he announced in muffled tones, "this is Prince Karadagh; well, let's get started."

The district attorney cast probing eyes on this exotic creature; he was a young and slender man with eyeglasses, the face of a Tibetan monk and delicate, thievish hands. Fancy-pants quack, the district attorney decided.

"Mr. Karadagh," Mr. Janowitz jabbered, "over here by this little table. There's some mineral water already there. Please, switch on that little floor lamp; we'll turn off the overhead light so it won't disturb you. There. Please, gentlemen, there should be silence. Mr.—eh, Mr. Klapka here brought some handwriting of some sort; if Mr. Karadagh would be so good as to—"

The district attorney cleared his throat briefly and seated himself so as to best observe the clairvoyant. "Here is the handwriting," he said, and he took an unsealed envelope from his breast pocket. "If I may—"

"Thank you," the clairvoyant said impassively. He took hold of the envelope and, with eyes closed, turned it over in his fingers. Suddenly he shuddered, twisting his head. "Curious," he muttered and bolted a sip of water. He then inserted his slim fingers into the envelope and suddenly stopped; it seemed as if his pale yellow face turned paler still.

There was such a silence in the room that a slight rattling could be heard from Mr. Janowitz, for Mr. Janowitz suffered from goiter.

The thin lips of Prince Karadagh trembled and contorted as if his fingers were clenching a red-hot iron, and sweat broke out on his forehead. "I cannot endure this," he hissed in a tight voice; he extracted his fingers from the envelope, rubbed them with a handkerchief and quickly moved them back and forth over the tablecloth, as one sharpens a knife, after which he once again sipped agitatedly from his glass of water and then cautiously took the envelope between his fingers.

"The man who wrote this," he began in a parched voice, "the man who wrote this...There is great strength here, but a— (obviously he was searching for a word) strength which lies there, waiting. This lying in wait is terrible," he cried out and dropped the envelope on the table. "I would not want this man as my enemy!"

"Why?" the district attorney could not refrain from asking. "Is he guilty of something?"

"Don't question me," the clairvoyant said. "Every question gives a hint. I only know that he could be guilty of anything at all, of great and terrible deeds. There is astonishing determination here...for success...for money... This man would not scruple over the life of a fellow creature. No, this is not an ordinary criminal; a tiger also is not a criminal; a tiger is a great lord. This man would not be capable of low trickery, but he thinks of himself as ruling over human lives. When he is on the prowl, he sees people only as prey. Therefore he kills them."

"Beyond good and evil," the district attorney murmured with unmistakable approval.

"Those are only words," Prince Karadagh said. "No one is beyond good and evil. This man has his own strict concept of morality; he is in debt to no one, he does not steal, he does not lie; if he kills, it is as if he checkmated in a game of chess. It is his game, but he plays it correctly." The clairvoyant wrinkled his brow in concentration. "I don't know what it is. I see a large lake and a motor boat on it."

"And what else?" the district attorney burst out, scarcely breathing.

"There is nothing else to see; it is completely obscure. It is so strangely obscure compared with that brutal and ruthless determination to bring down his prey. But there is no passion in it, only intellect. Absolute intellectual reasoning in every detail. As if he were resolving some technical problem or mental exercise. No, this man feels no remorse for anything. He is so confident of himself, so self-assured; he has no fear even of his own conscience. I have the impression of a man who looks down on all from above; he is conceited in the extreme and self-congratulatory; it pleases him that people fear him." The clairvoyant sipped his water. "But he is also a hypocrite. At heart, an opportunist who would like to astound the world by his actions— Enough. I am tired. I do not like this man."

"Listen, Janowitz," the district attorney flung out excitedly, "he is truly astonishing, this clairvoyant of yours. What he described is a perfect likeness. A strong and ruthless man who views people only as prey; the perfect player in his own game; a brain who systematically, intellectually plans his moves and feels no remorse for anything; a gentleman yet also an opportunist. Mr. Janowitz, this Karadagh pinpointed him one hundred per cent!"

"You don't say," said the flattered Mr. Janowitz. "Didn't I tell you? That was a letter from Schliefen, the textile man from Liberec, right?"

"It most certainly was not," exclaimed the district attorney. "Mr. Janowitz, it was a letter from a murderer."

"Imagine that," Mr. Janowitz marveled, "and I thought it was Schliefen; he's a real crook, that Schliefen."

"No. It was a letter from Hugo Müller, fratricide. Do you remember how that clairvoyant talked about a boat on a lake? Müller threw his brother from that boat into the water."

"Imagine that," Mr. Janowitz said, astonished. "You see? That is a fabulous talent, Mr. District Attorney!"

"Unquestionably," the district attorney declared. "The way he grasped Müller's true nature and the motives behind his actions, Mr. Janowitz, is simply phenomenal. Not even I could have hit the mark with Müller so precisely. And this clairvoyant found it out by feeling a few lines of Müller's handwriting—Mr. Janowitz, there's something to this; there must be some sort of special aura or something in people's handwriting."

"What did I tell you?" Mr. Janowitz said triumphantly. "If you would be so kind, Mr. District Attorney, I've never seen the handwriting of a murderer."

"With pleasure," Mr. District Attorney said, and he took the envelope from his pocket. "It's an interesting letter, besides," he added, removing the paper from the envelope, and suddenly his face changed color. "I...Mr. Janowitz," he blurted out, somewhat uncertainly, "this letter is a court document; it is...I'm not allowed to show it to you. Please forgive me."

Before long, the district attorney was hurrying homeward, not even noticing that it was raining. I'm an ass, he told himself bitterly, I'm a fool, how could that have happened to me? I'm an idiot! That in my hurry I grabbed not Müller's letter but my own handwriting, my notes on the trial, I shoved them in that envelope! I'm an imbecile! So that was *my* handwriting! Thanks very much! Watch out, you swindler, I'll be lying in wait for you!

But otherwise, the district attorney reflected, all in all, for the most part, what the clairvoyant had said wasn't too bad. Great strength; astonishing determination, if you please; I'm not capable of low trickery; I have my own strict concept of morality — As a matter of fact that is quite flattering. That I regret nothing? Thank God, I have no reason to: I merely discharge my obligations. And as for intellectual reasoning, that's also true. But as for being a hypocrite, he's mistaken. It's still nothing but a hoax.

Suddenly he paused. It stands to reason, he told himself, what that clairvoyant said can be applied to anyone at all! These are only generalities, nothing more. Everyone's a bit of a hypocrite and an opportunist. That's the whole trick: to speak in such a way that anybody could be identified. That's it, the district attorney decided, and opening his umbrella, he proceeded home at his normal energetic pace.

"My God!" groaned the presiding judge, stripping off his gown, "seven o'clock already; it did drag on again! When the district attorney spoke for two hours—but, dear colleague, he won it; to get the rope on such weak evidence, I'd call that success. Well, you never know with a jury. But he spoke skillfully," the presiding judge granted, washing his hands. "Mainly in the way he dealt with Müller's character, that was a full-fledged portrait; you know, the monstrous, inhuman nature of a murderer—it left you positively shaken. Remember how he said: This is no ordinary criminal; he isn't capable of low trickery, he neither lies nor steals; and if he murders a man, he does it as calmly as checkmating in a game of chess. He does not kill from passion, but from cold intellectual reasoning, as if he were resolving some technical problem or mental exercise. It was very well spoken, my friend. And something else: When he is on the prowl, he sees his fellow creatures only as prey—you know, that business about the tiger was perhaps a little theatrical, but the jury liked it."

"Or," the associate judge added, "the way he said: Clearly this murderer regrets nothing; he is so confident of himself, so self-assured—he has no fear even of his own conscience."

"Or then again," the presiding judge continued, wiping his hands with a towel, "the psychological observation that he is a hypocrite and an opportunist who would like to astound the world by his actions—"

"This Klapka, though," the associate judge said appreciatively. "He's a dangerous adversary."

"Hugo Müller found guilty by twelve votes," the presiding judge marveled, "who would have thought it! Klapka got him after all. For him, it's like a hunt or a game of chess. He is totally consumed

by his cases — My friend, I wouldn't want to have him as my
enemy."

"He likes it," the associate judge replied, "when people fear
him."

"A touch complacent, that's him," the presiding judge said
thoughtfully. "But he has astonishing determination...chiefly for
success. A great strength, friend, but—" The appropriate words
failed him. "Well, let's go have dinner."

Translated by Norma Comrada

The Case for the Defence

GRAHAM GREENE

I T WAS THE STRANGEST MURDER trial I ever attended. They named it the Peckham murder in the headlines, though Northwood Street, where the old woman was found battered to death, was not strictly speaking in Peckham. This was not one of those cases of circumstantial evidence in which you feel the jurymen's anxiety — because mistakes *have* been made — like domes of silence muting the court. No, this murderer was all but found with the body; no one present when the Crown counsel outlined his case believed that the man in the dock stood any chance at all.

He was a heavy stout man with bulging bloodshot eyes. All his muscles seemed to be in his thighs. Yes, an ugly customer, one you wouldn't forget in a hurry — and that was an important point because the Crown proposed to call four witnesses who hadn't forgotten him, who had seen him hurrying away from the little red villa in Northwood Street. The clock had just struck two in the morning.

Mrs Salmon in 15 Northwood Street had been unable to sleep; she heard a door click shut and thought it was her own gate. So she went to the window and saw Adams (that was his name) on the steps of Mrs Parker's house. He had just come out and he was wearing gloves. He had a hammer in his hand and she saw him drop it into the laurel bushes by the front gate. But before he moved away, he had looked up — at her window. The fatal instinct that tells a man when he is watched exposed him in the light of a street-lamp to her gaze — his eyes suffused with horrifying and brutal fear, like an animal's when you raise a whip. I talked afterwards to Mrs Salmon, who naturally after the astonishing verdict went in fear herself. As I imagine did all the witnesses — Henry MacDougall, who had been driving home from Benfleet late and nearly ran Adams down at the corner of Northwood Street. Adams was walking in the middle of the road looking dazed. And old Mr Wheeler, who lived next door to Mrs Parker, at No. 12, and was wakened by a noise — like a chair falling — through the thin-as-paper villa wall, and got up and looked out of the window, just as Mrs Salmon had done, saw Adams's back and, as he turned, those bulging eyes. In Laurel Avenue he had been seen by yet another witness — his luck was badly out; he might as well have committed the crime in broad daylight.

'I understand,' counsel said, 'that the defence proposes to plead mistaken identity. Adams's wife will tell you that he was with her at two in the morning on February 14, but after you have heard the witnesses for the Crown and examined carefully the features of the prisoner, I do not think you will be prepared to admit the possibility of a mistake.'

It was all over, you would have said, but the hanging.

After the formal evidence had been given by the policeman who had found the body and the surgeon who examined it, Mrs Salmon was called. She was the ideal witness, with her slight Scotch accent and her expression of honesty, care and kindness.

The counsel for the Crown brought the story gently out. She spoke very firmly. There was no malice in her, and no sense of importance at standing there in the Central Criminal Court with a judge in scarlet hanging on her words and the reporters writing them down. Yes, she said, and then she had gone downstairs and rung up the police station.

'And do you see the man here in court?'

She looked straight at the big man in the dock, who stared hard at her with his pekingese eyes without emotion.

'Yes,' she said, 'there he is.'

'You are quite certain?'

She said simply, 'I couldn't be mistaken, sir.'

It was all easy as that.

'Thank you, Mrs Salmon.'

Counsel for the defence rose to cross-examine. If you had reported as many murder trials as I have, you would have known beforehand what line he would take. And I was right, up to a point.

'Now, Mrs Salmon, you must remember that a man's life may depend on your evidence.'

'I do remember it, sir.'

'Is your eyesight good?'

'I have never had to wear spectacles, sir.'

'You are a woman of fifty-five?'

'Fifty-six, sir.'

'And the man you saw was on the other side of the road?'

'Yes, sir.'

'And it was two o'clock in the morning. You must have remarkable eyes, Mrs Salmon?'

'No, sir. There was moonlight, and when the man looked up, he had the lamplight on his face.'

'And you have no doubt whatever that the man you saw is the prisoner?'

I couldn't make out what he was at. He couldn't have expected any other answer than the one he got.

'None whatever, sir. It isn't a face one forgets.'

Counsel took a look round the court for a moment. Then he said, 'Do you mind, Mrs Salmon, examining again the people in court? No, not the prisoner. Stand up, please, Mr Adams,' and there at the back of the court with thick stout body and muscular legs and a pair of bulging eyes, was the exact image of the man in the dock. He was even dressed the same — tight blue suit and striped tie.

'Now think very carefully, Mrs Salmon. Can you still swear that the man you saw drop the hammer in Mrs Parker's garden was the prisoner — and not this man, who is his twin brother?'

Of course she couldn't. She looked from one to the other and didn't say a word.

There the big brute sat in the dock with his legs crossed, and there he stood too at the back of the court and they both stared at Mrs Salmon. She shook her head.

What we saw then was the end of the case. There wasn't a witness prepared to swear that it was the prisoner he'd seen. And the brother? He had his alibi, too; he was with his wife.

And so the man was acquitted for lack of evidence. But whether — if he did the murder and not his brother — he was punished or not, I don't know. That extraordinary day had an extraordinary end. I followed Mrs Salmon out of court and we got wedged in the crowd who were waiting, of course, for the twins. The police tried to drive the crowd away, but all they could do was keep the road-way clear for traffic. I learned later that they tried to get the twins to leave by a back way, but they wouldn't. One of them — no one knew which — said, 'I've been acquitted, haven't I?' and they walked bang out of the front entrance. Then it happened. I don't know how, though I was only six feet away. The crowd moved and somehow one of the twins got pushed on to the road right in front of a bus.

He gave a squeal like a rabbit and that was all; he was dead, his skull smashed just as Mrs Parker's had been. Divine vengeance? I wish I knew. There was the other Adams getting on his feet from beside the body and looking straight over at Mrs Salmon. He was crying, but whether he was the murderer or the innocent man nobody will ever be able to tell. But if you were Mrs Salmon, could you sleep at night?

Rumpole for the Prosecution

JOHN MORTIMER

A S ANYONE WHO HAS CAST half an eye over these memoirs will know, the second of the Rumpole commandments consists of the simple injunction 'Thou shalt not prosecute.' Number one is 'Thou shalt not plead guilty.' Down the line, of course, there are other valuable precepts such as 'Never pay for the drink Jack Pommeroy is prepared to put on the slate', 'Never trust a vegetarian', 'If Sam Ballard thinks it, then it must be wrong', 'Never go shopping with She Who Must Be Obeyed', 'Don't ask a question unless you're damn sure you know the answer', 'If a judge makes a particularly absurd remark, rub his nose in it, i.e. repeat it to the Jury with raised eyebrows every hour on the hour' and 'Never ask an instructing solicitor if his leg's better'. This last is as fatal as asking a client if he happens to be guilty; you run a terrible danger of being told.

But the rule against prosecuting has been the lodestar of my legal career. I obey this precept for a number of reasons, all cogent. It seems to me that errant and misguided humanity has enough on its plate without running the daily risk of being driven, cajoled or hoodwinked into the nick by Rumpole in full flood, armed with an unparalleled knowledge of bloodstains and a remarkable talent for getting a jury to see things his way. As everyone — except a nun in a Trappist order and the Home Secretary — now knows, the prison system is bursting at the seams and it would be out of the question for even more captives to arrive at the gates thanks to my forensic skills.

Then again, prosecuting counsel tend to be fawned on by Mr

Justice Graves and his like, characters whom I prefer to keep in a state of healthy hostility. Finally, I should point out that it is the task of prosecuting counsel to present the facts in a neutral manner and not try to score a victory. This duty (not always carried out, I may say, by those who habitually persecute down the Old Bailey) takes the fun out of the art of advocacy. There are many adjectives which might be used to describe Rumpole at work but 'neutral' is not among them. It is a sad but inescapable fact that as soon as I buckle on the wig and gown and march forth to war in the courtroom, the old adrenalin courses through my veins and all I want to do is win.

Bearing all this in mind, you may find it hard to understand how, in the case that came to be known as the 'Mews Murder', I took the brief in a private prosecution brought by the dead girl's father.

'All right, Mr Rumpole. You're out to protect the underdog, I understand that. I might say that I find it very sympathetic. You attack the establishment. Tease the judges. Give the police a hard time. Well, doesn't my daughter deserve defending as much as any of your clients?'

I looked down at the pile of press-cuttings on my desk and at the photograph of Veronica Fabian. She was a big, rather plain girl in her early twenties. I imagined that she had a loud laugh and an untidy bedroom. There was also, in spite of her smile, a look of disappointment and a lack of confidence about her, and I thought she might have been a girl who often fell unhappily in love. Whatever she had been like, she had died, beaten to death in an empty mews house in Notting Hill Gate. I didn't altogether understand what I could do in her defence, or how such an earth-bound tribunal as a judge and jury down the Old Bailey could now pass judgment on her.

'You want me to defend your daughter?'

'Yes, Mr Rumpole. That's exactly what I want.'

Gregory Fabian, senior partner in the firm of Fabian & Winchelsea, purveyors of discreet homes to the rich and famous, dealers in stately homes and ambassadorial dwellings, had aged, I imagined, since the death of his daughter. There is something squalid about murder which brings a sense of shame to the victim's as well as the killer's family. In spite of this, Fabian spoke moderately and without rancour. He was a slim man, in his early sixties, short but handsome, clear-featured, with creases at the sides of his eyes and the general appearance of someone who laughed a good deal in happier times.

'Isn't it a little late for that? To defend her, I mean?'

'There's no time limit on murder is there?' He smiled at me gently as he said this, and I was prepared to accept that his interest went beyond mere revenge.

'Justice! We haven't had much of that, sir. Not since they decided not to charge Jago. We just wanted to know how much that cost him. Whatever it was, he could probably afford it.' Up spoke young Roger Fabian, the dead girl's brother and the one who, being very close in appearance to his father, seemed to have inherited all the good looks in the family and left little for his sister. He looked what he probably had been, the most popular boy in whatever uncomfortable and expensive public school he had attended; but he bore his good fortune modestly, and even managed to slander the fair name of the serious crimes squad with a certain inoffensive charm. His habit of calling me 'sir' made me feel uncomfortably respectable. I wondered if all prosecuting counsel get called 'sir' at conferences.

'Why did the police let him go? That's what we want you to find out.'

'You were recommended to us as a barrister who didn't mind having a go at a man like Detective Chief Inspector Brush.'

Brush? The very copper who, in his salad days, had been the hammer of the Timsons and my constant sparring partner down the Bailey, now promoted to giddy heights in charge of a West London area, where he had brilliantly failed to solve the 'Mews Murder' and let Christopher Jago, the number one suspect, out of his clutches.

'They say you'll never be a judge, so you're not afraid of going for the police, Mr Rumpole.' Fabian senior managed to make it sound like a compliment.

'They said we weren't to mind about the soup or the tie or the cigar ash down the waistcoat.' Fabian junior was even more complimentary. 'And you don't care a toss for the establishment.'

'They said you'd do this job far better than the usual sort of polite and servile Q.C.' And when I asked George Fabian who they were, who spoke so highly of Rumpole, and he gave the name of Pyecraft & Wensleydale, our instructing solicitor and one of the poshest firms in the city, I could hardly forbear to preen myself visibly.

In answer to repeated inquiries from Pyecraft, Detective Chief Inspector Brush and his men had disclosed the gist of Christopher Jago's statement to them. He said he was a local estate agent, who had seen the For Sale notices outside 13A Gissing Mews, off Westbourne Grove, and wanted to view the property for a client of his own. He had rung Fabian & Winchelsea, and been put through to a young lady, believed to have been Veronica Fabian, who worked with her brother and father in the family business. He made an appointment to meet her at the house in question at eight thirty the following morning. The time was set by Jago, who was leaving that day to do a deal in some time-share apartments on the Costa del Sol. When Jago got to 13A Gissing Mews, the front door was open. He went in, expecting to meet Miss Fabian, whom he told the police he had never met before. The little mews house was still half-furnished and decorated, apparently, with African rugs and carvings. There were some spears fixed to the wall of the hallway, and a weighted knobkerrie, a three-foot black club, had been torn down and caused the fatal blow to the girl. Jago said he had knelt beside her body and tried to raise her head, during which operation his cuff had become smeared with blood.

Then there followed the events which might have made any family feel that they had good reason to suspect Christopher Jago. He said he panicked. There he was with a dead girl whose blood was on his clothing and he felt sure he would be accused of some sort of sex killing — one of the murders which had recently terrified the neighbourhood. He left the house, drove to the airport and went on his way to Spain. Two hours later, the owner of the mews called to collect some of his possessions, found the body and called the police. Veronica Fabian had died from extensive wounds to her skull. The only real clue was the name she had written against her eight thirty appointment in her desk diary: Arthur Morrison. The police spent a great deal of time trying to find or identify the man Morrison but without success.

As luck would have it, Jago had parked his car on a resident's parking place in the mews, and the irate resident had taken its number. When he got back to England, Jago was questioned as a possible witness. He immediately admitted that he had found the dead girl, panicked and run away. However, after several days when he was assisting the police with their inquiries (often a euphemism for getting himself stitched up) Jago was released to the surprise and fury of the surviving members of the Fabian family.

'You'd've charged him at least, Mr Rumpole, wouldn't you?' Fabian *père* sounded, as ever, reasonable.

'Perhaps. But I've grown up with the awkward habit of believing everyone innocent until they're proved guilty.'

'But you'll take it on for us, won't you? At least let a jury decide?'

'I'll have to think about it.' I lit a small cigar and blew out smoke. If Fabian *fils* had come expecting ash down the waistcoat I might as well let him have it. It's a curious English system, in my view, which allows private citizens to prosecute each other for crimes with the aim of sending each other to chokey, and I wasn't at all sure that it ought to be encouraged. I mean, where would it end? I might be tempted to draft an indictment against Sam Ballard, the Head of our Chambers, on the grounds of public nuisance. I had caught this soapy customer ostentatiously pinning up NO SMOKING notices in the passage outside my door.

'But we've got to have justice, Mr Rumpole. Isn't that the point?'

'Have we? "Use every man after his desert," as a well-known Dane put it, "and who should escape whipping?" ' I puffed out another small cigar cloud, hoping it would eventually waft its way in the general direction of our Head of Chambers who would, no doubt, go off like a fire alarm. I was thinking of the difficulty of having a client I could never meet in this world, whom I could never ask what happened when she went to the mews house to meet this mysterious and vanished Morrison or, indeed, whether she wanted such secrets as she may have had to be dragged out in a trial which could no longer have any interest for her.

'The power of evil is everywhere, Rumpole. As I'm afraid everywhere includes our own Chambers at Equity Court. That is why I have sought you out, although one doesn't like to spend too much time in these places.'

'Does one not?' I consider any hour wasted which is not passed with a hand round a comforting glass of Chateau Thames Embankment in Pommeroy's haven of rest.

'Passive alcoholism, Rumpole.' Sam Ballard, who, I imagine, gets his hair-shirts from the Army & Navy Stores and whose belligerent puritanism makes Praise-God-Barebones look like

Giovanni Casanova, had crept up on me at the bar and abandoned himself to a slimline tonic. 'You've heard of passive smoking, of course?'

'I've heard of it. Although, I have to say, I prefer the active variety.'

'Passive alcoholism's the same thing. Abstainees can absorb the fumes from neighbouring drinkers and become alcoholics. Quite easily.'

'Is that one of Matey's medical theories?' Sam Ballard, of course, had fallen for the formidable Mrs Marguerite Plumstead, the Old Bailey matron, and made her his bride, an act which lends considerable support to the theory that love is blind.

'Marguerite is, of course, extremely well informed on all health problems. So now, when we ask colleagues to dinner, we make it clear that our house is an alcohol-free zone.'

This colleague thought, with some gratitude, that the Bollard house in Waltham Cross would also be Rumpole-free in the future. 'But that wasn't why I wanted a word in confidence, Rumpole. I need to enlist your help, as a senior, in years anyway, a very senior member of Equity Court. A grave crime has been committed.'

'Oh my God?' I did my best to look stricken. 'Some bandit hasn't pinched the nail-brush again?'

'I'm afraid, Rumpole' — Bollard looked as though he were about to announce the outbreak of the Black Death, or at least the Hundred Years War — 'this goes beyond pilfering in the downstairs toilet.'

'Not nail-brush nicking this time, eh?'

'No, Rumpole. This time it would appear to be forgery, false pretence and obtaining briefs by fraud.' I lit another small cigar which had the desired effect of making Bollard tell his story as rapidly as possible, like a man with a vital message to get out before the poison gas rises above his head. It seemed that Miss Tricia Benbow — a somewhat ornate lady solicitor in whom Henry finds, when she enters his clerk's room with the light behind her, a distinct resemblance to the late Princess Grace of Monaco — had sent a brief in some distant and unappetizing County Court (Snaresbrook, Luton or Land's End, for all I can remember) to young David Inchcape whose legal career was in its tyro stages. Someone, as this precious brief was lying in the clerk's room, scratched out Inchcape's name and substituted that of Claude Erskine-Brown, who duly turned up at the far-flung Court to the surprise of Miss Benbow who had expected a younger man. An inquiry was instituted and, within hours, Sherlock Ballard, Q.C. was on the case. Henry denied all knowledge of the alteration, which seemed to have occurred before he entered the brief in his ledger, young Inchcape looked hard-done-by, and Claude Erskine-Brown, whose performances in Court were marked by a painstaking attention to the letter of the law, emerged as public enemy number one.

'That quality of evil is all pervasive.' The slimline tonic seemed to have gone to Ballard's head. He spoke in an impressive whisper and his eyes glittered with all the enthusiasm of a Grand Inquisitor preparing for the *auto-da-fé.* 'In my view it has entered into the character of Erskine-Brown.'

Not much can be said in criticism of that misguided, and somewhat fatuous, old darling with whom I have shared Chambers at Equity Court for more years than we like to remember. Claude's taste for the headier works of Richard Wagner fills him with painful longings for young ladies connected with the legal profession, whom he no doubts sees as Rhine Maidens or mini-Valkyries in wig and gown. In Court his behaviour can vacillate between the ponderous and the panic-stricken, so those who think unkindly of him, among whom I do not number myself, might reasonably describe him as a pompous twit. All that having been said, the soul of Claude Erskine-Brown is about as remote from evil as Pommeroy's plonk is from Château Latour.

'Claude would be flattered to hear you say he was evil,' I told our Head of Chambers. 'He might feel he'd got a touch of the Nibelungens or something.'

'I noticed it from the time we did that case about the dirty restaurant. He wanted to conceal the fact that he'd been dining there with his female instructing solicitor. From what I remember, he wanted to mislead the court about it.*

'Well, that's true,' I conceded. 'Old Claude, so far as I can see, conducts his love life with the minimum of sexual satisfaction and the maximum amount of embarrassment to all concerned. If you want to call that evil...'

'A man who wishes to deceive his wife is quite capable of deceiving his Head of Chambers.' For a moment I caught in Ballard's voice an echo of that moral certainty which characterizes the judgments of She Who Must Be Obeyed.

*See 'Rumpole à la Carte'.

'How do you know he'd deceive you? Have you asked him if
he put his name on the brief?'

'I'm afraid Erskine-Brown has added perjury to his other
offences.'

'You mean he denied it?'

'Hotly.'

'No one in the clerk's room did it?'

'Henry and Dianne say they didn't and I'm prepared to accept
their evidence. Rumpole, when it comes to crime, you have considerably more experience than any of us.'

'Thank you very much.'

'I want to undertake a thorough investigation of this matter.
Examine the witnesses. And if Erskine-Brown's found guilty . . . '

'What, then?'

'You know as well as I do, Rumpole. There is no place in Equity
Court for fellows who pinch other fellows' briefs.'

I gave Soapy Sam the chance of a little passive enjoyment of
the heady fumes of Château Fleet Street and thought the matter
over. Poor old Claude was probably guilty. The starring role played
by his wife, Phillida, now luxuriously wrapped in the silk gown
of Q.C., in so many long-running cases must have made him
despondent about his own practice, which varied between the
second-rate and the mediocre. The sight of a brief delivered by
a solicitor he fancied sufficiently to fill up with priceless delicacies
at La Maison Jean-Pierre to a white-wig must have wounded him
deeply.

Moreover, it had to be remembered that he had admitted young
Inchcape to our Chambers under the impression that he was
thereby proving his tolerance to those of the gay persuasion, only
to discover that Inchcape was in fact a closet heterosexual and
his successful rival for the favours of Mizz Liz Probert.* All these
were mitigating factors which would spring instantly to the mind
of one who always acted for the Defence. They were already
outweighing any horror I might have felt at the crime he had
probably committed.

'I'm sorry, Bollard.' Our leader was still alongside me, his nose
pointedly aimed from the direction of the glass that contained
my ever-diminishing double red. 'I can't help you. It's the second
time today I've been asked; but prosecution isn't my line of
country. Rumpole always defends.'

*See 'Rumpole and the Quality of Life' in *Rumpole and the Age of Miracles*, Penguin
Books, 1988.

Not long after that events occurred which persuaded me to change my mind, with results which may have an incalculable effect on whatever is left of my future.

It was that grim season of the year, which now begins around the end of August and reaches its climax in the first week of December, known as the 'build-up to Christmas'. I have often thought that if the Son of Man had known what he was starting he would have chosen to be born on a quiet summer's day when everyone was off on holiday on what the Timson family always refers to as the Costa del Crime. As it was, crowds of desperate shoppers were elbowing their way to the bus stops in the driving rain. More crammed aboard as we crawled through the West End, where the ornamental lights had been switched on. I sat contemplating the tidings of great joy She Who Must Be Obeyed had brought to me a few weeks earlier. That very night her old school friend, Charmian Nichols, was to arrive to spend the festive season *à côté de chez* Rumpole in the Gloucester Road.

Readers of these chronicles will only have heard, up till now, of one of the old girls who sported with my wife, Hilda, on the fields of Bexhill Ladies College when the world was somewhat younger than it is today. You will recall the redoubtable Dodo Mackintosh, painter in watercolour and maker of 'cheesy bits' for our Chambers parties, who regards Rumpole with a beady, not to say suspicious, eye, whenever she comes to call. Dodo's place, on this particular Christmas, had been taken by Charmian Nichols. Charlie Nichols, no doubt exhausted by the wear and tear of marriage to a star, who had been not only a monitor and captain of hockey, but winner of the Leadership and Character trophy for two years in succession, had dropped off the twig quite early in the run up to Christmas and the widowed Charmian wrote to Hilda indicating that she had nothing pencilled in for the festive season and was inclined to grant us the favour of her company in the Gloucester Road. She added, in a brief postscript, that if Hilda had made a prior commitment to that 'dowdy little Dodo Mackintosh' she would quite understand. She Who Must Be Obeyed, in whose breast Mrs Nichols was able to awaken feelings of awe and wonder which had lain dormant during our married life, immediately bought a new eiderdown for the spare bedroom and broke the news to Dodo that there would be no room at the inn owing to family commitments. You see it took

the winner of the Leadership and Character trophy to lure Hilda
to perjury.

'Hilda, dear. Why ever can't you persuade Howard to buy a
new Crock-a-Gleam? Absolutely no one plunges their hands
into washing-up bowls any more. Of course, it is rather sweetly
archaic of you both to still be doing it.'

The late Dean Swift, in one of those masterpieces of English
literature which I shall never get around to reading, spoke of a
country, I believe, ruled by horses, and there was a definite air
of equine superiority about La Nichols. She stood, for a start,
several hands higher than Rumpole. Her nostrils flared contemp-
tuously, her eyes were yellowish and her greying mane was
carefully combed and braided. She was, I had noticed, elegantly
shod and you could have seen your face in her polished little
hooves. She would, I devoutly hoped, be off with a thoroughbred
turn of speed as soon as Christmas was over.

'You mean, get a dishwasher?' Hilda no longer trusted me to
scour the plates to her satisfaction and Charmian had taken my
place with the teacloth, dabbing a passable portrait of the Tower of
London at our crockery and not knowing where to put it away.
'Oh, Rumpole and I are always talking about that, but we never
seem to get around to buying one.' This was another example of
the widow's fatal effect on She's regard for the truth; to the best of
my recollection the word 'dishwasher' had never passed our lips.

'Well, surely, Harold,' Charmian whinnied at me over the glass
she was polishing mercilessly, 'you're going to buy Hilda something white for Christmas?'

'You mean handkerchiefs? I hadn't thought of that. And the
name is Horace, but as you're here for Christmas with the family
you can call me Rumpole.'

'No, white! A machine to wash plates and things like that?
Charlie had far too much respect for my hands to let them get
into a state like poor Hilda's.' At this, she looked at my wife with
deep sympathy and rattled on, 'Charlie insisted that I could only
keep my looks if I was fully automated. Of course I just couldn't
have lived the life I did without our Plan-ahead "archive" freezer,
our jumbo-microwave and rôtisserie.' Something snapped
beneath the teacloth at this point. 'Oh, Hilda. One of your glasses
gone for a Burton! Was it terribly precious?'

'Not really. It was a Christmas present from Dodo. From what
I can remember.'

'Oh, well then.' Charmian shot the shattered goblet, a reasonably satisfactory container for Pommeroy's Perfectly Ordinary, into the tidy-bin. 'But surely Hammond can afford to mechanize you, Hilda? He's always in Court from what you said in your letters.'

'Legal aid defences,' Hilda told her gloomily, 'don't pay for much machinery.'

'Legal aid!' Charmian pronounced the words as though they constituted a sort of standing joke, like kippers or mothers-in-law. 'Isn't that sort of National Health? Charlie was always really sorry for our poor little doctor in Guildford who had to pig along on that!'

I wanted to say that I didn't suppose old Charlie had much use for legal aid in his stockbroking business, but I restrained myself. Nor did I explain that our budget was well off balance since our cruise,* which had taken a good deal more than Hilda's late aunt's money, that legal aid fees had been cut and were paid at the pace of a handicapped snail, and that whenever I succeeded in cashing a cheque at the Caring Bank I had to restrain myself from making a dash for the door before they remembered our overdraft. Instead, I have to admit, something about the condescending Charmian, as she looked with vague amusement around our primitive kitchen equipment, made me want to impress her on her own, unadmirable terms.

'As a matter of fact,' I said, casually filling one of Dodo's remaining glasses, 'I don't only do legal aid defences. I get offered quite a few private prosecutions. They can be extremely lucrative.'

'Really, Rumpole. Just how lucrative?' Hilda stood transfixed, her rubber gloves poised above the bubbling Fairy Liquid, waiting for the exact figures. The next morning, when I arrived at my Chambers in Equity Court, Henry told me.

"Two thousand pounds, Mr Rumpole. And I've agreed refreshers at five hundred a day. They've promised to send a cheque down with the brief.'

'And it's a case likely to last a day or two?' I stood awestruck at the price put upon my prosecution of Christopher Jago.

'We have got it down, Mr Rumpole, for two weeks.' I did some not so swift calculations, mental arithmetic never having been my strongest point, and then came to a firm decision. 'Henry,' I said, 'your lady wife, the Mayor of Bexleyheath...'

'No longer, Mr Rumpole. Her year of office being over, she has returned to mere alderman.'

*See 'Rumpole at Sea.'

'So, you, Henry' — I congratulated the man warmly — 'are no longer Lady Mayoress?'

'Much to my relief, Mr Rumpole, I have handed in my chain.'

'Henry, you'll be able to tell me. Does the alderman ever plunge her ex-mayorial hands into the Fairy Liquid?'

'Hardly, Mr Rumpole. We have had a Crock-a-Gleam for years. You know, we're fully automated.'

Well, of course, I might have said, on a clerk's fees you would be, wouldn't you? It's only penurious barristers who are still slaving away with the dishcloth. Instead I made an expansive gesture. 'Go out, Henry,' I bade him, 'into the highways and byways of Oxford Street. Order up the biggest, whitest, most melodiously purring Crock-a-Gleam that money can buy and have it dispatched to Mrs Rumpole at Froxbury Mansions with the compliments of the season.'

'You're going to prosecute in Jago then, Mr Rumpole?' Henry looked as surprised as if I had announced I meant to spend Christmas in a temperance hotel.

'Well, yes, Henry. I just thought I'd try my hand at it. For a change.'

Finally, my clerk declined a trip up Oxford Street but Dianne, who was busily engaged in reading her horoscope in *Woman's Own* and decorating her finger-nails for Christmas, undertook to ring John Lewis on my behalf. At which moment my learned friend Claude Erskine-Brown entered the clerk's room looking about as happy as a man who has paid through the nose for tickets for *Die Meistersinger von Nürnberg* and found himself at an evening of 'Come Dancing'. He noted, lugubriously, that there were no briefs in his tray — even those with other people's names on them — and then drew me out into the passage for a heart to heart.

'It's a good thing you were in the clerk's room just then, Rumpole.'

'Oh, is it? Why exactly?'

'Well. Ballard says he doesn't want me to go in there unless some other member of Chambers is present. What's he think I'm going to do? Forge my fee notes or ravish Dianne?'

'Probably both.'

'It's unbelievable.'

'Perhaps. We've got to remember that Ballard specializes in believing the unbelievable. He also thinks you're sunk in sin. He's probably afraid of getting passive sinning by standing too close to you.'

'Rumpole. About that wretched brief in the Rickmansworth County Court...'

'Oh, was it Rickmansworth? I thought it was Luton.' I was trying to avoid the moment that barristers dread — when your client looks at you in a trusting and confidential manner and seems about to tell you that he's guilty of the charge on which you've been paid to defend him.

'Rumpole, I wanted to tell you...

'Please, don't, old darling,' I spoke as soothingly as I knew to the deeply distressed Claude. 'We all know the feeling. Acute shortage of crime affecting one's balance of payments. Nothing in your tray, nothing in the diary. The bank manager and the taxman hammering on the door. The VAT man climbing in at the window. Then you wander into the clerk's room and all the briefs seem to be for other people. Well, heaven knows how many times I've been tempted.'

'But I didn't do it, Rumpole. I mean I'd've been mad to do it. It was bound to get found out in the end.'

Many crimes, in my experience, are committed by persons undergoing temporary fits of insanity, who are bound to be found out in the end but I didn't think it tactful to mention this. Instead, I asked, 'What about the handwriting on the changed brief?'

'It's in block letters. Not like mine, or anyone else's either. All the same, Ballard seems to have appointed himself judge, jury and handwriting expert. Rumpole' — Claude's voice sank in horror — 'I think he wants me out of Chambers.'

'I wouldn't be surprised.'

'What on earth's Philly going to say?' The man lived in growing awe of Phillida Erskine-Brown, Q.C., the embarrassingly successful Portia of our Chambers. 'I should think she'd be very glad to have you at home to do the washing up,' I comforted him. 'That is, unless you have a Crock-a-Gleam like the rest of us.'

'Rumpole, please. This is no joking matter.'

'Everything, in my humble opinion, is a joking matter.'

'I want you to defend me.'

'Do you? Ballard's asked me to fill an entirely different role.'

'You!' The unfortunate Claude gave me a look of horror. 'But you don't ever prosecute, do you?'

'Well' — I did my level best to cheer the man up — 'hardly ever.'

I passed on up to my room, where I lit a small cigar and re-opened the papers in the Jago case, which I read with a new interest since Henry had dealt with the little matter of my fee. I looked at the photograph of the big, plain victim and thought again how little she looked like her trim and elegant father and brother. I went through the account of Jago's statements, and decided that even the clumsiest cross-examiner could ridicule his unconvincing explanations. I turned the pages of a photostat of Veronica Fabian's diary and learnt, for the first time, that she had had six previous appointments with the man called Arthur Morrison, and I wondered why the name seemed to mean something to me. Then the door was flung open and an extremely wrathful Mizz Liz Probert came into my presence.

'Well,' she said, 'you've really deserted us for the enemy now, haven't you, Rumpole.'

'I haven't been listening to the news.' I tried to be gentle with her. 'Are we at war?'

'Don't pretend you don't know what I mean. Henry's told me all about it. In my opinion it's as contemptible as acting for a landlord who's trying to evict a one-parent family on supplementary benefit. You've gone over to the Prosecution.'

'Not gone over' — I did my best to reassure the inflamed daughter of Red Ron Probert, once the firebrand leader of the South-East London Labour Council — 'just there on a visit.'

'Just visiting the establishment, the powers that be, the Old Bill. Just there on a friendly call? How comfortable, Rumpole. How cosy. You know what I always admired about you?'

'Not exactly. Do remind me.'

'Oh, yes. No wonder you've forgotten, now you've taken up prosecution. Well, I admired the fact that you were always on the side of the underdog. You stopped the Judges sending everyone to the nick. You showed up the police. You stood up for the underprivileged.' Liz Probert was using almost the same words as the Fabians, but now she said, 'And you, of all people, are being paid by some posh family of ritzy estate agents to cook up a case against a bit of a naff member of their profession. They're narked he's been let free just because there isn't any evidence against him.'

'Let me enlighten you.' My tone, as always, was sweetly reasonable. 'There is plenty of evidence against him.'

'Like the fact that he never went to a "decent public school" like the Fabians?'

'And like the fact that he scooted out of the country when he found the body instead of telephoning the police.'

'Oh, I'm sure you'll find lots of effective points to make against him!' Hell hath no fury like an outraged radical lawyer, and Mizz Probert's outrage did for her what a large Pommeroy's plonk did for me — it made her extremely eloquent. 'You'll be able to argue him into a life sentence with a twenty-five-year recommendation. Probably you'll get the thanks of the Judge, an invitation to the serious crimes squad dinner dance and a weekend's shooting at the Fabians' place in Hampshire. I don't know why you did it — or, rather, I know only too well.'

'Why, do you think?'

'Henry told me.' Then she took, as I sometimes do, to poetry: ' "Just for a handful of silver he left us." You're always quoting Wordsworth.'

'I do. Except that's by Browning. *About* Wordsworth.'

'About him, is it? "The Lost Leader"? Well. No wonder you like Wordsworth so much.'

All this was hardly complimentary to Rumpole or, indeed, to the Old Sheep of the Lake District whose job in the stamp office had earned him the fury of the young Robert Browning. I wasn't thinking of this, however, as Liz Probert continued her flow of denunciation. I was thinking of the unfortunate Claude Erskine-Brown and the way he had spoken to me in the passage. He had seemed angry, puzzled, depressed, but not, strangely enough, guilty.

It's rare for a criminal hack to be invited into his customer's home. We represent a part of their lives they would prefer to forget. Not only do they not ask us to dinner, but when catching sight of us at parties years after we have sprung them from detention they look studiously in the opposite direction and pretend we never met. No one, I suppose, wants the neighbours to spot the sturdy figure of Rumpole climbing their front steps. I may give rise to speculation as to whether it's murder, rape or merely a nice clean fraud that's going on in their family. The Fabians were different. Clearly they felt that they had, as representatives of law and order, nothing to be ashamed of, indeed much to be proud of in the way they were pursuing justice, in spite of the curious lassitude of the police and the Director of Public Prosecutions. Mrs Fabian, it seemed, suffered from arthritis and rarely left the house so my discreet and highly respected solicitor, Frances Pyecraft (of Pyecraft & Wensleydale), and my good self were invited there for drinks. The dead girl's mother wanted to look us over and grant us her good housekeeping seal of approval.

'It's not knowing, that's the worst thing, Mr Rumpole,' Mrs Fabian told me. 'I feel I could learn to live with it, if I knew just *how* Veronica died.'

'You mean who killed her?'

'Yes, of course, that's what I mean.'

I didn't like to tell her that a criminal trial, before a judge, who comes armed with his own prejudices, and a jury, whose attention frequently wanders, may be a pretty blunt instrument for prising out the truth. Instead, I looked at her and wondered if couples are attracted by physical likeness. Mrs Fabian was as small-boned, clear-featured and neat as her husband and son. And yet they had produced a big-boned and plain daughter, who had stumbled, no doubt, unwittingly, on death.

'Perhaps you could tell me a little more about Veronica. I mean about her life. Boyfriends?'

'No.' Mrs Fabian shook her head. 'That was really the trouble. She didn't seem to be able to find one. At least, not one that cared about her.' We sat in the high living-room of a house overlooking the canal in Little Venice. Tall bookshelves stretched to the ceiling, a pair of loud-speakers tinkled with appropriate baroque music. The white walls were hung with grey drawings which looked discreetly expensive. Young Roger moved among us, replenishing our glasses. The curtains hadn't been drawn and Mrs Fabian sat on a sofa looking out into the winter darkness, almost as though she was still expecting her daughter to come home early on yet another evening without a date. Veronica's mother, father and brother, I imagined, never found it difficult to find people who cared about them. Only their daughter had to get on without love.

'She worked in your firm. What were her other interests?'

'Oh, she read enormously. She had an idea she wanted to be a writer and she did some things for her school magazine, which were rather good, I thought,' Gregory told me.

'*Very* good.' Mrs Fabian gave the dead girl her full support.

'She never got much further than that, I'm afraid. I suggested she came and worked for us, and then she could write in her spare time. If she seemed to be going to make a success of it — the writing, I mean — of course, I'd've supported her.' 'Just do a little estate agency, darling, until you publish a best-seller.' I could imagine the charm with which Gregory Fabian had said it, and his daughter, unsure of her talent, had agreed. A fatal arrangement; if she had stuck to literature, she would never have kept an appointment in a Notting Hill Gate mews.

'What did she read?'

'Oh, all sorts of things. Mainly nineteenth-century authors. She used to talk about becoming a novelist.'

'Her favourites were the Brontës,' Mrs Fabian remembered.

'Oh, yes. The Brontës. Charlotte, especially. She had a very romantic nature.' Veronica's father smiled, I thought, with understanding.

'This man Morrison,' I said, 'whoever he may be, keeps turning up in the desk diary. No one in the office's ever heard of him. He's never been a client of yours?'

'Not so far as I've been able to discover. There's no correspondence with him.'

'You don't know a friend of hers by that name?'

'We've asked, of course. No one's ever heard of him.'

I got up and crossed to the darkened window. Looking out, all I could see was myself reflected in the glass, a comfortably padded Old Bailey hack with a worried expression, engaged in the strange pursuit of prosecution.

'But in her diary she seems to have had six previous appointments with him.'

'Of course' — Mrs Fabian was smiling at me apologetically, as though she hardly liked to point out anything so obvious — 'we don't know everything about her. You never do, do you? Even about your own daughter.'

'All right, then. What do you know about Christopher Jago? You must have come across him in the way of business.'

'Not really.' Gregory Fabian stopped smiling. 'He has, well, a different type of business.'

'And does it in a different sort of way,' his son added.

'What does that mean?'

'Well, we've heard things. You do hear things . . .'

'What sort of things?'

'Undervaluing houses. Getting their owners to sell cheap to a chap who's really a friend of the agent. The friend sells on for the right price and he and the agent divide up the profits.'

'We've no evidence of that,' Gregory told me. 'It wouldn't be right for you to assume that's what he was doing. Apparently he's rather a flashy type of operator, but that's really all we know about him.'

'He's a cowboy.' Roger was more positive. 'And he looks the part.'

They were silent then, it seemed, for a moment, fearful of the mystery that had disturbed their gentle family life. Roger crossed the room behind me and drew the curtains, shutting out the dark.

'She wasn't robbed. She hadn't been sexually assaulted. So far as we know she hadn't quarrelled with anyone and Jago didn't even know her. Why on earth should he want to kill her?' I asked the Fabians and they continued to sit in silence, puzzled and sad.

'The police couldn't answer that question either,' I said. 'Perhaps that's why they let him go.'

I left the house on my own, as Pyecraft was staying to discuss the effect of the girl's death on certain family trusts. Gregory came down to the hall and, as he helped me on with my coat, he said quietly, 'I don't know if Francis Pyecraft explained to you about Veronica.'

'No. What about her?'

'As a matter of fact she's not our daughter.'

'Not?'

'No. After Roger was born, we so wanted a girl. Evelyn couldn't have any more children, so we adopted. Of course, we loved her just as much as Roger. But now, well, it seems to make it even more important that she should be treated justly.' Again, I thought, he was talking as though Veronica were still alive and eagerly awaiting the result of the trial. Then he said, 'There's always one child that you feel needs special protection.'

Christmas came and we sat in the kitchen round the white coffin of the Crock-a-Gleam which flashed, sighed, belched a few times and delivered up our crockery. As I rescued the burning-hot plates from a cloud of steam, the widow Charmian said, 'At least I've made Howard cough up a dishwasher for you, Hilda. I've managed to do that.'

'It wasn't you' — I had long given up trying to persuade our visitor to use my correct name — 'that made me buy it.' 'Oh?' Charmian was miffed. 'Who was it, then?'

'I suppose whoever killed Veronica Fabian.' I don't know why it was that Charmian gave me a distinct touch of the Scrooges. Later, when we opened our presents in the sitting-room, I bestowed on Hilda the gift of lavender water, which I think she now uses for laying-down purposes, and I discovered that the three pairs of darkish socks, wrapped in holly-patterned paper, were exactly what I wanted. Hilda opened a small glass jar, which contained some white cream which smelled faintly of hair oil and vaseline.

'Oh, how lovely.' She Who Must Be Obeyed was doing her best not to sound underwhelmed. 'What is it, Charmian?'

'Special homeopathic skin beautifer, Hilda dear.' Charmian was tearing open the wafer-thin china early-morning tea set on which we had, I was quite convinced, spent far too much. 'We've got to do something about those poor toil-worn hands of yours, haven't we? And is this really for me? She looked at her present with more than faint amusement. 'What funny little cups and saucers. And how very sweet of you to go out and buy them. Or was it another old Christmas present from Dodo Mackintosh?' It says a great deal for the awe in which Hilda held her, and my own iron self-control, that neither of us got up and beaned the woman with our Christmas tree.

After a festive season of this nature, it may not surpise you to know that I took an early opportunity to return to my place of business in Equity Court, where I found not much business going on. Such few barristers and clerks as were visible seemed to be in a state of somnambulism. I made for Pommeroy's Wine Bar, where even the holly seemed to be suffering from a hangover and my learned friend Claude Erskine-Brown was toying, in a melancholy and aloof fashion, with a half bottle of Pommeroy's more upmarket St-Emilion-type red.

'You're wandering lonely as a Claude,' I told him. 'Did you come up to work?'

'I came,' he said dolefully, 'because I couldn't stay home.'

'Because of Christmas visitors?'

'No. Because of the shrink.'

I didn't catch the fellow's drift. Had his wits turned and did he imagine some strange diminution in size of his Islington home, so he could no longer crawl in at the front door?

'The what?'

'The shrink. Phillida knows all about the case of the altered brief. Ballard told her.'

'Ah, yes.' I knew my Soapy Sam. 'I bet he enjoyed that.'

'She was very understanding.'

'You said you were innocent, and she believed you?'

'No. She didn't answer me. She was just very understanding.'

'Ah.'

'She said it was the mid-life crisis. It happens to people in middle age. Mainly women who pinch things in Sainsbury's. But Philly thinks quite a lot of men go mad as well. So she said it was a sort of cry for help and she'd stand by me, provided I went to a shrink.'

'So?'

'It seemed easier to agree somehow.' Poor old Claude, the fizz had quite gone out of him and he had volunteered to join the great army of the maladjusted. 'She fixed me up with a Dr Gertrude Hauser who lives in Belsize Park.'

'Oh, yes. And what did Dr Gertrude have to say?'

'Well, first of all, she had this rather disgusting old sofa with a bit of Kleenex on the pillow. She made me lie down on that, so I felt a bit of a fool. Then she asked me about my childhood, so I told her. then she said the whole trouble was that I wanted to sleep with my mother.'

'And did you?'

'What?'

'Want to sleep with your mother.'

'Of course not. Mummy would never have stood for it.'

'I suppose not.'

'Quite honestly, Rumpole. Mummy was an absolute sweetie in many ways, but — well, no offence to you, of course — she was *corpulent*. I didn't fancy her in the least.'

'Did you tell Gertrude that?'

'Yes. I said quite honestly I wouldn't have slept with Mummy if we'd been alone on a desert island.'

'What did the shrink say?'

'She said, "I shall write down 'fantasizes about being alone with his mother on a desert island'." Quite honestly, I can't go and see Dr Hauser again.'

'No. Probably not.'

'All that talk about Mummy. It's really too embarrassing. She'd have hated it so, if she'd been alive.'

'Yes, I do see. Excuse me a moment.' I tore myself away from the reluctant patient to a corner in which I had seen Mizz Liz Probert settling down to a glass of Pommeroy's newly advertised organic plonk (the old plonk, I strongly suspected, with a new bright-green label on the bottle). There was a certain matter about which I needed to ask her further and better particulars.

'Look here, Liz.' I pulled up a chair. 'How did you know all that about Christopher Jago?'

'You can't sit there,' she said. 'I'm expecting Dave Inchcape.'

'Just until he comes. How did you know that Jago didn't go to a public school, for instance?'

'He told me.'

'You met him?'

'Oh, yes. Dave and I got our flat through him. And I have to tell you, Rumpole, that he was absolutely honest, reliable and trustworthy throughout the whole transaction.' I had forgotten that Liz and Dave were now co-mortgagees and living happily ever after somewhere off Ladbroke Grove.

'What do you mean, he was honest and reliable?'

'Well. We got our place pretty cheaply, compared to the price Fabian & Winchelsea were asking for the other flats we saw. He never put up the price or let us be gazumped by other clients and he helped us fix up our mortgage. Oh, and he didn't conk me on the head with a Zulu knobkerrie.'

'Yes. I can see that. What else about him? Did he have a wife, girlfriend — anything like that?'

'Hundreds of girlfriends, I should think. He's rather attractive. Tall, fair and handsome. So you see, I shan't be giving evidence for the Prosecution.'

'I imagine from what you said, you wouldn't come and take a note for me? Act as my junior?'

'You must be joking!' Mizz Liz took a gulp of the alleged organic brew and looked at me with contempt.

'I'll have to ask your co-habitee.'

'Save your breath. Tricia Benbow's already briefed Dave for the Defence. He knows I'd never speak to him again if he took part in a prosecution.'

'Christopher Jago's gone to La Belle Benbow?'

'Oh, yes. He asked me if I knew a brilliant solicitor and said he preferred women in his life, so I sent him off to her.'

'But Dave Inchcape's not doing the case alone? I mean no offence to him but he's still only a white-wig.'

'He's got a leader.'

'Who?' A foeman, I rather hoped, worthy of my steel. Liz looked at me in silence for a moment, as though she was relishing the news she had to impart.

'Our Head of Chambers,' she told me.

'Heavens above!' I nearly choked on my non-organic chemically produced Château Ordinaire. ' "Thus the whirligig of time brings in his revenges." Rumpole for the Prosecution and Ballard for the Defence. He'd better sit close to me. He might catch some passive advocacy.'

On my way out, I had a message for Claude Erskine-Brown, who was still palely loitering. 'Come and help me in the "Mews Murder",' I said. 'Be my hard-working junior. Take your mind off your mother.'

'Rumpole!' The man looked pained and I hastened to comfort him. 'At least you'll find someone who's deeper in the manure than you are, old darling,' I said.

Being in possession of two such contradictory views of Christopher Jago as those provided by the Fabians and Mizz Liz Probert, I decided that a little investigative work was necessary.

I could hardly ask Francis Pyecraft to hang round such pubs and clubs as Jago might frequent, so I called in the services of my old friend and colleague, Ferdinand Isaac Gerald Newton, known as Fig Newton to the trade. You could pass through many bars and hardly notice the doleful, lantern-jawed figure, sitting in a quiet corner, nursing half a pint of Guinness and apparently engrossed in *The Times* crossword puzzle which he solves, I am ashamed to say, in almost less time than it takes me to spot the quotations. But he hoovers up every scrap of gossip and information dropped within a surprisingly wide radius. You can't make bricks without straw and Fig is straw-purveyor to the best Old Bailey defenders. Now he would have a chance, as I had, of seeing life from the prosecution side.

I met him a couple of weeks later in Pommeroy's. He was suffering, as usual, from a bad cold, having been up most of the night keeping watch on a block of flats in a matrimonial matter, but between some heavy work with the handkerchief he was able to tell me a good deal. Our quarry lived in a 1930s house near Shepherd's Bush Road, the ground floor of which served as his office. He drove an electric blue Alfa-Romeo, the car which had led to his arrest. He was well known in a number of pubs round Maida Vale and Notting Hill Gate, where many of the properties he dealt in were situated. He was unmarried but went out with a succession of girls, his taste running to young and pretty blonde secretaries and receptionists. None of them lasted very long and in the Benedict Arms, one of his favourite resorts near the Regent's Canal, the bar staff would lay bets on how soon any girl would go.

There was one notable exception, however, to the stage army of desirable young women. On half a dozen occasions, the suspect had come into the Benedict Arms with a big, awkward, pale and rather unattractive girl. They had sat in a corner, away from the crowd, and appeared to have had a lot to say to each other. When Fig told me that, the penny dropped. I smote the table in my excitement, rattling the glasses and attracting the stares of the legal hacks busy drinking around us. I had just remembered what I knew about Arthur Morrison.

On my way home I went to check the facts in the library, for Veronica Fabian had no doubt known a great deal more that I did about minor novelists in the last century. Arthur Morrison, a prolific author, was born in 1863 and lived on into the Second World War. His best-known book about life in the East End of London was published in 1896. It was called *A Child of the Jago*.

I put the *Companion to English Literature* back on the library shelf with a feeling of relief. God was in his heaven: the widow Charmian, despite a pressing invitation to stay from Hilda, had gone back to Guildford, and the first prosecution I had ever undertaken seemed likely to be a winner. As I have said, I find it very difficult to embark on any case without being dead set on victory.

'May it please you, my Lord, Members of the Jury. I appear in this case with my learned friend, Mr Claude Erskine-Brown, for the Prosecution. The Defence of Christopher Jago is in the hands of my learned friends, Mr Samuel Ballard and Mr David Inchcape.' As I uttered these unaccustomed words, I had the unusual experience of the scarlet Judge on the Bench welcoming me with the sort of ingratiating smile he usually reserved for visiting Supreme Court justices or extremely pretty lady plaintiffs entering the witness-box.

'Did you say you were here to *prosecute*?'

'That is so, my Lord.'

'Members of the Jury' — Mr Justice Oliphant, as was his wont, spoke to the ladies and gents in the jury-box as though they were a group of educationally subnormal children with hearing defects — 'Mr Rumpole is going to outline the story of this case to you. In perfectly simple terms. Isn't that right, Mr Rumpole?'

'I hope so, my Lord.'

'So my advice to you is to sit quietly and give him your full attention. The Defence will have its chance later.' This reference caused Soapy Sam Ballard to lift his posterior from the bench and smile winsomely, an overture which Mr Justice 'Ollie' Oliphant completely ignored. Ollie comes from the northern circuit and prides himself on being a rough diamond who uses his robust common sense. I hoped he wasn't going to try to help me too much. Most acquittals occur when the Judge sickens the Jury by over-egging the prosecution pudding.

So we went to work in Number One Court. The two neat Fabians, father and son, sat in front of me. The man in the dock couldn't have been a greater contrast to them. He was tall, two or three inches over six feet, with a winter suntan that must have been kept going with a lamp, as well as visits to Marbella. His hair, clearly the victim of many hours' work with a blow-drier, was bouffant at the front and, at the back, swept almost down to his shoulders. His drooping moustache and the broad bracelet of his watch were the colour of old gold and his suit, like his car, might have been described as electric blue. He looked less like the cowboy Roger Fabian had called him than a professional foot-baller whose private and professional life is in a continual mess. He lounged between two officers in the dock, with his long legs stuck out in front of him, affecting alternate boredom and amusement. Underneath it all, I thought, he was probably terrified.

So there I was, opening my case to the Jury in as neutral a way as I knew how. I described the little mews house as I remembered it when I went to inspect the scene of the crime: the cramped rooms, the chill feeling of the home unused, the African carvings and weapons on the wall. I asked the Jury to picture the girl from the estate agents' office, who was waiting in the hallway, with the front door left open, to greet the man who had telephoned her.

Who was it? Was it Mr Morrison? Or was that a name she used to hide the identity of someone she knew quite well? I took the Jury through my theory that the literate Veronica had picked the name of the author of a book with Jago in the title. Then I waited for Ballard to shoot to his feet, as I would have done had I been defending, and denounce this as a vague and typical Rumpolean fantasy. I waited in vain. Ballard was inert, indeed there was an unusually contented smile on his face as he sat, perhaps deriving a little passive sensual satisfaction from the close and perfumed presence of his instructing solicitor, Miss Tricia Benbow.

'The Defence will no doubt argue that there is a real Arthur Morrison who met Veronica Fabian in the mews and killed her before Jago arrived on the scene.'

Once again Ballard replied with a deafening silence as he stared appreciatively at the back of his solicitor's neck. My instincts as a defender got the better of me. Jago may have been a crooked estate agent with a lamentable private life and an appalling taste in suits, but he deserved to have the points in his favour put as soon as possible. 'That's what you're going to argue, Ballard, isn't it?' I said in a *sotto voce* growl.

'Oh, yes.' Ballard shot obediently to his feet. 'If your Lordship pleases. It will be my duty to submit to your Lordship, in the fulness of time and entirely at your Lordship's convenience, of course, that the Jury will have to consider Morrison's part in this case very seriously, very seriously indeed.'

'If there is a Morrison, Mr Ballard. We have to use our common sense about that, don't we?' His Lordship intervened.

'Yes, of course. If your Lordship pleases.' Ballard subsided without further struggle. The Judge's intervention had somewhat unnerved me. I felt like a tennis player, starting a friendly knock up, who suddenly sees the referee hurling bricks at his opponent.

'Of course, I can concede that we may be wrong about the reasons Veronica Fabian used that name when entering her eight thirty appointment.'

'Use your common sense, Mr Rumpole. Please.' His Lordship's tone became distinctly less friendly. 'Mr Ballard hasn't asked you to concede to anything. Your job is to present the prosecution case. Let's get on with it.'

The Fabians, father and son, were looking up at me, and it was their plea for justice, rather than the disapproval of Oliver Oliphant, which made me return to the attack. 'In any event, Members of the Jury, we intend to call evidence to prove that Jago was seeing the dead girl quite regularly, meeting her in a public house called the Benedict Arms and having long, intimate conversations with her. There will also be evidence that he told the police...'

'That he'd never seen her before in his life!' Mr Justice Oliphant was like the helpful wife who always supplies the punchline to the end of her husband's best stories.

'I was coming to that, my Lord.'

'Come to it then, Mr Rumpole. How long is this case expected to last?'

My reaction to that sort of remark was instinctive. 'It will last, my Lord, for as long as it takes the Jury to consider every point both for and against the accused, and to decide if they can be sure of his guilt or not.' I felt happier now, at home in my old position of arguing with the Judge. Ollie opened his mouth, no doubt to deliver himself of a little more robust common sense, but I went on before he could utter.

'The police decided not to charge Jago because there was no apparent motive for the crime. But if he knew Veronica Fabian, if they had some sort of relationship, they may have had to consider why he ran from that house, where Veronica was lying dead, and told no one what he had seen. Finally, Members of the Jury, it's for you to say why he lied to the police and said he never met her.' And then I repeated the sentence I had used so often from the other side of the Court. 'You won't convict him of anything unless you're certain sure that the only answer is he must be guilty. That's what we call the golden thread that runs through British justice.'

So we began to call the evidence, produce the photographs and listen to the monotonous tones of police officers refreshing their memories from their notebooks. When I was defending, such witnesses presented a challenge, each to be lured in a different way, with charm, authority or lofty disdain, to produce some fragment of evidence which might help the customer in the dock. Now all I had to do was let them rattle on and so prosecuting seemed a dull business. Then we got the scene of the crime officer, who produced the fatal knobkerrie, its end heavily rounded, still blood-stained and protected by cellophane, as was the three-foot black handle. Ballard, who had sat mum during this parade of prosecution evidence, showed no interest in examining this weapon and said he had no questions.

'What about the finger-prints?' I could no longer restrain myself from hissing at my so-called opponent, a foeman who, at the moment, was hardly being worthy of my attention, let alone my steel.

'What about them?' Ballard whispered back in a sudden panic. 'Jago's aren't there, are they?'

'Of course not!' By now my whisper had become entirely audible. 'There are no finger-prints at all.'

'Mr Rumpole,' the voice of robust common sense trumpeted from the Bench, 'I thought you told us you appeared for the *Prosecution*. If Mr Ballard wants to ask a question for the Defence no doubt he will get up on his hind legs and do so!' I rather doubted that but, in fact, Soapy Sam unwound himself, drew himself up to his full height and said, as though a brilliant idea had just occurred to him, 'Officer. Let me put this to you. There are absolutely no finger-prints of Christopher Jago's on the handle of that weapon, are there?'

'There are no finger-prints of any sort, my Lord.'

'I'm very much obliged. Thank you, officer.' Ballard bowed with great satisfaction and as he sat down I heard him tell his junior, Inchcape, 'I'm glad I managed to winkle that out of him.'

Later we got the officer who had been in charge of the investigation, Detective Chief Inspector Brush, and even though he was, for the first time, in recorded history, my witness, I couldn't resist teasing him a little.

'Tell me, Chief Inspector. After the body was found, you spent a good deal of time and trouble looking for Arthur Morrison.'

'We did, my Lord.'

'In fact Morrison was always your number one suspect.'

'He still is, my Lord.'

'You don't accept that Arthur Morrison and Jago were one and the same person?'

There was a pause and then 'I suppose that may be a possibility.'

'And that Arthur Morrison is nothing but a dead author.'

'I don't know much about dead authors, Mr Rumpole.' There, at least the Detective Chief Inspector was telling the truth.

'If you'd known that, whether or not Morrison existed, Jago had been meeting the dead girl regularly, would that have made any difference to the decision not to charge him?'

There was a long silence and then Brush admitted, 'Well, yes, my Lord. I think it might.'

'Let's use our common sense about this, shall we? Don't let's beat about the bush,' Ollie intervened. 'Jago told you he'd never met the girl. If you'd known he was lying, you'd've charged him.'

'Yes, my Lord.'

'Well, there we are, Members of the Jury. We've got that clear at last, thanks to a little bit of down-to-earth common sense.' Mr Justice Oliphant had joined me as leader of the Prosecution. And that might have been that, but there was one other question someone had to ask and I couldn't rely on Ballard.

'You first questioned Mr Jago because you had discovered that his car had been parked outside 13A Gissing Mews at the relevant time.'

'Yes.'

'You had no idea that he had been into the house and found the body?'

'At that time. No.'

'So he volunteered that information entirely of his own accord?'

'That's right.'

'Was that one of the reasons he wasn't charged?'

'That was one of the reasons we thought he was being honest with us, yes.'

I sat down, having made Ballard's best point for him. Of course he had to totter to his feet and ruin it.

'And, so far as that goes, Chief Inspector' — Ballard stood, pleased with himself, rocking slightly on the balls of his feet — 'do you still think he was being honest with you about the way he found the girl?'

'I'm not sure.' Brush paused and then gave it back to the poor old darling, right between the eyes. 'If he was lying to us about not knowing the girl, I can't be sure about any of his evidence, can I?' Mr Justice Oliphant wrote down that answer and underlined it with his red pencil. The Fabians looked as though they were slightly more pleased with the way Ballard was doing his case than with my performance, but no doubt they'd be too polite to say so.

At the end of our evidence we called my old friend, Professor Andrew Ackerman, Ackerman of the Morgue, with whom I have spent many fascinating hours discussing bloodstains and gunshot wounds. He testified that Veronica Fabian had died from a heavy blow to the frontal bone of the skull, consistent with an attack by the knobkerrie, Exhibit P.I. I asked him if this must have been a blow straight down on her head, and he ruled out the possibility of it having been struck from either side. From the position of the wound it was clear to him that the club had been held by the end of the handle and swung in an upward trajectory. I felt that his evidence was important, but at the moment he gave it, I didn't realize its full significance.

'So you're defending? I expect you have Mizz Liz Probert's full approval?' I was disarming in the robing-room, taking off the wig and gown and running a comb through what remains of my hair, when I found myself sharing a mirror with young Dave Inchcape.

'What do you mean?'

'Well, she thinks prosecuting's as bad as aiding merciless landlords evict their tenants.'

'I know she doesn't think you should be prosecuting.'

'And I rather think' I told him as I got on the bow-tie and adjusted the silk handkerchief, 'that Mr Justice Ollie Oliphant would agree with her.'

'By the way, I think we're doing pretty well for Chris, don't you? He's promised us a great party if we get him off.' Dave Inchcape had fallen into the defender's habit of first-name familiarity with alleged criminals. I wondered if it were ever so and the robing-room rang with cries of 'I think we're going to get Hawley off — Hawley Crippin, of course.'

I walked back to Chambers with the still despondent Erskine-Brown, who had just been cut dead by Ballard and La Belle Benbow as they were coming out of the Ludgate Circus Palais de Justice.

'By the way, Claude,' I said, 'what was that case you're meant to have pinched from Inchcape all about?'

'Please' — the man looked at a passing bus, as though tempted to dive under it — 'don't remind me of it.'

'But what was the subject matter? Just the gist, you understand.'

'Well, it was a landlord's action for possession. Nothing very exciting.'

'He wanted to turn out a one-parent family?'

'No. I think they were a couple of ladies in the Gay Rights movement. He said they were using the place to run a business. Why do you ask?'

'Because,' I tried to encourage him, 'the evidence you have just given may be of great importance.' But Claude didn't look in the slightest cheered up.

No two characters could have been more contrary that Christopher Jago and his defence counsel. Jago lounged in the witness-box, flashed occasional smiles at the Jury, whose female members looked embarrassed and the males stony-faced. He was a bad witness, truculent, defensive and flippant by turns, and Soapy Sam was finding it hard to conceal his deep disapproval of the blow-dried, shiny-suited giant he was defending.

As I had called several witnesses, who said they had seen him with Veronica in the Benedict Arms, Jago no longer troubled to deny it. He said he first saw her in the pub at lunchtime with another girl from Fabians' whom he knew slightly and he bought them both a drink. Some time after that he saw her eating her lunch in a corner, alone with a book, and he talked to her.

'What did you talk about?' I asked when I came to cross-examine.

'The house business. Prices and that around the area. I didn't chat her up, if that's what you're suggesting. She wasn't the sort of girl I could ever fancy, even if I weren't pretty well looked after in that direction.' He gave the Jury one of his least endearing grins.

'So why did you meet her so often?'

'I just happened to bump into her, that's all.'

'It's not all, is it? Your meetings were planned. She entered five or six appointments with Morrison in her diary.'

To my surprise he didn't answer with a blustering denial that he and Morrison were one and the same person. Had he forgotten his best line of defence, or was he overcome by that strange need to tell the truth, which sometimes seems to attack even the most unsatisfactory witnesses? 'All right then,' he admitted. 'She seemed to want to see me and we made a few dates to meet for a drink round the Benedict.'

'Why did she want to see you?'

'Perhaps she fancied me. It has been known.' He looked at the Jury, expecting a sympathetic giggle that never came. 'I don't know why she wanted us to meet. You tell me.'

'No, Mr Jago. You tell us.'

There was a silence then. Jago looked troubled and I thought that he was afraid of the evidence he would have to give.

'She was a bit scared to tell me about it. She said it would mean a lot of trouble if it got out.'

'What was it, Mr Jago?' I was breaking another of my rules and asking a question without knowing the answer. At that moment

I was in search of the truth, a somewhat dangerous pursuit for a defence counsel, but then I wasn't defending Jago.

He answered my question then, quietly and reluctantly. 'She was worried about what was happening at Fabians'.'

I saw my clients, the father and son, listening, composed and expressionless. They didn't try to stop me and by now it was too late to turn back. 'What did she say was happening at Fabians'?'

'She said they gave the people who wanted to sell their houses very low valuations. Then they sold to some friend who looked independent, but who was really in business with them. The friend sold on at the proper price and they shared the difference. She reckoned they'd been doing that for years. On a pretty big scale, I imagine.'

Gregory Fabian was writing me a note quite impassively. His son was flushed and looked so angry that I was afraid he was going to shout. But his father put a hand on his son's arm before he passed me his message. I remembered that Roger had said Jago practised the same fraud the Fabians were now being accused of.

'Why do you think she told you that?' I read Gregory's note then: HE'S TRYING TO RUIN US BECAUSE WE KNOW HE KILLED VERONICA. STOP HIM DOING IT.

'She told me because she was worried. I was in the same business. She wanted my advice. Like I said, perhaps she fancied me, I don't know. She said she hadn't got anyone else, no real friends, she could tell about it.'

I thought of the lonely girl who was trapped in a business she couldn't trust, pinning her faith on this unlikely companion. Perhaps she thought her confidences would bring them together. At any rate they were an excuse to meet him.

'Mr Jago, when you called at Gissing Mews that morning...'

'Like I told you. I was interested in the place for a client. I phoned Veronica and...'

'And you kept the appointment and found her dead in the hallway.'

'Yes.'

'Why didn't you telephone the police?'

'Because I was afraid.'

'Afraid you'd be arrested for murder?'

'No. Not afraid of that.'

'Of what then?'

There are moments in some trials when everyone in Court seems to hold their breath, waiting for an answer. This was such an occasion and the answer when it came was totally unexpected.

'I thought she'd been done over because she'd told me what the Fabians were up to. I thought, that might be you, Christopher, if you get involved any more.'

'*You* killed her!' Roger Fabian couldn't restrain himself now. Ollie Oliphant uttered some soothing words about understanding the strength of the family feelings, but urged the young man to use his common sense and keep quiet. I did my best to pull myself together and behave like a prosecuting counsel. I asked Jago to take Exhibit P.I in his hand, which he did without any apparent reluctance.

'I'm bound to put it to you,' I said, 'that you and Veronica Fabian quarrelled that morning when you met in the mews house. You lost your temper and took that knobkerrie off the wall. You swung it up over your head...'

'Like that, you mean?' He lifted the African club and as he did so all the odd pieces of the evidence came together and locked into one clear picture. Christopher Jago was innocent of the murder we had charged him with, and, from that moment, I was determined to get him off.

The case began and ended in the little house in Gissing Mews. I asked Ollie Oliphant to move the proceedings to the scene of the crime as I wished to demonstrate something to the Jury, having taken the precaution of telling my opponent that if he wanted to get his client off, he'd better support my application. So now the cold, gloomy mews house, with its primitive carvings and grinning African masks, was crammed to the gunwales with legal hacks, jury members, court officials and all the trimmings, including, of course, Jago and the Fabians. In one way or another, as many of us as possible got a view of the hall, where I stood by the telephone impersonating, with only a momentary fear that I might have got it entirely wrong, the victim of the crime. I got Jago to stand in front of me and swing the club, P.I, again in order to strike my head. I was not entirely surprised when neither Sam Ballard, Q.C. nor Mr Justice Oliphant tried to prevent my apparent suicide, although Claude Erskine-Brown did have the decency to mutter, 'Mind out, Rumpole. We don't want to lose you.'

Everyone was watching as the tall, flamboyant accused lifted the knobkerrie and tried to swing it above his head. He tried and failed. When I was cross-examining him, I remembered the cramped rooms and low ceilings of the mews cottage. Now as the club bumped harmlessly against the plaster, everyone present understood why Jago couldn't have struck the blow which killed Veronica Fabian. Whoever killed her must have been at least six inches shorter.

It was my first prosecution and I had managed, against all the odds, to secure an acquittal.

'You got him off?'

'Yes.'

A few days, it seemed a lifetime, later, I was alone with Gregory Fabian in his white, early Victorian house in Little Venice.

'Why?'

'Did you want an innocent man convicted? That's a stupid question. Of course you did.'

He said nothing and I went on, as I had to. 'You said there's always one child who needs protecting, but you weren't thinking of Veronica, were you? You were talking about your son.'

'What about Roger?'

'What about him? Odd, his habit of accusing other people of the things he did himself.'

'What did he do?' Gregory was quiet, unruffled, still carefully courteous, in spite of what I'd done to him.

'I think you know, don't you? The racket of undervaluing homes, so you could see them to your secret nominees. He accused Jago of doing that, just as he accused him of Veronica's murder.'

The house was very quiet. Mrs Fabian was upstairs somewhere, resting. God knows where Roger was. Even the traffic sounded far away and muted in the darkness of an early evening in January.

'What are you trying to tell me?'

'What I think. That's all. I'm not setting out to prove anything beyond reasonable doubt.'

'Go on then.' He gave a small sigh, perhaps of resignation.

'Veronica discovered what was going on and didn't like it. She asked Jago's advice, and I expect he told her to keep him well-informed. No doubt so he could make something out of it when it suited him to do so. Then I think Roger found out what his sister was doing. Well, she wasn't his real sister, was she? She was the loved girl, who had arrived after he was born, the child he was always jealous of. I expect he found out she had a date to meet Jago at the mews house. He went after her to stop her. I don't think he meant to kill her.'

'Of course he didn't.' The father was still trying, I thought, to persuade himself.

'He lost his temper with her. They quarrelled. She tried to telephone for help and he ripped out the phone. Remember that's how they found it. Then he took the knobkerrie off the wall. He's short enough to have been able to swing it without hitting the ceiling. But you know all that, don't you?' Gregory Fabian didn't answer, relying, I suppose, on his right to silence.

'You wanted Roger to be safe. You wanted him to be protected, forever. And the best way of doing that was to get someone else found guilty. That's what you paid me to do. To be quite technical, Mr Fabian, you paid me to take part in your conspiracy to pervert the course of justice.'

'You said,' he sounded desperately hopeful, 'that you couldn't prove it...'

'It's not my business to prosecute. It never has been. And it's not my business to take part in crime. I told Henry to send your money back.'

He stood up then and moved between me and the door. I thought for a moment that the repressed violence of the Fabians might erupt and he would attack me. But all he said was 'Poor Roger.'

'No, Poor Veronica. You should never have stopped her becoming a novelist.'

I walked past him and out of the house. I heard him call after me 'Mr Rumpole!' But I didn't stop. I was glad to be out in the darkness, breathing in the mist from the canal, away from a house silenced by death and deception.

I decided to walk a while from the Fabian house, feeling I had, among other things, to think over what remained of my life. 'Mr Rumpole, although briefed for the Prosecution and under a duty to present the prosecution case to you, took it into his head, no doubt because of the habit of a lifetime, to act for the Defence. So, the basis of our fine adversarial system, which has long been our pride, has been undermined. Mr Rumpole will have to consider where his future, if any, is at the Bar. In the absence of a prosecutor, you and I, Members of the Jury, will just have to rely on good old British common sense.' These were the words with which Ollie sent the Jury out to consider its verdict, which turned out to be a resounding not guilty for everyone, except Rumpole whose conduct had been, according to his Lordship, in his final analysis, 'grossly unprofessional'.

It was while I was brooding on these judicial pronouncements that I heard the sound of revelry by night and noticed that I was passing a somewhat glitzy art nouveau pub, picked out in neon lights, called the Benedict Arms. I remembered that this was the night of Christopher Jago's celebration party, to which he had invited not only his defenders, but, and in all the circumstances of the case, this was understandable, the prosecution team as well. I had persuaded Claude not to sit moping at home and I'd promised to meet him there. Accordingly I called into the saloon of the Benedict and was immediately told that Chris's piss-up was on the first floor.

I climbed up to a celebration very unlike our Chambers parties in Equity Court. Music, which sounded to my untrained ears very like the sound produced by a pneumatic drill pounding a pavement, shook the windows. There were a number of metalically blonde girls in skirts the size of pocket handkerchiefs and tops kept up by some stretch of the imagination and a fair number of men with moustaches, whom I took for downmarket estate agents. Like dark islands in a colourful sea, the lawyers had clearly begun, with the exception of the doleful Erskine-Brown, to enjoy the party.

'Thanks for coming,' Jago stood before me. 'Do you always work for the other side? If you do, I'm bloody glad I didn't have you defending me.' It was the sort of joke I could do without and then, to my astonishment, I saw him put an arm around Mizz Liz Probert and say, 'You know this little legal lady, I'm sure, Mr Rumpole? I told her she can have my briefs any day of the week, quite honestly!' And I was even more astonished to see that Mizz Liz, far from kneeing this rampant chauvinist in the groin, smiled charmingly at the man she thought had been saved from a life sentence by the efforts of her co-mortgagee.

Wandering on into the throng of celebrators, I saw Bollard in close proximity to his grateful instructing solicitor, Tricia Benbow. It seemed to me that Soapy Sam had been the victim of much passive alcoholism, no doubt absorbed from the glass he held in his hand.

Then, under the sound of the pneumatic drill, I heard the shrilling of a telephone and I was hailed by Jago, who had answered it.

'Mr Rumpole. It's your clerk. He says it's urgent.'

'All right. For God's sake, turn off the music for five minutes.' I took the telephone from him. 'Henry!'

'I've got an awkward situation here, Mr Rumpole. The truth of the matter is Mrs Ballard is here.'

'Oh. Bad luck.'

'She happened to come out of her sprains and fractures refresher course and she wanted to meet up with her husband. She said —' Henry's voice sank to a conspiratorial murmur in which I could detect an almost irresistible tendency to laughter — 'he told her he was going to a Lawyers As Christians Society meeting tonight and might be late home. But she wants to know where the meeting's being held so she can join him, if at all possible.'

'Henry, you didn't tell her he was at a piss-up in the Benedict Arms, Maida Vale?'

'No, sir. I didn't think it would be well received.'

'Why involve me in this sordid web of intrigue?'

'Well, we don't want to land the Head of Chambers in it, do we, Mr Rumpole? Not in the first instance anyway.' Our clerk was positively giggling.

'Where is the wife of Bollard now?'

'She's in the waiting-room, sir.'

'Put me through to her, Henry. Without delay.' And when Mrs Ballard came on the line, I greeted her warmly.

'Matey...I mean, Marguerite. This is Horace Rumpole speaking.'

'Horace! Whatever are you doing there? And where's Sam?'

'Oh, I'm afraid brother Ballard can't come to the phone. He's busy preparing to induct a new member.'

'A new member. Who?'

'Me.'

'You, Horace?' The ex-Matron sounded incredulous.

'Of course. I have decided to put away the sins of the world and lead a better, purer life in future.'

'But where are you meeting?'

'I'm afraid that can't be divulged over the telephone.'

'Why ever not?'

'For your own safety I think it's better for you not to know. We've had threatening calls from militant Methodists.'

'Horace. Are you sure Sam's all right? I can hear a lot of voices.'

'Oh, it's a very full house this evening. Hold on a minute.' I held the phone away from my ear for a while and then I told her, 'Sam really can't get away now. He says he'll see you back in Waltham Cross and don't wait up for him. He'll probably be exhausted.'

'Exhausted?' She sounded only a little suspicious. 'Why?'

'It's the spirit,' I said. 'You know how it tires him.'

'Is he filled with it?' Her suspicions seemed gone and her voice was full of admiration.

'Oh, yes,' I assured her, 'right up to the brim.'

I put down the phone and the blast of road-mending music was restored. I then approached our Head of Chambers, who was standing with Dave Inchcape — Tricia, the solicitor, having danced away with her liberated client.

'That was your wife on the phone,' I told him.

'Good heavens.' The man was still sober enough to panic. 'She's not coming here?'

'Oh, no. I gave you a perfect alibi. Tell you about it later. I'll also tell you my solution to the Case of the Altered Brief. I'm getting into the habit of solving mysteries.'

'I'd better go and find Liz.' Inchcape seemed anxious to get away.

'No, you stay here, David.' I spoke with some authority and the young man stood, looking anxious. 'We're all but toys in the hands of women and your particular commander-in-chief is Mizz Liz Probert. I know you come into the clerk's room early to see what's arrived in the post, all white-wigs do. To your horror you found you'd been engaged by a flinty-hearted landlord to kick two ladies, active in Gay Rights, out of house and home. How could you face your co-habitee, if you did a case like that? It was a matter of a moment, Members of the Jury,' I addressed an imaginary tribunal, 'for David Inchcape to scratch out his name and write Mr Claude Erskine-Brown in block capitals.'

'Is this true?' Ballard tried his best to look judicial, although he was somewhat unsteady on his pins.

David Inchcape's silence provided the answer.

* * *

I was rather late home that evening and climbed into bed beside Hilda's sleeping back. I had no professional duties the next day and wandered into the kitchen in my dressing-gown and with a head still throbbing from the pile-driving music at Jago's celebration. I found Hilda in a surprisingly benign mood, all things considered, but I also noticed something missing from our home.

'Where's the Crock-a-Gleam?' I said. 'You haven't pawned it? I know things aren't brilliant but...'

'I sent it back to John Lewis,' Hilda told me. 'We might get a little something for it.'

'Why?' I felt for a chair and lowered myself slowly into it. 'What's it done wrong?'

'Nothing, really. It just takes about twice as long to do the washing up as even you do, Rumpole. That's not it. It's *her*.'

'Her?'

'Charmian Nichols. She wrote to Dodo and said Christmas with us was about as exciting as watching your finger-nails grow. And when I think of what we spent on her wretched tea set. "Charming Knickers", that was her nickname at school. We got her completely wrong. There wasn't anything charming about her.'

'How do you know what she wrote about Christmas?'

'Dodo sent me her letter, of course. Well, after that, I couldn't sit and look at the dishwasher you bought just to please her.'

Wonderfully loyal group, your old school friends, I thought of saying that but decided against it. Then Hilda changed the subject.

'Rumpole,' she said, 'are things very bad?'

'No one wants to employ me. Not since I changed sides in the middle of a case.'

'You did what you thought was right,' she said, surprisingly sympathetically. But then she added, 'Do be careful not to do what you think's right again. It does seem to have disastrous results.'

'I can't promise you that, Hilda.' I made my bid for independence. 'But I can promise you one thing.'

'What's that?'

'From now on, old thing, I promise you, Rumpole only defends.'

The Judge's Wife

ISABEL ALLENDE

N ICOLAS VIDAL ALWAYS KNEW he would lose his head over a woman. So it was foretold on the day of his birth, and later confirmed by the Turkish woman in the corner shop the one time he allowed her to read his fortune in the coffee grounds. Little did he imagine though that it would be on account of Casilda, Judge Hidalgo's wife. It was on her wedding day that he first glimpsed her. He was not impressed, preferring his women dark-haired and brazen. This ethereal slip of a girl in her wedding gown, eyes filled with wonder, and fingers obviously unskilled in the art of rousing a man to pleasure, seemed to him almost ugly. Mindful of his destiny, he had always been wary of any emotional contact with women, hardening his heart and restricting himself to the briefest of encounters whenever the demands of manhood needed satisfying. Casilda, however, appeared so insubstantial, so distant, that he cast aside all precaution and, when the fateful moment arrived, forgot the prediction that usually weighted in all his decisions. From the roof of the bank, where he was crouching with two of his men, Nicolas Vidal peered down at this young lady from the capital. She had a dozen equally pale and dainty relatives with her, who spent the whole of the ceremony fanning themselves with an air of utter bewilderment, then departed straight away, never to return. Along with everyone else in the town, Vidal was convinced the young bride would not withstand the climate, and that within a few months the old women would be dressing her up again, this time for her funeral. Even if she did survive the heat and the dust that filtered in through every pore to lodge itself in the soul, she would be bound to succumb to the fussy habits of her confirmed bachelor of a husband. Judge Hidalgo was twice her age, and had slept alone for so many years he didn't have the slightest notion of how to go about pleasing a woman. The severity and stubbornness with which he executed the law even at the expense of justice had made him feared throughout the province. He refused to apply any common sense in the exercise of his profession, and was equally harsh in his condemnation of the theft of a chicken as of a premeditated murder. He dressed formally in black, and, despite the all-pervading dust in this god-forsaken town, his boots always shone with beeswax. A man such as he was never meant to be a husband, and yet not only did the gloomy wedding-day prophecies remain unfulfilled, but Catilda emerged happy and smiling from three pregnancies in rapid succession. Every Sunday at noon she would go to mass with her husband, cool and collected beneath her Spanish mantilla, seemingly untouched by our pitiless summer, as wan and frail-looking as on the day of her arrival: a perfect example of delicacy and refinement. Her loudest words were a soft-spoken greeting; her most expressive gesture was a graceful nod of the head. She was such an airy, diaphanous creature that a moment's carelessness might mean she disappeared altogether. So slight an impression did she make that the changes noticeable in the Judge were all the more remarkable. Though outwardly he remained the same — he still dressed as black as a crow and was as stiff-necked and brusque as ever — his judgments in court altered dramatically. To general amazement, he found the youngster who robbed the Turkish shopkeeper innocent, on the grounds that she had been selling him short for years, and the money he had taken could therefore be seen as compensation. He also refused to punish an adulterous wife, arguing that since her husband himself kept a mistress he did not have the moral authority to demand fidelity. Word in the town had it that the Judge was transformed the minute he crossed the threshold at home: that he flung off his gloomy apparel, rollicked with his children, chuckled as he sat Casilda on his lap. Though no one ever succeeded in confirming these rumours, his wife got the credit for his new-found kindness, and her reputation grew accordingly. None of this was of the slightest interest to Nicolas Vidal, who as a wanted man was sure there would be no mercy shown him

the day he was brought in chains before the Judge. He paid no heed to the talk about Dona Casilda, and the rare occasions he glimpsed her from afar only confirmed his first impression of her as a lifeless ghost.

Born thirty years earlier in a windowless room in the town's only brothel, Vidal was the son of Juana the Forlorn and an unknown father. The world had no place for him. His mother knew it, and so tried to wrench him from her womb with sprigs of parsley, candle butts, douches of ashes and other violent purgatives, but the child clung to life. Once, years later, Juana was looking at her mysterious son and realized that, while all her infallible methods of aborting might have failed to dislodge him, they had none the less tempered his soul to the hardness of iron. As soon as he came into the world, he was lifted in the air by the midwife who examined him by the light of an oil-lamp. She saw he had four nipples.

'Poor creature: he'll lose his head over a woman,' she predicted, drawing on her wealth of experience.

Her words rested on the boy like a deformity. Perhaps a woman's love would have made his existence less wretched. To atone for all her attempts to kill him before birth, his mother chose him a beautiful first name, and an imposing family name picked at random. But the lofty name of Nicolas Vidal was no protection against the fateful cast of his destiny. His face was scarred from knife fights before he reached his teens, so it came as no surprise to decent folk that he ended up a bandit. By the age of twenty, he had become the leader of a band of desperadoes. The habit of violence toughened his sinews. The solitude he was condemned to for fear of falling prey to a woman lent his face a doleful expression. As soon as they say him, everyone in the town knew from his eyes, clouded by tears, he would never allow to fall, that he was the son of Juana the Forlorn. Whenever there was an outcry after a crime had been committed in the region, the police set out with dogs to track him down, but after scouring the hills invariably returned empty-handed. In all honesty they preferred it that way, because they could never have fought him. His gang gained such a fearsome reputation that the surrounding villages and estates paid to keep them away. This money would have been plenty for his men, but Nicolas Vidal kept them constantly on horseback in a whirlwind of death and destruction so they would not lose their taste for battle. Nobody dared take them on. More than once, Judge Hidalgo had asked the government to send troops to reinforce the police, but after several useless forays the soldiers returned to their barracks and Nicolas Vidal's gang to their exploits. On one occasion only did Vidal come close to falling into the hands of justice, and then he was saved by his hardened heart.

Weary of seeing the laws flouted, Judge Hidalgo resolved to forget his scruples and set a trap for the outlaw. He realized that to defend justice he was committing an injustice, but chose the lesser of two evils. The only bait he could find was Juana the Forlorn, as she was Vidal's sole known relative. He had her dragged from the brothel where by now, since no clients were willing to pay for her exhausted charms, she scrubbed floors and cleaned out the lavatories. He put her in a specially made cage which was set up in the middle of the Plaza de Armas, with only a jug of water to meet her needs.

'As soon as the water's finished, she'll start to squawk. Then her son will come running, and I'll be waiting for him with the soldiers,' Judge Hidalgo said.

News of this torture, unheard of since the days of slavery, reached Nicolas Vidal's ears shortly before his mother drank the last of the water. His men watched as he received the report in silence, without so much as a flicker of emotion on his blank lone wolf's face, or a pause in the sharpening of his dagger blade on a leather strap. Though for many years he had had no contact with Juana, and retained few happy childhood memories, this was a question of honour. No man can accept such an insult, his gang reasoned as they got guns and horses ready to rush into the ambush and, if need be, lay down their lives. Their chief showed no sign of being in a hurry. As the hours went by tension mounted in the camp. The perspiring, impatient men stared at each other, not daring to speak. Fretful, they caressed the butts of their revolvers and their horses' manes, or busied themselves coiling their lassos. Night fell. Nicolas Vidal was the only one in the camp who slept. At dawn, opinions were divided. Some of the men reckoned he was even more heartless than they had ever imagined, while others maintained their leader was planning a spectacular ruse to free his mother. The one thing that never crossed any of their minds was that his courage might have failed him, for he had always proved he had more than enough to spare. By noon, they could bear the suspense no longer, and went to ask him what he planned to do.

'I'm not going to fall into his trap like an idiot,' he said.

'What about your mother?'

'We'll see who's got more balls, the Judge or me,' Nicolas Vidal coolly replied.

By the third day, Juana the Forlorn's cries for water had ceased. She lay curled on the cage floor, with wildly staring eyes and swollen lips, moaning softly whenever she regained consciousness, and the rest of the time dreaming she was in hell. Four armed guards stood watch to make sure nobody brought her water. Her groans penetrated the entire town, filtering through closed shutters or being carried by the wind through the cracks in doors. They got stuck in corners, where dogs worried at them, and passed them on in their howls to the newly born, so that whoever heard them was driven to distraction. The Judge couldn't prevent a steady stream of people filing through the square to show their sympathy for the old woman, and was powerless to stop the prostitutes going on a sympathy strike just as the miners' fortnight holiday was beginning. That Saturday, the streets were thronged with lusty workmen desperate to unload their savings, who now found nothing in town apart from the spectacle of the cage and this universal wailing carried mouth to mouth down from the river to the coast road. The priest headed a group of Catholic ladies to plead with Judge Hidalgo for Christian mercy and to beg him to spare the poor old innocent woman such a frightful death, but the man of the law bolted his door and refused to listen to them. It was then they decided to turn to Dona Casilda.

The Judge's wife received them in her shady living room. She listened to their pleas looking, as always, bashfully down at the floor. Her husband had not been home for three days, having locked himself in his office to wait for Nicolas Vidal to fall into his trap. Without so much as glancing out of the window, she was aware of what was going on, for Juana's long-drawn-out agony had forced its way even into the vast rooms of her residence. Dona Casilda waited until her visitors had left, dressed her children in their Sunday best, tied a black ribbon round their arms as a token of mourning, then strode out with them in the direction of the square. She carried a food hamper and a bottle of fresh water for Juana the Forlorn. When the guards spotted her turning the corner, they realized what she was up to, but they had strict orders, and barred her way with their rifles. When, watched now by a small crowd, she persisted, they grabbed her by the arms. Her children began to cry.

Judge Hidalgo sat in his office overlooking the square. He was the only person in the town who had not stuffed wax in his ears, because his mind was intent on the ambush and he was straining to catch the sound of horses' hoofs, the signal for action. For three long days and nights he put up with Juana's groans and the insults of the townspeople gathered outside the courtroom, but when he heard his own children start to wail he knew he had reached the bounds of his endurance. Vanquished, he walked out of the office with his three days' beard, his eyes bloodshot from keeping watch, and the weight of a thousand years on his back. He crossed the street, turned into the square and came face to face with his wife. They gazed at each other sadly. In seven years, this was the first time she had gone against him, and she had chosen to do so in front of the whole town. Easing the hamper and the bottle from Casilda's grasp, Judge Hidalgo himself opened the cage to release the prisoner.

'Didn't I tell you he wouldn't have the balls?' laughed Nicolas Vidal when the news reached him.

His laughter turned sour the next day, when he heard that Juana the Forlorn had hanged herself from the chandelier in the brothel where she had spent her life, overwhelmed by the shame of her only son leaving her to fester in a cage in the middle of the Plaza de Armas.

'That Judge's hour has come,' said Vidal.

He planned to take the Judge by surprise, put him to a horrible death, then dump him in the accursed cage for all to see. The Turkish shopkeeper sent him word that the Hidalgo family had left that same night for a seaside resort to rid themselves of the bitter taste of defeat.

The Judge learned he was being pursued when he stopped to rest at a wayside inn. There was little protection for him there until an army patrol could arrive, but he had a few hours' start, and his motor car could outrun the gang's horses. He calculated he could make it to the next town and summon help there. He ordered his wife and children into the car, put his foot down on the accelerator and sped off along the road. He ought to have arrived with time to spare, but it had been ordained that Nicolas Vidal was that day to meet the woman who would lead him to his doom.

Overburdened by the sleepless nights, the townspeople's hostility, the blow to his pride and the stress of this race to save his family, Judge Hidalgo's heart gave a massive jolt, then split like a pomegranate. The car ran out of control, turned several somersaults and finally came to a halt in the ditch. It took Dona Casilda some minutes to work out what had happened. Her husband's advancing years had often led her to think what it would be like to be left a widow, yet she had never imagined he would leave her at the mercy of his enemies. She wasted little time dwelling on her situation, knowing she must act at once to get her children to safety. When she gazed around her, she almost burst into tears. There was no sign of life in the vast plain baked by a scorching sun, only barren cliffs beneath an un-bounded sky bleached colourless by the fierce light. A second look revealed the dark shadow of a passage or cave on a distant slope, so she ran towards it with two children in her arms and the third clutching her skirts.

One by one she carried her children up the cliff. The cave was a natural one, typical of many in the region. She peered inside to be certain it wasn't the den of some wild animal, sat her children against its back wall, then, dry-eyed, kissed them goodbye.

'The troops will come to find you a few hours from now. Until then, don't for any reason whatsoever come out of here, even if you hear me screaming — do you understand?'

Their mother gave one final glance at the terrified children clinging to each other, then clambered back down to the road. She reached the car, closed her husband's eyes, smoothed back her hair and settled down to wait. She had no idea how many men were in Nicolas Vidal's gang, but prayed there were a lot of them so it would take them all the more time to have their way with her. She gathered strength pondering on how long it would take her to die if she determined to do it as slowly as possible. She willed herself to be desirable, luscious, to create more work for them and thus gain time for her children.

Casilda did not have long to wait. She soon saw a cloud of dust on the horizon and heard the gallop of horses' hoofs. She clenched her teeth. Then, to her astonishment, she saw there was only one rider, who stopped a few yards from her, gun at the ready. By the scar on his face she recognized Nicolas Vidal, who had set out all alone in pursuit of Judge Hidalgo, as this was a private matter between the two men. The Judge's wife understood she was going to have to endure something far worse than a lingering death.

A quick glance at her husband was enough to convince Vidal that the Judge was safely out of his reach in the peaceful sleep of death. But there was his wife, a shimmering presence in the plain's glare. He leapt from his horse and strode over to her. She did not flinch or lower her gaze, and to his amazement he realized that for the first time in his life another person was facing him without fear. For several seconds that stretched to eternity, they sized each other up, trying to gauge the other's strength, and their own powers of resistance. It gradually dawned on both of them that they were up against a formidable opponent. He lowered his gun. She smiled.

Casilda won each moment of the ensuing hours. To all the wiles of seduction known since the beginning of time she added new ones born of necessity to bring this man to the heights of rapture. Not only did she work on his body like an artist, stimulating his every fibre to pleasure, but she brought all the delicacy of her spirit into play on her side. Both knew their lives were at stake, and this added a new and terrifying dimension to their meeting. Nicolas Vidal had fled from love since birth, and knew nothing of intimacy, tenderness, secret laughter, the riot of the senses, the joy of shared passion. Each minute brought the detachment of troops and the noose that much nearer, but he gladly accepted this in return for her prodigious gifts. Casilda was a passive, demure, timid woman who had been married to an austere old man in front of whom she had never dared appear naked. Not once during that unforgettable afternoon did she forget that her aim was to win time for her children, and yet at some point, marvelling at her own possibilities, she gave herself completely, and felt something akin to gratitude towards him. That was why, when she heard the soldiers in the distance, she begged him to flee to the hills. Instead, Nicolas Vidal chose to fold her in a last embrace, thus fulfilling the prophecy that had sealed his fate from the start.

Translated by Nick Caistor

About the Authors

ALICE ADAMS (1926–　　), born in Fredericksburg, Virginia, is a novelist and short story writer. Her novels include *Families and Survivors* and *Superior Women*. Her most recent novel is *Caroline's Daughters*.

ISABEL ALLENDE (1942–　　), born in Chile, now lives in Venezuela. Her first novel was *The House of Spirits*, which was followed by *Of Love and Shadows*, and *Eva Luna*.

MARGARET ATWOOD (1939–　　), born in Ottawa, Canada, is a novelist, short story writer, and a poet. Her novels include *The Edible Woman, Surfacing, Life Before Man*, and *The Handmaid's Tale*. Her short stores are collected in *Dancing Girls* and *Bluebeard's Egg*.

LOUIS AUCHINCLOSS (1917–　　), the author of more than 40 books of both fiction and non-fiction including *The Golden Calves, Diary of a Yuppie* and *Skinny Island*. He practiced law for more than 40 years at a Wall Street law firm.

MADISON SMARTT BELL (1957–　　) is an American novelist and short story writer. His novels include *Waiting for the End of the World, The Washington Square Ensemble, Doctor Sleep, Straight Cut* and *The Year of Silence*.

LARRY BROWN (1947–　　) has written an anti-war novel, *Dirty Work*, and two collections of short stories, *Big Bad Love* and *Facing the Music*. His most recent novel is *Joe*.

KAREL ČAPEK (1890–1938), born in Bohemia, was perhaps the leading figure in Czechoslovakian literature in the first half of the twentieth century. His plays "R.U.R." and "From the Life of Insects" were hits on Broadway in New York City. His novels include *War With the Newts*, a trilogy of novels, *Hordubal, Meteor*, and *An Ordinary Life*. Čapek also published several volumes of short stories, including *Wayside Crosses* and *Painful Tales*.

CHARLES W. CHESNUTT (1858–1932) was born in Cleveland, Ohio. His novel *The Marrow of Tradition*, published in 1901, was acclaimed by William Dean Howells, a leading literary critic. Chesnutt was, in addition to being a writer, one of the first black lawyers. His short stories were collected in *The Wife of His Youth and Other Stories of the Color Line*.

R. SARIF EASMON (1913–   ) is a prominent Sierra Leone author and playwright. His most recent book is *The Feud*, a collection of short stories.

IAN FRAZIER (1951–   ), born in Cleveland, Ohio, was an essayist and journalist on the staff of *The New Yorker*. His books include *Dating Your Mom* and *Nobody Better, Better than Nobody* (1987). He won the 1989 National Book Award for his work of non-fiction, *Great Plains*.

WILLIAM GADDIS (1922–   ), is a novelist and short story writer whose novels include *The Recognitions*, *JR*, and *Carpenter's Gothic*.

ELLIOTT STANLEY GOLDMAN was born in 1913 and grew up in Pittsburgh. His stories appear frequently in the *Atlantic*, and his first novel, *Big Chocolate Cookies*, was published in 1988. *Earthly Justice*, winner of the first annual William Goyen Prize for Fiction, is his first story collection.

NADINE GORDIMER (1923–   ), born in Springs, South Africa, is a novelist and short story writer. In 1991, Gordimer was awarded the Nobel Prize for literature. She has published 10 novels and nine collections of short stories. Her novels include *A Guest of Honor*, *The Conservationist*, and, most recently, *My Son's Story*.

GRAHAM GREENE (1904–1991) born in Hertfordshire, England was an editor on the London *Times* and is a prolific novelist and short story writer. His many awards include the Hawthorne Prize (1940), the James Tart Black Memorial Prize (1949), The Catholic Literary Award (1952), The Boys Club of America, Junior Book Award (1955), the Balliol College, Oxford Prize (1966) and the Legion d'Honneur (1969).

HARVEY JACOBS (1930–   ), born in New York, is a playwright and short story writer. His awards include the Earplay Award for Drama from the Writers Guild of America, and the Playboy Fiction Award.

B.S. JOHNSON (1933–1973), born in England, is a novelist, poet and short story writer whose works include *Albert Angelo, House Mother Normal* and *Christie Malry's Own Double Entry*. He won the Gregory Award in 1962.

WARD JUST (1935–   ), born in Waukegan, Illinois, is the author of fourteen books, including the novels *Jack Gance* and *The American Ambassador* as well as several collections of short stories. His ninth and most recent novel is *The Translator.*

FRANZ KAFKA (1883–1924), born in Prague, Czechoslovakia, is the author of *The Trial, Amerika,* and *The Castle.* His short stories were collected in *Franz Kafka: The Complete Stories.*

GARRISON KEILLOR (1942–   ), born in Anoka, Minnesota, is a raconteur and writer. His radio program, "A Prairie Home Companion," was heard by millions. His books include *Happy to Be Here* and *Lake Wobegon Days.*

LOWELL B. KOMIE (1927–   ), a lawyer practicing in Chicago, has published *The Judge's Chambers*, which was the first collection of short fiction published by the American Bar Association. He had also published short stores in *Harper's, Chicago Magazine* and *Student Lawyer,* the magazine of the Law Student Division of the American Bar Association.

GIUSEPPE DI LAMPEDUSA (1896–1957) was born in Italy. He is the author of *The Leopard,* which was published posthumously, and was awarded Italy's highest award for fiction, the Strega Prize.

J.S. MARCUS (19__–   ), of Milwaukee, Wisconsin, has published stories in *The New Yorker, GQ, Harpers* and *Anteus.* His first collection of short stories, *The Art of Cartography,* was published in 1991.

HERMAN MELVILLE (1819–1891), the author of *Moby Dick, The Confidence Man,* and *Billy Budd,* among many other novels and shorter works, was born in New York City.

JOHN MORTIMER (1923–   ), born in London, England, was a Barrister-at-law, and is an award-winning novelist and playwright. His awards include the Italia Prize (1957) for the play "The Dock Brief," The Writers Guild of Great Britain award (1969) for "Voyage Round My Father" and a Golden Globe Award nomination (1970) for the screen play "John & Mary."

FRANK O'CONNOR (1903–1966) is an Irish master of the short story. Richard Ellmann has edited *Collected Stories: Frank O'Connor.*

CYNTHIA OZICK (1928–   ), born in the Bronx, is a novelist and short story writer. Her novels include *Trust* and *The Cannibal Galaxy.* She has published several volumes of short stories including *Levitation*. Her most recent book is *The Shawl: A Story and a Novella*.

JAMES REID PARKER's (1909–1984) stories have appeared in *The New Yorker*. A collection of his legal stories was titled *Attorneys At Law*.

BENJAMIN PERET (1899–1959) is the French author of *Death to the Pigs, and Other Writers*. He was intimately involved in the Surrealist movement of the 1920s.

IRWIN SHAW (1913–1984) is the author of *The Young Lions, Rich Man, Poor Man* and *Beggar-Man, Thief* among other novels. His short stories have appeared in *Collier's, Esquire, Harper's, The New Republic, The New Yorker* and many other magazines. *Short Stories: Five Decades* is a collection of his short fictions.

ISAAC BASHEVIS SINGER (1904–1991) won the Nobel Prize for literature in 1978. Born in Lublin, Poland, Singer resided in New York City. Nevertheless, he continued to write his short stories and novels in Yiddish. His novels include *Enemies — A Love Story*. His last novel was *Scum*.

MARIAN THURM (1952–   ), born in New York City, is a novelist and short story writer. Her short story collections are *Floating* and *These Things Happen*. Her novels include *Walking Distance, Henry in Love*, and, most recently, *The Way We Live Now*.

PAUL WEST (1930–   ) has published a dozen novels, among them *Rat Man of Paris, The Very Rich Hours of Count von Stauffenberg, The Place in Flowers Where Pollen Rests, The Women of Whitechapel and Jack the Ripper* and *Lord Byron's Doctor*, which became a bestseller in France and was shortlisted for both the Medicis and Femina prizes. His short stories have been collected under the title *The Universe, and Other Fictions*.

THOMAS WOLFE (1900–1938) was born in Asheville, North Carolina and educated at the University of North Carolina and at Harvard. His novels include *Look Homeward Angel* and *You Can't Go Home Again*.